C000130165

Praise for Eric L. Harry and *Pandora: Outbreak*

"Like Crichton and H.G. Wells, Harry writes stories that entertain roundly while they explore questions of scientific and social import."
—*Publishers Weekly*

"Harry's vision of an apocalyptic plague is as chilling as it is plausible. This masterful thriller will leave you terrified, enthralled, and desperate for the next entry in the series."
—**Kira Peikoff**, author of *No Time to Die* and *Mother Knows Best*

"After a devastating epidemic that changes the very nature of humans, two sisters, an epidemiologist and a neurobiologist, hold the key to humanity's survival."
—*Library Journal*

Also by Eric L. Harry

Pandora: Resistance

Eric L. Harry

REBEL BASE BOOKS
Kensington Publishing Corp.
www.kensingtonbooks.com

To the extent that the image or images on the cover of this book depict a person or persons, such person or persons are merely models, and are not intended to portray any character or characters featured in the book.

This book is a work of fiction. Names, characters, places, and incidents either are products of the author's imagination or are used fictitiously. Any resemblance to actual events or locales or persons living or dead is entirely coincidental.

REBEL BASE BOOKS are published by

Kensington Publishing Corp. 119 West 40th Street New York, NY 10018
Copyright © 2020 by Eric L. Harry

All rights reserved. No part of this book may be reproduced in any form or by any means without the prior written consent of the Publisher, excepting brief quotes used in reviews.

All Kensington titles, imprints, and distributed lines are available at special quantity discounts for bulk purchases for sales promotion, premiums, fundraising, and educational or institutional use.

Special book excerpts or customized printings can also be created to fit specific needs. For details, write or phone the office of the Kensington Special Sales Manager: Kensington Publishing Corp., 119 West 40th Street, New York, NY 10018. Attn. Special Sales Department. Phone: 1-800-221-2647.

Rebel Base and the RB logo Reg. U.S. Pat. & TM Off.

First Electronic Edition: January 2020
ISBN-13: 978-1-63573-016-6 (ebook)
ISBN-10: 1-63573-016-3 (ebook)

First Print Edition: January 2020
ISBN-13: 978-1-63573-019-7
ISBN-10: 1-63573-019-8

Printed in the United States of America

Author's Note

In the late 1960s and early 1970s, scientists confidently foretold the impending collapse of civilization due to the human population explosion. Their predictions of famine, pollution, soaring commodity prices, and desperate poverty were proved completely wrong in every detail. Food production skyrocketed. Air and water quality improved dramatically. Commodities grew ever cheaper. Wealth accumulated at prodigious rates. The human race produced not only more people; it produced a network of ever more brilliant, ambitious, innovative, and driven geniuses, who pushed science and technology to previously unimagined heights. But what happens if the population collapses? Would the effects of a demographic implosion be worse than its opposite, undoing the benefits of specialization, trade, and productivity? Would humanity ultimately return to stone tools and the cave? This book explores the beginnings of a world in which peak person has come and gone.

Chapter 1

THE SHENANDOAH VALLEY
Infection Date 61, 2030 GMT (4:30 p.m. Local)

"Dad, do I shoot?" Noah's fifteen-year-old daughter Chloe whispered from the door on the opposite side of the barn.

A thirtyish man held a revolver to the head of a taller fiftyish woman in hospital scrubs and wearing a surgical mask. Noah and Chloe were unseen and only thirty yards from where the pair stood at the fence, but that was too far for Noah to see their eyes. The supposed female hostage's hands were bound behind her, but…something wasn't right.

"Dad?" Chloe said quietly while squinting into her assault rifle's scope. "I think I got the shot." Her mouth was open and her breathing steady, like their private instructors had taught. Her blond hair, cut short for the apocalypse, was pulled back from her face in a tiny ponytail by a blue band so that it didn't spoil her aim.

Noah looked up at the turreted tower—a last minute addition while prepping for just this sort of confrontation—atop the main house forty yards from the barn. His wife Natalie had joined their thirteen-year-old son Jacob behind their two rifles.

"Dad?" Chloe asked. "Make a freakin' call. Should we just give 'em some food? Or do I shoot? Jake and Mom are twice as far, and *Mom*…Your call." Noah's heart was pounding. His stomach threatened to cramp. He had to force his breathing past the bands of tension strapped around his chest.

"You're runnin' outta time!" the man with the pistol shouted toward Jake and Natalie. It sounded scripted; unemotional. That also described the man's calm hostage, who scanned the house and, now, the barn. "She's gonna git shot if you don't hand over fifty pounds of food and/or ammunition." There it was. The passive voice. Not, "I'll shoot her." He'd lost his "I."

"I think they're both bad," Chloe said in a voice warped by her press on her AR-15's stock. "Something's not right."

"I got the shot," Noah said quietly, which drew his daughter away from her sight. "Get ready." His crosshairs danced across the man's face, straying onto the torso and head of his captive. If the bullet clipped the metal fencing that diagonally crisscrossed his round, magnified view, it could deflect into the face of the woman. Or it could miss both and, if they're legitimate, get her shot in the head by her supposed captor. Noah's throbbing heart kept him from filling his lungs. His right hand took its orders from his right eye. The crosshairs traversed the man's nose repeatedly. Each time his trigger finger added a feather's weight. *Now. Now. Now—*

Bam!

The infected man's head was flung backwards and he dropped straight to the ground past lifeless knees. *Crosshairs don't lie,* his instructor had said.

The female hostage swung a pistol around and fired straight at Noah.

A bullet slapped the wall above him and clattered through the barn as Noah dove onto the chickenshit covered floor.

Noah heard three shots. He crawled back into the doorway with his rifle. The woman lay draped over the man. Neither moved.

Bam! The top of the woman's head exploded. It was Chloe. "Just making sure."

"Clear!" came Jake's call in a voice breaking with puberty, or anxiety, or both. "Clear!" came Natalie's call from beside him in the tower.

"Clear!" came Chloe's high-pitched shout.

Noah saw no movement by the gate or in the downward sloping woods beyond the fence where the two bodies lay. "Clear!" He led his daughter on a stooped run back to the front door of the main house.

Natalie came down the spiral staircase to meet them—a mid-thirties version of their teenage daughter. "I missed her with my first shot." She sounded pissed. "Fucking *animals.* They would *never* have left us alone. And trying to *trick* us. Use our *emotions* to…to kill and…." Natalie wrapped her arms around Chloe, hugging, kissing, and stroking her head. "I'm just so glad," kiss, "that you're both safe." Kiss. Tears welled in her eyes, and she sniffed. "But I hit that *bitch* with my second shot. Mother*fuckers.*"

Noah nodded toward Chloe. "*Na*talie," he said as softly as he could manage.

"*What?*" His wife was on an emotional rampage. "It's kill or be killed, Noah. Don't you forget that. Don't you go…go *wobbly* on us." Two people had just tried to kill her children. She turned to Chloe, but shouted up the staircase, "Jake! Listen up! There's *us*. *This* family. And there are targets—everyone else—who you've gotta be ready to kill to protect *us*. *This* family. From now, till this is all over, if it's ever over. Keep your weapons close and your*self* ready. Always figure out how you're gonna hit every single target around you, and be ready because situations can change in a split second." She grew angrier by the word. "And there are people like those two *vermin* who *need* to be killed. Hold your head up, and get ready. Because *this* family is gonna survive. We can do this."

She took off back up the spiral staircase. "Jake! Anything moving?"

"No."

"Then keep your head down."

"Then how do I know if anything's moving?"

Noah turned to Chloe, who arched her eyebrows at her mother's comments then sank onto the arm of the sofa. "What *next?*" she said, shaking her head. "I thought Infecteds were supposed to be, like, brain damaged or whatever. They tried to *trick* us. I didn't think they were that *smart*."

"Obviously they're not smart enough," her mother yelled downstairs. "Noah, what tipped you off?"

He thought for a moment. "The woman wasn't terrified."

The window in the living room exploded into shards. Noah and Chloe dropped to the floor. Both Jake and Natalie fired several shots. "You okay down there?" Natalie asked.

"Yeah. How many?"

"Can't tell!"

More glass shattered. Noah crawled to the open door. Natalie called out to him to be careful as bullets peppered the front of the house.

"There are a coupla people!" Jake shouted. "Behind some bushes to the right of the barn! Their cover is bad! Say the word!"

"Wait for me!" Noah rose despite the sporadic fire and dashed past a crouching Chloe for the spiral staircase. He climbed the stairs to the Tower's opening and crawled over to Jake and Natalie.

"They're right there." Jake enlarged the photo he'd taken on his iPhone and pointed toward a thick clump of foliage. His finger was shaking.

"Alright. On the count of three, we all get in a slit and start firing back at those bushes." The shots were coming their way every few seconds, but seemed random. "Don't hold back. Even if you miss it'll force their heads down. Let it loose. Okay?"

Jake and Natalie nodded. Noah counted down. On the beat after he said, "One," they all rolled into firing positions and began a steady stream of shots—one per second per person—until a man in a jacket holding a rifle began hopping downhill on one leg. Jake hit him squarely in the side, and he fell into the weeds.

A bullet slapped the stone six inches from Noah's head, sending a spray of rock chips onto his face and a fine mist of dust into his eyes.

"There are more on the right!" Jake cried out.

Before Noah could object, Jake slithered over and began firing toward the small gate leading up to the hunting cabin. Noah and Natalie joined him, ignoring the questions from his daughter below asking what was happening. When Noah slipped his rifle through another slit, he saw a man grab the small gate and immediately jerk his hand back as he fell to the ground. The electric charge in the fence had done its thing.

As the man scrambled to his feet—*Bam!*—Noah's 5.56mm round struck his center mass and he never rose again. Jake was plinking away at a woman who was literally hopping and weaving her way away from the gate as if dodging his shots. She fell and curled into a writhing ball. *Uninfecteds,* Noah thought. *She felt pain.* He fired at the targets—anyone not this family, just as Natalie had instructed—no matter their *Pandoravirus* status.

When a woman and a boy rose to flee, both fell. The woods were still, but for their writhing and moans of pain. Noah and Jake ceased fire. Natalie fired two shots. The first at the boy, and—as Noah and Jake watched in horror—the second at the uninfected woman, his mother, who crawled back for him. "Got 'em," was all she said. She turned to Noah. "We need to talk about this. Downstairs. Jake, keep your head down. Use your phone."

Sitting on the stairs leading down to the basement where the kids slept, Chloe demanded and got a recount of what had just happened. Everyone was hyper and cotton mouthed. Then Natalie said, "Chloe, your father and I need to talk."

"About what's going *on*? I wanta be here for that."

"Chloe," Noah began to explain, "there are some things your mother and I—"

"No," his wife interrupted. "Let her stay." They all sat on stairs just below ground level. *"Jake?"* Natalie shouted, looking up in his direction. "Everything quiet?"

"All clear," he replied. "Just me and a bunch of dead people."

"You're gonna have to go clean that up," Natalie told Noah. "Before…"

"What?" Chloe asked in the silence. "Before they start to smell or something?"

"It's not just the smell," Noah said. "Bodies carry diseases, not just *Pandoravirus.*"

"But it's *dangerous* to go out there," Chloe noted correctly.

"It's even more dangerous *not* to," Noah replied. "Patrolling, remember? We can't let them settle in just outside the fence and take shots at us when we least expect them."

"We can't even move around the property anymore," Natalie said. "I can't get to the grow labs. Chloe can't get to the barn. We're trapped. And they know we have stuff. Food and ammunition, that's what those first two wanted. How long, Noah?"

He had no idea what she meant. "How long till *what*?"

"How long can we hold out here? How long can we stay lucky?"

"Well...you gotta consider the alternatives, which are piss poor."

"What are they? Our options?"

Chloe's head went back and forth between her parents like at a tennis match.

"We could stick it out here, no matter how bad it gets. Or we could try to make ourselves useful to Emma's new community and hope to avoid her deciding to eradicate all Uninfecteds. Or we can make a run for it."

"Make a run for it?" Chloe asked. "Where?" But before anyone could answer, she said, "I'm down for that. Getting the hell outta here."

Natalie and Noah were clearly undecided. And unlike their kids, they were exhausted from the responsibility. At least Noah was.

"It's gonna be dark soon," Natalie said. "Better clean up those bodies. Be careful."

Chloe chortled. "*Be careful*. Just go outside the fence, bury a bunch of *Pandoravirus*-infected bodies, and fight off any attacks. But be *careful*."

"You're coming with me. Your mother and Jake will cover us."

There were so many bodies that Noah had to use the little Bobcat to dig a trench. When the hole was getting deep enough, more shots rang out, but it was over almost as soon as he'd found good cover. "Two more!" Natalie called out from the Tower. Noah turned off the electric fence and had Chloe take cover beside the handle in the barn so that she could reelectrify it quickly. He then donned gloves and a mask and began dragging bodies through the gate to the mass grave. He tried not to look at them. But when he used the Bobcat to dump the first load of dirt into the trench, he saw—staring back up at him—the lifeless eyes of a woman wearing makeup and earrings. He quickly dug another trench to be filled with people to be killed later.

Chloe electrified the fence, trotted back across the yard to the main house, and joined Noah and Natalie on the floor in the foyer beneath the level of the windows. Broken glass covered the sofa and chairs.

"I vote we make a run for it," Chloe repeated. "They're gonna keep coming."

"But out there," her mother replied, "it's just us versus them. No walls, no towers, no fence."

"Chloe," Noah said. "Why don't you head downstairs and take a break?" He expected an argument. Instead, their teenage daughter crawled along the antique runner to the top of the basement stairs.

In the silence following, Noah said, "In answer to your question...no. I don't think this is gonna work." He shrugged. The sound of buzzing outside from the drone's little electric motor confirmed that Jake was keeping an eye on things. "All this..." Noah said, feeling utterly defeated. "I don't know what I was thinking. How I thought this might work."

"Don't you dare!" Noah looked at his wife with a start. "You don't have the right to give up." She was angry...with *him*. "You don't get to quit. You have to fight...for *us*!"

As if on cue, Jake shouted down from the tower. "More on the way! I count four!"

From the basement, Chloe cried, "Ahhhh!" The footfalls of her boots were heavy on the wooden treads until she got down on all fours, struggling to keep her rifle slung over her shoulder.

Natalie was first off the floor with her rifle. She glared once more at Noah before he followed and both ascended the spiral staircase to join Jake in the tower.

* * * *

Things grew worse as the evening wore on. The number of near misses mounted. Sometimes, the smack of a bullet a foot away was noted by a "Jeez!" or a *"Shit!"*; other times, they were too busy returning fire. But each close brush with death left its mark on its would-be victim, and doubly on their parents. After darkness fell, the cumulative toll of the fear, adrenaline, and stress was written on all four faces of the Miller family.

In between assaults, Noah began to prepare. Down in the basement, he distributed among the four huge backpacks of all the food, water, ammunition, and camping and survival supplies that would fit. Several times, he completed the process only to find that the packs were far too heavy. Out came water and some food. In went ammunition. The net savings in weight, therefore, was modest. He tucked a few small bars of gold into his pack, but left in the safe $9 million worth at the last quote he'd heard before the exchanges closed.

Another attack began with several shots fired by Jake from the tower. Noah grabbed his rifle and, on the spur of the moment, a nylon sack filled with hand grenades, courtesy of his sister Isabel's Marine boyfriend. He hit the stairs just as all hell broke loose. "Noah! Noah!" Natalie was shouting from the tower. "There are a lot of them!"

He had left Chloe crouching beside the open front door peering into the darkness.

"Lock that door and keep low!" Noah shouted, panting as much from the anxiety as from exertion as he climbed the spiral staircase. In the tower, he found Natalie and Jacob blazing away, and ducked as grit from the stone wall above their heads rained down with each shot fired in return.

"They made it to the fence behind the barn!" Jake took the time away from his rifle to shout. "They've got big bolt cutters. We don't have a shot from up here!"

Natalie never stopped firing. She barely winced as her face lit with each blast from her AR-15. If only she were a good shot.

Noah knelt above his prone wife and took aim. The security lamps in the trees around the property began to explode and fall dark as the attackers shot them out but revealed their positions with muzzle flashes.

"Noah!" Natalie took the time to say while inserting a new magazine into her rifle with quivering hands. "They're coming inside! There are too many of them!"

There was motion inside the barn. The second time Noah saw it, he squeezed off a round. The barn flickered with a half dozen shots that forced him down behind the crenelated tower wall. Stones behind them spat debris from new pockmarks.

"Chloe!" Noah called down the stairs. "Get away from the front wall! They're inside the fence! If you see movement, shoot through the door or windows!"

"Okay!"

Too many rounds hit the tower to raise a head to return fire. Natalie, Jake, and Noah all lay flat under a rain of fragments shot loose from the walls and roof above them. Noah dragged the nylon sack over and extracted a smooth, round grenade. Jake and Natalie stared back at him in amazement. Natalie nodded her encouragement. He grabbed the first grenade and its handle—its *spoon*—firmly in his right hand, and had to pull with effort the metal pin, bent ninety degrees, out through its hole. The unrelenting fire his way made exposing himself even for a quick throw dangerous, but the barn was a long way away.

Noah readied himself. "Chloe, get down!" he called out. In what he perceived was a slight lull, he rose to one knee and put everything he had into a throw, grunting as he flung the grenade as far as he could toward the barn. He dropped back to his belly and reached for another grenade.

The brief but shocking blast was of a higher order of magnitude than the firearms, even the shotguns, and it must've been triply stunning to the people in the barn, whom it silenced for a moment.

Noah threw another. From his high vantage, he saw it bounce once and skitter into the dark structure, which exploded in light and flame and boiled with smoke. Noah even heard a distinct scream. He grabbed another and, with less fear of being shot, hurled a third grenade, which again bounced inside. It burst with a chest thumping thud, and the barn became consumed in fire. "They're running!" Jake said.

Natalie, Jake, and then Noah resumed firing. But they weren't all running away. A few crossed from the barn toward the house. Most didn't make it. One or two did. *"They're downstairs!"* Natalie said, terrified, as the guns all fell silent. "Be careful." Noah nodded and crawled toward the spiral staircase.

At the bottom, in the darkness, Noah got a wave from Chloe, who had taken cover behind a plush armchair in the living room opposite the double storm shutter clad windows. The twin sheets of metal were filled with holes, and bright light from the remaining security illumination and the fire in the barn shone through them like flickering stars. Noah heard Natalie ask Jake in a whisper if he saw anything, and Jake's reply of, "Nuh-uh."

Noah aimed his rifle at the front door. Propped up beside it, however, was the shotgun and, in a crouch, he went to get it.

"Dad. *Dad!*" came Chloe's breathless whisper.

He returned to the living room in a crawl and she pointed at the windows. The light from holes was extinguished one by one as a human form pressed against the shutters and tried to peer into the room.

Quickly, before the form could disappear, Noah raised the shotgun, flicked the safety off, took aim at the target's chest, and pulled the stiff trigger.

The roar and brilliant flash of the gun overwhelmed his senses to such an extent that he missed the recoil and only felt the pain in his shoulder when he coughed from the smoke. A tightly packed pattern of holes admitted even more light through the shutters where the attacker's chest had been.

There was another, single shot from the tower. "Got him!" Natalie called out, presumably felling the last of the fleeing attackers. The blaze from the flaming barn danced across the living room walls. The apocalyptic light show in their darkened refuge's living room made it official. *Time to go*, Noah now knew for sure.

Chapter 2

THE SHENANDOAH VALLEY
Infection Date 63, 2145 GMT (5:45 p.m. Local)

Emma Miller approached the ranch style home warily. At her side was Fred Walcott, the cowboy hat wearing local sheriff. Hiding in the thick woods were Emma's former roommates at the NIH hospital in Bethesda—Dwayne Bullock, a Marine Lance Corporal and former Beijing embassy guard, and Samantha Brown, the slender twelve-year-old with every strand of her long blond hair in place. Her father had been the U.S. ambassador to China when she and then Dwayne had caught SED—Severe Encephalopathic Disease—from infection by *Pandoravirus horribilis*. Emma made sure Sam was behind cover. She was too high functioning an aide to lose. Not so Dwayne's small militia of ragtag Infecteds—dullards all—who awaited orders to attack.

"That's far enough!" shouted the potbellied man in the front doorway maybe twenty yards away. He was obscured by the screen door and framed in the darkness of the home behind him, but it was clear that he held a long gun.

Walcott obviously knew the man. "Randy, we're goin' around, spreadin' the word that there have been some changes in town."

"What kinda changes, Sheriff?" There was a smaller figure beside him—Randy's wife, Emma surmised.

"Well, the virus came through," Walcott replied. "There was some trouble, but it's mostly passed. This young woman here, Dr. Emma Miller, is in charge now."

There was a brief, whispered exchange behind the screen door. "Who put *her* in charge?"

"I have a proposal to make," Emma called out. "If you agree to abide by the Rules, we can all work together and survive."

"Who's *we*?" Randy asked, now pressing against the screen.

"The survivors," Emma answered. "In this area."

There was more whispering. "Are you *infected*?" came their next question. Emma caught Walcott's questioning glance before she simply nodded. Randy stepped back into the shadows. The only thing they could see clearly now was the muzzle of his weapon. "Git the *hell* off my prop'ty, Walcott! What the hell do you think yer *doin'* here?"

Walcott shrugged, and turned to leave until Emma said, "This is your last chance!"

They waited on more debate in low but urgent tones. Finally, Randy said, "What does that mean?"

"If you don't join us, you'll run out of food and supplies and try to come and take them. We can't wait for that to happen. You'll be a danger to the community. So, we'll have to kill you all," she said simply and honestly. They might as well have all the relevant information before they made their decision.

There were full-on arguments now from inside the house. "There's a bunch of 'em in there," Walcott said softly. He was fidgeting and growing increasingly anxious.

"Breath in through the nose, and out through the mouth," Emma advised.

The door opened. Walcott flinched. Emma caught his hand before he drew his pistol. With parting arguments cast over their shoulders, four people emerged—a couple and a young boy and girl—and rapidly approached the infected emissaries, but not too closely. "We'll join up," the woman said.

"You'll agree to abide by the Rules?" Emma asked.

The woman's husband began to whisper something, but the woman gathered her two children into her arms and said, to Emma and Walcott, "You'll treat us fair, right?"

"Yes, ma'am," Emma said. "The Rules will be clear. If you follow them, there will be no punishment and your needs will be taken care of to the maximum extent possible. If you break the Rules, however, the punishment could include death."

The woman's husband shot her a look. But his wife hugged her son and daughter to her as if they were human shields. "We agree."

Walcott directed them off toward the flatbed of a pickup truck, politely keeping his distance and leaving them in the open air with the two other

Uninfecteds who'd agreed so far. They exchanged nods of greeting but said nothing and stared at their feet.

Emma and Walcott met Dwayne by the highway. "I can't tell how many are in there," Emma said.

"Should I ask those people who just left?" Dwayne replied.

"No. Let's not put their loyalty under too much stress yet. As a matter of fact," Emma said, turning to Walcott, "have your deputy drive them into town before we kill everyone in that house."

Walcott gave the orders. The pickup departed with its wide-eyed Uninfecteds. "It still makes sense," Walcott said, "to just infect 'em all. I don't trust 'em otherwise."

"And you trust Infecteds?" Dwayne asked.

"Infecteds will kill ya at the drop of a hat," the sheriff replied, "but they're not as devious. I never know what Uninfecteds are thinkin'. Plannin'. Infecteds are simple. They ain't plannin' nothin'."

Emma was ready with what was becoming her stock reply to the suggestion that Uninfecteds all be forcibly infected. "Half would die, and we're already short of manpower and skills. Plus, you'll be surprised at how useful the Uninfecteds will be. They're industrious and innovative."

"And devious," Walcott repeated.

"So don't trust them. But also don't trust Infecteds. Follow the Rules and be fair about them, and we'll end up with the right population after a while. Now, kill them all."

Dwayne organized the attack. Four men crept toward the house holding Molotov cocktails. Three lit rags protruding from beer bottles and hurled them onto the roof of the one story house. The fourth man had trouble with his lighter. By the time he rose from behind a wood pile to throw his bottle, he was shot from a window.

Randy sat in the gasoline flames spreading from the bottle he'd dropped. He emitted no shouts of pain. He didn't flail his arms and legs in panic. His clothes and skin quickly blackened and drooped from his seated frame before he toppled over dead.

The roof was ablaze. Smoke poured like an upside down waterfall out the upper few inches of the front doorway, and began escaping open windows all around. Emma checked her watch. They should be able to get to a couple more houses before dark.

The screen door burst open as the coughing man from before rushed out. He swiveled his shotgun left and right, but he was squinting through watery eyes and couldn't find a target. A rapid succession of single shots riddled him as his gun *boomed* and a tree branch dropped to the ground next to his body. A woman appeared, hands raised in surrender, with a young child clinging to her legs. They were easy shots. There was more shooting from the rear of the house as its other occupants fled straight into Dwayne's people. It was over in minutes.

When Dwayne approached Emma, she said, "Maybe we shouldn't do it this way. Burning down a perfectly good building, probably filled with supplies, just to get at the people inside seems wasteful. See if you can figure out another way to flush them out."

Dwayne asked Walcott how much tear gas he had during their walk to the trucks for the short trip up the highway to the next house. Samantha had marked it on her map with a big capital "I" for Infecteds.

Chapter 3

Isabel Miller was totally exhausted; a fact she denied with an increasingly fake smile every time Rick Townsend asked if she needed a break. She wasn't one of Captain Rick's Marines, so he had no idea what her limits were. Nor did she, but Isabel understood that the harder they pushed themselves, the sooner they'd catch up with her brother Noah and his family, who had fled their compound just before Isabel and Rick arrived.

The tree-lined highway along which they trudged shrank over the hours from a ribbon of asphalt many miles long, to a stretch of pavement no further than the crest of the hill ahead. Beyond that, she could see neither the road nor the dangers that awaited them.

Her long brown hair was matted by sweat and slowly coming loose from its tight bun just beneath her Kevlar helmet. Her spine felt like shattered glass from the heavy pack she carried but seemed ominously to be falling numb. Her feet, knees, and shoulders ached, and her thighs burned. Her hands flirted every so often with a quiver. The evening air was growing chilly, but in body armor and boots she produced heat that even damp camouflage clothing couldn't shed. Sweat poured down her face, her ribcage, and in the little valley in the small of her back. Still more worrisome, despite the sweat she felt the onset of chills like the first warning of a fever but more likely the first symptom of physical collapse. She had to will herself to take each step like in the unnatural gravity of some supermassive planet.

All conversation had finally halted. Gone were the little personal trivia games of earlier in the day. "Okay, here's something you don't know about me," she had said cheerfully. "I always sneeze twice. Not once. Not three times. Twice." Now, Isabel set her sights in silence on objects ahead. A bare white trunk of a rotten tree. A yellow road sign warning drivers of a junction. An abandoned, rusting junker in the roadside ditch. She plodded along until reaching those bite-sized milestones, then found another.

When Rick stopped, dropped his pack beside the road, and knelt amid some litter, Isabel grew annoyed. She had *told* him she didn't need a break. He was manufacturing one nonetheless. If Isabel took her pack off and sat, she knew she wouldn't rise again.

"Come *on!*" she snapped. Rick raised the trash and sniffed. Isabel rolled her eyes. "Seriously? Are you from some lost tribe of green-eyed Wisconsin dairy farmers?"

"These are MREs. Five of 'em. Still fresh."

"You think it's theirs?"

"No soldier worth his salt would've eaten a meal right on the side of a highway."

"They're tired." Isabel set her sights on the toppled trash cans ahead. "Let's go."

Rick hoisted his huge backpack into the air and, in one motion, slung its straps over both shoulders. After buckling it into place, he hopped once without leaving the ground, and off they went.

Isabel's shoulders were so red as to practically be bloody where her own straps, though broad, cut a little more into her with each step. By the time they reached the overturned plastic trash cans, her vision had tunneled. All she could see was her next goal—a handmade sign, drooping from the mailbox where it hung.

What did the sign say? Only a few dozen more steps would tell. How long had it been since the apocalypse began? Two months? Uncollected trash swirled with every gust. Every car or truck seemed to be rusting. Half the trees were rotting. Maybe this impoverished part of rural Virginia had looked more or less the same before the outbreak, but it seemed inevitable that the rest of America would quickly join it.

"Take cover!" Rick called out, startling Isabel, whose thoughts had long ago turned inward. He dragged her off the road onto uneven ground. She fell heavily and tried to land on her pack but painfully smashed her hip into the ground amid the scraping branches of thick brush. Rick's joining her suggested this was his intended destination.

Three cars raced by them at highway speeds. After just seconds, the civilian convoy had receded and all was quiet again save the rustling of the branches in the wind and the settling of roadside rubbish in the caravan's wake.

"Alright. All clear." Rick rose. Isabel, however, did not. "You *okay*?"

"I just wanta ress here for a minuh." She felt invisible inside the leaves and weeds and vines. A shiver rippled up her spine. She didn't even bother to flick away the bug that alit on the tip of her nose as her eyes had drifted closed. "Juss a minute."

"Not here," Rick said cruelly. "Come on."

He pulled Isabel to her feet as she complained in moans and groans and a poor attempt at a whimper. Everything hurt ten times worse than before the cars had passed. To her utter disbelief, he directed them uphill. She grunted in time with each dig of her boots' toes into the loose soil. Each step up the hill was an act of superhuman willpower. For the first time in her life she didn't trust her legs, which might buckle on any step. The noises she made evolved slowly into an imitation of sobbing. Real sobbing took too much effort.

Rick finally said they could stop. Isabel unceremoniously dumped her pack onto the dirt and curled up on the ground beside it into a ball of soreness. She closed her eyes, hugged herself against the threatening tremors, and took inventory. Neck—sore. Shoulders—sore. Back—sore. Feet—

* * * *

Isabel awoke with a start to Rick's gentle nudging. In the dim twilight, she stared at his boots as he squatted on his haunches beside her. Her head lay on his rolled up jacket. His sleeping bag covered her. When she looked up at his head, she gasped. All she saw were otherworldly night vision goggles under the brim of his helmet.

Her cyborg boyfriend said, "Time to get going."

"It's nighttime," she objected.

His binocular goggles nodded. "Your brother and his family will bed down for the night. That's when we can make up ground."

The pain from her muscles, chaffed skin, and blisters on the soles of her feet hurt with undiminished force. But at least her limbs no longer trembled.

They quickly reached the previous milestone on which Isabel had set her sights and stopped to read, in the fading light, the handmade sign that sagged from the mailbox. It was written in black marker on a white poster board like from some child's school supplies. "To Whom It May Concern. Bobby McKeever turnt and kilt his wife and kids (Louise, Mary Elizabeth, Bobby Jr., and baby Luke, all buried in back). The house is contaminated. Bobby is a white male, fifty-six, about five foot ten and 180 lbs. If you see him, kill him."

That warranted no more than a glance at Rick before they marched on in silence.

The houses that they passed were widely spaced and dark. Once, they again skidded into the ditch alongside the highway and watched a truck pass. Night fell. Milestones disappeared, but Isabel found the darkness contributed to the blankness into which she happily descended. After passage of a not insignificant amount of time—she scrupulously avoided actually checking her watch—they crested a rise and saw, up ahead, a house that, while not brightly lit, leaked enough light to suggest life inside. Rick's goggles glanced her way. *Yeah, I see it.* That house, set back from the highway, became Isabel's next goal.

The only sound was from a generator, whose engine noise stood out amid the silence of the empty road. At the foot of the meandering driveway, the mailbox read "Rawls." Rick headed up toward the house.

"Where are you going?" she asked.

"They may have seen your family. Let's go ask. Plus, we could use a water refill."

"Okay, but…but let's be careful. They're probably jumpy."

"You *think*?"

Sarcasm. That was new. Even Rick must be tired. She hadn't asked, but his pack looked half again as heavy as hers. Of course, he was twice her size, so—

"Dad!" they heard from the darkness ahead.

Without being told, Isabel joined Rick behind a rock retaining wall. The lights in the house went dark. The generator sputtered to a stop. All was now dark and still.

Isabel jumped when Rick shouted, "*Hello?* We're not here to cause trouble!"

At first, Isabel thought there would be no answer. But after what could have been a pause for an unheard debate, a man yelled, "You're on our property! You're trespassin'!"

"I'm an American Marine!" Rick replied. "We're searching for some people and wanted to ask if you've seen them!"

Another pause. This time, they heard what could only have been a muted argument growing heated. Finally, they heard, "Come on up!" from a woman, not the man.

"No funny business!" added the man.

They headed up the driveway slowly. "There's a man and a woman," Rick whispered, "just to the right of the house by the garage." His eyes behind the glowing goggles surveyed a scene that was, to Isabel, vague dark shapes amid even vaguer and darker shapes. "Boy off to the left in a duck blind at the far corner of the house. They've all got long guns."

"What's a duck blind?"

"It's, like, a...a camo tent with straps and pockets that hold foliage."

"Oookay." She could see nothing, but she gripped her carbine tightly. "I'll be on the lookout for that, then."

"That's close enough!" came the disembodied voice of the man.

Rick and Isabel stopped about fifteen meters from the house next to the front walk.

"My name is Captain Rick Townsend, USMC. This is Dr. Isabel Miller. We're looking for a group of five people—two men, a woman, and a boy and girl, both teenagers. They should've come down this highway sometime yesterday."

Again, there was more hushed discussion from beside the house. Isabel glanced up at Rick even though there was no information to be gleaned there other than that his eyes were wary and darting in the glow from the small screens. "There's good cover," he whispered, "in a culvert about three or four steps to our right rear."

Isabel turned to look but could make nothing out.

"We can show you a picture," Rick tried on the homeowners. "And we could use a refill of some water for the road, if you can spare it."

The couple's argument was halted by the women, who said something in a rising voice that ended with, "...we just ask!"

The man addressed Rick from the darkness. "We ain't seen nobody passin' by. But we'll give you your water, if you agree to take care of a problem we got."

"What problem?"

"There's this gang of Infecteds livin' down at the stream in back. Been harassin' us. Stole our dog and done God only knows what to her."

"They's starvin'," the woman added in explanation.

"They's desperate," the man continued. "And we're scared of 'em. We got kids."

"What do you want us to do?" Rick asked.

"You're the military. Go down there and take care of 'em."

"You mean chase them off?"

"No. They'll just come back."

"So, *kill* them?" Rick clarified.

"That'd do it," replied the man from the shadows.

Isabel whispered, "For some fucking *water*?"

Rick apparently agreed. "Sorry, but I don't think we're going to take you up on that. Good luck to you."

Isabel turned to leave. Rick followed but walked backwards and kept his goggles on the house.

"Wait!" the woman said. "Don't go."

* * * *

After a long explanation about how they were both vaccinated and immune from *Pandoravirus*—"So it really works?" asked the woman, Helen Rawls—and amazing hot showers for both Rick and Isabel while the other stood guard outside the bathroom door, everyone sat down to a well-lit dining table. Rick and Isabel wore their one set of fresh camo trousers, blouse, and underwear while their filthy other set was being washed. The generator masked all sounds from outside the house. The teenage boy from the duck blind, and a previously unseen girl of around eight, stared silently at their two guests.

Rick kept nervously glancing at the heavy drapes that covered the windows. "So, there's nobody on watch?"

"They usually only come around late at night or right before sunup," said Helen.

"And they haven't attacked the house?" Rick asked.

"No," replied Helen's husband, Thomas. "They just steal stuff. Lost a hoe from the shed."

"And Mister Sniffles," said the little girl. "Our doggie."

Isabel glanced at Rick. "I thought the dog was a *she*?" Their M4s were propped against the wall behind them. Isabel lowered her hand to her lap nearer the butt of her pistol in its holster.

"She was a female," Helen Rawls replied. "But the kids both agreed that cats were girls and dogs were boys, so we named her *Mister* Sniffles. She had a cold when we got her as a puppy."

"We kept her chained up out back on a dog run," Thomas Rawls explained. "The chain had been chopped through."

"And he didn't bark," said the boy. "He always barked at everybody."

The table fell silent as the parents looked at their daughter, who was on the verge of tears. "He barks all the time." Her lip quivered. She had probably already guessed that Infecteds had killed her pet. She probably didn't understand that they may have eaten her too.

"You're a doctor?" Helen asked.

"A neuroscientist. Dr. Isabel Miller."

"Hey," Thomas said. "*Hey!* I saw you on *TV*. You're the one whose twin sister..."

Isabel nodded. "Yeah. I went on CNN to talk about the virus. My sister was an epidemiologist who got infected when *Pandoravirus* first broke out in Siberia."

Something was wrong. Helen and Thomas exchanged sidelong glances, fell quiet, and picked at the delicious, fresh green beans and venison.

Finally, Isabel broke the silence. "I'm sorry, but did I miss something here?"

Rick, Isabel, and the little girl looked from face to face. Thomas Rawls said, "We don't want any trouble." That was even more bewildering. "We just wanta live our lives here, not...not choose sides or anything."

"I'm sorry. But I still don't understand."

The husband and wife stared silently at each other before Helen said, in an urgent whisper, "Tell your sister that we'll do whatever they say."

"Well..." Thomas began to modify, but his wife silenced him with a hand on his forearm. It took another round of Isabel's polite what-the-hell-are-you-talking-about queries, minus the profanity, for Thomas to explain. His cousin and his cousin's family from up in Staunton had stayed with them the previous night. They, too, were fleeing down the highway and had urged the Rawls's to join them. "But we got our supplies, and our garden," Thomas reasoned again—to his wife, not Isabel, to whom he finally turned. "Your sister..."

He searched his memory for her name. "Emma?" supplied Isabel.

"Right, Emma Miller. She held a meetin' at the Staunton Holiday Inn. My cousin took a video on his phone and showed it to us. She basically said join up, or else. Either you're with 'em, or again' 'em. And she had all these rules."

"Like no," Helen added before lowering her voice, "s-e-x."

She glanced at her daughter, who said, "I can spell, Momma."

"The point is," Thomas continued, "that if you break her rules, they'll kill ya. Who knows how, or where, or when, or who decides. No trial, or probation, or community service, or jail time. Just...." He made the slashing sign across his throat and a sickening sound to go with it. "My cousin up and took off. A bunch did. The Uninfecteds, at least."

Helen was waiting impatiently for him to finish. "So when you see your sister, tell her that the Rawls family is, you know, behind her 100 percent. Restore order, stop the violence, give everybody jobs. All the things she said in her little speech. It's just, you know, we're good right where we're at. We won't bother nobody."

Isabel was nodding. That sounded like Emma. Helen and Thomas, however, took her nod for more than it meant, smiled, and seemed greatly relieved. Helen even dumped more green beans on Isabel's plate. She didn't refuse them, but shared half with Rick.

Finally back on the highway after packing their freshly washed spare clothes, Isabel could spot no landmarks on which to focus. Instead, her goal was more figurative. She headed not for a physical milestone, but a concept. She would find and reunite with her family, like the Rawlses stuck together...before it was too late.

Chapter 4

"It's a trap," said Noah Miller's daughter Chloe.

Noah's wife and kids were exhausted after hiking only eleven miles on the first day. He'd hoped to make twenty-four miles a day on their 1,260 mile journey from Virginia to Texas. But complaints about sore backs and blistered feet had led to frequent breaks. Now, they had been stopped cold by a little girl playing in the road at sunset.

His family and the eighteen-year-old neighbor boy Margus Bishop lay on a hillside surveying the odd scene. Chloe and Jake peered through the scopes on their AR-15s. Noah searched the ditches and fields alongside the road with binoculars. His only concern was the dark opening of a large drainage pipe under the highway twenty yards from where the girl sat on an upside down plastic bucket.

"Why would a ten-year-old girl," his wife Natalie asked, "wearing her frilly white *Easter* dress and pigtails, be out playing on a highway just before dark with absolutely no one else in sight? In the middle of a pandemic? It's beyond weird. She must be infected."

The little girl seemed absorbed in scraping a stick along the pavement between her patent leather dress shoes. Her long hair was braided, and her play seemed listless and aimless. "Maybe she's waiting for a ride to come pick her up?" Noah suggested.

"After doing *what?*" Natalie replied. "Why is she even here, and alone?"

"Maybe she's been orphaned," Noah threw out with flagging conviction.

"It's a *traa*ap," Chloe repeated in a singsong voice with one eye to her sight.

"We can't stop every time we see someone on the road. We'll never even get to Tennessee, much less Texas."

"There's a car," Natalie said. Everyone turned. A dusty sedan with what looked like gold New York license plates approached slowly. Its headlights were off despite the growing darkness.

"I'll go flag it down," Jake said, rising.

"Wait!" Noah snapped. "We don't know anything about them."

"Yeah, but Dad—"

"Just *wait!*"

The car passed, rounded the bend, and stopped short of the girl, who rose to stand, motionless, in the middle of the road. Their headlights came on. The girl's head jerked to the side as she shielded her face from the glare.

Natalie said, "Pupils must be popped. She's infected."

"Yeah," Noah had to agree. "But they see what we see. And she isn't armed."

The driver's door opened. "Dad!" Chloe said. "It's a *trap.*"

"They're closer to the scene than us," he reasoned as even Natalie raised her rifle to her shoulder. "They may see things we can't."

"He's talking to her," Natalie said as she squinted through her own scope, "but the girl isn't answering."

Noah raised his binoculars just as a line of motley figures came racing out of the concrete pipe almost even with where the car had stopped. "Look out!" Chloe shouted.

The car's driver jumped back inside.

"Dad, I'm shooting!" Chloe said.

One attacker with a large chunk of concrete shattered the driver's window. Another man reached inside the car.

Chloe's rifle shot flame a foot out the end of its barrel.

The car was thrown into reverse, dragging and felling attackers.

Jake's rifle blazed too, as did Natalie's and Margus's.

Attackers stabbed knives into the rear tires like spear wielding native hunters taking down big game. Sparks flew from the rims of the car's wheels.

"Dad...*shoot!*" Jake called out.

The driver was easily hauled out through his shattered window, but the passenger, a woman, still wore her seatbelt and had to be cut from it, screaming.

Noah opened fire. Not at the attackers who beset the luckless couple, but at the others whose attention had turned toward them and who raced back toward the shelter of the pipe. They were only a hundred yards away. He was pretty sure he hit all four of them.

Within seconds, both the mob of attackers and their two victims lay unmoving on the highway. His family's weapons fell silent.

"We shoulda stopped 'em," Jake said in a quaking voice. Noah knew he was right.

Jake's sister kept her eye to her scope. "There's that little girl." Noah raised his binoculars. The girl's pigtails danced as she ran away along the roadside ditch, clearly visible in the car's headlights.

His binoculars shook when a shot rang out. "Chloe!" Natalie shouted. When Noah reacquired his view of the girl, she lay face down amid the weeds. Noah and Natalie turned to their daughter, whose rifle was still raised to her cheek. *Bam!* Flame again shot out, lighting the hillside beneath her. Chloe returned their looks. "She was still *moving.*"

Jesus, Noah thought before finding Natalie's gaze on him. "We have to go check on them," she said.

"Maybe we should make camp around here and work our way past them tomorrow after the sun comes up."

But Natalie said, "Noah, that was a young couple. What if...?"

He caught her eye and shook his head. But Chloe asked, "What? What if *what*?"

"They might have a baby or young child in that car," Natalie answered.

"Oh. Jeez. Let's go." It was Chloe and Jake hoisting their heavy packs on their backs that decided it. Noah disagreed, but he'd proven his decision making suspect. As they descended the hill, he said to Natalie, "We can't take a baby with us, Nat."

Chloe replied. "Are you gonna put the little thing out of its misery, or leave it in its car seat till it dies? And it's not an *it*, you know. It's a little he or a little she."

"How the hell could we take care of a baby?" Noah rebutted. "You know how much noise they make. Plus baby food. Diapers. We can't take that on."

When they reached the highway, they donned disposable gloves and masks. The car's headlights still shone and the engine groaned. It was in gear, but stuck on a body pinned under its rear rims. The seatbelt warning *binged* insistently. "Find cover," Noah said as they neared the ambush site. "Keep rifles on both ends of that pipe. I'll check the car out."

"Be careful," Natalie said from behind, which annoyed Noah immensely. They shouldn't even be doing this. The interior and exterior lights of the car lit a scene littered with carnage. The driver lay still amid a tangle of bodies. His one remaining eye stared unblinking at the sky. One of his attackers, however, was still breathing. Noah's aim followed the rising and falling chest up his bloody torso, past his bloody neck, to his still intact head. *Bam!* Bits of his cranium skittered across the pavement. The pile fell still.

He went around to the other side of the car. An Infected leapt out at him. He fired while backpedaling but missed. Three shots rang out. The attacker bounced off the car's trunk before sliding to the pavement and face planting on asphalt. Noah put an insurance round into the back of the woman's head, then took a deep and steadying breath. On the far side of the car lay the other victim of the Infected ambush. Three attackers lay dead around her, all men. One already had his trousers lowered. Noah gritted his teeth in anger before putting bullets into those three Infecteds even though none showed any signs of life.

He crept closer. A young Asian woman whose blouse had been torn open had been cut up badly by the knife used to free her from her seatbelt. Deep slashes oozed from her face, neck, shoulders, and abdomen. Frothy orange blood bubbled slowly at the ragged puncture wound in her throat. She made an inhuman noise with the last air to pass her windpipe. *God, please forgive me,* he prayed before shooting her.

Noah's head began to spin. A prickly feeling spread across his chest and arms. He wanted to sit, to curl up and wrap himself in a tight embrace guaranteed to ward off the impending shakes.

But instead, he slowly, and with dread, raised his flashlight to search the car. It held supplies, but no car seat. "It's empty," he informed his family in a voice that fluttered and shook, but he heaved a huge sigh of relief. He would not have to face the dilemma he feared of finding a baby in back. And his family had survived an ambush into which he would have led them had Chloe not been as paranoid as she was. Noah turned the car and its headlights off. With Jake covering him, he confirmed that the Infecteds he had shot beside the road were all dead and the pipe from which they had emerged was empty. They grabbed two gallons of water from the car to replace what they'd consumed and hurried past the awful scene.

When they reached the little girl's body, their daughter left the highway. "Chloe!" Noah called out.

She kicked the little girl with her boot, ready to fire, then turned her over and thumped her eye with the flick of her finger. The girl didn't flinch. "Little *bitch!*" she cursed at the corpse as she kicked her again and threw her Latex gloves atop the small corpse.

An hour later, they set up camp and ate in sullen silence until Chloe asked, "Did you let that car go by to see if it was an ambush?"

"No!" Noah replied. "*Jesus*, Chloe."

It was hard to tell in the darkness and ensuing silence whether she believed him.

Chapter 5

THE SHENANDOAH VALLEY
Infection Date 65, 1315 GMT (9:15 a.m. Local)

Emma thought that the first day's work assignments went well. Samantha had prepared all the work cards and used pushpins to affix them to the cork bulletin board next to the few Rules, which hadn't changed overnight.

"Don't lose the pins," Samantha called out to the crowd in her high-pitched voice.

An Uninfected retrieved one that had fallen when he pulled the three by five card off the board. On the card, as on all the others, Sam had printed in her cheery red handwriting, various day jobs and a few more permanent positions.

"I think the Uninfecteds appreciate the smiley face," Samantha suggested to Emma. She stepped forward and took a card from an elderly woman, pinning it back to the board. "That job requires too much physical labor." The masked octogenarian now waited on the twelve-year-old. "You could take *that* job. All you have to do is identify the bodies before burning. Check them for driver's licenses and stuff. Or you could do that one down at the bottom. Cleaning up after meals in the dorm and washing the dishes."

The woman, strangely expressionless for an Uninfected, selected the latter card. "Thank you, dear."

Upon returning, Samantha said to Emma, "She seems nice. But I can never tell what they're thinking."

"They're always thinking something," Emma cautioned.

When the last of the Uninfecteds had selected a job and cleared away, it was the Infecteds' turn. There were some minor scuffles. Two Infecteds tugged on the same job card. Samantha again admonished them about the pushpins, speaking to the Infecteds more harshly, Emma noted, than she had to the old uninfected woman. One infected man stepped on the toe of another, who threw an elbow into his ribs. The two men had to be pushed apart by Dwayne, who shouted, "Hey!" and drew his pistol.

"Don't lose those pins!" Samantha added.

One of the men said, "Why do the Uninfecteds get first choice?"

"Because you're contaminating this area with *Pandoravirus*," Emma replied.

"*So*. That's their problem."

Dwayne aimed his pistol straight at the man's face and looked at Emma, who shook her head. He let the complaining man live.

But Samantha was writing something in her blue spiral notebook. "Mr. O'Keefe complains a lot," Emma read over the girl's shoulder.

When the town square had cleared and everyone had presumably headed off to work at their assigned jobs for the day, Emma convened a meeting in Sheriff Walcott's office with her roommates from the NIH hospital— Dwayne and Samantha—but excluding the relatively incompetent Dorothy Adams, a housewife who had been touring the Great Wall when the virus rampaged across China. "We should have someone in here representing the Uninfecteds," Emma suggested. "Any candidates come to mind?" No one had any names to propose. "Be on the lookout for anyone who seems to be an organizer type. I'd rather them be in here talking to us than out there talking to the Uninfecteds."

Dwayne and Walcott stared back at her blankly. Samantha wrote Emma's order in her notebook and said, "I'll find someone."

"So, Dwayne, how did it go down at the county road junction last night?"

"Fine. They were all infected, and they'd collected a good amount of food and weapons by ambushing passersby. We lost two. They lost eleven. Five more are in the jail cells in back. Do you want me to kill them?"

Emma said, "No. I'll talk to them first."

She quickly gave them their tasks. Walcott and his two surviving deputies she sent out with Dwayne's team to continue clearing houses in the valley and foothills around town. "Try to avoid burning houses down," she reminded him. "If they're uninfected and refuse to join, try executing hostages until they come out. Otherwise, pin them down inside and start tossing infected bodies or body parts in."

"And still kill them all when they come out?" Walcott asked. "No second chances?"

"No second chances. Our credibility is at stake. But you can take prisoners. You can use them as hostages at the next house."

"It's so crazy," Samantha said, "that Uninfecteds give up just because we're executing strangers. Weird. What do we do if the holdouts are *Infected*? They won't care that we're throwing contaminated body parts at them or executing hostages."

"Those you may have to burn out." Emma tasked Samantha with checking on how the assigned work was progressing. "You won't scare the Uninfecteds. You're too young. But if you see anyone slacking off, or any Uninfecteds that seem to be organizing a resistance, write down their names and we'll take care of them later. Try smiling. The Uninfecteds will let their guard down. Practice." Samantha opened her mouth and bared her teeth. "Keep practicing. Use a mirror."

"Dwayne," Emma said, "I hear the Uninfecteds are organizing defenses down in Rawley Springs. When will we be ready to move on them?"

"We're down to twenty-two guns we can count on. Sheriff Walcott may turn up some more today, but unless you let me start recruiting among the Uninfecteds we'll have to use up most of those twenty-two in any fight with Rawley Springs."

"When will you be ready to go if you do plan on using them all up?"

"As early as tonight. We'll at least whittle down the numbers in Rawley Springs for a next try in a few days once we've built our forces back up."

"And you trust your people will die for you?"

"No," Dwayne responded. "It's very different than leading Marines. Infecteds will run away if they see what's coming as certain death. But they all caught the virus and turned in the last week or so and are still pretty addled."

"Not very deep thinkers, eh?" Samantha tried out her latest version of a smile.

"Try keeping your eyes open," Emma advised. Samantha rubbed her jaw to loosen it.

Emma dismissed them and headed to the back of the sheriff's offices. Four men and one woman stared out through bars at Emma with fully popped and black pupils. "We're organizing a community to provide for its members' needs."

"What's the catch?" asked a middle aged man.

"You have to follow The Community's Rules."

"And what happens if we don't?" persisted the stubble faced man.

"You'll be punished. Executed."

"Who makes up these Rules?"

The talkative man must have been the group's leader. None of the others seemed the least bit curious. *"I do."*

Off to the side, unnoticed at first by Emma, a young man in his twenties leapt to his feet and, seething with adrenaline, lunged for the bars and grabbed for her with claw like hands at full extension. *"Aaaaarrh!"* he screamed, grimacing, tainted spittle spraying from his mouth, fingernails just inches from an unflinching Emma.

She turned to Walcott's deputy and nodded. His pistol shot rang out, and the Infected man rocked back and then slumped, one arm caught in the bars and preventing him from reaching the concrete floor.

The four other Infecteds didn't react at all. Three stared at the middle aged man, who in turn held Emma's unblinking return gaze. "If we agree to join, what do we get?"

She held her hand out to the deputy, who handed Emma his pistol. She raised it, took aim, and shot the man in the forehead. He crumpled dead to the floor. The other three now looked at Emma, not at the dead man. "You get to live," Emma said in answer to their former leader's question. "And all your needs will be taken care of."

The two men and one woman joined, casually stepping over the bodies of their former comrades. Emma radioed Dwayne. "I've got three more guns for your force."

Chapter 6

Isabel and Rick surveyed from a distance the carnage spread across the state highway. "Jesus," Isabel said. "What a bloodbath."

They left their packs in the roadside ditch and approached the car carefully, M4 carbines at the ready. Several times, Rick halted Isabel, ten meters behind him, with a raised hand when his senses alerted. But after each, they resumed their slow progress until they reached the car, whose flat back tire had rolled to a stop against one of the dead.

The car windows were smashed. An Asian woman, who had been cut out of her still clasped seatbelt, lay dead beside the passenger door.

"Let's go," Isabel whispered, though they appeared to be alone.

Rick was kneeling next to one of the dead. "These people must have attacked this car and killed the driver and passenger."

"But who killed *them*?" Isabel asked, searching the dark ridges and trees all around.

He drew a large, black, serrated knife from its sheath. Isabel cringed, thinking he was going to conduct some kind of roadside autopsy. But he rolled a body over and pried a flattened and warped bullet from the bloody asphalt beneath where the dead man's head had lain. Rick held the smushed bullet up to Isabel. "Kill shot to the head. 5.56mm."

"That's the same ammo Noah and his family use," Isabel noted, her hopes rising.

"Whoever it was, they tore these attackers up."

After retrieving their packs, they proceeded past the massacre. "Look." Isabel pointed into the ditch ahead. "It's a little girl."

Rick knelt beside her corpse. "Two shots in the back."

"Jeez," Isabel muttered. If Noah and his family had done this, how much had they changed since she'd last seen them less than two weeks earlier?

* * * *

After the sun had risen on a bright day, they came upon a barricade across the highway right at the city limits of a small town, as delineated by a road sign. Three men with hunting rifles manned the far side. Rick and Isabel approached slowly; Rick with his right hand raised instead of resting on his M4s grip.

"That's close enough!" shouted one of the men. His rifle rested on his hip and, like the others, eyed them from behind sunglasses. All three wore hats and caps of various sorts. "Town's closed!"

"I'm Capt. Rick Townsend. This is Dr. Isabel Miller. We're on official U.S. government business."

The three sentries held a brief sidebar discussion before the spokesman asked, "What kinda doctor is she?"

"I'm a neuroscience professor!"

"Sorry. Like I said, the town is closed. Head thata way." He pointed to the road that led off at a right angle. "It rejoins the highway on the other side of town. I wouldn't bother any landowners along the way. They're all shoot-first types these days."

"Has the virus made it down here?" Rick asked.

"*Oh* yeah. They's everywhere."

Isabel said, "Can I show you a picture and ask if you've seen some people we're looking for?" She pulled her cell phone out of her pocket and approached the barricade.

"Iz!" Rick snapped. He aimed his rifle in the air over the heads of the men at the barricade ahead, whose rifles and shotguns were now aimed at Isabel.

"Take it easy," she said to the town guards in a plaintive tone. "Jeez."

"Why ain't you wearin' gloves and masks?" questioned one of the men.

"We're immune. We've been vaccinated."

After a brief, hushed discussion, their original challenger said, "Bullshit! Ain't nobody around here got any of the vaccine yet."

"*We* have. I'm from the White House and he's from the Pentagon."

"Right. And I'm the King of...of wherever."

Isabel tried again. "Have you seen a family—husband with dark curly hair, pretty wife and daughter with short blond haircuts, and a tall and skinny thirteen-year-old boy?"

"And that other kid," Rick prompted.

"Oh, and a grown boy, but we don't know what he looks like."

Again, there was a whispered conversation. "Yeah, we seen 'em. Armed to the teeth, like you."

Isabel grinned at Rick. "How long ago? Where'd they go?"

The main guy pointed up the hill along the route they'd been directed. "They come walkin' up yesterday just like you. 'Bout midafternoon, I'd guess."

"Thank you! And good luck!"

She again grinned at Rick as they detoured around the town.

"Say!" called out the sentry from the behind them. "That vaccine really work?"

"Yes! It does!"

"Tell 'em to send us some ASAP! Every day, somebody else gets sick!"

The road wound into the foothills and was slower going than the flatter highway. Despite Isabel's dozen major aches, which had merged into continuous pain from her shoulders to the soles of her feet, her pace quickened. They were gaining on Noah. "We're less than a day behind! And they're following the map they left for us."

Isabel couldn't tell where Rick's eyes were looking behind his sunglasses, but his rifle was just beneath his chin and its butt rested firmly against his shoulder. She raised her own M4 but saw nothing at which to aim.

"Do you smell that?" Rick asked.

Wood smoke was mixed with a vaguely nauseating smell. Rick led them off the lane and up a scrub covered hillside. A column of gray smoke rose above the forest. Rick dumped his pack and crouched as they neared the crest. Isabel did the same and felt she might escape the bonds of gravity with each lighter, springier step.

"They're burning bodies," Rick reported from behind binoculars.

Isabel borrowed them as Rick continued his observation through his M4's scope. A man and a woman tossed a corpse onto a flaming stack of the dead. "They're not wearing protective gear."

"I noticed," Rick replied, squinting slightly.

Isabel scanned the bodies awaiting cremation and the pile of gear obviously salvaged from them. Rick said, "Your brother's stuff was all camo, right?"

"Yeah. It's not them. Whatta we do? Those Infecteds are right by the road."

"I don't see any weapons." Rick lowered his carbine. "Let's just head on past."

To Rick's aid in donning her pack, Isabel contributed several grunts of exertion and hisses of pain before they proceeded up the road past the funeral pyre. When the man and woman, who neglected even to wear a scarf or bandana against the overpowering stench, turned toward them, Rick raised his right hand as before. But his left, Isabel noticed, gripped his carbine's forward grip, ready to raise it into firing position.

The couple returned his wave awkwardly and tossed a fresh body—a naked child—into the crackling blaze. Rick and Isabel passed, cringing but without incident.

A half mile farther they came upon a crazed Infected teenager, who was pulping a body in a front yard with a shovel, alternately pounding it with the shovel's flat head and jabbing its blade edgewise into the corpse, fully committed to its complete dismemberment. Other, calmer Infecteds kept a wary eye on and steered a wide path around the grunting boy as they systematically looted their murdered neighbors' home and carried out sacks of food and jugs of water. Spray painted across the front door, which dangled from its hinges, was the warning, "Infecteds Will Be Shot on Sight!" And true to its word, the front porch was littered with bodies.

Rick stopped and listened, Isabel imagined, for a scream coming from that overrun house. She was greatly relieved not to have heard one. "Nothing we can do here," he said.

There were random gunshots, however, in the distance. Isabel looked Rick's way at each one. Sometimes they rose to a crackle of fire from multiple weapons, but mostly they were just the *pop* of a single shot. They grew louder with each hill crested.

Finally, Rick left the road, and they climbed a hill and found a vantage point among the trees. "Someone is attacking that house up ahead. The one with the white camper parked beside it with the electric cables running into the house."

Isabel took the binoculars from him and found the house he described. A loud report of a rifle or shotgun fired at attackers in a ditch was accompanied by a flash from the windows of the house. "I can't tell who's infected and who's not," she said.

"Does it matter?" Isabel eyed Rick in surprise after that fatalistic remark. "I mean they could all be Infecteds, or all Uninfecteds, or even mixed. We can't stop and intervene in every fight we come across, Isabel. We'll never catch up with your brother."

What followed was the worst moral crisis of Isabel's life to date. It lasted far longer than the ten minutes it took to circumnavigate the firefight. She couldn't even see the house from the streambed through which they waded, but she could hear its defenders. "Go away! Leave us alone!" a woman shouted. Her only reply was a few gunshots, which she returned. Isabel thought they had escaped with her conscience only bruised until, as they climbed back up onto the road, they heard, at the very limit the sound could travel, a crescendo of shouts from the woman and high-pitched shrieks from a number of children.

We could have killed those attackers, Isabel tormented herself in condemnation, *or tried.* Racked with guilt, she couldn't bring herself to look up at Rick, and he said nothing as his sunglasses scanned the road ahead. "They're evil," she said softly for fear her voice would break and tears would flow.

"Who? Infecteds? I thought you, you know...?"

"Was on their side? I was...I guess. 'Cause of my sister. But not anymore. The things they do. The outrages they commit without any compunction whatsoever. Murder comes as easily to them as saying hello is to an Uninfected. How can you not conclude, like some of those people on TV I used to think were nutcases, that the only good Infected is a dead Infected? Even Emma. What atrocities will she commit before things settle down, if they ever do?"

"I thought you said we shouldn't hold their crimes against them because they're incapable of moral judgment, and it's not their fault that they got sick and brain damaged."

"I said that? Well, that doesn't make as much sense as it did back at the NIH lab."

With every step, they drew closer to Noah. He, his family, and the other Uninfecteds, as imperfect as they had proved to be throughout human history, were nonetheless on a higher evolutionary rung than Infecteds. They, and only they, were worth defending.

Chapter 7

Emma and Samantha waited just outside the glare of the studio lights as the anchorman and woman at the local television station completed their news broadcast.

"With the outbreak in Kanyakamari in the far south," the blank faced woman read, "authorities in New Delhi report that *Pandoravirus* has now reached every region of India. An overloaded ferry filled with refugees attempting to escape the pandemic capsized during the night in the Gulf of Mannar, with the apparent loss of all aboard, estimated to be twelve hundred people. The government in Colombo has denied any responsibility although it has closed all ports and ordered their navy to fire on any craft attempting to enter Sri Lankan waters."

The camera cut to the woman's male partner, whose eyes were black like the female broadcaster's. "Closer to home, Rawley Springs, Lacey Spring, New Market, and Newport have all joined a new and growing community formed in the wake of SED's passage through the Shenandoah Valley."

A woman with bright green darting eyes, wearing a mask and gloves with a face shiny with perspiration, directed Emma to a chair just outside the camera's shot. With hands shaking in what Emma presumed was fear, she attached to the collar of Emma's simple white blouse a microphone, and ran the wire over her shoulder and out of view.

"The fighting in Rawley Springs was intense but brief, with heavy casualties on both sides," the announcer continued. "The casualties were lighter in Lacey Spring, but New Market agreed to join The Community without a fight. WHSV-TV is pleased to have the leader of The Community, Dr. Emma Miller, in our studio. Dr. Miller? Welcome."

Emma said, out of habit, "Thank you for having me," even though there had been no invitation. A few hours earlier, the few defenders of Harrisonburg's outlying TV station had been overwhelmed by Dwayne's quickly growing army.

"Tell us about your new community," asked the man interviewing her.

"We are organized around three principles: voluntary agreement to an evolving social contract, work in exchange for satisfaction of basic needs, and punishment for violations of the social contract. Every morning at eight o'clock, we publish any amendments to the Rules proposed for the coming day. All citizens then either head off to their assigned jobs or have a reasonable amount of time—currently two hours—to depart the area governed by The Community if they do not agree to abide by the amended contract."

"And what sort of terms does this contract provide?"

"Well, the core sets out the basic Rules," Emma explained, turning to the camera and her audience in the wider region beyond it. "All Community members age fourteen and up must accept work at one of the posted jobs. No one may commit any violence not sanctioned by The Community. No gatherings larger than six people per ten square meters are allowed other than as called for by work commitments. Things like that. Then, as events dictate, we provide special Rules, sometimes on a temporary basis. For instance, one special Rule placed on each town's bulletin board this morning and posted on The Community's Facebook page is that no Community members are to approach the city limits of Harrisonburg."

"And why that rule?"

"We would like to offer to the residents of Harrisonburg membership in The Community, and we would like to avoid violence preceding that offer, if at all possible. And your list of towns that have joined is incomplete. Already this afternoon, Grove Hill joined us, Shenandoah fell after about an hour-long fight, and fighting continues in McGaheysville even though Penn Laird to their west has already agreed in principle to join once a corridor along Highway 33 is opened to them."

"Quite impressive gains," said the newsman, which even to Emma's ear sounded odd due to his total lack of inflection or emphasis. His off camera partner sat inert at the news desk and staring blankly into space, presumably not even listening. "And I presume, given that the remaining uninfected employees of our studio have been asked to remain in their jobs, that your Community includes both Infected and Uninfected members?"

"That's right. The Community is open to all who agree to abide by the Rules."

"And what if someone does not comply with them?"

"They'll be punished." The anchorman nodded at the plan's reasonableness and didn't ask follow-ups like, *Punished how?* But Emma caught sight of the small huddle of Uninfected studio workers, just outside the glare of the lights, who locked arms or held hands.

"You mentioned," said the newsman, referring to a paper he held, "that you are hoping to incorporate Harrisonburg into your Community without violence. But the population of Harrisonburg has swollen to nearly a hundred thousand people with the arrival of refugees from Northern Virginia and beyond, many of whom are housed in empty dormitories and academic facilities at James Madison University. Reports that we have aired here on Channel 49 are that militias were being organized to quell the violence that is running rampant in the overcrowded and under resourced town. Would they not represent a significant security, or *military* challenge for you?"

"Yes, but not an overwhelming one," Emma replied honestly to what she guessed was a question scripted by an uninfected producer. "Our intelligence indicates that Harrisonburg is down to only a few days of food left. The Mennonites who live in and around Harrisonburg have already sought our protection as they are some of the principal victims of looters' violence, and we have agreed to a side contract with them to provide security assistance until the situation in the area is resolved. We expect that, if no overarching agreement is reached with the remaining local government, there will be ample opportunities for similar side deals as conditions deteriorate. Our Community is rebuilding, working the farms and fields, distributing food, water, and medicine, and maintaining law and order. Those things should be appealing to the citizens of Harrisonburg and to the refugees who've found shelter there, and we should be able to avoid a direct assault on the town. If not, every day we grow stronger and Harrisonburg more desperate."

"Do you not fear the military forces of the United States?" the man read.

"Yes, we do. Of course we have taken note of the substantial firepower still deployed by the U.S. armed forces, and of the tremendous destruction they wrought before evacuation of the government from the District of Columbia. But that withdrawal left the Norfolk naval base and its associated facilities as the nearest large concentration of military forces. And it's worth noting they lie over 200 miles from here, and would have to fight their way through Richmond, which is in total chaos, and negotiate or force their way through the Neutral Zone declared in and around Charlottesville, at least until that fails."

"But you need only look up at the sky," the newsman said—*his own observation?*—"to see, from the numerous jet contrails, that the airpower in Norfolk is still strong. Were they to come to the defense of Harrisonburg, do you think you could prevail in a fight?" That question was far too complex. He was definitely reading an uninfected person's script.

"Yes. Eventually. But we don't believe the military will be able to aid Harrisonburg given the other demands they're facing. Norfolk is still facilitating the withdrawal of forces and government personnel not just from the District of Columbia, but from the Acela corridor and all across New England. Those evacuees are transiting through Norfolk to bases in southern Florida and Cuba. Given all those demands, Norfolk hasn't even been able to forestall the collapse of civil government in Newport News and Hampton, which are just across the James River, and are barely maintaining order in Virginia Beach now that *Pandoravirus* has broken out there. They had to complete the withdrawal of Marines and FBI from their facilities in Quantico by air and sea, not overland, so Harrisonburg way down here is a little outside their area of operations."

The anchorman nodded sagely, although the gesture was empty, not indicative of too much active cognition. "Is there anything else you would like to inform our viewers?"

"Yes. Beginning tomorrow morning at eight a.m., we will broadcast the full list of Rules that constitute our social contract. Every member of our Community will be charged with viewing those Rules at one of our growing number of bulletin boards, online, or on-air broadcasts by this and other stations, or assuming the risk of an unknowing violation. And secondly...perhaps we should get your station manager over here."

Beside the glare of the studio lights, the uninfected woman who had ushered Emma to her chair touched her chest, and Emma nodded. Reluctantly, she departed her small clutch of Uninfecteds and tentatively joined Emma and the two anchors behind the desk. The station manager was standing, so Emma rose. "As you can see, she is uninfected and unharmed. We harbor no ill will toward anyone and wish only to provide for the safety, health, and needs of the members of our Community. We welcome all who wish to join us to work together for the common good."

Emma held her hand out to the station manager, who stared down at it for a moment before awkwardly taking it in her own, gloved hand for a ceremonial shake.

Eric L. Harry

The red light atop another studio camera lit, and the female anchorwoman seated at the desk stirred from her reverie. "Thank you, Dr. Miller. Moving on to the weather, we are sad to announce the death an hour ago of Butch Figgens, WHSV's long-time meteorologist, and extend our sympathies to his wife and three children." Neither sadness nor sympathy were evident in the woman's voice. "But it looks like we are in for a cold snap this weekend. The chance of rain rises to 90 percent tomorrow night, and temperatures the following day are expected to fall into the forties. *Brrrr,*" she read tonelessly.

Chapter 8

Noah's Apple Watch vibrated. Although he was deep in an almost narcotic sleep, he woke—confused—to a shot of adrenaline. *Where am I?* He removed his watch and placed it on its charger, which was plugged into an active wall outlet.

The dark shapes of his wife and daughter lay still as death in their sleeping bags. But on closer inspection, they breathed steadily.

There was a fluttering sound. A flag flapped in the steady, cold breeze. It was the pin in a golf green a few dozen yards away. The smell oriented him. His family slept on the hard concrete slab of a semi-enclosed and filthy bathroom. But at least the roof's overhang provided them shelter from the rain that had pelted the area throughout the night.

He grabbed his AR-15 and went to relieve his son, who was on watch. Jake was sound asleep.

"Jake!"

His teenage son started and raised his head. "What? I was awake."

"No, you weren't!"

"What is it?" Natalie whispered from the darkness.

"Dad?" Jake pled softly.

Noah hesitated before saying, "It's nothing. Go back to sleep."

Noah grabbed his son's skinny arm and dragged him out across the sodden ground toward the copse of trees they used as a latrine. *"Jake,* Jesus! You know what's at stake! You can't *do* that! We're all *counting* on you!"

"I know, I know." His words were catching in his chest. His son was crying. "I'm *sorry*. I don't know *what* happened. It got cold, so I got in my sleeping bag, and—"

"How can I trust you to take a watch, Jake?"

"You *can*! I promise! I'm *sorry*, Dad. It'll never happen again!"

Noah was too exhausted to do anything more than sigh. "Go get some sleep." Jake wrapped both arms around Noah, hugged him against his still heaving chest, and apologized again. He, too, was bone weary—his nerves frayed and emotions raw. In four days of walking, from dawn to dusk, they had traveled 115 miles. Only 1,145 miles to go.

His sniffling almost fourteen-year-old wiped away his tears and trudged toward the reeking bathroom. His back was lit by dim flashes originating over the treetops.

"Hey Jake. What's that?" Noah pointed in the direction of the flashes to the south.

"I dunno. Lightning?"

Noah decided to clear the cobwebs by patrolling their position. His rifle—magazine full, round chambered, safety on, always—was gripped firmly in both hands. Most of the ground outside the overgrown fairways, which offered good sight lines from the bathroom, was soggy from the rains, which if the lightning was any indication might not be letting up. Noah kept his family in sight as he circumnavigated the perimeter. He remained just inside the tree line, ready in an instant to shoot anyone he might surprise there.

When he reached a utility road that ran to the equipment barn housing the golf carts, he saw, in the distance, that the flashes weren't lightning. They were explosions coming from the direction of Roanoke. What he had hoped might be a momentary sanctuary—a respite from the travails of the road—had now turned into an obstacle to be bypassed. A few extra hours of walking before they got back on course.

He cut across the fairway to the opposite rough and the cover offered there by a smattering of trees. From that side, he made his way past the bathroom.

Even without the heavy pack, his every step brought pain. Both of his shoulders were bloody and raw from his pack's straps. He kept trying to stretch the ache from his back, but his body stubbornly refused him any relief. His thighs and knees were sore. The soles of his feet in his damp boots were on their second round of blisters. They would all need to care for their feet better in the coming days to avoid crippling medical complications.

The fighting in Roanoke did not appear to be by the military. There were no long strings of explosions from bombers, or steady pummeling from artillery, or tracers fired from the air to the ground. The fighting seemed sporadic, disorganized...primitive.

Natalie was waiting for him. "You should sleep, sweetheart," she whispered.

"I need to check our rations and water, then check everyone's feet for blisters, then make sure the rifles have all been cleaned adequately, then—"

"You need to rest, Noah. The kids need their father, and I need my husband. None of us needs an exhausted, sick, braindead wreck. You need to take care of yourself before you can take care of us. Go have a bite to eat. I'll stand watch."

* * * *

By the time they had each taken a shockingly cold but therefore highly invigorating shower in the country club's locker rooms, the sun was rising above the mist. Margus bore the shower with surprising dignity, but the sting of the spray elicited squeals from Noah's children. Afterwards, they all seemed more animated than they had been in days.

"I spy," Jake said when back on the highway, "with my little eye, something black."

Chloe said, "That's too vague."

"No, it's not. Those are the rules. Right Mom and Dad?"

"You're too close together," Noah said from up front.

"Okay. I spy, with my little eye, something black in the sky. *Hey.* It even rhymes."

"That smoke?" Chloe replied.

"See. That made it *too* simple."

"Take cover!" Noah snapped on seeing the approach of trudging human forms.

They scrambled into the woods, randomly dashing to both sides of the highway and quickly settling in behind their rifles. About a dozen people, not in any tactical formation or even necessarily members of the same group, slowly passed. Many wore bandages and limped. Few carried any supplies. Children were carried in their parent's arms or held hands, several still wearing pajamas and animal themed fuzzy slippers. They must have been uninfected given that they still cared for their young, but they looked as dazed and insensate as the most out of it Infected.

No one said a word when back on the road. They were more alert than before and barely made it another mile before having to take cover again. As the refugee traffic grew thicker, they abandoned the main road altogether, when they could, and began taking a series of trails, streams, and paths roughly paralleling it.

When they rounded a bend on a country road in the hills above the highway, there was no hiding from the gathering of a dozen or so people milling around a mailbox. They were presumably locals, and immediately tapped neighbors on shoulders until most turned and stared as the armed Miller entourage neared.

A couple of men wore pistols on belts. Noah stopped his family at sixty or so yards and waved. He received a half-hearted reply in kind. A man and a woman approached them tentatively. The attention of the group was split between the newly arrived Millers and the sounds of distant shouting from the road ahead.

At about twenty yards, the welcoming committee halted. "Y'all ain't sick, are ya?" shouted the man with a holstered pistol.

"No!" Noah replied. "We're from up in the Shenandoah. We're just passing by."

"Well, you're welcome to pass on through. But there's a little trouble up ahead. Some half naked guy, prob'ly from town, is rantin' and ravin' like a madman. Musta caught it and gone nuts or somethin'."

Noah raised his white N95 mask and led his similarly masked entourage up the opposite side of the road to keep some distance from the locals until they spotted the man, a hundred yards away, darting aimlessly this way and that. He wore only a ripped and tattered hospital gown that barely hung across his shoulders. When he whipped around as if startled by something behind him, his skinny white torso and buttocks were displayed, as were the IV tubes still taped to the needle running through his gown and into the back of his hand.

"We figured he'd just tire hisself out," said the woman from across the asphalt road. "But he's still goin' strong after 'bout two hours." The infected man was snarling, throwing his head about to confront imaginary threats, each of which seemed to spark anew a rush of adrenaline and paranoia. "We keep callin' 911, but we cain't get through."

Noah looked at his wife before saying, "We'll take care of it." Natalie didn't object.

The dozen local residents, half children, half adults, watched in silence as the Millers and Margus, clean but wearing filthy camouflage and combat boots, marched past.

"Safeties off," Noah commanded quietly as they descended the hill. Without being told, Natalie, Chloe, Jake, and Margus spread out across the road to Noah's left and right to clear their lines of sight to the berserk Infected.

"Are we just gonna...?" Chloe began.

Noah looked back over his shoulder at his daughter and saw the locals herding their children into the nearest house. Two couples embraced, with one of the women shielding her face from what was about to happen. "He'll make a hostile move. When he does, I'll shoot."

"We'll all shoot," Natalie said.

"No. Waste of ammo."

At fifty yards, the infected man still paid them no mind. At thirty, his head jerked up, his fists clenched, he unleashed a furious yell, and he charged. All five assault rifles rose, but only Noah's *cracked*.

The man staggered. *Pop. Pop.* Both Chloe and Natalie fired their rifles. The man lay sprawled on his back, spilling toxic fluids onto the pavement. Jake, who had held his fire like Margus, admonished his sister and mother. "Dad said not to waste ammo."

Noah turned back to the residents and waved. One man returned the gesture. Most turned away. They wound a wide path around the man, who leaked pathogens onto the pavement. Jake said to Chloe, almost in a whisper, "I spy, with my little eye, something red." Noah glanced at his wife, but Natalie seemed concerned only with the open windows of the trailer home they passed, the woodpile behind which someone could be hiding, and the abandoned car that could conceal potential attackers.

Chapter 9

ROANOKE, VIRGINIA
Infection Date 70, 1515 GMT (11:15 a.m. Local)

Emma didn't ask for Dwayne's binoculars. Efficiencies were gained by a division of labor. When Dwayne completed his survey of Roanoke's smoky skyline, she asked, "What do you see?"

"Looks like the Infecteds and Uninfecteds are going at each other pretty hard."

"The Uninfecteds will be scared," Samantha noted. "It should be a good time to offer them order and security."

Emma said, "Let's make it a good show of force to back up our offer." They drove into the chaos of Roanoke with two dozen buses, trucks, and vans.

* * * *

Walcott's pickup—blue lights flashing—led the way with Emma in the passenger seat holding the handset for the PA system. The trucks behind them were filled with food, water, and medicine for those joining, and one hundred armed fighters for everyone else.

The sounds of gunfire grew ever louder. "There they are," Sam said from the cab's back seat. Walcott turned down the block where fighting raged and pulled to a stop seventy-five yards from the nearest combatants, who were hiding behind a car whose glass was shattered.

The shooting died down as Infecteds and Uninfecteds alike turned to assess the arriving convoy. Dwayne had all one hundred fighters dismount. The Infecteds were highly compliant...up to a point. *But*, Emma noted, they lacked any initiative. There were no sergeants providing small unit leadership. No lieutenants and captains upon which hierarchical organizations were built. They went where Dwayne directed and stood there, waiting, as Dwayne spaced them out.

Emma raised the microphone to her mouth. "My name is Emma Miller," boomed her voice over the loudspeaker atop the sheriff's truck. "We're here to offer you, Infected and Uninfected, one and only one chance to join our Community. You'll get order, security, an end to the violence, and the necessities you need to survive. All we demand from you in return is that you follow our Community's Rules. You must work. You must not commit violence except as directed for defense of The Community. We post all the Rules every morning, and if you disagree with any you will be allowed to leave. If you stay, however, you must obey the Rules or else be punished."

Among the nearest combatants, heads turned and debates erupted. They were Uninfecteds. Their infected opponents at the far end of the block were more subdued and much quicker to agree. They stood up from behind stone retaining walls, green electrical transformer boxes, and the steps up to the front porches of the middle-class ranch-style homes. They lowered their weapons and awaited Emma's instructions.

The Uninfecteds, in contrast but as they always did, had questions. Emma met their representatives on the overgrown front lawn half way to their improvised barricade of cars, trucks, riding mowers, and a pile of bricks from a nearby construction site. "That's close enough!" a middle aged man called out from twenty yards away. His eyes nervously darted toward the hundred guns behind Emma. His voice was loud enough to be heard by the dozens of Uninfecteds behind the barricade and in the doorways of the overcrowded houses on both sides of the street. "What kinda *community* are you talkin' about?"

"It's a community of Infecteds and Uninfecteds living together in peace," Emma replied, tailoring her messaging to Uninfecteds' sensibilities. Offering them the one hope, she had noted on prior recruiting visits, they most valued. "Violence serves no purpose. We offer order. We put everyone back to work to provide for the common good."

"You're infected?" the man asked. "*All* of you?"

"No. Our Community includes both Infecteds and Uninfecteds."

The man scanned the forces behind Emma. She turned to look. A hundred men and women carrying arms of every kind imaginable stood passively, stoically, awaiting orders. "None of them looks uninfected to me. Nobody's wearin' a mask."

"Our uninfected citizens are doing different jobs. But we will welcome you into our Community with open arms."

"It's a trick!" yelled a woman from one of the doorways. "It's a trap!" came from another. The Infecteds down the block, for their part, mostly just waited. One, however, was having trouble containing her anxiety. Two of her comrades yanked the shotgun she held from her hands, agitating her further. The young woman held her ground, but stomped and grimaced and clenched her fists and groaned loudly enough that Emma could hear her almost a football field away.

The uninfected representative took a silent poll of the faces around him. Others joined him to discuss the offer in whispers. "What will you do if we *don't* join?"

"Nothing," Emma replied, "for now. But you won't be members of The Community, and you won't have its protections or supplies from our stores. If we succeed in signing up everyone else here in town, you'll be isolated, and you'll be viewed as hostile and eliminated." Another half dozen people joined the uninfected spokesman and their hushed discussions raged.

A single shot startled everyone. The Uninfecteds dropped to the ground and turned their weapons back toward their infected opponents down the block. But it quickly became clear that the Infecteds had simply eliminated the source of the continuing disturbance in their midst. A man stood over the body of the previously agitated young woman with his pistol waiting to see if a second shot was required. It wasn't.

After another huddle of Uninfecteds, their spokesman said, "Okay. We'll join. But we can quit any time, right?"

"No." Emma's reply confused them. "You can only quit from eight to ten o'clock in the morning, after the Rules for that day have been posted."

A series of silent shrugs signaled the final vote. "Okay. We're in if *they* join." The man jabbed his thumb over his shoulder at the Infecteds behind him.

Chapter 10

OUTSIDE ROANOKE, VIRGINIA
Infection Date 71, 2030 GMT (4:30 p.m. Local)

Isabel was nearing the end of her night's sleep. But it hadn't been at night, and there had been precious little sleep. The sun had been bright. The ground had been hard. She took a deep breath that was exhaled as a frustrated sigh. She turned from her aching right side to her sore back, and then to the tender muscles on her left.

Rick breathed steadily. He lay on his back sound asleep with the crook of his elbow covering his eyes. It had been too hot when the sun shone directly on where they lay amid a clump of bushes. Now it was too cool in the shade. She felt a dozen itches all at once, and periodically gave each a dismissive scratch in a grand tour of her unwashed body.

It was only an hour or so before their *day* began. Like vampires, they slept for a few hours while the sun was high. They climbed atop as precarious a perch as possible—crumbling, sheer walls and loose rocks beneath them—so that Rick too could get some rest. Rick liked to hike in the darkness, when his night vision goggles gave them an advantage. But to Isabel, stumbling blindly, the gloom alternately filled her with dread at imagined threats, or numbed her into a dangerous stupor through which she floated along mile after mile.

She rolled over again in jerky movements as if to punish the ground beneath her. Rick had laid out a couple of mats whose solar cells charged his night vision goggles, their radios and flashlights, and the satellite phone Isabel had been given when sent by the president to confirm that the newly developed vaccine in fact worked. The same vaccine that had spelled the president's own doom. Was it an unfortunate coincidence that President Stoddard had been among the unlucky 6 percent to contract *Pandoravirus* from vaccination? Or a plot by Gen. Browner, Chairman of the Joint Chiefs of Staff?

The green light blinked on the sat phone. It was fully charged. She wondered if it still worked…and whether there was anyone left to answer it.

Isabel rolled onto her back and heaved a long sigh. She had a headache that emanated from behind her eyes, which she rubbed. The late afternoon sky was a pale and featureless blue save a thin jet contrail high above. The white streak, tight and crisp at the jet's exhaust but ragged and diffuse the farther behind it fell, didn't track from one horizon to the other. It twisted and turned. Here almost a figure eight. There three quarters of an oval. It was loitering in the sky near Roanoke a day's march behind them.

She had to stifle the cough she felt coming, and unwrapped one of the lozenges from Rick's plentiful supply. The cough drop had grown sticky from her body heat. She peeled the paper from it in strips.

The sound of an engine gave Isabel all the justification she needed to wake Rick. She reached over and gently shook his shoulder. "Car," she whispered.

He raised his rifle before his eyes were clear of their sleepiness. Both peered down the shortened barrels of their carbines toward the road forty meters beneath their perch. It wasn't a car, but a truck with a cherry picker in back. It slowly passed their encampment and pulled onto the shoulder of the highway about a hundred meters past them.

Two men in white hardhats got out. One climbed into the basket in back. A whirring sound announced its slow rise into the air. At the top of a wooden telephone pole, the worker draped heavy rubber mats over wires. His colleague sat on the rear bumper. The lounging man didn't smoke, or drink, or surf the Internet on his phone. He just sat there.

It took Rick and Isabel three minutes to pack their gear and head down to the road. The two workers both stared at them. At about forty meters, Rick raised his right hand. "Hello!" Both his and Isabel's rifles were slung unthreateningly across their chests, but the workers remained wary. "We're just passing by!" They approached the truck slowly. The fists of the man at the rear of the truck were balled tight. The man in the raised basket gripped its edges like he feared an imminent fall. Both wore sunglasses.

"Infecteds," Isabel whispered.

"Yep. If it comes to it, you take the guy on the ground."

"'Kay."

When they were close, Rick said, "We're heading south. You guys heard any news from down that way?"

The worker on the ground said, "There's fightin' all the way to Tennessee."

"Any places we should take special care to avoid?" Rick asked.

"Are you Uninfecteds?" asked the man above them in the basket. Rick nodded. "You should steer clear of Blacksburg, then."

"Oh yeah? Why's that?"

"They're Infecteds and are shootin' any Uninfecteds they see. They refused to join. There's trouble comin'."

Isabel asked, "They refused to join what?"

"The Community," replied the lineman standing at the rear bumper.

"What community? Who's in charge of this community."

"Some lady. Looks a lot like you."

"Is her name Emma? Emma Miller?"

"Yeah, that's it," said the man in the basket. "Miller."

"And you two joined?"

Both nodded. "Got the old jobs back," said the man on the ground. "Two meals a day. A roof. No more lootin'. Blood pressure meds comin' real regular."

"And all you've gotta do is agree to live by her rules?" Both men nodded. "Out of curiosity, have you ever seen anyone punished for violating those rules?"

The two workers looked at each other, then shook their heads. But the man in the basket said, "We did see a crowd down in Roanoke that got too big. They were handin' out food—the Uninfecteds on one side of the highway, Infecteds on the other. When it looked like they were gonna run out, the Infecteds started crowdin' up. The deputies used a bullhorn to try to spread 'em out, but they didn't listen."

"They got all quiet like," said his partner. "Stopped and stared right at the people handin' out the food. We were workin' on the lines 'bout a quarter mile down the road."

"I was up in this same basket," said the other worker from on high. "The Uninfecteds ran away. The deputies brought up trucks filled with armed folks. They kept shoutin' over the bullhorn, 'Disperse! Disperse!' But the mob attacked the trucks and got shot up. Musta kilt a hun'erd."

"More," said his partner. "That's one of their biggest rules." The man finally calmed enough to settle again onto the truck's rear bumper. "No crowds. They stagger the times you can come look at the new rules based on your last name. You know, A through E from eight to eight thirty. F through J from eight thirty to nine. That sorta thing."

"Any of the rules cause you any problems?" Isabel asked.

The two men exchanged a glance. "Yeah," said the man on the rear fender. "No sex unless you get a permit, even if you're married and your husband or wife survived. And the office that hands 'em out is only open till five o'clock, and we work most days till six or later."

"I told you, Hankins," said his coworker up in the basket. "First thing you gotta do is get yer wife or some lady friend to cosign the form. *Then* you take it to the window and show 'em your work card. You gotta get three days punched to get a permit, and that's only good for two weeks."

"No. First thing is to get a copy of the *form*. They was out when we went by there on our lunch break. If they don't get more soon, I may just have to head west."

"What's west?" Rick asked the man sitting in front of him.

"They call it the Exclusion Zone," replied the other man up in the bucket. "He wouldn't last ten minutes up in them mountains afore somebody shot his ass. Most ever'body who quits heads that way, and they're the hard cases. The ones who know they cain't control their urges and are gonna be put down soon enough."

Rick and Isabel eyed each other before showing the man at the rear of the truck the photo of Noah's family on Isabel's phone. The worker seemed surprised by how close they approached. He removed his sunglasses and squinted in the sunlight, then looked up with black eyes and shook his head. "You're perty close. Hope you don't get sick."

"Much obliged," Rick said, touching the mostly imaginary brim of his Kevlar helmet. Both white hardhats bobbed in nodded reply before Rick and Isabel walked on. When they were around the bend in the highway and out of sight of the electric utility crew, Rick said, "*Sex* permits?"

Isabel sighed. "Emma was always a bit of a control freak. I couldn't be her lab partner in high school because her procedures drove me fucking crazy."

They walked mostly in silence after that. Isabel's muscles warmed and felt less sore, at least until they stopped for a break. The soles of her feet, however, and the raw skin atop her shoulders where her pack's straps bore down both stung from injury and sweat.

"Maybe we should get one of those sex forms," Rick said out of the blue. It was growing darker and he took off his sunglasses.

"I'm not consenting to anything until I've had a shower."

"Probably never find a notary public out here anyway."

Isabel snorted more out of politeness than amusement.

Darkness always fell more slowly than it should. First, their sunglasses came off, seeming to extend the daylight further. Then, Isabel's eyes kept adjusting as the sun sank, dragging out the lingering twilight. The official beginning of the night wasn't the nautical sunset, or astronomical sunset, or when a few lights became visible here and there. No, the official onset of darkness came when Rick lowered his night vision binoculars from atop his helmet and his eyes began to glow behind them.

There was occasionally dim starlight and moonlight on clear nights like this one. And every so often, when the power in the area was on, they passed an incongruous, brightly lit billboard advertising a local insurance broker or brake repair shop. But most of the houses were either totally dark and seemingly abandoned, though maybe they weren't, or leaked light muted by thick blankets nailed over the openings, indicating that they meant to be left alone...or else.

Shortly after night vision goggle sunset, they approached a nondescript house that glowed brilliantly. The trash cans along the highway were filled with neatly bagged rubbish and encased in mesh fencing to repel wild animals. The mailbox read, "Wilson Family."

"What is it?" Isabel asked.

"A little weird, is all," Rick said, surveying the drive, front lawn, and house, from which the faint sound of music could be heard. "I know we're not writing reports to the Pentagon anymore, but...."

"You know what they say about curiosity. But if you insist...whatever."

They ditched their heavy backpacks just off the road. She felt almost joy to be out from under the ridiculous burden, even if they were wasting their time and taking some unknowable amount of risk on a totally unimportant detour.

They tracked alongside the driveway through the relatively thick brush of the woods. Branches dragged across her body armor, scratched at her exposed and damp neck, and scraped her raw and wind chapped hands, which gripped her M4's plastic pistol grip and foreguard.

They lay on the ground at the edge of the rutted flat area at the top of the drive. Country music emanated from the house. Enough light streamed through the trees from the stars and low hanging, nearly full moon to give Isabel a general view of the yard. But the garish illumination from the windows spotlit areas with almost shocking displays. The house's flower beds were ringed by low fencing that appeared would be ineffective even against rabbit intruders. A gazebo sat beside a dry swale that hinted at an intermittent stream. A concrete fountain had a broken bowl and a moss-covered statue of a naked cherub at its center. There were a couple of homemade birdhouses, some chimes under the eaves, two large and two small pink plastic flamingos, and crosses standing in front of each of two freshly dug graves—one adult sized; one child sized.

Isabel glanced at Rick's glowing eyes, which darted this way and that, searching, she knew, for danger. There was no garage. Two pickup trucks were parked under their respective discolored and mildewed plastic roofs, which were held aloft by rickety metal poles. A plastic shed, leaning too dramatically for the doors to close, housed what looked like a lawn mower and gardening implements.

Through the picture window across the front of the house she could see a glowing TV screen in the living room. Its picture changed and its music fell silent, but Isabel couldn't tell much about what she was seeing until Rick handed her his binoculars.

The house was neat and tidy inside. A man sat in a reclining chair watching TV while eating dinner from a metal tray balanced on his lap. On screen were images of large explosions in the distance that shook the camera a half second after the detonations. In place of the previous music, they could hear through the open windows the *booms* like in an old war movie. But it wasn't a movie, it was the news. Some of the blasts shown on TV were visible over treetops and at a distance, their targets unseen. When the locale changed, others flung cars skyward, left all the windows on entire city blocks shattered, and toppled trees clinging tenaciously to urban life and metal poles secured firmly to the pavement. The view switched to a local anchorman in a studio. Isabel couldn't hear any audio or see his eyes, but guessed they were black given the total absence of expression on his face.

The picture was replaced with a graphic. The two columns of bullet pointed text was too small for her to read, but the heading—"Today's Rules"—told her all she needed to know.

A preteen girl wandered into the living room. The man paid her no attention. She sat in a chair and stared into space. She moved not a muscle. Her hands were wedged between her thighs. Her head was tilted slightly, and her gaze was generally downward. The two said nothing to each other. The girl was uninterested in the TV news, which ended while Isabel and Rick lay there watching. A clock face appeared in place of the broadcast, and the country music returned. The man continued staring at the TV as if waiting for the second hand to sweep past twelve, then waited again.

A superimposed scroll rose past the clock. Isabel missed the heading, but squinted until she picked up a word here and there. "Backhoe operator," she caught on one line. "7:00 am, Costco parking lot," she read three listings later.

A dog out back began barking. Rick's rifle reacted, changing its aim. "Bo?" came the high-pitched call of the little girl. The screen on the front door clapped shut loudly. The eleven- or twelve-year-old appeared in the bright porch light carrying an impossibly large hunting rifle. "Beau-re-*gard*! What is it, boy?"

The dog, obviously tied up, was barking with wild abandon.

Rick aimed at the girl. *"Riiick,"* Isabel whispered, shaking her head.

"Is anybody out there?" the girl called out. From inside, her father said something. "But if we *do*," the girl replied, "he could run off like last time." He again spoke, but she remained unpersuaded. "But they could *hurt* him. He's more use bein' a guard dog here at the house." She raised her voice and shouted, "If anybody's out there, go away!"

Rick turned to Isabel. "They've got hot food. A bed. A shower."

"So...what? You wanta *kill* them? For a fucking *shower*?"

"Hello!" the girl shouted in their direction. Then, "I thought I heard somebody," in the direction of her father, who joined her at the front door carrying a shotgun.

"No, I don't mean kill them," Rick replied. "Jesus. Maybe they'd invite us in like that last house."

"Those people were *Un*infecteds. These look pretty infected to me."

They made their way back down to the highway and shouldered their heavy packs. Isabel took a few seconds attempting first to brush free the prickly burs stuck to her body armor and magazine pouches, then peeling them off individually like Velcro seeds in the glow of her penlight.

"Let's get going," Rick said, nervously scanning in all directions.

"One sec," Isabel said, tugging at what appeared to be the last of the little pests.

Both heard the low rattle of a guttural warning. Two eyes glowed from the ditch in the feeble and inadequate illumination of Isabel's penlight.

The dog attacked with a sudden growl that became a continuous bark and rose in volume with each bounding leap it took toward Isabel.

Bam! Bam-bam! Three brief, jarring strobes flashed from the muzzle of Rick's rifle. The first illuminated a crouched German shepherd, fangs bared. The second a confusing tumble of fur and skittering claws. The third a whimpering pile of dying family pet feebly licking fatal wounds inches from Isabel's boots.

"Beauregard?" came the little girl's high-pitched shout from the distance.

Chapter 11

Chloe Miller found life along I-81 to be strangely comforting. South of Roanoke, the highway was filled with stranded refugees. Normal people, like them, with no Infecteds anywhere to be seen. But rumors of Infecteds on both sides of the narrow ribbon of concrete abounded.

The drama of the road, however, had given way first to blisters, then to boredom. She picked up her pace until she caught up with her brother. "Hi."

"Dad said ten meter spread," was Jake's only reply.

"Dad said ten meter spread," she repeated in a mocking tone. "You've been such a kiss ass ever since you fell asleep on watch."

"I did not! How did you know?"

She ignored his question and they walked through the hills in silence past millions of trees, any one of which could hide an attacker that could put a bullet straight through their chests. "Have you ever thought about the last thing you'll do before you die?" When Jake seemed confused, she amended her question. "I mean…we could get shot any second now. We may not even see or hear anything before—*bang*—it's all over. And what would the last thing we did be? Scratch an itch on your nose? Yawn? Look up at those big birds circling something dead in the woods?"

"Vultures," Jake supplied.

"My point is, you know, anything we do could be the last time we do that thing. The last drink of water. The last time you stretched your back on a rest break. The last breath. Doesn't that make everything seem more special, more important than normal?"

"I *guess*. I dunno. Everybody has a last breath, I s'pose. But these days, it's not that special. Everybody's dying. There's nothing that special about it."

He didn't get it. Chloe heaved a big sigh. "Okay. How about this one? How much longer would you have to live before you'd consider this whole survival thing to be a success? Like, if some magical genie could offer you a deal and say that you'll live for X amount of time, how much time would he have to offer before you'd accept the deal?"

"And stay uninfected?" Chloe nodded to him. "Uhm, maybe, say, three months?"

"Three *months*?" That was a *lot* shorter than she was expecting. "Jeez. I was thinking maybe a coupla years or something. You'd really take...?"

"Chloe! Jake!" their dad yelled back at them. Without another word, Chloe slowed to allow Jake to pull ahead. Margus, trailing them, came to a stop to maintain the spacing, but he swayed from one boot to another as he waited for Chloe to resume her progress. The subtle movement back and forth—one foot this way, one foot the other—was to make a sniper's aim more difficult. Standing totally still was too easy a shot.

Chloe's mind blanked until they approached another roadside collection of stalled vehicles. People stirred around the cars and trucks, which still provided them shelter and a store of presumably declining stocks of food, water, and supplies. She gripped and regripped her AR-15. Her right thumb rested on its selector switch, ready to flick it forward at a moment's notice.

"Where you guys from?" asked a cute boy about her age as she passed his immobile SUV.

Chloe stopped and smiled, trying to look pretty but not straying too close. She hadn't bathed in days, plus there was the whole *Pandoravirus* thing. "D.C. You?"

"New York." His hair was a little shaggy, and a lot hot.

"New York *City*?"

"That's what people mean when they say New York."

"Chloe!" her dad called sharply from up ahead.

"Hold up a minute!" she shouted back and turned to the boy. But she could only think to say, "What are you doing?"

"In theory, fleeing." He shrugged. "My parents are off looking for gas. You guys are just hoofing it?"

"Yeah. Taking in the sights. Fresh air and exercise." She smiled. "And meeting interesting people."

Her flirtation went right over his head. Was she suddenly hideous looking or something? "Where you headed?" he asked.

"I dunno. Texas or something."

"Jeez. Long way. Looks like you've got enough guns, though. My dad has this old shotgun that's been in the family for, like, a hundred years. And we spent my college fund outside Philly buying this." He retrieved a black revolver from the seat behind him, which he handled, Chloe thought, a little carelessly. "Six bullets. I'm supposed to save three."

"What? Like, for you and your parents?"

"Chloe!" her dad interrupted as he headed back her way. But the boy nodded.

She gave him one more smile before her father dragged her off. "Dad," she whispered, "can I give him my pistol?"

"*What?* No!"

She sighed. "It's *heavy*, and I still have the AR. All they've got is antique *crap*."

"No, Chloe. And stop talking to people. Try not to make eye contact."

He resumed his position at the head of their single file column. Margus, who brought up the rear, had kept his distance behind her but had maintained his fixed gaze on the boy, especially after he flashed his pistol. Now, she felt his eyes on her...probably. She was wearing baggy camouflage clothes, and nothing was certain anymore.

"Hi!" she said to an African American woman with three kids at a semipermanent camp around an old station wagon, whose hood was propped open and doors flung wide.

"Do you have any food?" the woman asked, approaching Chloe too closely.

"Wait. Stop! Get back!" Chloe backpedaled as the woman neared and swung the AR-15's barrel toward the threat.

A jarring shot rang out. Margus lowered the aim of his smoking rifle straight at the starving woman, who instantly hunched over and cowered beneath bowed shoulders and lowered gaze as if expecting a rain of thudding blows.

"That's your only warning!" Margus shouted as everyone within sight stared at the confrontation, many reaching for whatever firearms they had handy. "*Back* off!"

The woman returned to hug her two young sons and wiry daughter to her sides. She never again raised her gaze toward Chloe, who felt extremely guilty. Was Margus a racist or something? "Sorry," Chloe said so softly the woman didn't hear. Chloe's mother, father, and brother, who had each taken cover behind abandoned vehicles, all resumed their steady march southward.

Margus passed the African American family's station wagon with his rifle at the ready and its aim never straying from the woman, then pivoted and walked backwards while riveting his attention on the poor, hungry, stranded people.

About a mile farther down the highway, a little boy, who was trying to play with a flat tire by rolling it with difficulty along the shoulder, waved at Chloe with a hand that was grimy and blackened by the tire's road dirt. Chloe tucked in her chin and ignored him, entertaining herself instead by noting in silence the license plates of the cars she passed. Few were from Virginia. Most had Pennsylvania, Connecticut, Massachusetts, or New York plates. When she saw a tag from Vermont, where the *P.* had first broken out in America, she looked around to share the exciting find. But only Margus was close enough to hear her, and he was kind of a jerk.

Not actually a jerk, really, just standoffish. "Some boys are shy," her mom had said the night before when the girls and boys had separated for their respective sponge baths. "You've only paid attention to the confident boys who hit on you. But there are lots of nice, decent, kind boys out there who just aren't comfortable coming up to talk to a pretty girl."

"Whyyy?" she had asked.

But her mother had given up with a shake of her head.

Chloe glanced back again, and again found Margus returning her gaze. That didn't seem too freaking shy. He was carrying his rifle in both hands, at the ready like he was in the army. Which, technically, they all believed he still was, though no one dared ask him for fear that it was a huge secret. *"AWOL,"* her dad had told her mom in a whisper when they had thought Chloe was asleep. *"Desertion?"* she had replied. "They're shooting people for that."

So Margus was, like, a criminal. That kind of made him a little more interesting.

Chloe slowed, but Margus slowed too. Finally, she turned and walked right up to him. If he wouldn't talk to her, she would talk to him. "So, Margus, you were in the army?"

Margus's soldier on patrol playacting grew awkward, and he lowered his rifle. There wasn't anyone around anyway. "Virginia National Guard."

"And you're…taking a break?" He said nothing as they walked side by side. "It doesn't matter to me. I mean, it seems like the smart thing to do. Virginia basically doesn't exist anymore. And I suppose you wanted to get back to help your parents."

"Lotta good that did." Again, he mumbled barely audibly.

"How'd they catch it?"

"They insisted on keepin' the store open." He shrugged, frowning. "All they had left on the shelves were some stupid games for car trips, over the counter meds, and a bike tire pump. They didn't even raise their prices."

"Somebody came in the store who was sick?"

He shrugged. "I'd taken the predawn watch and was catchin' some shut-eye. When they didn't call me for breakfast, I came lookin' for 'em. My Ma had thrown up in the store, and my Pa was moppin' it up. I shouted at him to get away, but…it was too late. They both turned a few hours later. I thought they'd both die 'cause I wasn't able, you know, to get too close and help. But they helped themselves, and when they woke up, they was turned."

"I'm sorry." Margus paid her no attention. The scowl returned to his face.

"I ain't done too much good anywhere I been, it turns out."

When the silence wore on, Chloe said, "Well, you're sure helping *us* out." Margus snorted. "My dad says you went to Iraq."

"Naw. I joined too late. It was my unit that went. They were gonna send me over after trainin' me up, but my unit was in the last month of its deployment and it wasn't worth it. I appreciate your mom and dad takin' me in. Sharin' your supplies. And this rifle. All I had before was my ole .22 I got when I was a boy."

The conversation died when she couldn't think of any follow-up questions. "What were your plans from before?" the question finally came to her. "I mean, I know you had the National Guard gig, but…?" She had been worldly enough not to ask what colleges he'd applied to, which was a standard and safe question back at McLean High School.

"Git a job. My parents paid me for workin' the register, but they couldn't really afford it long run. I thought I'd gotten a job down at the renderin' plant. They were s'posed to let me know. But then the news about the virus hit, and…"

She considered asking what *renderin'* was, but instead said, "Was it hard? Leaving, I mean…your unit?"

He surveyed the stinking bus they passed, which had rolled onto its side off the Interstate and burned down to a barely recognizable frame, scorching the grass all around. "They gave us orders to redeploy to Texas." Again, he laughed sourly. "Instead of gettin' a free ride with my buddies courtesy of Uncle Sam, here I am…headin' to Texas on foot."

The conversation again died. But this time, it was mostly because Margus's attention was drawn to their surroundings. He craned his neck to peer all around, even behind them, and finally pulled out the small, handheld radio that her dad was constantly recharging whenever they found power. "Mr. Miller, you read me?"

A crackling, "Yes, Margus. Copy."

Margus's nervousness suddenly infected Chloe. She grabbed her rifle's pistol grip and front guard. There were cars lining the highway, but no people. The car nearest them was filled with holes in the windshield and open driver's door.

"Mr. Miller, there's no people around these cars. Somethin' don't feel—"

Boom. Boom. Boom. Three gunshots—loud—rang out from the hill on the left side of the road. Chloe was already stooping and running, but Margus grabbed her arm painfully and dragged her in the opposite direction— toward the gunshots—before taking cover behind the hulk of a car.

"Leave your gear behind!" someone shouted down from the hillside above them after those first three shots. He was clearly giving orders to her father, who was at the head of the column maybe sixty yards beyond Chloe and Margus. Her mom and Jake were safely behind the cover of bullet riddled cars of earlier refugees who, presumably, had strayed into the same trap. But her dad was exposed as he lay behind a pile of trash. Chloe and Margus, by lagging behind to talk, appeared to be just outside their killing zone. "Leave your weapons and packs and other gear," came the ambusher's shout, "walk on past, and we'll let you live!"

"Come on!" Margus said. He took off running up the hillside from which the voice had called down. After hesitating, Chloe followed. No shots rang out. They hadn't been noticed amid the wreckage from past atrocities or during their run up through the thick trees.

Margus dumped his pack and Chloe did the same. "What're we doing?"

"I'm gonna go fuck them up. You stay here and guard our shit."

"No. I'm gonna go too. I'll help...fuck them up."

He directed Chloe to a spot downhill and behind him, and both slowly climbed uphill toward the ambushers' elevation. Both held their rifles to their shoulders ready, as taught, to fire at a moment's notice. Chloe peered just over the rifle sights, but repeatedly lowered her right eye to the optical sight to be ready to acquire a target in the crosshairs in an instant.

Her father, ever the lawyer, was arguing. "We don't want trouble! You obviously don't mean to kill us or you would've hit one of us! We'll pull back, but *with* our gear!"

When the attacker replied, he sounded shockingly close to Chloe. Margus lowered himself to the ground with his palm patting down. Chloe got down, her eyes darting now back and forth between Margus's hand signals and the ambusher's voice. "You don't seem to understand your situation here! But you are correct! If we'd wanted, we coulda hit any one of ya, or maybe all three! That tends, however, to piss any survivors off and make 'em wanta fight it out! We're willin' to go there if you insist, but we thought we'd be polite and ask first!"

Margus pointed at Chloe and made a sweeping motion around behind him to a place uphill. Chloe nodded, crawling backwards, and edged her way in a crouch up the slope past Margus. Her heart was pounding, but not from exertion. Her shallow breaths dried her mouth, and when she tried to swallow she couldn't. Gone were her aches and pains and boredom. She paid little attention to the back-and-forth parlay in which her father engaged. Chloe's focus was on not making any noise.

She climbed until she reached a wall of sheer rock and crumbling dirt and worked her way forward on her belly, careful not to shake foliage on passing or trigger little avalanches of rock or dirt. When she saw Margus, he pointed at the ambushers and raised three fingers. Chloe saw nothing on the wooded hillside and shook her head. Margus raised his AR's scope to his eye in demonstration.

Chloe peered through the magnified sights, searching the hillside for—

A head. A woman with flecks of gray in her messy hair. The muzzle of the woman's hunting rifle, aimed at the road, poked out through brush. She hadn't dug a hole or prepared her position in any way other than to pile up branches in front of a log. About four yards beyond her—so close Chloe could almost hit both with one shot—was a boy about Jake's age. He, too, had a rifle and lay behind the far end of the same log. She couldn't see the man who shouted, "Last chance!" at her dad.

When Chloe caught Margus's eye, she shook her head and raised only two fingers. Not knowing how else to say it, she held her right forearm up like it was the log, and lay her finger across it like the two ambushers' rifles, one at each end.

Amazingly, Margus understood her pantomime and nodded. He pointed at her, raised one finger and then two, and pointed at the log. He then pointed at himself, raised a third finger, and pointed at the third target she couldn't see. She nodded, failed again to swallow, and lowered her eye to her scope. In her peripheral vision, she saw Margus raise five fingers, then four, then three, then drop his hand to his rifle.

She aimed right at the curly haired woman's head. At thirty yards, it was—
Crack!

The woman turned, wide-eyed, to look straight at Chloe's crosshairs. Chloe's finger twitched. *Bam!* Her rifle kicked. A giant mass blew out the back of the woman's head. Both the log and her son's face were coated with gore.

The boy behind her, aghast and in horror, cried, "Dad!", got no reply, and took off.

"Cease-fire," Margus said, but too late. *Bam!* Chloe hit the boy in full stride squarely between his shoulder blades. He dropped his rifle, arching his back as if to stretch out a kink, looking skyward through the canopy of trees toward the sunlight, and collapsed without any attempt to break his fall.

She glanced at Margus, who was staring at her until he turned back toward the three fallen ambushers. "Anybody else out there?" he shouted. "Now's your last chance to give yourselves up!" His radio crackled. Margus said something too quietly for Chloe to make out, looking up at her midway through his little confab.

"Stay here!" Margus told her. "But cover me!" She lowered her eye again to her sight. Margus went forward, keeping his distance from the dead. They could be infected. "All clear!" he finally shouted.

Chloe safed her rifle, brushed herself clean, took a deep and steadying breath, and joined Margus at the same time as the rest of her family. Her dad was sweating profusely and looked freaked.

They stood the requisite ten meters from the dead, though that was probably excessive since they no longer appeared to be breathing. Or so she thought.

"Hey!" Jake said. "That one's still alive." It was the boy Chloe had shot—in the back—as he ran away. *After* Margus had called cease-fire. The others joined Jake, but Chloe stood off by herself, searching the ground beside her boots. "Whatta we do?" Jake asked.

Chloe allowed her eyes to stray toward the wounded boy. He lay on his stomach, and his back rose and fell rhythmically. His jeans had sagged, revealing underwear with cartoon images from SpongeBob SquarePants.

"I shot him," Margus announced, glancing at Chloe. "I'll finish it."

He raised his mask and put on a pair of blue Latex gloves. No one said a word, but Chloe's parents and Jake exchanged looks. The wounded boy wore a knife in a scabbard on his belt. Margus squatted beside him, put a gloved hand on the boy's head, said a silent prayer with his eyes closed, drew the boy's knife, and plunged it straight through his back between his shoulder blades a few inches from the gunshot wound.

Chloe heard a gasp. It was probably her mother, but she imagined it was the boy.

Margus rose. "Are...are you gonna leave him like that?" Jake asked in a voice that quaked, but not from puberty. The knife handle protruded from the boy's back at a right angle. Margus extracted it and tossed it down the hill along with his gloves.

As they headed back down to the Interstate, Chloe fell in alongside Margus. "I...I guess I owe you one," she said without catching his eye. He didn't ask what she meant.

In the ditch just off the shoulder they came across the bodies of a middle aged man with a bald spot on the top of his head and a woman with long gray hair. Both had been killed by single shots to the backs of their heads. The man's front pants pockets and jacket pockets were all turned inside out. An ancient double barrel shotgun lay beside them, cracked open and empty of its shells, which the ambushers must have deemed the only thing worth taking. Margus again donned his mask and a new pair of gloves to pick up the man's wallet, which had also been rifled through but left behind. "Andrew Potter, New York, New York," he said after checking the man's driver's license. He then took the plastic card and grotesquely inserted it into the dead man's mouth, eliciting looks of alarm and disgust from Chloe's mother.

When Margus turned to Chloe, she averted her eyes. After their brief thaw on the highway before, they resumed a chilly distance. Chloe's family thanked Margus, but had trouble describing his good deed, mumbling only, "you know, for what you did."

"Counter ambush," Margus supplied. "Always depart your line of advance on the ambushers' side." They retrieved their packs and resumed their column with ten meter spreads and paid much more serious attention to the terrain they approached. Chloe let the tears flow, but avoided any other outward manifestation of the crushing guilt she harbored. No bucking chest, hiccupping gasps, or contorted face, just tears that went unnoticed by her newly threat aware family. And she especially avoided any eye contact with the one person who knew the reason for her guilt, who walked ten meters behind her and couldn't see her face.

Chapter 12

As the sky grew brighter, the spooky mist along the Interstate began to lift. There were people sleeping in the stalled cars Isabel and Rick passed, but no one stirred. Isabel was exhausted from their mind-numbing march and looked forward to finding a campsite for their one midday rest.

"Hey!"

Rick and Isabel both slewed their carbines toward the startling call, which came from a mop headed teenage boy. They relaxed.

"Sorry. I didn't mean to scare you. Are you headed south?"

"Yeah," Rick replied.

The boy approached them. Too close; not for Isabel and Rick, who were now immune, but for his own safety had they been contagious. "My mom and dad went down that way yesterday morning. They said they'd be back by sundown, but they weren't. Sophie and Andrew Potter. My dad has, like, a bald spot." His hand patted the curly top of his head. "My mom looks like, you know, an old hippie. Long gray hair, baggy corduroys, a green army shirt—like yours, only not camouflaged. Like from Vietnam. I'd show you a picture if my phone had some juice." He still clung to the useless, dark device.

"What do you want us to do?" Rick asked. It sounded somewhat cold to Isabel, but it was probably just fatigue: physical, and emotional.

"If you see 'em...I dunno. Tell 'em Barry is waiting. Right where they told me to!"

"Your name is Barry Potter?" Rick said.

"I know. They fucked me. My real name is Berrigan—named after some antiwar dude that nobody remembers but was their, like, hero—and *Barry* is what stuck."

"Sorry 'bout that. If we see 'em, we'll give 'em the message." Rick headed off.

He seemed annoyed when Isabel showed the boy her cell phone and asked, for the thirtieth or fortieth time, "You haven't by any chance seen these people, have you?"

"Yeah."

"Okay, thanks for….Wait. You *have* seen them?"

"Well, her. The hot blond chick. And *this* dude. Her dad or whatever. I'm pretty sure the others were up ahead. Plus there was another guy with short hair, like yours," he said to Rick.

"You *saw* them?" Isabel repeated, unable to believe the boy's answer.

"Yeah. Like I said. They came through yesterday before dark. Headed south, too."

"All of them? Five people? All alive?"

"Yeah." He looked up while seeming to count. "Yeah, five. Sounds right."

"Thank you. *Thank* you!" Isabel repeated. She grinned broadly as she rejoined Rick, feeling energized.

From behind, the boy said, "You can't spare any food, can you? I'm, like, starving."

"Sorry, buddy," Rick replied over his shoulder without even looking.

They got a few steps before Isabel whispered, "Not even *one* MRE?"

Rick huffed and stared skyward in obvious irritation. "Isabel, you've probably asked me that two dozen times. If you'd given food away every time we passed pitiful people, we'd be out by now."

"Yeah, but that boy helped us. And he's alone, waiting for his parents."

"Okay, listen. I'm not gonna do this. You wanta give somebody some rations, go right ahead. You don't need my permission."

"Okay." She returned to the boy's SUV. "Here ya go."

"Wow! Thanks, ma'am."

Ma'am?

Isabel felt pleased with herself. Rick seemed less pleased. Despite muscles deadened to numbness, Isabel increased her pace. As the sun rose, so did the first people. Men relieved themselves in bushes. Children gathered sticks for fires. One couple even called out to Rick, "Like some coffee, soldier?"

To Isabel's surprise, he accepted their offer, which she politely declined. Rick downed the metal cup filled with jet black coffee in two long swigs. He thanked the rough looking pair, both of whom were missing teeth but seemed to be adapting better to life alongside the freeway than most. He then spent the next half mile spitting stray grounds of coffee from his mouth.

"You know," he said, more talkative after the caffeine, "I was about half a day away from suggesting that we were never going to find your family, and figured maybe two days away from convincing you."

"O ye of little faith."

"And I assume you wanta press on straight through the daylight?"

"You assume correctly. I do."

The sun was visible through the treetops. Rick stopped, fastened the flexible solar panel atop his enormous backpack, and plugged in the portable battery, then hoisted the entire load onto his back with a grunt. He seemed utterly spent, and she began to worry about him for the first time. She had always just assumed he had no practical limits and could endure anything she could times two, or ten. But he barely slept during most of their daytime rests, which she had just cancelled, in between his patrols of their campsite's perimeter. The limits of his physical endurance were now plainly within sight. There was no telling how long his emotional stamina would hold after all the stress he had endured in monitoring the approach of the pandemic first in Asia and then with her in the Northeastern U.S. And he was presumably worried about his family in Wisconsin. Rick wasn't exactly the brooding sort, but he wasn't brooding's opposite either.

She vowed to keep him under a more watchful eye even as his attention darted from thick tree trunks, to abandoned vehicles, to highway overpasses, to pillaged gas stations. His eyes, she noticed, had grown red and bleary.

After several hours on the road, Rick said, "Let's spread out." Isabel tried to find the reason for his anxiety, but saw nothing. The road ahead was empty. The cars on either side abandoned. On closer inspection, however, she noted one troubling fact. Every car they passed was peppered with bullet holes. "Off the road," came Rick's curt command.

They proceeded slowly along the ditch beside the highway. Rick held his M4 to his shoulder about ten meters in front of her, crouching slightly, swinging his carbine left and right as his attention switched from the shot up cars to the dominating hillside above them. Isabel raised her carbine also, but all seemed still.

Rick raised his right hand, sank to a knee, and peered through his binoculars. Isabel knelt with difficulty beside a bullet riddled car and scanned the woods above through her M4's sight. They resumed their march but halted again on finding two bodies in the ditch. The man had a bald spot splattered with blood. The woman, with stringy gray hair, also matted with blood, wore a green U.S. Army fatigues blouse. Rick pulled a driver's license from the man's mouth.

He looked up at Isabel. "Andrew Potter," is all he said before returning the license to the dead man's mouth.

"Why are you doing that?"

"GIs started putting dog tags in casualties' mouths in Vietnam. Napalm melts 'em if they aren't protected. It makes IDing the body easier."

"Gross. That kid who's with Noah's family is in the army or reserves or whatever. Do you think maybe he put the driver's license there?"

"Maybe."

Isabel was uneasy. "Do you think *they* killed them? That boy's parents? Caught 'em trying to steal food or something?"

"I doubt it. They were both shot execution style—in the back of the head."

"We need to go back for that boy," Isabel said. "He's all alone… for good, now. He'll never know what happened to his parents unless we tell him."

Rick didn't say anything for a long while. "It's daylight," he finally noted. "Your family is presumably up and moving south. Right now, we're maybe a half day's march behind 'em. We go four hours back for that boy, then four hours to return here, we're a day and a half behind your family, and physically spent."

She knew what the only right answer was. But as she knelt over that boy's dead parents, she felt an obligation.

"I told you, Isabel, I'm not gonna keep being the bad guy. But do you know how many millions of orphans there must be right now? A lot of 'em younger and less capable of taking care of themselves than that boy?"

"But he's…." She stopped herself. It wasn't fair to count on Rick to make the hard but correct decisions. "No. You're right. Let's go." She rose and took off.

Rick waited beside the bodies. "We could bury them."

"No. Then, if the boy comes looking, he'll never find them."

"I could tack his driver's license to a grave marker."

"No. Let's go. We're close. And, obviously, it's dangerous here. My brother may have survived *this*, but every minute counts. They could get in big trouble at any time."

Rick surprised Isabel again when, still on one knee, he closed his eyes and moved his lips in silent prayer, which had never occurred to her to do. She briefly shut her own eyes and thought, *God, please take care of that boy. And all the other orphans. Thank you. Oh, it's Isabel. Isabel Miller. Goodbye. Amen.*

Chapter 13

The representative of the Uninfecteds at the first meeting of Emma's council, who wore a blue mask and gloves, clear plastic goggles, and an impermeable white one piece suit with a hood, stared back with an inscrutable expression as the other members of Emma's advisory board, all infected, gathered around the conference table. He was the picture of an outsider.

"Reports?" Emma said, turning first, as always, to Dwayne and Sheriff Walcott.

"I'll handle the external," Dwayne said. Walcott nodded. "There's still a lot of military traffic to our east, mostly heading south along I-95. None of it threatens us directly, but it could if the order was given. The Marine and naval bases around Norfolk are still active. Shipping arrives and departs without difficulty. The USS George H.W. Bush and Gerald R. Ford and their air wings are fully operational along the coast. Their two battle groups are ranging up and down the Atlantic seaboard, but sorties only rarely come this far inland."

Samantha asked, "What are all those planes we keep seeing up in the sky doing?"

"They look mainly to be military transport aircraft shuttling equipment and personnel between Naval Station Norfolk and points west, presumably Texas, and south, down to Florida and Guantanamo Bay. I did get a cell phone picture," he walked around the table to show Emma, "of what looks to me like a high altitude drone that was orbiting I-81, presumably monitoring the progress of refugees heading south to warn towns and cities in their line of advance what's coming."

Emma asked, "How should we handle those refugees? Most are stuck where they are with no fuel and declining stocks of supplies. I keep hearing that violence is rising."

"They're almost all Uninfecteds," Walcott said. "The people I've sent out that way—should they be called deputies...?"

Emma shook her head. "No. We'll come up with something else to call them."

"And what should we call *you*?" asked the Uninfecteds' representative out of nowhere. "People have been asking, ya know. President? Governor? What?"

Emma shrugged. "Chief...Epidemiologist."

The man stared back at her, but any expression was hidden by his mask and goggles. Not that it would've communicated much to Emma, although she was getting better at reading the highly expressive faces of Uninfecteds.

Walcott waited patiently. *No,* Emma decided. Walcott wasn't patient; he wasn't even there until Emma turned to and prompted him. "You were saying?"

Walcott continued as if there had been no interruption. He could, Emma knew, have sat there for hours awaiting his cue. "The men I sent out to the Interstate yesterday evenin' started takin' fire as soon as the refugees saw they were infected."

"Did you lose people?" Dwayne asked.

"Not many. I got on the radio and ordered 'em back."

Emma asked, "Are those people able to keep moving? Or are we stuck with them?"

"They're flat outta gas," Walcott said. "They ain't goin' nowhere 'cept on foot."

Emma turned to the uninfected council member. "Why don't you send out feelers? Explain to those people on the highway the benefits of joining us and make the offer?"

"The offer...*or else*?" He was shaking his hooded, goggled, masked head. "I didn't sign up for that. And the *or else* part would better come from one of you, wouldn't it?"

"All right," Emma replied. "I'll go." She and Samantha turned to Dwayne. But, as high functioning as even he was, no ideas occurred to him. "Will you get together the show of force to go with me?"

"Yes, ma'am."

Samantha shot Emma a look—lips pinched, eyes wide—but that expression was either too complex or too muddled to decipher. Most likely, it was some form of commiseration with Emma at Dwayne's lack of initiative. Or it could just be Samantha's failed attempt at some other meaningful look. "So," Emma wrapped up, "lots of forces along the coast; none up this way?"

Dwayne bobbed his head in confirmation.

Emma turned to Walcott. "What about internal security?" When he seemed unable to formulate an answer to such a general question, she rephrased it. "Have we had any crowd control issues?"

"Yes." After that appeared to be the end of his answer, she asked him for details. "When the—whatever we're gonna call the deputies—approached Lynchburg on 460, they ran into a mob and some heavy fighting in a suburb called Montview. And up at the old River Ridge Mall, there was a crowd of a couple of thousand fully charged up Infecteds facing off against thirty or so well armed Uninfecteds. One of my men got sucked into the crowd and had to be dragged away and slapped out of it. We gotta warn people about the dangers of even straying *close* to a crowd. They left there before the crowd tipped over, but when that happened there was gonna be a whole lotta violence."

"And those poor Uninfecteds...." the PPE-clad Uninfected began, but didn't finish.

"Is that all you have to say?" Emma asked. The man nodded with a rustling of disposable suit fabric, but seemed confused. "In the future," she explained, "please speak in complete sentences so we know what you mean." Another rustling nod. Emma turned back to Walcott. "Let's set those southwestern suburbs of Lynchburg as the northeastern limits of our Community for the time being."

No one said a word even though Emma and Samantha scanned the faces of the men and women gathered around the table. "Does that make sense?" Emma asked Dwayne.

"Yes. We shouldn't get any closer to Norfolk. They're bombing Richmond and Virginia Beach around the clock. They may move on to Hampden Sydney, which is getting close to Lynchburg and possible contact with their long range patrols."

"But we need more resources," Samantha said. "We've only got the southern Shenandoah Valley down to Blacksburg. We need factories, farms, mines, and people."

Again, Emma and Samantha scanned the table for suggestions. Again, there were none. And again, Samantha gave Emma a look. Emma needed to get together with the girl to agree upon a common interpretation of all her attempted expressions. "Don't we have an offer expiring down at the college?" Emma asked Walcott.

The sheriff said, "Technically. But we sent Uninfecteds down to Radford University to extend the offer, and the people we sent went over to the other side."

No one even glanced at the uninfected representative, but the man said, "Don't look at me. I had nothing to do with them. It just proves my point. You shouldn't send us out to…to *extend* any *offers.*"

The words he used were correct. But his intonation suggested a subtly altered interpretation that, when Emma checked, was also lost on Samantha, who shrugged.

Emma turned to Walcott. "When are we supposed to hear back from the college?"

"Dwayne's still gatherin' up batshit crazies, so they were s'posed to give 'em four more days. But we ain't heard a peep out of 'em and they stepped up work on their *de*fenses after the Uninfecteds went over to 'em."

"Dwayne, if they say no, what should we do?" Dwayne gazed back at Emma blankly. "Are they a threat to us if they just stay holed up on their campus?"

"Yes. They're on this side of the New River, and the orders were to secure everything *to* the river." It seemed not to occur to him that those were *Emma's* orders, which Emma could change as the situation warranted.

"They've got supplies," said the uninfected man from the far end of the table. "They're not roaming around. They're just hunkering down where they are."

"But supplies run out." It was Samantha. *Good point,* noted Emma's inner advisor.

Emma turned to Dwayne. "Prepare to…what would you call it in military terms?"

"Reduce their lodgment?"

"Prepare to reduce their lodgment," she reiterated with the correct vocabulary. "No more extensions of the deadline."

"They're not bothering anybody!" said the uninfected rep. "They're mostly college kids who couldn't make it home."

Emma polled the faces around the table. No one seemed the least bit persuaded by the uninfected man's argument. Samantha, who was the only person Emma really trusted to think issues through, noted, "They'll keep attracting Uninfecteds. They'll be an example to everyone who's considering our offer. And they'll be a threat when they run out of food."

"An attack could attract the military," the uninfected man said, but in a quiet, tired sounding voice. "If they call Norfolk and say they're under attack by an organized force of Infecteds, the navy and Marines might send troops. Or at least bombers."

"Could they make it there?" Emma asked Dwayne, who nodded. She waited for more, to no avail. "*Will* they send help?"

"No. It's too far to keep them resupplied, so they won't have much staying power. And they're busy much closer to home, particularly in Richmond and along the roads out of D.C."

"The Uninfecteds could, you know," interrupted their representative, "help you out. Not immediately, but eventually. If...if you'll allow us to be armed."

"No," Emma replied. "Your people already ignored all our demands that they turn over their personal weapons, and we haven't forced the issue. Yet. And just in the last twenty-four hours, there've been...how many killings?"

Walcott said, "By Uninfecteds? They killed thirty-seven Infecteds, and six Uninfecteds, not counting what's going on along I-81."

"But most of those killed," Samantha reasoned, "were out of control crazies or people breaching the peace. Those killings were justified, and kinda did your job for you."

Walcott did not disagree. And the uninfected man, for some reason, said, "Thank you, little girl." Samantha again tried her smile, but it was toothy and the man for whom it was intended looked down at his lap, ending Sam's latest effort at body language.

There being no more discussion around the table, Emma repeated to Dwayne, "Get ready to reduce the lodgment at Radford University."

Chapter 14

The first sign of trouble ahead that Noah noted was the Interstate contraflow. A moving vehicle always attracted attention. One heading the wrong way—*toward* the north and the virus, in the opposite direction of the slow river of humanity—redoubled Noah's scrutiny. Then came more, eventually clearing the two northbound lanes of semi resident pedestrians and their refuse. Half an hour later came people on foot, clutching weapons and shouting at anyone who strayed too close. Little, terror stricken groups of families or bands of strangers, who knotted up in circles and raised weapons whenever approached.

"Just tell us what's happening down there?" Noah heard a girl ask.

"Stay the fuck back!" was shouted from a tight cluster of three, who raised masks and long guns, back-to-back like in some gladiatorial game. "One more step and I shoot."

Everyone scurried off the highway when another car raced north, engine revving.

Who had that much gasoline? They weren't government, or some well provisioned local warlord's militia. They must be using some precious last drops of fuel to flee something…terrifying. And another curious fact: the people on foot looked far more jumpy and less talkative even than the southbound mainstream refugees fleeing the Northeast.

A car stopped fifty yards ahead for its occupants' bathroom break. A woman with a shotgun escorted three little kids into the woods. A man and a boy with rifles stood outside the car's doors. A small crowd was gathering.

Noah, at the front of his family of four plus Margus, quickened his pace.

"...are killin' the Infecteds, and the Infecteds are killin' the Uninfecteds," was the first thing Noah heard the driver say. "So far, the Tennessee National Guard is winnin', but you know how this goes. There's no way to get through the fightin', and it's blowin' back up the highway in this direction."

Upon the return of the women and kids, the driver and the boy took their rifles to the woods for their own relief. The children returned to their accustomed spots in back without instruction, and the woman sat behind the wheel with her shotgun in the passenger seat and an automatic in her lap. "That's close enough!" she warned, flashing the pistol.

Crowds were drifting nearer the car. Noah was just trying to get some information.

"Where are you backtrackin' *to*?" asked a middle aged woman from the roadside.

"I ain't tellin' you *shit*. Git back. *Back*." She was now waving the pistol. Noah motioned Natalie off the opposite side of the road. His wife relayed his command back down the highway. Noah saw Margus, fifty yards behind, disappear from sight. Natalie settled to the ground with nothing but the top of her blond head and the muzzle of her rifle showing over the road's shoulder. People beside stranded cars nearby began to react to the standoff at the stopped car by seeking cover—some casually; others with undisguised urgency.

"All I can say is," the woman in the car snarled, "you people are all *fucked*." A three car caravan raced past at speeds too fast and margins too narrow for Noah's comfort. He began to shy away from the tense scene. "In a few hours," the woman continued in a sadistic taunt meant, presumably, to intimidate the growing crowd, "there's gonna be a whole *horde* of those motherfuckers. Runnin' away from the killin'. Runnin' right the fuck *over* every last one a you. Ya know what I'd do? Run. Anywhere but south. Hey! Hey git back! Get the fuck.... Hey! I'll shoot! I'll shoot, mother—!"

Noah took off just as the first shot rang out. Multiple gunshots erupted, he saw over his shoulder, both from and at the car, whose windows began shattering as the crowd around the car either fell, ran, or fired.

Noah slid painfully onto the shoulder with a grunt and dumped his pack. Natalie's rifle rested atop her pack a few yards away, and her eye was behind her sight as the volume of gunfire from the highway rose. The new fire came from the trees above the road. The father and son had returned and were shooting anyone and everyone near their car. "Please! Stop shooting!" one woman shouted where she cowered before she was shot dead.

"I got one in my sights," Natalie said, not in a whisper, but aloud and calmly.

"What?"

"The boy from the car. Should I shoot?"

"What?"

"Noah. They're firing in this general direction. They're *murdering* people trying to crawl to safety off that highway."

"This isn't our fight, Natalie," Noah replied through gritted teeth. *"Jesus."*

"What's goin' on?" Margus's voice crackled over the radio.

"Two men on the hill with rifles shooting anything that moves," Noah replied. "A woman and three kids in a car…" Jesus. Their car was riddled. The glass pocked or mostly gone. He could hear, between the sporadic gunshots, a crying child and a loud moan.

Finally, when the shooting subsided, the father raced down the embankment to the car as his son presumably covered him. His wail made Noah's eyelids too heavy to keep open.

"Daaad?" his son called out.

"Oh, *God*!"

Noah got on the radio. "Head to that stream down the hill to our right. Where all those other people are headed."

Amid the scratch of the radio's sign on and sign off, Noah heard, "Got it."

"Dad! Dad! What is it?" the boy shouted from the hillside.

"It's…It's…Your mother. And Becka. And…Oh, *God*!"

Natalie wouldn't look at the car or the carnage around it. The senseless slaughter had ended as quickly and inexplicably as it had begun. Noah and Natalie hurried down the hill to escape the moans of the wounded, the inhuman howls of loved ones, and the cries for help—"Is there a doctor anywhere?"—from both sides of the pointless tragedy.

* * * *

Chloe squatted beside the little trash strewn stream tossing rocks into the water. But she was jittery, Noah noticed. Her hand quivered as she picked up small stones.

"It was like a fucking horror movie," said the man talking to Margus, whom Noah joined, from the prescribed safe distance of ten steps. He and his grungy wife were both the color of the surrounding soil. Their backpacks were dusty, their boots mud caked, and their jeans stained.

"Infecteds just kept coming and coming," the couple reported. "The town, Bristol, is right on the border, and it's split in two by the infection. Everybody on *this* side of town is infected, and everybody on the other side is trying to drive them out. The Tennessee Guard is shelling the hell outta the Infecteds. That's sending them back up the highway this way in a fucking frenzy. We hitched a ride in the back of a pickup until it ran outta gas and everybody then went their own way."

Chloe asked in bewilderment, "Why'd they shoot that woman and her kids?" She tossed a last rock from her perch atop a ledge and rose. Noah hadn't even realized she was listening to their conversation. "That woman on the highway up there? What was that?"

No one had an explanation. "Dunno, honey," the man said. "Everybody is killing everybody these days. But say, we're headed back toward this detour someone mentioned off I-81, up through the mountains, and around Bristol. Why don't you folks join up with us? Marco and Laura Moretti from Ocean City, New Jersey. We're self-sufficient. We're both armed, and we could share turns on guard. We'd get a lot better sleep with more people."

But Noah shook his head and said, "No. Thanks. Let's go."

"Yes, *sir*!" Chloe replied under her breath. Noah pointedly ignored her.

There was a crackling rumble from the sky that seemed to dissolve not into distinct echoes, but into the crinkly *whoosh* of noise scattered by the trees and hills. Another rattling string of staccato bursts followed the first like distant firecrackers, but instead of *pops* they made *booming* sounds. "Artillery," Margus said in a worried tone.

When Chloe, Natalie, and Jake all stared at Noah, he said, "Those are the good guys...fighting back. Let's head their way."

"You know," persisted the man from New Jersey, "when they fire those big guns, they kill whoever happens to be on the receiving end ten miles away. Good guys, bad guys—everybody dies. There's a whole lotta Infecteds, folks, between here and those troops in Tennessee, who, by the way, are turning everybody back. Let's take this detour together."

Noah spent a long time looking at Natalie, trying to guess at her opinion. But she gave him no clues. He took a deep breath. "No. We're headed south."

"Awright. Good fuckin' luck to you." The man turned to leave.

His wife hesitated. "If you're stuck for a place to hole up before nightfall, we stayed at this old abandoned barn last night. You could see a long way across open fields." She gave directions to Noah before her husband dragged her away.

The Miller family plus one set off toward the magical barn after Noah's inspiring words—"Five meter spread." When they angled back up the hill to the more open Interstate, the light was better. But the explosions on the horizon ahead sounded nearer and more prominent. *That* was where Noah was leading them.

They passed a steady parade of slouching refugees heading in the opposite direction. A girl a little younger than Chloe said casually, in a sing-song voice, but ominously, "You'll be *sooor*ry."

Chloe stared at Noah, but said nothing. To Noah her look communicated only one thought—*My life depends entirely on you.*

* * * *

It was dark when they found "the barn," which was a total pile of shit. "Really glad we hiked all the way up *here*," Chloe said. The relic had no roof. The house accompanying it had long ago burned down, leaving an ancient bad smell. Chloe dropped her pack, righted a low, overturned stool, and sat. "Ahh. All the comforts of home."

"Good walls," her dad said, slapping the thick stones that rose a grand total of about three feet off the ground. "Top of the hill. This side has great sight lines across the pastures. The other side is too steep to climb. This'll do."

Margus took the empty doorway to cover the road up from the highway. Chloe's dad spread the four members of his family at intervals along the stone wall looking out over the moonlit fields below. They had ceased paying attention to the artificial thunder. There was no gunfire, but there were clusters of explosions, then a respite, then another dozen *booms*, all close enough to illuminate briefly the dark horizon to the south. "What's the watch schedule?" Jake asked.

"No watches tonight," Chloe's father replied.

"What?" Chloe said. "After what those people told us, we're not posting a *watch*?"

"No." It was her mom. "Tonight, everyone's on watch. An all-nighter."

Chapter 15

The jogging was difficult under the weight of Isabel's huge and cumbersome backpack. "Shouldn't we...drop these...packs?"

"No," Rick replied tersely. The sound of gunfire toward which they ran was close. Steady. One *crack* from a rifle every second or two, sometimes randomly overlapping. "This is it," Rick said at the broken sign, the remaining bottom half of which warned that something was, "Out!"

The dirt drive up the hill was more of a rutted track. The small bridge across a stream had mostly collapsed, but one beam was passable on foot. They could now see the flashes of individual rifle fire from the top of the hill.

Bam! Isabel jumped when Rick felled a single, previously unseen woman in the woods off to their right. His muzzle flash illuminated two more men. *Bam-bam!* They both fell. One tried but failed to rise. Neither made any sounds of pain or distress—Infecteds.

Isabel was swiveling her carbine, aiming at shadows, looking for targets at all points of the compass but finding none before they finally spotted the ruins of a barn ahead from which rifle fire blazed like camera flashes. One bright flame and loud *crack* accompanied a passing *sssszzt* sound that sent both Rick and Isabel to ground.

"U.S. Marine!" Rick shouted. "We're comin' in!"

"Make it quick!" a man or boy replied from behind the barn's low walls.

They rose and ran in a stoop toward the roofless structure, which was silhouetted against the flashes of more rifle fire. The barn was just where the woman had said it would be. After Isabel and Rick had ignored the warnings of the New Jersey couple and refused their invitation to join them on their detour around the besieged Tennessee town, the woman had whispered, "And my husband didn't tell you the truth. We *did* see your family. We told them about this barn we'd found where they might stand a chance to make it through the night."

The man in the barn fired again and again to either side of them. "Get inside! *Now!*" Rick and Isabel practically dove through the opening and collapsed behind a wall. The shooter kept up his fire, which Rick joined.

Isabel dropped her heavy pack and rolled toward the opening to assume a prone firing position. The edge of the woods forty meters away was alive with dark, moving targets. Isabel fired at the shapes and hit one. Two. Missed the third. Rapid shots erupted from a newly arrived defender and spent cartridges rattled around the rubble. "Aunt *Isabel?*" she heard Chloe cry.

Chloe lay beside Isabel and they stole a brief hug before returning to their weapons. The teenage girl's smooth skin was warm on Isabel's cheek.

Both plinked away at the dwindling number of profiles in the woods. "We need help over here!" came a voice Isabel recognized as Noah's. She saw her brother firing his rifle over the stone wall. While Rick and Margus kept shooting down the road, Isabel and Chloe scrambled to Noah's side of the old barn and raised their rifles onto the cold stone. Isabel could make out figures approaching across the fields below. She jumped when Chloe's rifle blazed. Isabel quickly engaged running targets too numerous to count. Even at the greater distance and in the poor light, her shots hit more than they missed.

"Isabel! What are you...?" Noah had made his way over to her, but took no time away from his rifle to embrace her.

"We've been looking for you," Isabel explained in between shots.

"Lucky *you*,"—*bam!*—"You found us!"

Natalie arrived to say, "There's too many of...! *Isabel?*"

The confused reunion was interrupted by their steady fire at the onrushing Infecteds. "And Rick's with me!" Isabel added. She looked over at Rick, who appeared to be on the satellite phone as Margus redirected his fire from the road to the pasture filled with targets. Isabel aimed at dark, onrushing Infecteds in the field below and added her fire, hitting someone every couple of rounds.

"We can't hold this place!" Natalie shouted at her husband between shots. "There are too many of them! Noah, we've gotta drop everything and run! *Now!*"

Rick arrived with a scraping slide. He held the glowing sat phone Isabel had been given by the president's aides in upstate New York.

"We're making a run for it!" Noah announced to Rick

"Negative!" Rick replied. "Take cover! Fire in the *hole!*" he shouted at Jake. "Fire in the hole!" went a shout Margus's way.

"Jake, get down!" Natalie added before joining everyone on the ground at the base of the barn's wall. All sounds of their gunfire fell quiet. The only noise was a distant but rising howl or growl from hundreds of voices drawing ever closer. It was the same sound Isabel had first heard on the bridge in upstate New York. It was the sound that presaged the end. As it grew louder, she reached for her pistol. Rick's hand stopped hers. He shook his head.

An eerie noise like a blend of whistling and cutting descended from the night sky.

BOOOOM!

The stunning burst shocked Isabel. She felt the blast wash over her. It seemed to suck the breath right out of her chest. Her ears rang with tones. It was impossible at first, to make sense of anything.

"Fuuuck!" Chloe cursed. "What was *that?*"

Rick peered over the wall through goggle clad eyes with the sat phone to his ear. "Drop one hundred! Fire for effect! I say again, drop one hundred! Fire...for...effect!" He pressed himself to the ground beside the rest of them and said, loudly enough for Jake to hear in the distance, "Get as low as you can! Hug the ground! Plug your ears!"

"What?" Isabel asked.

She heard the same whistling and cutting sound as before, but times a dozen. Her fingertips found her ears just in time. *B-B-B-B-B-B-B-BOOOOM!*

Just as her brain was beginning to register the stupendous series of explosions that landed seemingly right on top of them, there came another. *B-B-B-B-B-B-B-BOOOOM!* And another. The sickening jolts—each its own sharp shock to her senses—were followed by still another, which rattled Isabel's chest and frayed her nerves as debris rained down and an acrid smell fouled her nose. She coughed and thought she might vomit.

The barn alit in another string of blinding strobes as the ground beneath her shuddered. Thudding blast waves pounded their tiny refuge. Charred wood bracing snapped and splintered. Bits of stone sprayed from unseen impacts. The boy by the door lay in a fetal ball. Isabel jammed her eyes shut and clenched her teeth in a grimace.

The growing pall of smoke made Isabel nauseous. Or at least she thought it was the smoke. It could just as easily have been the shaking that her insides were taking, or the clench of all the muscles in her body as if that might fend off errant shrapnel. The condition grew worse the longer the barrage continued. She coughed and coughed until she did throw up. But no one noticed. Everyone was preoccupied by the same explosive tumult.

When the volleys finally ended, Rick was back on the satellite phone. He then raised his rifle and fired off a steady stream of shots before finally Noah, then Natalie, then Jake and Chloe and the guy by the doorway joined him.

When Isabel rose, grit cascaded off her. She found a spot atop the stone wall to steady her carbine, but smoke partially obscured the field. A hundred fires, however, lit the smoke and everyone passing through it, whom Isabel's loved ones steadily cut to pieces. Most of the Infecteds were staggering, drunk from shock or wounded in myriad ways. Their clothes were ripped into shreds and hanging from their torsos, as was the occasional limp limb. Their bodies looked blackened and sometimes visibly smoking in the flickering light. Isabel found only one target at which to aim before Rick shouted, "Cease-fire!" She never squeezed her trigger hard enough to release a round, and her would-be target stumbled and fell on her own.

It was the end of the unwholesome slaughter, but it wasn't a merciful end. Two helicopters wheeled into sight amid the glow from the blazes beneath them. The smaller one orbited the smoking pasture firing its machine gun into the few pathetic Infecteds struggling to stand upright. The larger one thundered right over their wreck of a barn stirring dust and dirt and ash into the air in its hurricane force down blast before landing in a clearing between the barn and the remnants of a fire ravaged house.

Rick helped everyone toss their heavy packs through the open doorway of the ubiquitous Black Hawk, which took off the moment Rick clambered aboard last.

When the door closed, and the relative silence descended on the shell shocked survivors, Noah crawled over to her and said, simply, "Oh, God, Isabel." He looked older, tired, his brown face chapped and riven with deep creases of worry. They hugged. Isabel cried, but no tears came out. She was surprised when she felt Noah's chest bucking against hers.

Chapter 16

"Ten minutes," Dwayne announced to Emma on the hill overlooking his operation.

Samantha, who had just discovered coffee, asked, "Should we attack exactly at six o'clock? Shouldn't we pick some other time than on the hour? Isn't that too obvious? Won't they be expecting it then?"

Dwayne said nothing. He wasn't as high functioning as the twelve-year-old. Maybe no Infected was except Emma, and possibly not even her.

The eight eighteen wheelers made beeping sounds as they backed up to the breaches quietly cut into the fence surrounding the college. "Maybe you could shut off the *beeping*? That sounds really loud. Someone might hear it in those dorms." Samantha hyperactively rocked from tiptoes to heels and back. Men stood at the rear of the trailers ready to throw open the doors and hide behind them. The campus was dark and quiet—asleep. Dwayne's best fighters had killed the three college students and one faculty member they encountered—two on a foot patrol; two in a listening post—silently, with knives. The overcrowded, overconfident Uninfecteds lay undefended before them.

"It's oh-six-hundred," Dwayne said. He turned to the trucks, raised his arm, and dropped it like the starter with a flag at an auto race.

They heard loud, grating sounds as the rear doors of the trailers were unlatched, and groaning noises as the doors swung open. Nothing happened.

No crazed Infecteds streamed out to storm the dorms filled with sleeping students and displaced townsfolk.

"I thought you said these were totally out of control Infecteds," Emma remarked.

Dwayne said, "We haven't fed them in days. They should be starving."

"Or maybe they all killed each other during the drive over here," Samantha suggested. "Or maybe they suffocated, or got overheated? Did you check?"

"How many of them are in there?" Emma asked.

"About sixty per truck. We may have lost some, but surely not all."

"They're packed too tight," Emma said. "They're in a trance. Go trigger them."

Dwayne headed down the hill. As Emma was thinking how terrible Dwayne was at taking initiative, Samantha said, "Dwayne is great at following orders. He's a really good choice for heading up the security people. I wonder if the Marines taught him that, or if he was good at following orders first and that's why he *became* a Marine?"

"However much coffee you had this morning," Emma said, "was too much."

Dwayne was unable to anticipate problems, or take ownership of his job, or think for himself. And Dwayne was one of the best performing Infecteds she had. Walcott was a cretin by comparison, sometimes standing like a statue for hours until racing off to urinate.

A pistol shot rang out. Dwayne had climbed up onto the front of a trailer and fired into a vent. His men did the same on the others. "They're making a lot of noise," Samantha muttered as she clasped both hands behind her back and swiveled from side to side. "What are those thingies—*cattle prods*—they would be quieter."

Alarms began sounding and lights came on all across Radford U. "They're awake now," Samantha said, "but look. The crazies are leaving the trailers." Dozens, then hundreds of Infecteds leaped out and landed on top of each other, dragging themselves to their feet and charging into the open on the campus's wooded grounds. "I hope they don't disperse too much. They're gonna get slaughtered, and if they lose their mob mentality they may come running back *this* way."

Dwayne rejoined them. *Good job,* Emma considered saying. But Dwayne was infected and cared not a whit for praise. "Next time use cattle prods. They're quieter."

"We may need more crazies," Samantha said. "Look. They've made it to all four of those dormitories, but it looks like they're getting shot up pretty fast."

"You said most are newly turned, right?" Emma asked Dwayne.

"Very fresh. Some are hurt, though. It was the only way we could grab 'em."

Samantha remained skeptical, so Emma said, "They're extremely contagious. By nightfall, people will be turning and they'll finish whatever's left of the Uninfecteds here. Dwayne, keep an eye on things. We've got to go parlay with the mayor of Blacksburg out on Highway 460 at sunup."

On the walk to Sheriff Walcott's truck, Samantha said, "Virginia Tech probably still has a lot of smart scientists and engineers. It'd be nice if we didn't have to kill half and trash the brains of the rest by infecting them all, like here."

Emma agreed. "We're still experimenting. Trial and error." Walcott stared out the front windshield, motionless. He didn't even start the engine. "Sheriff Walcott?" Emma said. "We've got a little drive ahead of us. Do you need to go to the bathroom?"

"Yes!" he said as he opened the door, ran toward the edge of the woods, and fumbled frantically to unzip his fly.

Samantha shook her head and made a face in Emma's direction. "Just to be clear," Emma said, "that expression you just made was intended to convey...?"

"Disbelief," the girl explained. "I may not have done it right. But surely he knew that his bladder was full. Right?"

"Based on my sister's research, he probably didn't feel enough discomfort to motivate him to address his bladder. And thinking ahead to the drive to Blacksburg when the urge to urinate would become overpowering, is the kind of planning he's shown himself to be incapable of in enforcing the Rules. He and Dwayne both. You've got to follow up on every task they're given or everything will come to a complete stop."

"I'll keep that in mind," Samantha said.

Emma felt a frisson of anxiety, but why? What had triggered it? Emma clenched her fists and her jaw, and turned to the girl. Sam's face was reflected in her window as she stared into the darkness...lost in thought? *Why is she thinking?* asked the voice in Emma's head. And when Samantha had said, *"I'll keep that in mind,"* what did *that* mean?

"I'll do a history of the pandemic," Samantha said. For reasons unclear, she drew a smiley face in the patch of window fogged by her breath. "I'll need to define its phases. The Outbreak. The Killing. I'll record everything that's happened since The Outbreak, and how and why The Killing is happening. I'll need to interview everyone to document their perspectives before something happens to them and their data is lost. I'll start with the Uninfecteds. They're a *whole* bunch more talkative. I'll need a lot more people to do the interviewing. Teachers, librarians, accountants—whatever they are. There are bound to be plenty of them, and they're probably not good for much else."

Walcott slammed the door, affixed both hands to the wheel, and stared out over the hood into space. "Blacksburg?" Emma prodded. He started the engine and drove off.

Emma was practically quivering with tension as Samantha rattled off more of her plans. Emma's breathing grew ragged. Her shoulders and thighs felt tense. And she now realized the reason for it all. Samantha had cavalierly committed to memory Emma's *pointer* about how best to command the two chiefs of security forces. And Emma hadn't paid much attention to the girl's writing of an official history until she switched from saying *we* to saying *I* everywhere. *She's writing an official* history?

It was the voice that formalized the threat, bombarding Emma from within. *She's preparing for* your *job. That's the surest way for her to survive. And the best way to take your job is to kill you. Therefore, the best way for you to stay alive may be to kill* her.

"Sound good?" Samantha said.

"Hmm? What?"

"When the kids go back to school we can teach them the history of The Community and how to be good citizens."

"Members. It's a contract, not a country." Emma sat on her vibrating hands.

"But one day it'll be a country. *The* country. Right?" Emma couldn't safely answer without betraying her anxiety. "Well, that's what *I* think, anyway."

Chapter 17

BRISTOL, TENNESSEE
Infection Date 79, 1430 GMT (10:30 a.m. Local)

"What did they say?" Noah asked as Rick Townsend returned to the high school's utility closet—their quarters.

The Marine looked up from the satellite phone and shook his head. "When it broke out at the community college and spread to Bristol's airport, we lost the fuel there and the chance to get a fixed wing in. And the helicopters diverted, or took off headed west, or were destroyed on the ground. That leaves us depending on the army or Marine Corps cobbling a long-range mission together. They'll need a big-assed helicopter from up at Fort Campbell, Kentucky, or a tilt-rotor Osprey from Virginia Beach, midair refueling along the way to Texas, and combat search and rescue at points in between."

"Wait a minute," Natalie said. "That airport is *behind* us. West of here. Right?"

Rick nodded. "Yeah. Looks like we're cut off."

"You mean surrounded," Natalie said. "Be*sieged.* You notice no one has offered us any hot meals or anything. No food at all. We're still eating that crap in baggies we lugged in here. So, they're running out of food, and now they're surrounded?"

"At least we've got showers with hot water," Chloe said in a faux chipper tone.

"Great," her mother replied. "In a month, we'll all be freshly bathed *skeletons.* Noah, is the plan to *wait* here? See which gets here first—

a-a helicopter from Kentucky, or an outbreak, or a horde of Infecteds overrunning their defenses, or-or *starvation*? We should've stayed with Emma. I know family doesn't mean anything to her anymore, but it's not like she's killing uninfected people just for the *hell* of it."

"You wanta go back?" Noah asked. It wasn't a question, but it ended Natalie's unproductive recriminations. "Whatta you think, Rick? Should we make a run for it while the situation out there is still fluid? How would we best do that?"

Rick wore a scowl and rubbed his chin. "There are two ways. Exfiltration—sneaking out of here undetected—which means we should split up into smaller groups; say pairs. Or a breakout—fighting our way out—which means we should all go together, and maybe bulk up by recruiting other guns. But what we really should do is stay. Things are bad here, and will keep getting worse until this town falls, just like all the rest. *But*, for *now*, we can sleep through the night, rest, and recharge. As long as we have any prospect of an airborne evacuation, we should stay... at least until the end gets very near."

"This sucks." To Noah's surprise, it wasn't Chloe, it was Natalie. His well-rested, freshly showered, recently fed warrior wife, who on the road had been steely, had somehow, illogically, grown disgruntled on rescue. "I don't like this one fucking bit. This room smells like...like detergent, and vomit, and pardon me, *men*, but body odor. Plus Chloe and I passed a half a dozen leering would-be *rapists* between the showers and here. And everyone we've met have all had this look, you know, like sizing us up before slitting our throats to take our *crappy* food. And after that's gone, what's next? Cannibalism? And *they're* on *our* side, not some clawing mob of Infecteds! How long? How long, Noah, can we keep beating the fucking odds?"

"Mo*oom*?" Chloe whined.

Natalie caught herself, sighed, and deflated visibly. "Oh, I'm sorry, sweetie." She cradled Chloe's head. "Mommy's just tired. Just...blowing off steam. We'll be.... We'll be fine. Shh. Shh. Shh."

Rick's troubled visage contrasted with his reassuring tone. "They're evacuating the air assault school at Fort Campbell, about 350 miles west of here, to Texas. I've just gotten them to ask for volunteers. For a crew that'd be willing to fly 350 miles, the *wrong* way, to come pick us up, then try to make it all the way to Texas with no refueling or CSAR. No rescue team ready to come pick us up if we sustain damage, or run outta gas, or have engine trouble. That means we, and that all volunteer crew, could end up putting down...wherever."

"Yeah," Natalie said. "But it wouldn't be here. And it'd be closer to Texas. Do you think anyone will? Volunteer, I mean?"

"Yeah. Probably." Rick's reply seemed to depress him further. He was putting more lives at extreme risk and must feel the full weight of that responsibility. Isabel saw it too, rubbed Rick's arm, and lay her head on his shoulder. Rick seemed to relax as he inhaled Isabel's hair. It was so intimate that everyone found a reason to look away. But not before Noah and Natalie both noticed Rick dry the tears that welled in his eyes.

Chapter 18

NEW ROANOKE, VIRGINIA
Infection Date 80, 1700 GMT (1:00 p.m. Local)

Emma's meeting of The Community council gathered around a conference table in Roanoke's city hall. No one said a word except the three Uninfecteds, who huddled tightly together along a wall of glass and whispered through masks.

"Are these their new representatives?" Emma asked. Samantha nodded. "Where's the old one?"

"Dwayne said they found his body at Radford University. He must've... what's the word for when you switch sides to the enemy?"

"Defected. But they weren't the enemy."

"What were they then?"

Emma didn't exactly know how to answer that question. "An...obstacle. Let's take our seats." Emma sat at the head of the table next to Sam.

The Uninfecteds found the most distant and isolated spots.

"The first order of business," Emma said, "is garbage collection." One of the Uninfecteds glanced quickly at her two seatmates and tentatively raised her hand. "Yes?"

The woman's eyes, which were visible above her mask, darted about as everyone turned her way. "I...I just thought.... Since this is our first meeting, maybe we should discuss *preliminaries* before we dive right into the issues."

"What preliminaries?" Emma asked.

"Well, like...what *is* this meeting? What are we doing here?"

"This is the organizational meeting of The Community council," Samantha replied. "We manage The Community."

The woman unsuccessfully sought the support of her two mute male colleagues. "Is...is that what we're calling this...whatever we are? *The Community?*"

"Do you want to propose a different name?" Emma asked.

The confused woman's companions supplied no clarity. "It just sounds...generic."

Emma didn't understand. "There's our Community, and other communities. It seems like a pretty clear distinction."

That apparently settled the matter. "Okay," replied the uninfected woman. "And we are here...*why?*"

"To give advice. Consider new Rules. Interpret old ones. Hand down punishments. Allocate resources. Establish security strategy. Whatever The Community needs."

"But we thought *you* made all the decisions."

"I do. But I value opinions. So...garbage collection."

"Does that include collection of the dead?" asked Sheriff Walcott. "'Cause they're startin' to get perty smelly down by the old train station."

"Sure," Emma replied. "Garbage *and* body collection."

* * * *

They spent the next half an hour making productive decisions. There would be twice daily body collection and once weekly trash pickup. Food distribution to infected and uninfected areas to be either directly to dormitories or employers, in some cases, or to designated stores for people to visit. Numbered cards to be printed up each month with thirty-one boxes into which holes would be punched to indicate collection of that day's rations. Master lists with the names of all Infecteds and Uninfecteds in The Community and their associated ration card numbers. And mandatory reporting of deaths.

The uninfected woman representative again interrupted. "Aren't we kind of overlooking some pretty major foundational questions?"

"Like what?" Emma asked.

"Like.... First off, my name is Jane Finch. Hi, everybody."

None of the Infecteds made any move to respond until Samantha said, in an uncertain tone, "Hi," and waved, but only just her fingers.

"And this is Miles Jordan." The middle aged white man to her right nodded. "And this is Kwame Walsh." The youngish black man to her left stared back at the silent Infecteds without making any move.

"Hi," Sam repeated, waving her entire hand this time while watching it, presumably to confirm that this gesture appeared more appropriate. *Is she training herself to pass as an Uninfected?* asked the companion voice in Emma's head. That *would be tricky.*

The Infecteds' spokeswoman, Jane Something—Emma looked over at Samantha's notes and read, "Jane Finch"—looked around the table waiting for something to happen.

"All right then," Emma said, continuing the meeting, "we probably ought to use the master rolls of members to ensure that everyone is productively employed."

"Excuse me," Jane Finch said. "Sorry. Sorry. I…. It's just…. I understand we're called *The Community.* But before we decide on all these details… are we a democracy? We had a poll, of sorts, yesterday, and the three of us were elected representatives of the Uninfecteds. It wasn't a perfect process. I mean, there are probably tens of thousands of Uninfecteds in these southwestern Virginia counties—"

"Hundreds of thousands," Samantha interrupted. "Counting refugees."

"Right. But we put up flyers in a bunch of the uninfected neighborhoods announcing our meeting, and it was well attended, and we had a vote. I was just wondering, how did you decide who all would be here from, you know, your side?"

"We didn't," Emma said. "I told people what time the meeting was."

"Well, not to be critical or anything, but that's not very democratic."

"This isn't a democracy."

"What is it then?"

"It's a community, like we established. You belong, or you don't. Your choice."

"And you'll just…decide, for us all, what the Rules are? You alone?"

"Yes."

Emma scanned the faces of the Infecteds lining both sides of the table. They could not have been less interested in the conversation… except Samantha. She screwed up her mouth, knit her brow, and cast that expression toward Emma, who was perplexed by it. "Quizzical," Samantha whispered, and Emma nodded.

"That's just the way it's gonna *be?*" Jane Walsh persisted, her voice rising. No one said a word, not even her uninfected colleagues to whom she had turned. "Okay. Fine. If you're all on board, why rock the boat?"

Samantha leaned over to Emma and whispered, "There is no boat. She's saying she's not going to make any more trouble."

"I understand," Emma replied out loud since everyone surely had heard Sam's unnecessary translation of idiomatic English. "It's time to move on to punishments." Emma turned to Walcott. "What are the numbers?"

"There haven't been any punishments yet," the sheriff replied as he pulled the small notepad from the breast pocket of his khaki uniform blouse. "There are 1,369 people in detention as of bed check this morning. We've lost quite a few in detention, you'll understand. Of the ones remaining, there were 275 rapists, 311 guilty of murder or felonious assault, 296 property thieves, 419 job no shows, and 68 others."

"Okay," Emma said. "Let's get them processed today." Walcott nodded. "Next up, Dwayne? What about reports of some reconnaissance patrol sighting?"

"Hold on a sec," interrupted Jane Finch again. "I'm really sorry, but…. What was just decided? About punishing all those people?"

"It was decided to proceed with punishment," Emma replied. "Today, if feasible."

"What…what about a *trial*?"

"We don't have the resources for a thousand trials. And there are more to come."

"Okay. No trials. But…who decides on the correct punishments? I mean, rape versus…being absent from your *job…?*"

"Imprisonment costs too much," Emma answered. "The punishment is execution."

Walcott interrupted. "I just wanta make a point. We don't execute *real* crazies. Not formal-like. We shoot 'em right on sight unless Dwayne has put out a call for some more."

"Thank you for the clarification, Sheriff," Emma said. She wanted to show the Uninfecteds that she had not forgotten how to be polite.

"And I have enough for Winston-Salem tomorrow," Dwayne told Walcott. "But we may need more for Greensboro, Durham, and Raleigh next week, if they resist." Samantha whispered for Dwayne to thank Walcott. "Thank you," Dwayne added. Walcott nodded.

Samantha smiled at Jane Finch, sort of, then nodded for Emma to continue now that their manners had been put on full display.

The Uninfecteds were whispering, which was impolite. Jane Finch emerged from the private conclave and said, "How many of those people you're killing are uninfected?"

Walcott flipped pages in his little pocket notebook. "*Sixty*...seven. We had a bunch turn in a little mini outbreak while in detention, you understand."

"There'll be trouble," Jane said to Emma. "They all have families. Friends."

"How many people are we talking about if we round them up, too?" Emma asked.

"That's...that's not what I.... They haven't *done* anything."

"But you just said they'll cause trouble once the sentence is carried out."

"Yes, but.... Look, do anything you want with your people. But if you execute every uninfected man, woman, and God forbid *child* you arrest, and *then* kill all their families and *friends*...." She was doing so well until totally failing to make any point.

"I think she means," Samantha supplied, "that the Uninfecteds will revolt. And that makes sense. It's even possible the Infecteds will rebel too. It's a breach of the contract to execute someone who hasn't broken the Rules. It's a breach of the peace."

"*Exactly,*" Jane Finch said. "A breach of contract. Thank you, Miss...."

"Brown. Samantha Brown. And you're welcome, Ms. Finch." Again Sam bared her straight white teeth.

"They were given fair warning by publication of the Rules," Emma said, "not to murder, rape, steal, or miss work. Housing them in jail requires significant resources and is too burdensome for an economy that's struggling to feed The Community's swollen population and deal with major security issues internally and externally. Execution also provides the deterrent benefits of reinforcing The Community's commitment to the Rules."

"So have a trial," Jane Finch proposed. "We've got lawyers and judges. We know how to try people. Why reinvent the wheel?" Emma had to hush Samantha, who tried to explain there was no wheel. "We don't want rapists and murderers going unpunished either. Let's just make sure we're not executing innocent people."

"Alright," Emma said, persuaded. "Jane Finch, get with Samantha and create a court system. But I decide on guilt or innocence, and on the punishment, which will more likely than not be severe. And the trials will be quick, with no appeals. I don't have time for the old way of doing these things."

"What do I do about the current detainees?" Walcott asked.

"Execute the Infecteds. Hold onto any Uninfecteds you detain until we can give them a brief hearing."

"Thank you," Jane Finch replied, which thanks were repeated by both of her previously silent colleagues. That reinforced, to Emma, the importance Uninfecteds ascribed to manners and politeness.

Chapter 19

Chloe's father insisted that they gear up for their walk around town, and Aunt Isabel's Marine boyfriend agreed. But Chloe's shoulders were still sore. "I understand taking weapons. But why take our freaking *back*packs?"

Her mother explained. "Because your dad said so."

"We don't want anyone stealing our stuff," her dad said. "Plus, listen to that." Even from their basement closet they could hear the constant rattle of guns and an occasional *boom*. Aunt Isabel's boyfriend had spent the previous boring evening doling out cough drops, which Chloe and Jake considered candy, as prizes for correct guesses, and teaching them to distinguish between artillery, tank guns, and demolition charges. It was part macabre party game, and part campfire ghost story.

B-b-b-b-b-boom. "Arty," Chloe muttered to herself.

"What?" her irritated mother shot back, spoiling for a fight.

Chloe huffed. "Artillery, Mom. Probably 155s." *Whatever they are.* "Weren't you paying attention last night?"

Her mother bristled, but Chloe's dad said, "Listen up. Maintain tight spacing. Five meters max. Keep ten meters from anyone we meet. *Anyone*, Chloe. Anyone begging for supplies, flash your weapon and...."

"...and *use* them if you have to," Chloe completed. "We know, Dad. We're not newbies." Ka*boooom*! Chloe could feel the explosion through the soles of her boots. "Demo*lition*?" Chloe asked Rick.

The Marine nodded. "They're taking down buildings to clear their sight lines."

"Rounds chambered," Chloe's dad said. "Safeties on."

There were a series of *clacks* and *clicks*.

"You sure we should be doing this?" Chloe's mother asked her husband.

"*You're* the one who said the kids were going stir-crazy down here."

"Yeah, but that was before World War III started up there."

They left their basement utility closet fully outfitted for war. At the top of the stairs sat a well-armed police sergeant with a radio. "You leavin' us?"

"Just goin' for a walk," Chloe's dad replied in near native dialect.

The man eyed their weapons and equipment with a brow raised in skepticism. Chloe gathered that attempting to flee the besieged town was a popular pastime.

Chloe filled her lungs with the cool air outside but coughed at the smoke and winced at the smell, both of which hinted at fighting, despair, death, decay, and collapse. Columns of smoke too numerous to count rose from all points of the compass forming sheer canyon walls defining the town's defensive lines, which had constricted noticeably since their arrival four days earlier. A low pall pressed down upon Bristol—probable site of humanity's next miserable last stand—and cast grimy buildings and trash strewn streets in the gray light of sieges past. Chloe wanted to ask why they were trapped there and not taking their chances on the open road. Judging from the sounds of the guns, there were lots and lots of Infecteds. But their single file column assumed the imperatives of combat readiness—360 degree vigilance and rigid noise discipline—without needing any command.

They were in the eye of a storm, and Chloe felt its dangerous presence all around.

First went Dad. Mom followed. Then Jake. Then Rick and Aunt Isabel. Chloe stayed close to them. Margus brought up the rear, as usual. All held weapons at the ready like on the highway, and all were stooped under their heavy loads.

"Can you spare some food?" asked a grimy woman pushing a baby stroller.

"Stay back!" Margus snarled. Chloe raised her mask, then her rifle, joining Margus's in a final warning to the woman.

"Back...*please!*" Chloe begged as the woman reached the life defining ten meter mark. Chloe aimed carefully enough to miss the stroller. But what was the point? If she killed its mother, she killed the baby.

The woman turned the stroller aside. It was empty. Maybe her baby was already dead. Or maybe the stroller was a prop to elicit pity or to distract from some danger. Chloe's rifle swung all around before settling back on the whimpering woman. Or maybe the carriage was just to cart around supplies.

"I need food. Please. We're starving. I've lost my milk. I need to eat."

The plea tugged at Chloe's heart, but not her dad's. "Let's go! Keep up!"

Go where? They left the forlorn woman, who stared silently at their passage.

"Sorry," Chloe turned back to say.

They reverted to silence, only it wasn't silent. *Boooom!* Main tank gun, Chloe guessed, because artillery fired in bunches. *B-b-b-b-boom!* Now *that* was artillery. Seconds later, the distant *c-c-c-c-crump* announced arrival of the shells. Chloe knew the sound, feel, and smell of that mini apocalypse from the night Rick had gotten them rescued.

"One call does it all," Rick had replied when Margus asked how he had managed to *"drop the hammer"* on the Infecteds at the barn. Apparently, Rick's satellite phone call had gone to the White House switchboard, which had relocated somewhere, and been transferred to the military and down the chain of command with surprising efficiency. Had it not happened quickly, Chloe knew, bits of her body—minus the top of her head—would litter that burned-out barn.

Her reflection off the dark windows of the Subway sandwich shop danced as explosions' shock waves rattled the glass and Chloe's insides. She hoped they would soon return to their cramped and smelly basement.

"Stay back!" her dad shouted to a gaggle of beggars. "This is your last warning!" That shout, and the half dozen rifles aimed their way, scattered the ten or so people into subgroups, which hurried away separately. It was their eyes that haunted Chloe. Wide. Sunken. Desperate. Terrified and terrifying. It was like Uninfecteds were transitioning to Infecteds even before arrival of *Pandoravirus.*

Chloe waited until Margus twirled around to walk forward. "This is a really stupid idea."

"No shit." He looked left and right then spun to check the rear.

"What do you think is gonna happen? With this town, I mean?"

"They're surrounded. They're runnin' outta everything. Nobody's comin' to help. Same as happens everywhere else, I s'pose."

"Quiet!" snapped her dad.

They passed people here and there. A line of civilians with empty gas cans. *You're dead,* Chloe thought. Troops guarding a water tower. *Dead.* A family much like Chloe's, apparently making a run for it, but much more poorly equipped. *Definitely all dead.* Men pushing a pickup truck piled high with belongings while a woman steered. *Them too.* A crowd waving papers at troops in gas masks guarding a grocery store. *Bet you didn't realize it, but it's the end of the line.*

At an intersection, there was a much louder *b-b-b-b-b-boom*, causing Chloe to duck reflexively. Huge guns in an empty lot recovered from their recoil and smoked as troops clad in rubber suits and gas masks reloaded with well-choreographed movements. *C-c-c-c-c-crump.* Someone, somewhere, was getting blown to pieces. For what? No matter how many the big guns killed, the artillerymen would all soon be dead or turned.

"Halt!" came a shout from ahead.

Rick, right hand raised from his rifle's trigger, approached a sandbagged pit across the street. Chloe couldn't hear their conversation, but the soldiers kept pointing in various directions and shaking their heads.

Chloe drifted closer to Margus. "You think we're going to get out of here?"

"Sounds like Cap'n Townsend is havin' trouble findin' us a ride."

Was that his answer? That sounded like a no. "Maybe we should, I dunno, just not be here when, you know, it happens? Maybe sneak out or something? *Exfiltrate?*"

Margus snorted as he looked around. "Sneak out? Through *that*?"

Flashes barely preceded the *thumping* of explosions and boiling clouds of smoke. There was a constant background rattle of gunfire.

"We're headed back," Rick called out from thirty yards ahead, chopping his hand and pointing back toward the high school. "Margus, you take point!"

The normally serious boy now turned grave as he led them back from their abbreviated stroll. Chloe didn't follow, but hung back as Rick, Isabel, Jake, and her mom passed. No one said a word. All grasped their weapons tightly and eyed every broken window or smashed doorway of the thoroughly looted town.

"What's going on?" she asked her father. "I thought we were taking a look around."

"We did." Even fifteen minutes above ground had been deemed too great a risk.

"But I heard you tell Mom we were gonna scout ways out of here."

Her dad, now doing the Margus spin to check behind them every few steps, said, "Change of plans. Those soldiers said the quarantine facility is filled to the brim. They're getting ready to...to clear it out."

"What does that mean—clear it out? How? Let all those Infecteds *go*?"

His eyes darted toward her, and he shook his head. It told Chloe everything she needed to know. They were getting ready to slaughter thousands of captive Infecteds, or try to. Which gave Chloe the answer to another of her questions. The end was nearer than she had thought. They had days, at most; hours, in the worst case.

A sudden fusillade of gunfire erupted from a few blocks away, much louder than the sounds of fighting from the town's perimeter. The avalanche of sound rose and rose until everyone in their small procession had come to a stop and stared toward its source.

"Let's go!" her dad said. "Safeties off!"

Chloe felt a sudden rise in anxiety as she clicked her rifle to *Fire*. But it wasn't fear; it was dread. She didn't want to resume killing Infecteds, especially fellow citizens of their newly adopted home town of Bristol who had managed to hurl themselves out of windows or somehow dodge machine gun bullets only to run into the Miller family out for a stroll.

Crack. It was Margus's rifle. *Pop-pop-pop-pop.* Rick and Aunt Isabel had joined in. The first of the onrushing Infecteds came pouring down the side street toward them. Aunt Isabel was directly in their path. Mom, Dad, and Jake took cover—prone behind the curb or kneeling behind a concrete trash receptacle—and flashes from their rifles joined the furious fire from Rick and Isabel's weapons.

Chloe lay prone in the middle of the intersection. There were dozens of Infecteds fleeing the slaughter at the smoking warehouse, and they were bearing down on Aunt Isabel. A man with one side of his shirttail untucked. *Bam!* Chloe's shot went in his chest and out his back, and he landed on his knees and then face. A middle aged woman whose hospital gown flapped loosely around her flabby frame. *Bam! Bam!* How had she missed that first shot? A little boy, arm bloody and eyes black. *Bam!* The high powered round was really overkill for his small body. *Bam!* The face of a man in the blue coveralls of a paramedic cratered sickeningly.

Men, women, and children recoiled as if hitting an invisible force field sagging ever closer to Aunt Isabel. Rick knelt above her as rounds flew and Infecteds fell. In the end, Chloe was reduced to shooting squirmers and crawlers before Rick yanked Aunt Isabel to her feet and they all took off jogging, if you could call it that. Their heavy packs slowed them to little more than a fast, springy walk.

"Stay back!" came Margus's shout, followed instantly by a single shot from his rifle. The man who fell looked uninfected. By the time Chloe passed, his family had gathered, sobbing, around the man's last breaths, and the man's wife shouted obscenities at her. Seconds after her dad passed them, the woman and her children were tackled, pounded with fists, and stomped with heels by the Infecteds that had overtaken them.

By the time they reached the door leading back into the high school, a huge tank was restoring order. Two crewman manning machine guns atop the monster raked the area clear of life while rumbling slowly down the street, sweeping fire at anything that moved. Rick and Jake helped Aunt Isabel back to her feet after she collapsed, trembling and sobbing, from near death at the hands of the onrushing horde. It was the reaction of Aunt Isabel—a grown-up—that brought home to Chloe how close their call had been. They must have shot thirty or forty Infecteds who had escaped the slaughter at the quarantine center. Had there been fifty or sixty, they might all have died. And if they had been a minute or two slower getting off the street down which the tank carved its deadly path, they would have died by its guns. Once again, they had just barely escaped death.

But for how long? Was Chloe's life still just beginning, or was it very near its dismal end? She took one last look at the contracting walls of smoke and one last deep breath of the distinctly acrid stench. The mechanical clatter of metal treads on concrete and shuddering rips of fire from its guns were the new chirps and tweets of nature. Would this be her last glimpse of sunlight filtering dimly through a canopy of smoke? The last kiss of cool air on her cheeks before hearing the animal howl storm down the stairs toward their dungeon? *Save one round,* she reminded herself as her father dragged her through the door. *One round is all it would take.*

Chapter 20

"Raleigh Court is first," Samantha informed Emma. "The Uninfecteds there seem real nice. They made those cookies I brought to work yesterday."

Emma had parked the Honda CRV, which belonged to Roanoke's public works department, at the end of the block opposite the barricades, and walked toward the armed men manning them. The middle aged, middle-class houses on the tree-lined street were presumably previously tidy. Now, however, the lawns were overgrown and filled with trash. Many had obviously been looted, and their inessential contents discarded in trails from front doors to the sidewalk. Some were burned to stinking shells.

"Halt!" came a shout from behind a mask. Armed uninfected men challenged them from thirty yards away—Dwayne's uninfected troops assigned to guard the Uninfecteds they were guarding anyway before being assigned by Dwayne.

Emma raised her hands as if in surrender. Samantha did the same in imitation. "I've come to talk to your people! I'm Emma Miller!"

"We know who you are."

Although they didn't sound friendly, Samantha said, "See? They know you."

The guards pulled a metal bike rack aside with a grating sound to open a narrow pathway through the barricade, which was built from a tumble of appliances and heaps of lumber haphazardly piled atop layers of collected debris, all anchored by three automobile hulks. The barrier ran across the sidewalks and lawns all the way to the two homes on opposite sides of the street.

"Thanks!" Samantha said as she and Emma, hands still raised, stumbled over the unsteady footing in the gap. None of the uninfected men dared come close enough to render aid.

"Everybody's at the middle school," said the elder most among the Uninfecteds. He pointed down the street, but neither Sam nor Emma saw any schools.

"Can you show us where?" Emma asked.

Looks were exchanged. The man seemed put out by the request and huffed before heading down the street. The two Infecteds followed, slowly lowering their hands.

Strangely, things were even filthier *inside* the uninfected neighborhood. Garbage was piled on the curb in front of every house. At the bottom of the piles, the refuse was in bags. At the top, it was loose and being spread by the wind. The smell of human waste was strong.

"Is the sewage system working?" Emma asked their silent escort.

He snorted with barely a glance over his shoulder. "Right."

"Is that a yes, or a no?"

The man stopped. Samantha kept walking to close the distance, but Emma reached for her arm just as the man took his shotgun off his shoulder. "There ain't *nothin'* workin' 'round here." He headed off again.

Samantha wrote, "Nothing is working in Raleigh Court," in her spiral notebook. When she pressed her pen to the ruled paper to make a period, they followed the man.

One house drew Emma's attention. It was draped in yellow police tape, but also bullet-riddled, burned, and roofless. Red biohazard tape still crisscrossed its strangely intact front door. "What happened there?" Emma asked.

Their escort didn't have to look back to know the house to which she referred. "They got quarantined."

"Where are its occupants now?"

"Still in there, I s'pose."

Samantha wrote in her notebook, "Uninfecteds killed the Infecteds in quarantine." It was presumably her small contribution to the research on The Killing.

Emma asked Samantha, "How's it going with organizing the research teams?"

"Pretty well." Sam flipped pages in her notebook. "They're asking about peoples' experiences since The Outbreak. How many they've killed. How many members of their family they've lost. Whether the interviewees are refugees, and if so from where. That kind of stuff." Their guide glanced over his shoulder at them. "They turn in their notes at the end of the day and we are typing it all up. Some of it's useful, but sometimes the interviews kind of break down."

"Come up with procedures—prompts—to get them unstuck. A script. And we ought to standardize the questions or they're going to produce all kinds of inconsistent data. Remember, we want to understand behaviors—infected and uninfected—so we can manage them and anticipate problems." There was another peek by the eavesdropping Uninfected. "How about the outreach teams?"

"The first ones are heading north tomorrow," Sam replied. "They've got copies of the latest Rules and a brochure this uninfected guy made with colorful pictures of Infecteds and Uninfecteds working together to repair the conveyor belt at a sawmill. The Uninfecteds even took off their masks to show their smiles, but they weren't happy about it."

"Where are the first teams going?"

"Sixty people are heading up the coast toward D.C. and the Northeast, and twenty toward Chicago and the Upper Midwest. They'll peel off two person teams when they reach recruitable communities, and they'll try to report in periodically. They'll also document local histories to add to our research. Do you think people will join when there's no threat of force to back it up?"

"Trial and error, remember? If it doesn't work, it cost only eighty people."

Their shotgun toting host pointed with a gloved hand. People filed into the Patrick Henry Middle School. "Aren't you coming?" Emma asked.

"Naw, not me." She and Sam headed for the school. "You have masks and gloves?" he called out from behind them.

"I turned two and a half months ago," Emma said.

"Fifty-seven days ago for me," Samantha added.

"So, we're hardly contagious at all."

"Still...." That was all the man said. After exchanging brief looks with Samantha at the mystifying truncation of his sentence, Emma extracted from her backpack a mask and latex gloves, which she carried for the comfort of Uninfecteds. Samantha found only a mask in hers. "Here," said their escort, handing her a pair of disposable gloves.

"Thank you." They walked on toward the middle school alone. "See," Samantha said from behind her mask. "They're very helpful. And a lot of Infecteds are real jerks."

But Emma had her doubts. The man hadn't seemed too nice. Samantha had this vision of a future, Emma realized, that was far rosier than Emma's. Maybe the little voice in Samantha's head was an optimist. But the one in Emma's head definitely was not.

At the door into the school's auditorium, the converging crowd did a double take. Although they, too, wore protective gear, they instantly made way as everyone recognized Emma. "Thank you," Samantha said as the door was held open by a masked woman who squinted, held her breath, and leaned as far away from them as possible.

Inside, the loud buzz of conversation rapidly fell silent. Metal chairs facing the podium on stage scraped noisily as shoulders were tapped and heads were turned. The room was full, and people lined the far walls as Samantha and Emma walked alone down the central aisle. "Hi. Hi. Hi," Sam kept repeating. Some of the Uninfecteds, especially the children, replied in kind. Even though light streamed through the high windows of the basketball gym, the cavernous space seemed dark and the still air thick with stale sweat.

An unshaven man, incongruously wearing a rumpled suit and unstarched white shirt with a loosely knotted tie, descended from the stage. His graying hair was unwashed and unkempt. Samantha's long blond hair, Emma noted in contrast, was clean and perfectly straight. "Hi," Sam said. She turned to Emma. "This is the man I was telling you about."

"Richard Ames." The man clasped his hands behind him.

"Emma Miller. Pleased to meet you." She used words that were now mere habits and whose linguistic origins were quickly being lost.

Ames motioned toward the steps up onto the stage like a glib master of ceremonies or an unctuous undertaker. Samantha sat on the front row facing the stage. One by one, Uninfecteds all around her rose after hushed debates and went to stand along the walls of the packed auditorium. Undaunted, Sam kept saying, "Hi. Hi. Hi," as her neighbors departed until she was separated from the others by five empty rows behind her and ten empty seats to her side.

Emma was not introduced. The undertaker bid her take to the podium with an outstretched hand. "Hello," she said to the crowd. But the room and the audience were large and her voice muffled. She lowered the mask.

There were gasps, and people on the front row across the aisle from Samantha rose even though they were fifteen feet away. "I'm not really that contagious. Neither is Samantha. By the time Infecteds' pupils return to normal a couple of weeks after infection, you can't catch *Pandoravirus* through the air anymore, only through bodily fluids."

The reasoning, or social discomfort, or both were sufficient for many of the reluctant Uninfecteds to return to their seats.

"I am Dr. Emma Miller. I'm an epidemiologist who contracted *Pandoravirus* in Siberia on Infection Date 7 while deployed on a World Health Organization surge team. This is Samantha Brown. Her father was the U.S. ambassador to China." Samantha stood, turned, and waved, but got silence in return. "She was infected when the virus reached Beijing on Infection Date...?"

"Twenty-four," Sam squeaked in her juvenile voice. "Glad to see you all." Her wave was again met with no replies.

"So, we're well past the two week mark and don't need to wear protective gear."

"We'll wait till we get the vaccine," someone called out from the crowd.

A general disturbance arose. Questions arose about when that would be. Some sounded hostile. Samantha had worn an ill-fitting and frilly dress for this first meeting with Uninfecteds, and sat with her blue gloved hands primly folded across her notebook.

You should've brought security, said the voice in Emma's head. A rush of anxiety caused Emma to grip the podium tightly. In through the nose; out through the mouth.

"We obviously," Emma said in a vibrating voice, "don't have the vaccine yet."

More shouts arose. Emma cobbled together a question from the disparate snippets she heard while locating the emergency exit to her right ten sprinted paces away. "We don't have any contact with representatives of the former government or military." More shouts. "But we've got more pressing matters to discuss."

"Pressing for *you!*" came a reply that rose above the others.

"If we establish contact with the former government, which is off in Texas—"

"They're in Tennessee," came an interruption.

"They're closer than *that,*" a man said, turning and craning his neck to address the first person to interrupt. "There's a whole bunch of Marines and sailors over at Norfolk."

"Samantha will put your concern on her list," Emma said. Sam opened her notebook and held her pen at the ready, but had no idea what to write. "We will inquire about the vaccine." After an exaggerated bob of her head, Sam made that notation. "In the meantime, I'm here to answer any other questions you might have about the new government."

"When are the elections?" came a question.

"What elections?"

"For...the new government."

"There are no elections planned."

After a silence, an uninfected woman said, "Who made *you* head honcho?"

It was a good question. Samantha listened with pen in hand. "No one. I made myself head honcho, although my title is technically Chief Epidemiologist."

Again, the room fell silent.

"Where'd you take the people you arrested?" came from the back corner.

"For violating the Rules?" Emma clarified. "They're awaiting trials."

An even deeper stillness settled in after that response. Emma gripped the lectern tighter. Samantha remained at ease. Her feet, in black patent leather shoes and lacy socklets, didn't quite reach the floor and swung forward and back with her ankles crossed.

"For not feelin' up to *work*! One fuckin' *day*! You gonna fuckin' *kill* 'em?"

A quarter of the auditorium joined in the chorus of anger. Another quarter tried to calm them. But fully half the room sat stock still and awaited Emma's response.

"The Rules say you have to work."

The disturbance grew. Samantha looked over her shoulder one way, then the other.

"Which brings me to my first point," Emma said in a raised voice, quieting the commotion. "You need to follow the Rules."

"Whose fuckin' rules...?" shouted a man in back, who was muscled out of the room. After the door closed with a *bang* that caused the most rapt Uninfecteds to jump, the disturbance continued indistinctly in the lobby outside.

"You must follow the Rules, leave during the prescribed exit time, or be punished. Those are the same choices you were given when you first joined, and they're the same choices you're given each morning when the Rules are updated."

A man, wearing a mask and baseball cap that made identification difficult, said, "What if we don't *wanta* leave our homes...*or* follow your Rules?"

The answer seemed straightforward, so Emma glanced at Sam. She made some kind of face hidden behind her mask and shrugged. "Then you'll be executed, as I mentioned."

That satisfied them. After another long pause, the next questions centered on getting a greater variety of food delivered to their barricades. "We're awfully tired of tofu."

Samantha noted the complaint. But it occurred to Emma that her audience didn't fully appreciate the situation. "We're getting you enough calories to maintain your body weight. Right now, we have a lot of soybeans, but that will change as different crops come in or new food supplies are located. But since you don't venture out of your neighborhood much except on work details, let me tell you what's going on out there. People are starving. *Pandoravirus* crossed into the U.S. on Infection Date 39—forty-three days ago. Almost all economic activity, including agriculture, came to a halt before we restarted it. If it weren't for the massive number of fatalities from the disease and from the fighting, we'd be completely out of food. As it stands, we've got...how many days of food supplies currently?"

Samantha flipped pages, still swinging her skinny white legs. "Twelve days."

"Twelve days of food left." There was a stir as heads turned to seatmates. *Tell them more,* came the voice. "In the Exclusion Zone—in the Appalachian Mountains to the west—we've had seven credible reports of cannibalism—"

"Eight," Samantha corrected, finding the right page. "There was that hog rendering place Walcott found last night outside Danville that was selling meat."

"*Eight* cases of cannibalism," Emma amended. They were listening now. "Our Community's goal is to provide you with enough to eat that you don't start killing each other for food. Variety and taste are things we'll work on after the crisis passes. But I hope you see why we need every member—Infected and Uninfected—to work every day."

"But do you have to *execute* people?" came a woman with long, almost white hair, who rose with a slight scrape of her chair. "Can't you show some *decency*? Some mercy?"

"No. We thought about it, but we just don't have the resources to jail people. And as I assume you know, we're culling the Infecteds rather more aggressively. If an Infected shows an obvious inability to maintain self-control, we're shooting them on the spot. That reduces the number we feed and should prove to you that we're committed to maintaining order. And if you've watched the news on TV you should appreciate how preferable order is to what's going on everywhere else in the world."

"But," the woman said with a strange emphasis, "mass *murder*?"

"Most of the executions are Infecteds. What were the numbers?"

Samantha again found the right page. "I'd have to do the math. But two days ago, we executed 1,302—" There were gasps that confused Samantha. "Uhm, all of those were Infecteds, pending trial of the eighty-nine Uninfecteds in detention. Yesterday, we executed 467 Infecteds.

Today—you haven't approved these executions yet," she said, looking up from her notes to the podium, "—but we've rounded up another 278 Infecteds for execution, and only eleven Uninfecteds for trial."

"How about you let *us* try Uninfecteds?" came a request. "We'll take care of it."

Emma shook her head. "No. You won't punish them. We will. And we'll keep you safe and fed. All we ask for in return is that you obey the Rules. If you can't, you're free to go. But if you stay, the Rules and the punishment for breaking them are nonnegotiable."

A man stood and hurled his metal chair against the wall, making a huge racket. "You got my *son*, you fucking bitch! You let him go today," he said, shaking a fist but being restrained, "or this is fucking *war!*" Uninfecteds hustled the man toward the rear door. "You touch one hair on his head...!" he shouted through his struggles.

The door again closed with a *bang*.

"Any other questions?" There were none.

Outside, Samantha said, "That went well, don't you think?"

No, Emma didn't think it went well. Was there some way to woo Uninfecteds back into the fold? Or were they going to be a threat, perpetually, until they were eradicated or infected *en masse*? They couldn't get by without them now, when their Community hovered on the edge of collapse. But the day would come when the economy improved.

"I think they're a *big* help," Samantha said, waving at and greeting every staring Uninfected she passed. "They're a lot better workers than Infecteds. You tell them what to do, and it gets done. I was out at the pits where they're filling sandbags, and they'd run out of bags. The infected workers and foremen were just standing around in the hot sun, but an uninfected man came up and said they could cut up the canvas from the awnings of the stores at a nearby shopping center. I put him in charge, and an hour later they were filling these colorful, peach-striped sandbags. I think they're great, the Uninfecteds. *Hi!*" she said to a woman.

The woman whisked two small children across the street to the opposite sidewalk.

Chapter 21

Rick Townsend returned to the claustrophobic utility room in the basement of the high school with deep concern etched on his face. "Is there a problem?" Noah's sister Isabel asked. "Is the helicopter still coming?"

"Yes, and yes. The Black Hawk is still coming, but the situation up there has gone from bad to worse. Everybody should get up and get packed."

That stirred the Miller family and Margus into action.

"What's it like up there?" Noah asked as he stuffed the pockets of his backpack with the gear he had removed during their week-long stay in the besieged town.

"Falling apart. There are outbreaks all across town, and every E-2 out there is firing at shapes and shadows. We need to decide whether to stay down here, where it's safer, or move over to the LZ, where it's not, before all the lines collapse."

"What do *you* think we should do?" Isabel asked. It annoyed Noah that she so totally relied on whatever her boyfriend thought.

Townsend filled his lungs deeply. "It's a close call. But…."

When he didn't finish his comment, Natalie asked, "But what?"

"When things go, they go fast. Right now, most everybody's still following orders and holding positions, but they're watching for signs. There won't be any orders to abandon ship, but in the end, it'll be every man for himself. I vote we go now, and defend that LZ…in case we're the only ones left *to* defend it."

Without any debate, it was decided. They would go, because Townsend said.

The lights flickered at the sound of a loud explosion outside, which Noah felt through his feet. Wide eyes flitted up, or toward the open doorway, or at each other. Another explosion plunged the room into total darkness. There were curses and confusion from the corridor outside. Rick flicked on his flashlight just before Noah found his own by feel.

"I don't fuckin' know!" a soldier shouted from the hallway. "I ain't heard from the CO since yesterday! And the first sergeant didn't come around this mornin'."

The flashlights panned wildly as backpacks were hoisted onto shoulders with grunts. Noah's family searched nooks and crannies for forgotten gear and checked each other out like at the beginning of a morning's march on the road.

"Everyone ready?" Noah said.

"Anyone need to go potty?" Natalie asked.

"Natalie," Noah said, "I don't think—"

Townsend interrupted. "Good idea. No telling when we get our next biological break." But no one needed to go. They all marched out of the utility room and labored toward the stairs under heavy loads.

"You leavin' too?" one of the soldiers at the door asked Townsend. Noah couldn't hear the Marine officer's reply, but by the time Noah passed the two Guardsmen were in a heated argument. "They ain't gonna tell us *shit*! It don't happen like that. Try and get 'em on the radio. *Try*. Ain't nobody answerin'."

Outside, the night alit with flashes marking front lines that seemed close in all directions. The Infecteds that pressed in on the beleaguered town were either crazy, or starving, or semi-organized killing parties, and therefore in every case homicidal. Thick curtains of smoke, visible in each roaring explosion, formed the eye wall of their *Pandoravirus* disaster. Noah had to walk briskly to keep up. Townsend was in a hurry. The only sounds were the guns and explosions mere hundreds of yards away and their boots crunching through debris in between. A second story window shattered—a stray round or shrapnel?—and rained glass near a ducking Chloe. Noah was too tense to rebuke her for her subsequent cursing.

He couldn't even see Townsend and Isabel at the head of their column. Natalie was hunched over and aiming her rifle at every dark hiding place they passed. Chloe's head turned left, right, left, right, and she too stooped low. Behind Noah, Jake seemed alert and Margus walked backwards bringing up the rear.

A civilian couple carrying a toddler raced along the sidewalk from one doorway to the next on the opposite side of the street. "You're going the wrong way!" the mother holding the child called out to them before making the next dash into the shadows.

Noah picked up his pace, passing Chloe and joining Natalie. "Did you hear them?" Noah whispered. "That woman said we're going the wrong way."

"Rick knows what he's doing," was Natalie's curt and irritating reply. The sights they passed were randomly illuminated by the booming main guns of tanks. Gone was all concern about collateral damage or noncombatant casualties. Noah and Natalie's rifles found possible targets everywhere. A shattered glass door to a hair salon. An overturned portable generator.

Noah jogged ahead to find their new leader. He was out of breath when he pulled even with Rick and Isabel. "That woman back there," Noah said, panting, "said we were headed…the wrong way. There must be… trouble ahead."

"Yeah?" came Townsend's reply from behind glowing night vision goggle lenses. "There's trouble in every direction." He slowed at an intersection long enough to look both ways. Not for traffic, but for jumpy, trigger-happy troops or coiled and crazed Infecteds.

Noah followed him across the street. "Do you know what we're heading into?"

"No. But I know where that Black Hawk is supposed to pick us up."

On the far side of the intersection, Noah waited until Isabel arrived. Both ducked as a thunderous *boom* rattled the few remaining intact windows. "This is insane!"

"Just do what Rick says," Isabel replied, entrusting blind faith in the Marine.

At the next intersection, Townsend stopped to talk to two helmeted, prone men. Noah kept going, intending to join them, but Isabel grabbed his arm. "What? I don't even get to listen?"

"Jesus, Noah. Let Rick do his job."

Townsend might be responsible for Isabel, but Noah was responsible for his family. It wasn't an obligation he was willing to delegate. He joined the kneeling Marine beside two soldiers, one of whom was saying, "… about an hour ago. Since then, we've had no contact with anybody beyond this point, sir."

Townsend turned to Noah. "The LZ is two blocks past this line, which might be the last one that's intact."

"Can you radio the crew? Give them new coordinates?"

Townsend shook his head. "Nope. I've got their frequency, but no luck so far. The only contact I've had is via sat phone with Fort Campbell, where the Black Hawk took off a while ago in the middle of a shitstorm. Now, I can't even raise Fort Campbell."

"Do you know it's still coming?" In the darkness, Noah could discern no reply.

"What's up?" Isabel asked, joining them.

Townsend said, "We're gonna have to go out there and secure the LZ ourselves."

"Okay," she said in what Noah thought was naïveté. "Let's *do* it."

"Can't we get some help?" Noah said, turning to look at the dark, prone forms of the nearby soldiers. If they heard his request, they ignored it.

"You're not gonna fuckin' shoot us, are you?" Townsend said to the Guardsmen.

"No, sir," came one soldier's reply. It somehow seemed inadequate.

"Get on the radio and pass the word that we're heading out," Townsend ordered.

"Sir, it's just me and my fire team, plus those two cops across the road. Five of us. That's the only contact I've got. As a matter of fact, if you'd give us the order to pull back from here, that'd be good enough for me."

"I'll tell you what," Townsend said. "If you see a Black Hawk take off from that grocery store parking lot down the street, you've got my permission to pull back. We came from the high school. That's where I'd head."

"Yessir! Thank you, sir."

"But if you don't see it in about fifteen minutes or so, we're comin' back this way and I expect to see you here. Don't bug out till we're airborne or back inside, got it?"

"Yes, sir. Good luck, sir."

Townsend crossed the next street. As Isabel followed, Noah heard, "Lucky bastards," from one of the soldiers, and, "Maybe," from the other.

Noah caught up with Townsend and Isabel at the edge of a low wall beside a dark parking lot, which was filled with debris. The lampposts were all lying flat on the ground, having been cut at about waist level. Broken wooden pallets, crates smashed open, and plastic wrap and Styrofoam peanuts were all that remained of the airlifted supplies that had once been flown into the impromptu heliport.

Chloe, Jake, and Margus finally gathered around them.

"This is a free fire zone," Townsend informed them all. "Anything you see—anyone—is a threat. If they make a move toward you, or they're armed, drop 'em. Don't worry about any niceties like challenges or warning shots. First shot center mass. Got it?"

Noah's children both nodded. Townsend rose to head into the parking lot, but Isabel stopped him. "Look!" Three people ran out through the blackened doorway of the grocery store. They didn't seem to be together, but they ran toward where Noah and the others lay on the street. Townsend, who wore night vision goggles, stared down the barrel of his carbine.

Bam! One of the three people fell. *Bam-bam-bam-bam!* The other two fell.

Townsend looked around. He hadn't fired his weapon. The shooters had been Chloe and Natalie. Their three targets lay still. "All right," Townsend said. "Let's go."

They crossed the parking lot. Townsend steered them clear of spots littered with discarded and bloody bandages, IV drip bags and hoses, dark stained swabs, and other refuse from first aid that might, now, harbor viral contaminants. He placed each member of their group behind whatever cover was available roughly in a broad circle around the cleared landing zone. Jake lay behind an overturned gurney. Townsend stacked a few crates around where Natalie settled. Chloe's position was beside the broad cylindrical concrete base of a severed lamppost. Margus covered the open doorways and shattered windows of the grocery store from behind some shopping carts. Isabel was put next to a car resting on its rims. And Noah got a position with nothing but the concrete curb for protection. He guarded against intruders from the street from beside his bulky backpack.

Not seconds after Noah settled into place and raised his rifle, a man rounded the building along the street ahead. He was ranting and throwing his arms in the air as if explaining something to someone seen only by him. "Back! Run back! He said it. They said. Stay back! Back, back-back-back!"

He was demented. Insane. Rick was thirty yards away.

"Dad!" Chloe called to him.

The crazy man heard her. "What? Who's there? *Who*, who-who-who!" He headed for Noah's daughter, lurching one way, then the other. The demons in his damaged head spoke through him. "Come out, come out, little girl, wher*ever* you are!"

The man stopped and stood straight up as if for a better view. *Bam.* At first Noah assumed he must have missed. The man jumped on hearing the shot, but just stood there. Noah lined up a second shot, but his target dropped to one knee and both hands, tried to rise, and rolled onto his back. "Been shot. Shot. Been shot," he muttered until falling quiet.

Bam! Bam-bam! Margus shot another two people exiting the grocery store. The woman screamed in agony...uninfected. "Oh! Jared? God! *Ow!*" *Bam!* That shot ended it.

Natalie, Chloe, and Jake all began firing. Noah could see multiple dark forms emerging from an alleyway beside the store but couldn't get a clear enough aim to help.

"Noah!" came Townsend's shout as he raised his own carbine to his shoulder. Flame shot from its muzzle.

Noah turned. A half dozen people were rushing straight toward him and growling or groaning in the way of Infecteds. He fired twice but missed. They didn't scatter or take cover even when Townsend's shots struck home and felled members of their group.

At fifteen yards—close enough for Noah to see the fixed grimace, bared teeth, and wide eyes of the berserk gray haired woman—his third shot struck home. The woman's steady snarling rose an octave before being choked off like a dog's growl by a brief yelp. A young boy of ten or so raced past her. *Bam.* Noah couldn't miss him at point-blank range.

There was a loud *pop.* The parking lot bloomed with orange light and filled with a hissing sound, followed by two more *pops* and *hisses* as the flares Townsend tossed illuminated the helicopter's landing zone. But the sky was silent save the ever present roar of fighting that rose intermittently and ferociously from every direction.

"Let us in!" shouted four people—three adults and a child— from the street.

"No! Stay back!" Noah shouted. The people ignored him. "Last warning!"

Bam! Townsend shot one of the adults. The others gathered around the wailing wounded man, shouting at him to, "Hold on! Stay with me! We'll get you help!"

Another much larger crowd appeared on the street. "Townsend!" Noah shouted. The shouts from the three surviving Uninfecteds nearer them were much louder. Noah fired at the multitude of targets, as did Townsend and the others. The three unwounded Uninfecteds began firing, too, but their shrieks pierced the night and what little remained of Noah's failing composure as the Infecteds bludgeoned, stabbed, and tore the life from them.

But for their pause to rip apart the hapless Uninfecteds, whom they must have been chasing, they would have immediately overrun Noah's position. Noah and Townsend fired repeatedly at their stationary targets, who presented themselves mainly as dark profiles against backlighting from flames down the street. *Bam-bam-bam.* The flickering light from the flares was now dying. *Bam!* Noah shot an Infected who raised one of the dead Uninfected's rifles. Townsend added more illumination with a *pop, pop, pop*, which lit the masks of rage that were the Infecteds' faces. They didn't bite their victims on the ground beneath them—*bam*—but they looked feral enough *to* bite as they flailed at the bodies with wild abandon. A man raised what looked like a table leg over his head. *Bam.* Noah dropped him. A woman came back up with a hand full of torn clothing. *Bam.*

From behind that group of murderers came a much larger mob. "Town*seeeend*!" Noah shouted, rising up to kneel on the pavement for a better shot. *Bam-bam-bam-bam-bam-bam.* Half his shots struck home. Only those stopped the Infecteds. The rest raced straight for him undeterred. There were too many, too fast, too unafraid. This was the end.

Explosions forced Noah flat to the ground. Townsend was firing grenades from the launcher underneath his carbine's barrel. The grenades hit a wall next to the parking lot. An abandoned bus on the street. A tree, whose upper half collapsed straight to the grassy median beneath it. Each burst of a rifle grenade felled several Infecteds, often causing Noah to reacquire new targets. But still they came. Twenty yards. Fifteen yards. Too many. It was no use. He pulled the pistol from its holster and raised its muzzle to his mouth.

"Noah!" Natalie cried.

The sky shrieked like the howl from an otherworldly alien weapon. The parking lot was lit by fire and erupted in geysers of pavement shot skyward in long strings that passed within yards of where he lay, shredding the onrushing attackers as Noah cringed and curled in a fetal ball. A helicopter orbited the blazing scene. The multiple barrels of a gun in its door spun and spewed flame six feet from their muzzles.

Noah raised his rifle again. Infected attackers disappeared limb by limb. Heads exploded. Shoulders were sheared from torsos. Pumping thighs left their knees behind. Bodies spun, and twisted, and contorted not from pain but from the sheer violence of the metal rain that minced their flesh, cracked their bones, and pummeled the earth around them.

"Mount up!" Townsend shouted as the helicopter's gun fell silent and the aircraft almost crash landed in the parking lot. All the accumulated trash left the ground at once and swirled in an eddy rising into the orange light of the flares and fires like the rapture. "Leave them!" Townsend shouted at Isabel and Natalie as they dragged their huge packs across the pavement toward the Black Hawk, which had huge bomb-looking tanks slung under each of its stubby winglets.

Noah looked down at his pack. Everything he owned in the world, from toothbrush to bars of gold, was in it.

"Now, Noah!" Townsend shouted at him.

Noah left his pack and raced toward the helicopter, whose helmeted crewman was waving vigorously for everyone to hurry. Noah had to squint against the dust as he entered the fury of the downdraft. The pilot was keeping the rotors churning at high speed.

His outstretched hand collided blindly with the fuselage. The crewman grabbed Noah's rifle so Noah could climb aboard. But Noah was aghast when the man simply tossed the rifle to the ground outside. Natalie tugged on Noah to pull him further inside. Townsend threw his own carbine out the door. The aircraft lurched skyward. Not one of them had a pack or a rifle. Before the door closed, at Townsend's urging they stripped off their webbing, ammo pouches, dump pouches half filled with mostly empty mags, belts, holsters, body armor, and helmets, and tossed them all out. The door gunner pulled his multibarreled weapon from its mount and heaved it into the black night air. Two large metal ammo boxes followed, then two other crates laden with indeterminate contents.

In the quiet after the side door slid shut, Noah looked around. Something was wrong. Natalie one, Jake two, Chloe three, Isabel four, Townsend five. Me six. He counted again. One, two, three, four, five, six. "Where's... where's *Margus*? We've gotta go back!" Chloe broke down and sobbed. Natalie slid over and put an arm around her, but looked confused. "We *left* him there?" Noah cried.

"He was shot, Dad," Jake said in a quivering voice. Tears welled up in his eyes. "Bad. He couldn't...he couldn't breathe. He kept gurgling... saying...." Jake began sobbing.

Chloe repeatedly banged the back of her head against the bulkhead—not gently—and stared into space, face glistening with tears. She completed her brother's sentence in a drained monotone. "He kept saying *shoot me. Shoot me*. He was...drowning...in his own blood. His eyes were... bugging out. He was turning purple and shaking. He was so, so scared, *Dad*." She collapsed into the arms of her mother, who looked in distress at Noah, then at Jake.

"Jake," Noah said, feeling a quiver ripple along his torso, "Jake, did... did you...?"

Jake shook his head. *Oh-thank-God!* But his son stared down at his now wailing, twisting, squirming, kicking sister, who kept screaming into Natalie's lap. "Mommy! Mommy! *Mommyyyy!* Make it stop! Make it *stop!*"

"Chloe did it," Jake whispered. "He kept telling Chloe you owe me. You owe me."

Chapter 22

"They're in here." Dwayne nodded to the guard, who opened the door for Emma.

Emma entered the hotel conference room to find a dozen U.S. Army soldiers in full combat gear, minus their weapons and radios, on the carpet sitting with their backs to the walls or lounging on the floor. All wore gloves and most wore masks, which one hurriedly slid back into place after taking a sip of coffee from a Styrofoam cup.

Another rose. "This is Capt. Williams," Dwayne said before turning to the officer. "Sir, this is our Chief Epidemiologist." The man's eyes flitted back and forth between Dwayne and Emma as if he had no idea what to do or say.

"How do you do, Capt. Williams?" Emma said.

He looked around at his men before replying, "I'm, uh...We're fine. I guess."

"Is there anything we can get you? Have you been fed?"

"Yeah. We got some chow." Nothing seemed amiss in his response. "We'd like to get our gear back."

"First, I'd like to ask you some questions."

"*More* questions?"

Dwayne explained. "Samantha's interviewers spent most of the night with them. They were uncooperative."

The army officer said, "They were asking things we can't talk about. Our deployments. Missions we've been on. Engagements we've had and the casualty counts."

"They're compiling a history of The Outbreak and The Killing," Emma explained, hoping that would clarify things. "They weren't asking for military secrets."

"Yeah, well, there's a protocol, when you've been...detained." He turned to Dwayne. "You understand, don't you?"

Dwayne turned to Emma. He obviously did understand his fellow soldier.

"What were you doing outside New Roanoke?" she asked the captain.

"*New* Roanoke?"

"That's what we're calling it. Why were you spying on us?"

The army officer hesitated. He turned back around to his men. Dwayne had called them a "Special Forces A Team." The captain said, "That's a perfect example of what we're not allowed to talk about. It's in the Geneva Convention, Dr. Miller."

He knew Emma's name. "Okay. But what did you see?"

"We saw you murdering people."

Dwayne filled in the blanks. "They were on a hill observing the executions. When we started shooting the *Un*infecteds who got convicted at trial, they fired on us. We lost twenty-nine dead from their attack, and from when we maneuvered against them."

"Some of your men were only *wounded*," the captain said in a voice that rose nearly to a shout, "that *you* shot! Your *own* wounded, for the love of God!"

"We don't have good trauma care," Emma explained. "How many did *you* lose?"

"We, uh.... None. The Lance Corporal here had vehicles and numbers, and got around behind us. But listen. My men couldn't just stand down and observe that...*slaughter*."

"They were executions," Emma replied. "Those people broke the Rules."

"There were old *women*, and...and we saw at least two children. They were Infecteds, but still..."

Dwayne noted, "You only fired on us when we started killing *Un*infecteds."

"The Infecteds weren't even *complaining*. They just *stood* there. The Uninfecteds were on their knees and *begging* you! How can you...?" He was suffering some distress. "You people don't even get what I'm talking about, do you?"

Emma and Dwayne exchanged a look. "No," Emma replied.

After a long silence, the captain asked, "So...what happens now?"

His eleven men stared back intently, not moving a muscle, awaiting her answer. "If we let you go, do you agree not to come back again? A contract?"

The captain said, "Yeah. Sure."

"Because if you *do* come back, you would be breaching your contract. Breaking the Rules. You understand the punishment for that?" Capt. Williams took a moment, then nodded. "Dwayne, get agreements from them individually and take down their names. And please tell your commanders, captain, that we are not hostile to your forces. We're only trying to restore order and get the economy back on its feet to stave off mass starvation. If, however, they send more forces into our territory, and we capture them, we're most likely going to execute them. Can you please pass that along?"

"Well, yeah. I can. But are you sure that's the message you wanta send?"

"I thought, in the spirit of neighborliness, that it was preferable to warn them instead of demonstrating our intentions by executing you. But if you're suggesting that the message would have greater impact if we returned your bodies with a note pinned to them—"

"No. I'm not saying that. I'm saying that, if you haven't noticed, the United States military has the ability to retaliate…massively."

"We have noticed. I'd prefer to use our resources to restore economic productivity and not make war. Ultimately, however, every contract requires all parties agreeing. I've made an offer—you leave us alone, and we'll leave you alone—and your commanders must decide whether to form a contract, or reject my offer and suffer the consequences."

"I'll…pass that along."

"Thank you." Emma instructed Dwayne to take the A Team to the current frontier between Community territory and the lawlessness beyond, and to return their equipment and weapons upon release. "Good luck to you, Captain Williams."

Although she had intended no humor in her farewell, the soldier snorted. "Same to you, I guess, Dr. Miller. I hope you can live with your conscience."

He means me, said the voice in her head. *And I'm fine with the executions.*

Chapter 23

Their miraculous rescue from Bristol, Tennessee, had been no cause for celebration. Chloe lay curled up and blessedly catatonic after putting Margus Bishop out of his misery with a bullet. Townsend had whispered to the door gunner, "Do we have enough fuel?" The man had crossed his fingers in reply. They had no gear or weapons. If they were forced to put down, they would be at the mercy of soulless Infecteds and desperate Uninfecteds.

"Those poor people," Natalie said.

"Who?" Noah asked.

His wife seemed shocked by Noah's callousness. She must be referring to the abandoned defenders of Bristol. But his heartlessness was necessary. They were doomed, like everyone before them. All Noah could think was what happens if they run out of gas.

Noah stared out the side windows as the dark wooded terrain slid by. The crew chief began visiting the cockpit. First, it was once every half hour. After one such trip, the noncom warned them the external fuel tanks were dry and being jettisoned to save weight. Even so, there were gasps when the helicopter lurched skyward.

As time went by, Jake, Natalie, and Isabel fell asleep one after the other. "Mississippi River," Townsend announced as a milestone. Its black water glistened in the moonlight. The crew chief's visits to the front soon came every fifteen minutes, then ten, then five.

"How're we doin'?" Townsend asked him.

The man in the oversized helmet waggled his hand. "If we run out of fuel and have to auto-rotate, it'll be a hard landing. I'll crack the door open so it doesn't jam if the airframe gets warped. Give me a second to check on the rotors before we exit, then follow me out and get away. Even though there won't be any fuel, there's lots of other flammable fluids. Engine oil, hydraulic fluid, grease. And that engine, the main shaft, the exhaust—they're all gonna be white hot." The crewman returned to the cockpit, and stayed there.

Noah listened to the sounds. The thrum of the engines seemed steady. But every time the pilot adjusted the throttle, or the *whop-whop* of the rotors chopped at the air differently, or an up or downdraft abruptly altered their straight and level flight, the breath froze in Noah's lungs. Only when they kept flying did he resume breathing.

When the sun rose, they were lower. They were losing altitude. Townsend noticed it too. He held a sleeping Isabel lovingly: one hand on her head; the other on her arm. With her head in his lap and her face relaxed, she looked much as Noah remembered her the day he went off to college and didn't wake her from her nap on the couch. He always regretted not saying goodbye to her. She was napping from exhaustion at crying over him leaving home forever, fearing that to mark the end of their family. The real end came several years later with the death of their parents on a dark and icy road.

Townsend turned from the window, where the treetops were sliding beneath them. "He's staying low," Townsend whispered to Noah, "in case he loses power. He'll disengage the main rotor shaft so it'll keep windmilling and provide at least *some* lift."

"Should we get them up and into seatbelts?"

Townsend shook his head. "Better to be flat on the deck. Reduces spinal compression if we drop straight in."

The engine sputtered, but just once. Noah and Townsend caught each other's eye but said nothing. The copilot was leaning sideways and cranking a lever back and forth while contorting himself to read a gauge. The pilot's jaw was clenched into a grimace as he had one hand on the stick and the other on the throttle, feathering the blades' angle to eke out the maximum lift possible from each rotation. The crew chief between their chairs was pointing and shouting. The engine sputtered again.

Noah closed his eyes. *Dear God, please!*

There was a bump, then another. Noah looked out the window. They were rolling…on the ground. His family was roused from their deep sleep.

They were taxiing past aircraft of all descriptions when the engine spat and puffed and conked out. The spinning rotors wound down with a dying whine.

"Where are we?" a bleary eyed Natalie asked, blinking to clear her vision while staring out through the grimy windows. The crew chief returned to the cabin...grinning. "Welcome to Texas."

The pilot and copilot high fived each other and the crew chief. But the slowly rising Millers were more subdued.

"What's that about?" Natalie asked as she watched the crew's celebration.

"We made it," Noah replied.

Natalie seemed confused. "Okay, but...was that ever in *doubt?*"

Noah shrugged. They could see movement outside. A soldier in full protective gear—charcoal suit and hood, gas mask, gloves—appeared in the window and startled Chloe, whose eyes were puffy and red. "Dad? Is everything okay?"

"Yeah," he said, though he was beginning to wonder.

Natalie and Isabel both started when a pelting spray lashed the window through which they peered. Suds followed, and long brushes on poles after that. Jake said, "Do they think helicopters can catch the *P.* or something?"

The stench of scalding steam filled the cabin as water drenched the hot engine. Finally, there was a rap on the door. The crew chief slid it open. The air outside smelled of detergent. A soldier power washed the last suds from their aircraft's decontamination off the concrete into a muddy pit half filled with blackish water.

When everyone climbed down, they were ordered out of their gear. When it became clear that meant strip naked, Noah objected. "This is my wife and *daughter* and *sister.*"

"Everybody! Now!"

"Daaad?" Chloe whined.

"Come on, Chloe," said her mother as she unbuttoned her own trousers.

Their embarrassment was short lived. The freezing spray almost knocked Noah to the pavement. Hands that had covered privates now protected faces from the powerful stream as bodies doubled over.

"Fuck!" Noah shouted. "Take it *easy!*" He gasped for air. Soon, they were covered in suds and scrubbed with brushes, restoring a modicum of privacy before that was robbed from them again by the rinse cycle. As suddenly as the decontamination had begun, it was over.

Chloe was crying, doubled over behind arms and hands. Noah backed up to her to shield her from prying eyes. Jake and Natalie did the same from the other sides. Noah didn't look Isabel's way but saw out of the corner of his eye that she hugged a naked Townsend. Rough towels were extended on the ends of poles. The cool air on their wet skin and hair left them shivering.

There were no rides. The small bedraggled band of soaked immigrants, clad only in soggy towels, shuffled barefoot past crews and soldiers. Men arming and fueling fighter bombers, teams of heavily armed soldiers on one kneepad waiting on preflight checks, helicopters disgorging stretchers atop which lay wounded clad head to toe in plastic baggies pierced only by the mouthpiece of a snorkel on the inside connected to a cylindrical filter on the outside, and huge transport aircraft unloading artillery and armored fighting vehicles or loading cargos of supplies on pallets.

"My feet hurt," Jake said as he tried walking on the rims of his soles. Noah had tried first aid on the boy's blisters, but they had all been bloody and burst when he last tried to unstick his socks from his skin.

"Hang in there, buddy," Noah said. "We're almost there." But it was Chloe that concerned him most. She was hunched over holding the top and bottom of her towel closed, shivering quietly, mouth ajar, face a blank, staring wide-eyed at nothing. Noah put an arm around her, but she didn't even notice.

They arrived at a tent outside a large hangar. There was a single gas heater like on a restaurant's terrace. Noah and Townsend let the women and Jake huddle nearest to it. A female airman in full protective gear issued them jumpsuits that looked like prison wear and paper thin slippers. They were cheap, but everyone hurriedly scrambled into them with backs turned. The women began drying their stringy hair with their towels. It was then that Noah noticed the armed guards who had accompanied them at a distance. They held rifles at the ready.

"Who's first?" asked the African American woman who'd brought the prison wear.

"Me," Noah said when no one else spoke up. He followed her behind an opaque plastic curtain and sat in a folding chair. She settled behind three rough wooden planks spanning two rusty metal barrels. It looked less like a desk than a barricade. There was a pistol in a holster beside her hanging from a hook on the tent post.

"Name."

"Noah Miller."

"Places you've been in the last thirty days?"

"Uhm, the Shenandoah Valley, in Virginia. I-81 down past Roanoke." Her eyes darted up at him. "And Bristol, Tennessee."

"Have you had contact with anyone who might have been exposed to *Pandoravirus*?"

She looked up when he snorted. "You're *serious*?" Apparently, she was. She didn't get how ridiculous her question sounded. And he didn't realize until then that this was the old world, where encounters with homicidal Infecteds was still only as seen on TV. "Uhm…we had, I guess, what you'd call encounters. We killed a bunch of them."

"How close did they get to you?"

Noah thought back to the landing zone. "Fifteen or so yards. Maybe ten."

She rose, strapped on her pistol belt and holster, rounded the barricade, and rolled a device across his forehead. She noted the results on a form before prying his eyes open with gloved fingers and flashing a penlight past pupils that responded, he hoped as he winced. She put a green ring binder on the planks and opened it to plastic, three hole punched sleeves.

"Tell me what you see."

Noah leaned forward. It was a photo of a family laughing at a picnic. Paper plates rested atop a checkered blanket on a grassy hillside. All of the plates except one contained hot dogs and French fries. On the exception, however, were the smashed contents of a dead cat, whose entrails dangled off the plate like road kill.

"Jesus Christ," Noah replied, cringing and looking up aghast. "You want me to describe…?"

She turned the page. "What about this?"

He immediately searched for something out of place and disgusting. A family in church clothes singing from a hymnal in their pew. Nothing fucked up there. "Looks like an ordinary family at Sunday…."

She flipped the page. Noah winced and turned away. "Jeez. Is that some kind of cannibal…*kitchen* or something?" She wasn't interested in his answers. She stared at his face, which contorted with revulsion. One dismembered torso whose limbs and head had been stacked atop it, and one wedding cake being shoved into a pretty bride's mouth later, he was through and wearing a plastic bracelet like when checking into a hospital.

It took fifteen minutes for his group to process through. Noah tried to go thank the helicopter crew for rescuing them, but had to settle for a wave and a shouted thank you when one of the armed guards stopped him.

His reassembled group were issued masks and gloves, which they donned. "Where are we going now?" Noah asked.

"Temporary quarantine," the airman said as they climbed into the back of a canvas-covered truck. Although no one raised objection, he quickly added, "*Temporary* quarantine, not *quarantine*." Noah wasn't sure he understood the difference, but the airman's stressing of the word *temporary* was vaguely reassuring.

That reassurance evaporated when they reached the sandbagged gates through the double fences guarded by machine guns and snipers in raised manlifts. Natalie, Isabel, even the kids exchanged looks of concern. Inside, however, they found row after row of white, nondescript mobile homes. "At least it's not open air," Isabel said.

They were led to a no frills trailer home that troops in full protective gear and hardhats were leveling while other troops kept watch over them with assault rifles. When the driver opened the home's front door, it crackled and squeaked like it was the first time it had been entered. Inside smelled of plastic. He tried the switch on the wall repeatedly, but no lights came on. He leaned back out and said, "Hey! No power."

One of the soldiers who was packing up the huge wrenches they'd used for the leveler waved and went over to plug in a thick orange cable with a snap of electricity. The cheap fluorescent lighting in the trailer flickered until it came on. Or mostly came on. One lamp on the low ceiling continued its flicker even after the airman banged on the fixture a few times with the back of his closed, gloved fist.

"Home sweet home," said the airman through his mask.

"For how long?" Townsend asked.

"Fuck if I know. Two meals a day—eleven hundred and eighteen hundred. There's a cold shower in your unit if you can squeeze inside the thing, and one hot shower at the admin building per week." He read a piece of paper taped to the inside of the flimsy front door. "Yours is on Tuesdays."

"Wait," Natalie said. "We're *all* staying in here?" She looked around. There was one bedroom, and one sofa.

"*I'm* sorry," the man replied. "Did you reserve a *suite*?"

"Airman!" Townsend snapped. Although the man had no reason to know that Townsend was an officer, stripped as he was of his uniform and insignia, the tone of his voice—and maybe his short Marine haircut—evoked a quick, "Sorry. Yes, ma'am. All of you. Bed check is between twenty-one hundred and twenty-three hundred hours. You gotta all be here for that, or there's a helluva shitstorm."

He tapped the doorframe to signify the end of their orientation, and closed the door behind him. Natalie began looking in cabinets and closets. The meager bedding, airline pillows, and cheapest possible towels they had been supplied were wrapped in plastic and stacked atop the coffee table. Townsend peered out the filmy window at the streets and alleyways and the innumerable mobile homes arrayed in all directions. "Where is everybody?" Isabel asked on joining him.

"Probably baking a pie to welcome us," Chloe suggested sarcastically. Sullenly.

Jake made a face. "Where are they gonna get stuff to make a *pie*?"

Noah opened the door and stepped outside. Townsend and Isabel joined him. Behind them, Natalie gave orders to her kids to collect all the cushions, linens, blankets, and pillows out of which they would fashion beds for everyone.

We made it, Noah thought in an attempt to rejoice at the accomplishment. But not Margus. He didn't make it. And not, he feared, some part of his daughter's humanity, which she left back at that nightmarish landing zone.

Chapter 24

NEW ROANOKE, VIRGINIA
Infection Date 85, 1200 GMT (8:00 a.m. Local)

Emma Miller convened a meeting of The Community council at Samantha's request. For some reason, the girl had invited no uninfected representatives.

The twelve-year-old opened her notebook. Dwayne and Walcott waited patiently to be addressed or for the meeting to end. If Dwayne still heard voices in his head, he didn't show it. And Walcott clearly heard nothing. Dorothy, on the other hand, sat at the far end and didn't seem to know who to look at. She had been invited by Samantha out of tradition, presumably, since they, minus Walcott, had all been roommates at the NIH lab in Bethesda.

"I wanted to report some preliminary numbers," Samantha said, "from the census." She referred to her notebook. "The Community consists of eight counties in the Roanoke and New River Valleys: Allegheny, Montgomery, Bedford, Floyd, Botetourt—weird name—Craig, Franklin, and Roanoke. I've included the towns of New Roanoke, Blacksburg, Lynchburg, Salem, Covington, Bedford, and Radford, but have excluded Lexington and Virginia Tech until Dwayne figures out how to deal with them."

She looked up at Emma, who decided not to interrupt.

"One of our interviewers is really smart—almost as smart as some of the *Un*infecteds. She was, if you're interested, one of the scientists at the NIH lab where they experimented on us. She caught *Pandoravirus* while getting out of D.C. Anyway, I borrowed her from the interview teams documenting the history after The Outbreak for work on the census, and she estimates the pre-outbreak population of our territory at 475,000, of which 228,000 have died from the disease and violence. But there are also about 190,000 refugees from up north, making our total population around 412,000, plus or minus."

"How are we going to feed all of them?" Dorothy—surprisingly—asked.

"We need to get people farming," Emma said. "Less sweeping and road repair. More farming jobs on the boards."

Samantha made a note on the last page of her notebook, but no one else moved. Emma couldn't imagine how she could manage everything without the girl. She showed almost as much initiative as an Uninfected. "What else?" Emma asked.

"Well, except for spikes during Dwayne's operations—and executions, of course—most of the deaths these days come from encounters by Infecteds or Uninfecteds with the 7,500 or so crazies still roaming around, or from those crazies' starvation, exposure, or accident. They don't even know to get off the streets at night. Sheriff Walcott and I hit one yesterday in his truck and broke a headlight, right Sheriff?"

"What?"

"Never mind. Anyway, Dwayne needs new ones almost every day because of spoilage, and hundreds after every attack, and stocks are running low. The Selective Eradication police are trying to tase them, or use rubber bullets, or capture them with nets or traps, but about half they injure so badly, or they're already so beat up and ratty, that they're useless. And given that the rate of infection has fallen because the Uninfecteds have figured out hygiene and isolation—and as order was reestablished—we're down to only a few hundred new infections a day, with crazies being only about 10 percent of the half who turn."

Emma knew she was over reliant on Samantha, so she asked Dwayne, "What's your plan?" When he failed to reply, she rephrased her question. "How are you going to get enough incompetent Infecteds as fodder for your military operations?"

Still, nothing. Emma was forced to turn back to Samantha, who consulted her notebook like a junior version of Emma, whom the girl had carefully observed at the NIH hospital. "I can think of three options." It was thinking like that that left Emma unable to imagine replacing Samantha with another Infected. Could she risk putting an Uninfected in such a key position? "Option one would be to infect more Uninfecteds." That was why Samantha hadn't invited any Uninfecteds to the meeting. "But it would take about 1,000 Uninfecteds to yield fifty crazies. It seems ridiculously inefficient to lose 1,000 decent workers just to get fifty short-term...what did you call them, Dwayne?"

"Hm? Oh, berserkers."

"*Berserkers.* I like that."

"What are the other two options?" Emma asked. Walcott and Dwayne didn't appear to be listening anymore.

"Head into the Exclusion Zone and round them up there," Samantha proposed. "That violates our contract with Norfolk, if you can call it that since they never replied to Dwayne's messages. But there are more crazies running around up there now than down here in the territory we've pacified. And they keep coming down out of the mountains looking for food or sex, so we could characterize our incursions as security operations."

"And your third option?"

"Change tactics...and forces. Use stable, normal Infecteds for Dwayne's attacks. And maybe use Uninfecteds, too."

No way, came the voice in Emma's head, whose opinion Emma would need time to consider. "Dwayne, what do you think about that?"

"About what?"

"Using regular Infecteds for your forces...and/or Uninfecteds?"

Emma waited as he considered her hypothetical. "Um...well, I don't think the trick with the trucks would work with Uninfecteds."

"No," Emma said. "It won't."

"And if we fill those trucks with *regular* Infecteds, the crowd behavior will take hold. But when we stampede 'em, they'll fan out, cool off, and either go to ground or run away if the enemy fire is stiff."

"What if you change *tactics*?" Samantha asked, not waiting on Emma. Dwayne had no idea what she meant. "Instead of trucks full of crazies, what if you raised a *real* army?"

That, too, momentarily stumped Dwayne. He hadn't once, apparently, ever considered that alternative. "We could train them to use small arms, fire and maneuver, basic orienteering, comms, logistics. But...." They waited.

"But what?" Emma finally prodded.

"Why would they fight?"

Samantha said, "Because it's their job."

"Yeah," Dwayne replied, "that works...to a point." He fell quiet.

"To *what* point?" Emma asked.

"To the point where it makes more sense to run away than follow orders. They wouldn't charge an enemy if that meant a high risk of death. They wouldn't care if we branded them cowards or traitors, or shot deserters if the risk of death from the enemy was even more certain. And once one turned tail, they'd all run. Crowd behavior in reverse."

"What about the Uninfecteds?" Samantha asked. "If we risked arming them?" Dwayne had little idea how to respond. "What makes Marines fight?" Sam asked.

"Love of country. Love of the Corps. The respect of your fellow Marines. Pride."

"Would you or your *regular fighters* charge an enemy position if it meant almost certain death?" Emma asked.

Dwayne blinked several times before replying. "No."

"But U.S. Marines or army soldiers would?"

"Yes."

Emma returned the gaze of Sam, who said, "Then we'd better not fight U.S. Marines or Army, I guess."

A single shot rang out. Their heads turned to the window. Emma asked, "What about, instead of just shooting people who fail temperament testing, using *them*?"

Dwayne addressed another apparently novel question. "No. They're too *high*-functioning. We've made the mistake before—more than once—of misidentifying a crazy. They were competent enough to escape, and twice those escapes involved prematurely triggering attacks by the real crazies. We lost over a dozen of my regular fighters in one."

There was another, single shot down the street outside the church where they were doing the testing. "A lot of failures today," Samantha mused. "We should've anticipated this problem." She wasn't looking at Emma, who hadn't imagined a *lack* of crazed Infecteds being problematic. But Emma couldn't help but feel Samantha was being critical of her judgment. "We're *victims of our own success*," Samantha said, recollecting from somewhere the old saying, which seemingly greatly impressing both Dwayne and Walcott, who nodded in recognition of the comment's profundity.

Samantha filled the void left by Emma's increasingly anxious silence. "The outreach teams say there are plenty of crazies roaming around Ohio, Pennsylvania, and West Virginia."

"They're too far away," Emma replied. "Most wouldn't survive shipment. But since you brought it up, how are the outreach teams doing?"

"Great. They've gotten a whole bunch of interest. In fact, they've asked if you could get on a call, if the phone lines are working, or the radio with prospective new towns and communities to answer their questions."

"What questions?"

"Like what benefits do they get if they join? What will it cost them? Can we send troops one day to help with their security, or food, or do they send those things our way?" When Emma had no immediate answers, Samantha said, "I was talking to an uninfected lawyer working in body disposal who said he was an expert in franchising, whatever that is, and he can draft contracts that address all our issues. He's probably just trying to get out of body disposal, but…"

"I'll meet with him," Emma said, intrigued that there was a form of ready-made contract dealing with all those things. She turned back to Walcott.

"Sheriff, send your SE police up into the Blue Ridge and Allegheny Mountains—into the Exclusion Zone—and start rounding up crazies there. Avoid contact, if possible, with anyone else. Dwayne, send a message to Norfolk that this is just a border security issue, not an attempt at westward expansion."

Dwayne looked at Samantha, who said nothing, before turning back to Emma. "Yes, ma'am," he replied. But his delay in responding—and his check of Sam—had been significant. *Uh-oh,* said the inner voice as Emma's anxiety spiked.

* * * *

When the meeting ended, everyone left except Samantha. "Was there something else?" Emma asked.

"I'm worried about the executions," the girl said. *Again!* came the voice in Emma's head. "The Uninfecteds are really upset about them."

"We held trials, just like they wanted. And I released a good number of accused Uninfecteds when the evidence against them seemed weak. What more could they want?"

"I was talking to a doctor," Samantha said. "A psychiatrist. She said—"

"An uninfected psychiatrist?"

"Yes. She said that Uninfecteds are suffering from," Sam searched her notebook, "traumatic stress disorders, and their health, productivity, and loyalty to The Community are suffering as a result."

Emma had heard of soldiers suffering post-traumatic stress disorder after war. "Samantha, there's not much I can do about what they went through when the infection broke out and The Killing began. They're just going to have to toughen up and get over it."

"I'm not talking about that, although she did mention preexisting psychological damage from The Killing. What she was talking about was the threat of execution hanging over them. She said they were falling ill from immune systems weakened by the stress and fear of being detained, tried, and executed." Samantha rose from her seat at the table. "Would you follow me down the hall? I want to show you something."

"I don't have time to talk to some uninfected psychiatrist, Sam."

"It's not that. Just give me a couple of minutes."

Emma followed Sam down a back hall toward the employee parking lot of the city hall building. One of Dwayne's troops stood guard, and opened a door beside him when Samantha and Emma arrived. Curled up in a small broom closet, cowering in a fetal ball in the corner, was a quivering man. "Come on out," Samantha said in her high pitched voice. "Come on. *Come* on."

The shaking man crawled out on all fours and, at Sam's urging, reluctantly rose to his feet. He was stooped, arms wrapped around himself, wincing, looking anywhere but at the two infected women and his armed guard, and he was crying.

"What's your name?" Samantha asked. The man cringed and shut both eyes, loosing a whimper like an abused animal on seeing a raised hand. "What's your name?"

"Buh-Buh-Bob," he finally managed. He tried to look up at Emma, but he was too busy twitching, and serious tics caused not only his eyes, but his entire face to seize. He abandoned the effort and half turned away, lowering his gaze.

"This is what the doctor was talking about," Samantha said to Emma. "Look at him. How can we expect someone like him to work productively, or do much of anything at all for that matter?"

"Where did you find him?" Emma asked.

"He was next up to be shot. I thought he was a perfect example of what that woman was talking about." The man was almost doubled over, as if he were experiencing severe abdominal distress. He clutched himself in an embrace that seemed less for comfort than to prevent uncontrolled shaking of his limbs. His lips quivered, and he was pale. "Apparently, the Uninfecteds are all so worried about getting arrested and shot that they are suffering from," again Sam consulted her notes, "*mass psychosis,* or something like that. It's causing them to fall ill, to contribute only as much labor as is minimally required to avoid detention, and to plot and scheme against The Community, which raises the potential that they might rebel against it."

Emma tilted her head as she studied the man. He really did seem ill. It wasn't agitation, a feeling with which she was familiar. It was debilitating fear—a term whose definition she recalled, but which she could not, no matter how hard she tried, conjure up. "And this...whatever is all because he was going to be executed? Are you sure?"

"Watch this. Pardon him."

"What?" Emma asked.

"Pardon him. Call off his execution, and watch."

Emma shrugged. "I hereby pardon you of your offense, whatever it was."

The man looked at her out of the corner of his eyes, but seemed hesitant. Slowly, and by degrees, he turned to face her and Samantha and straightened up. His arms uncrossed. "Re-really?" Emma nodded. "Thank you! Thank you! *Thank* you!" Gone was the stuttering, the quivering, the cowering, the tics. He faced them both fully. "If you weren't infected, I'd kiss your feet. And I swear by all that's holy, I'll never touch a child again as long as I live! I *swear* it!"

"See?" Samantha said.

"It's remarkable," Emma had to admit on seeing the man's transformation.

"The psychiatrist lady said that every Uninfected is suffering from," she found the term in her notebook, "*anticipatory* trauma—which is a small fraction of what this man was suffering from—just at the possibility of being executed someday."

"Can I go?" the man asked. Emma nodded. The man glanced once at the armed guard, then walked toward the door at the end of the hall, looking over his shoulder, hastening his pace, and finally running full speed through the door, which burst open.

The guard closed the closet door and departed in the opposite direction.

"So what do you propose that we do?" Emma asked.

"Stop executing Uninfecteds for minor offenses," Samantha said in a tone suggesting it was a trial balloon.

"I suppose that was the psychiatrist's suggestion."

"Yes. The lady doctor said," Samantha found her note, "punishment should be *com-men-su-rate* with—meaning proportional to—the crime."

"I know what commensurate means. Let me think about it."

Samantha eyed Emma, but said nothing. She was thinking. Emma couldn't imagine *what* she was thinking, but her agitation spiked again and she left the girl immediately.

Chapter 25

"I don't *wanta* go for a walk," Chloe said. She lay on the thin, hard cushions of the dining table's banquette, where she slept. "I did a lifetime's worth of walking down that miserable highway." She looked around at the flowery plastic curtains, fake wood veneer paneling, and cheapest imaginable gray carpeting. "I'm good right here."

Aunt Isabel was staring at Chloe's mother, who turned back to Chloe. "It'll do you good to get some air. Improve your mood. Come on. Let's go."

Her father added, "We need to stay in shape. We don't know what's gonna happen."

Chloe rolled her eyes, huffed, and joined her parents and brother in the fading sunlight on the muddy street outside. She looked up and down the unending rows of white mobile homes. "Nobody else is outside."

"I've seen people," Jake replied, getting her next eye roll.

The mobile home's door closed behind Chloe and the latch *clicked* from the inside. "Aren't Aunt Chloe and Rick coming?"

"No," was all her mother said before she and Dad took off down the street.

"Wait," Chloe said on catching up with her parents. "Are they...? Is *that* why we're going for a walk?"

"They need alone time," her mom replied before leaving her children behind.

"Sure," Chloe mumbled. "How soon we forget."

"What?" Jake said. "I don't get it."

"I guess everybody's over Margus, now." Chloe looked back at their mobile home. Jake just looked confused. "They're *doing* it, dorkus."

"Doing what?"

"Jesus. *It. Sex.*"

"Aunt Chloe? And Capt. *Townsend?*" *Jesus Christ.* "But it's, like, still *daylight.*"

Chloe caught up with and fell in alongside her parents. People stared at them from behind sealed windows. "So, how come you guys never send *us* out for walks?"

"*Chloe.* None of your business!"

"It *is* my business. I mean, you did before. All the time. Now... nothing? *Ever?*"

"Chloe," her dad said in a strained tone, "*drop* it. Please."

"Are you gonna get divorced?"

"*Divorced?*" Jake replied in alarm.

"No one's getting divorced," Chloe's mother snapped. "They're a new couple. Things are different." But her father stared at her mother. "*Seriously?*" her mom said to him.

Chloe cringed and fell back in with Jake, who asked, "What was that about?"

"Don't ask. It's too gross."

Curious eyes peered out through curtains that snapped closed. "I feel naked out here," Jake said, "without my rifle."

"Not nearly as naked as Aunt—"

"Chloe!" her mom shot back.

At one slightly wider intersection of rutted pathways, they saw two children—a boy and a girl—a couple of rows over. "Why don't you go say hello?" Chloe's mom suggested.

"They're, like, *kids*," replied Chloe. "Younger than *Jake*."

"So? Just remember to keep your distance."

Chloe and Jake slowly approached the children, with Jake's cursory wave getting returned by both. At about fifteen yards, Chloe said. "Hi. What're your names?"

"Campbell," said the little girl. "And my brother's name is Porter." Chloe introduced Jake and herself and asked how old they were. Their answers—nine and eleven—caused Chloe to look back at her parents to deride their stupid idea. But they were arguing, with her mom clearly being the angrier of the two.

"Where you from?" the boy named Porter asked.

"D.C.? You?" Jake replied.

"North Dakota. At least, that's where we lived last. Our daddy's in the Air Force. He says they're gonna let us out soon. He may go to work in that big building there." They pointed past the barbed wire topped fence at a hangar. "He fixes planes. What does your daddy do?"

"He fixes lawsuits," Chloe answered. "Does anything ever happen around here?"

The two kids laughed and the boy said, "A coupla nights ago, there was a big siren and all the lights came on and a bunch of soldiers came in and the speakers said to stay indoors."

"There was shooting," his sister said.

"I was *getting* to that," Porter admonished, arching his eyes in an angry face.

"Infecteds?" Chloe asked.

"Pro'lly. It came from over there." The boy pointed toward the gate.

"Kids!" shouted Chloe's pissed-off mom. "We're *going!*"

"Why do you always ruin my *stories*?" Porter complained to his sister.

The Millers resumed their walk. Chloe's parents no longer seemed on speaking terms. When they reached the next intersection, they saw a white mobile home that was scorched and blackened above the windows and the door. Yellow police tape encircled it, and a red biohazard sticker barred entrance. The walls and windows were riddled with bullet holes.

"They were pointing this way, not at the gate," Chloe said before relating what she had learned from the kids, embellishing details of the skirmish to make it more interesting.

Jake finally spoke up. "Like I was saying, I wish I had my rifle."

Chloe's parents pivoted and headed back. Had they been gone long enough? How long did it take? When her mother tried the door, it was unlocked. Everything seemed the same as when they'd left, except Aunt Isabel cuddled with Rick on the banquette where Chloe slept. Surely, they didn't…! Not right there!

Chloe's dad opened drawers in the kitchen. From one, he extracted a long wooden spoon handle. From another, a cheese grater. Both were courtesy of local charities, like the clothes they all wore. He settled in over the trash bag and began sharpening the wooden spoon with the cheese grater.

Without asking any questions, Rick searched the mobile home, pried loose a long metal door pull on the utility closet, and strained to straighten one end from which protruded a sharp screw. Aunt Isabel sat on the steps leading to the front door and began whittling on the end of a broom handle, using the metal edge of a tread as her tool. Jake brought back inside the larger rocks from the gravel strewn about the mud. Chloe lay back down on the banquette before her mother shook her still sore shoulder roughly. "Ow!"

"Oh, please. Get to work."

Chloe sighed dramatically as she rose, found some loose metal window trim, and began wrapping the less sharp end with tape someone had used to patch up a crack in the bathroom door.

* * * *

After dark, there was a loud rap on the door of the mobile home. They had seen the flashlights approaching and heard the rumble of a Humvee with its machine gunner on top.

Chloe hid her shiv under the cushion of the banquette.

Rick opened the door. A man in a gas mask and covered head to toe stood there with his pistol holstered but with several men holding rifles just behind.

"Bed check," came his muffled comment. He tracked mud inside on his disposable booties. "Miller, Isabel?" Aunt Iz raised two fingers. "Captain Rick Townsend?" Rick said, "Present." He went down the list on his iPad and got replies from each of them as he checked off boxes with a stylus. "Have a good night."

Chloe's mom got the broom to sweep the mud out, but saw its needle sharp handle and hid the makeshift weapon.

Half an hour later, all the sodium lamps outside began winking off, and the quarantine facility fell truly dark except along the perimeter fencing. Chloe's mom and dad slept in the lone bed at the far end of the trailer. Jake in the hallway leading to their bedroom. Chloe on the banquette, lying curled up on her side to fit. Across the room, Aunt Iz lay on the sofa and Captain Rick on the floor beside her. *Aw,* Chloe thought as her eyes adjusted to the darkness and she saw that they were holding hands.

* * * *

Wah-wah-wah-wah!

They had never heard the quarantine camp's alarm before. It took everyone a moment to realize what it was as the lights outside began to come on. Chloe peeked out the curtains until her father snarled at her to get down on the floor.

"What's goin' on?" Jake said after Chloe's mom tripped over him and cursed.

A sudden fusillade of gunfire sent everyone to the floor. A machine gun rattled. Chloe scanned the walls and ceiling for any sign of light through puncture holes.

"Listen up!" It was Rick. "If this camp is turning, we head away from the main gate! The fence closest to us is on the side by the hangar and tarmac, where the lights are brightest! So we should head the *opposite* direction! *Away* from—"

Before he could even finish his instructions, which had Chloe's full attention, the shooting died down. Like the last kernels of corn to pop in the microwave, there were three more spaced, single shots, and then silence but for some shouting. A loudspeaker announced something no one could understand. The adults allowed themselves to look out windows on all sides. After another inaudible loudspeaker announcement, the lights began falling dark again. Chloe could smell plastic or rubber burning.

"Everyone go back to sleep," her dad said.

Sleep! What a crazy stupid idea. But as Chloe lay there, trying to eavesdrop on the whispers between Aunt Isabel and her boyfriend, who curled up together and barely fit on the sofa, Chloe's thoughts grew more random. She had never gotten to snuggle with *her* boyfriend—or ex-, Justin—whose body parts now presumably rotted away with the rest of his family in the upstairs closet of his McLean house. And the curly haired boy from New York on the shoulder of I-81—what way had he died? And why was Aunt Emma wearing a helmet and riding atop a military truck in a parade while confetti drifted down, Chloe and her cheer team shook pom-poms and did high kicks, and Margus lay bleeding at their feet?

Chapter 26

NEW LYNCHBURG, VIRGINIA
Infection Date 87, 2230 GMT (5:30 p.m. Local)

"It's the same as yesterday," Samantha said to Emma. "I thought you'd wanta see it." They walked the leaf strewn streets of the walled, uninfected neighborhood escorted by two of Dwayne's guards, both infected, and two of his uninfected guards from the barricades. The two pairs of armed men eyed each other warily. All four Infecteds wore masks and gloves in deference to the sensibilities of the uninfected members they passed as families filled the streets, jogging in large numbers at exactly the appointed time. "You see? They *do* respect the Rules. They're all getting in shape just like you told them to. I think they'll make *great* members of our Community."

Samantha had increasingly become the leading champion of the Uninfecteds. Dwayne didn't seem to care much for them, and would probably eradicate the lot of them if given his choice as that would simplify his concerns about security. Walcott didn't seem to care about anything at all. He simply did what he was told, and nothing if told nothing—a stereotypical Infected, even though he too was classified *high-functioning*.

"Have you improved on the test we were using to categorize Infecteds by mental capacity?" Emma asked. "To reduce the amount of waste?"

"Sorta. I mean, I'm only twelve. But fewer people are failing, so…. I'm gonna have that NIH scientist lady who's been helping me on the census and interviews work on that next. But do you know who we could *really* use to make that test better?"

My sister, came the voice. "My sister?" Emma said aloud.

"*Yes.* How'd you know that was what I was gonna say?"

"Just a guess."

They passed a white haired lady in her front yard kicking one heel back, then the other, twisting her torso in time with her movements. "Hi!" Samantha said, waving to the woman, who hesitated before replying after some apparent confusion…or fear.

The joggers who passed them steered clear, sometimes veering all the way up onto overgrown front lawns. "If we keep getting refugees," Emma said, "we're going to need to pack people in more tightly. How densely populated is this neighborhood?"

"We'll have that info in our census. But most houses seem occupied, and some are already full because people took in relatives or friends."

"We need more food!" shouted a woman in a large group that jogged past. She was shushed by her fellow, running Uninfecteds.

"They already get more food than Infecteds," Samantha noted in confusion.

"Start weighing people," Emma said. "Add that to your census data. We can reweigh them in a month. If weights begin falling—or rising—we'll need to adjust rations."

"You know Dwayne thinks the uninfected farmers are hiding food."

"*Hoarding.* Let's make a special point of weighing the farmers and their families first. If nothing else, it'll let them know we're on the lookout for hoarders."

Samantha's gaze followed passing joggers until she walked backwards. An uninfected boy in their ranks was ogling her, too. "What's the legal age for hooking up?"

"For *what?*" Emma asked as they passed an entire household under the tattered net of a driveway basketball hoop doing jumping jacks.

"Sex. We got a permit request by a boy who's sixteen and a girl who's fifteen. The uninfected woman who's running the DMV turned it down, but…I was wondering."

"You're too young. You should wait. You're not physically mature."

"Wolver*ines!*" shouted a young man who jogged past before he, too, was silenced by shoves from his fellow runners, all young uninfected men.

"*They're* cute," Samantha said, again turning.

"What does *Wolverines* mean?" Emma asked.

Samantha shrugged. "The woman at the DMV said it was immoral. Unmarried sex, I mean. We don't even have any way to *marry* people. *Should* we?"

"Don't worry about morality. We've already outlawed murder, assault, rape, theft."

"What about, like, being *nice* to each other?" Samantha's voice always rose in pitch when she was uncertain. A tree had fallen across the road, presumably in the big storm from the day before, and many of the joggers had stopped to help move it. Emma watched as an uninfected man directed the others. People with tenuous handholds or footing responded with directions or requests for pauses. Emma marveled at how coordinated they were for such an impromptu endeavor. They self-organized and cooperated.

"What about picking your nose or peeing in public?" Samantha asked.

"If you want to add Rules like that, go ahead."

"Really? I can add Rules?"

"You can *propose* Rules. But should we execute someone for picking their nose?"

"It *is* unsanitary." Samantha had a point.

Despite the chill, a teenage boy lifting the heavy trunk had removed his shirt. The thin sheet of boyish muscles stood out from his hairless torso. Samantha was mesmerized. When the boy looked their way, she waved. The boy seemed paralyzed by uncertainty.

She doesn't just like boys, came the voice. *She likes* uninfected *boys.* They turned the corner onto a block filled with groups doing calisthenics. "Samantha?"

The girl seemed startled. "What?"

"Do you like uninfected boys more than infected boys?"

Samantha stared at the sidewalk beneath their feet. "I guess. Why do you think that is?" Emma had no idea, and the voice ventured no guesses. "They're more interesting," Sam said. "They're always thinking. Sometimes they laugh and smile, and that looks cute. I saw a boy yesterday clearing the railroad tracks outside Copper Hill who was playing a guitar during his break. He was sweaty, and his hair was, like, in his eyes so he kept flicking his head." She imitated the motion. "And his eyes were *so* green. Like yours."

"Is that why you're going back to Copper Hill tomorrow? I saw it on your calendar."

"Well...you said it was important to get those tracks clear."

She was being deceptive. How much had her mind recovered? How close was she to wholly uninfected behavior? There must be other Infecteds who, over time, would also revert somewhat. At least those who, like Samantha—and Emma—had received excellent medical care immediately postexposure. Their more limited damage had greater potential for recovery. It also made their behavior less trustworthy, and more in need of monitoring.

Samantha's interest in boys was less sexual than it would become as she grew up. It was more...*emotional*? Was a boy crush a precursor to love? Was that even possible?

Samantha's head tracked a mop headed, light skinned African American boy, who returned her wave with one of his own before both caught Emma looking at them.

The world had completely changed once already. Was it possible it might yet change again? If an Infected could fall in love, or anything close to it, she couldn't be counted on. She would protect the object of her affection over other conflicting priorities like following the Rules. If Uninfecteds became unmanageable and Emma decided to eradicate them, what would Samantha do? *And if* Sam *can feel love,* the voice said, *what about* you? Emma felt nothing save the occasional but growing twinge of sexual desire. The risk that she might develop emotions and the irrational behaviors they caused was a serious concern. Emma surveyed the next half dozen men and boys they passed. *Yes, no, yes, yes, no, yes.* She would have sex with many of them, but felt nothing more.

"Should I go to Copper Hill," Samantha asked, "or not?"

"Go." Emma would have Dwayne assign a bodyguard to escort her and to report on the girl's behavior around the hair tossing, guitar playing boy. But, Emma knew, it would be a huge loss to The Community if Samantha turned out to be untrustworthy.

Chapter 27

There was a loud rapping on the thin trailer door.

Isabel was folded into Rick's arms. She felt his muscles grow taught as he sprang from the sofa with the pointy metal door pull in his hand. She got her sharpened broom from under the sofa and took up a position beside the door. In the dancing beams of flashlights from outside she saw Jake, Noah, and Natalie appear with their own improvised weapons.

Rick ignored the knocks and calls to, "Open up!" until everyone appeared ready.

A half dozen soldiers in protective gear awaited them on the street. "Dr. Isabel Miller?" Rick made way. Isabel peered around the doorframe. "We're here to take you downtown. To military headquarters. You're being released from quarantine."

"What about everyone else?"

"My orders only mention you."

"Well *I'm* not going without everyone *else*. If I'm healthy, so are they." She declined to mention her vaccination.

The confusion created by her apparently unheard of refusal to exit quarantine was resolved quickly over the radio. "All of you, gather your things."

That took two minutes. The Miller party—apparently, now, the *Isabel* Miller party—followed the guards down dark, empty lanes toward the well-lit front gate wearing an unsightly assortment of outdated, frayed, and ill-fitting clothes donated by area churches. Curtains were pulled aside as people peered at the departing souls, not knowing whether they were lucky or doomed. Another family, waiting in a tight huddle outside the gate—wrapped in blankets and looking exhausted, dripping wet, and traumatized—were escorted into quarantine, possibly to their old trailer.

Troops at the canvas covered army truck were armed but wore no protective gear. Either the Miller family was now reliably certified healthy, or the troops had been vaccinated.

Off they drove. The only words spoken were by Isabel's brother, Noah, who said, "Once again, Isabel, I guess we should thank you for this."

Isabel made a face and shrugged. The ride down the empty highway seemed to be going quickly until they slowed to a stop. The canvas at the rear was pulled aside. A bright flashlight was shone into their eyes, causing flinches and averted gazes. "You need to look into the light," came the stern command from the helmeted soldier in a gas mask.

One by one, the flashlight ruined their night vision. Isabel saw sandbags and machine guns spanning all four lanes of the northbound Interstate except for the one lane through which they passed. The roadblocks were repeated once every few miles until they exited the Interstate and were ordered to dismount.

The skyline of the city, mostly dark at that hour, loomed before them. Their truck did a three-point turn and headed back the way they had come. The Miller family passed on foot past last pupil and temperature checks before zigzagging through a narrow passage of towering tan sandbags. Two Humvees awaited them on the city side.

Foot patrols by small units used flashlights to peer under mounds of cardboard rubbish or dying islets of greenery dotting the concrete desert. Everyone was armed, tense, and looked ready to kill.

The Humvees stopped in front of yet more walls of sandbags at the foot of a well-lit glass office tower. More perfunctory pupil and temperature checks admitted them into the lobby, which bustled with men and women in the differing camouflage gear of various service branches. The new arrivals were processed singly in separate cubicles.

"Full name? Social Security number? Residence address? Occupation?" The bored functionary tapped on a laptop. The expected glossy photos of splattered corpses and puppies sniffing daisies never appeared. A printer hummed. The uniformed bureaucrat trimmed and laminated the printout in a practiced routine as Isabel wondered why she was there? What happens next? She knew those questions would be answered in time, not here by the soldier with the scissors. At least they were out of quarantine.

She hung the ID around her neck by its strap. When everyone had theirs on, an army captain approached Isabel. Although she had passed the infection checks, she had no way of proving she was immune. The man was taking no chances and kept his distance. "Dr. Miller? Follow me, please."

"What about them?" she asked, turning back to Rick and Noah's family.

"The commissary is closed, but there's always coffee."

"We'll be okay," Noah assured her. She gave Rick a peck on the lips and a squeeze of his hand before following her escort to the elevators.

The floors whizzed by and her ears popped. They exited onto an upper level lobby filled end to end with cots and both she and her escort had to endure yet more pupil and temperature checks. A scanner beeped after reading the QR code on her ID. Isabel's handwashing was monitored by a nurse. "Use the brush to get under your fingernails." Isabel scrubbed until her fingers hurt. All that remained of the nail polish after her last manicure months earlier was a tiny strip of red enamel hugging her cuticles.

The view over the city outside the floor to ceiling windows was probably spectacular. But the streets and highways, still bathed in light, were totally devoid of traffic.

The captain rejoined her after his own bathing ritual and they boarded an elevator for another ascent. It opened onto what looked like a lawyer's office, with noise and activity everywhere. A man and a woman sat behind the receptionist's desk wearing camouflage and side arms. They scanned Isabel's ID before the captain led her past outer offices with windows, which were occupied by senior officers, based on their ages and insignia. The inner, smaller, windowless offices held either junior officers or two sergeants sitting on opposite sides of a single desk. All seemed to be on laptops or phones. Everything had the appearance of a normal day at work but for the fact that everyone wore camouflage and was armed.

"Dr. *Miller*?" came the booming voice instantly recognized by Isabel. The hulking frame of Marine General Browner, Chairman of the Joint Chiefs of Staff, met her at the door of his large corner office. He extended his right elbow toward her. She met it with a bump. "Glad you decided to rejoin us. We can sure use your help."

A blanket was neatly folded at the foot of a simple folding cot opposite the small pillow at its head. He ushered Isabel to a guest chair in front of his cluttered desk. As Browner gave his assistant some instructions, Isabel gleaned as much information as she could from the mounds of books, papers, maps, and photographs lying before her. A ring binder's label read, "West Coast Evacuation Plan." The top photo on a stack looked to be navy ships exiting a harbor—San Diego, she guessed from the "Padres" sign on the stadium—with the skyline behind the ships lit only by blazing high-rise fires. A bound directive entitled, "Temporary Regulations," was incongruously stamped with a diagonal and red, "TOP SECRET." How were people supposed to follow top secret regulations?

"Enjoying your eye fuck?" Browner growled.

"Pardon me? Oh. I'm sorry, I was just—"

"That's okay. You're cleared Top Secret, or you'd never be in here." Browner sat in the plush swivel chair. "So you made it all the way from…" Browner consulted the desktop monitor, "the Shenandoah Valley to Bristol, Tennessee—on foot—250 miles through Injun Country? Not too shabby. And Captain Townsend is with you?"

"He's downstairs. So is my brother, his family, and…." Margus was dead. "What's going on?" she asked when what she really meant was, *Why am I here?*

The Marine found something in what she said amusing, and snorted. "Same ole apocalypse. But we're making progress with our vaccine production. About 20 percent of my troops have been inoculated."

"What do you do with the ones who turn?"

"Boy, you get right to it, don't you?" Isabel wasn't sure what he meant, but guessed she had a habit of raising uncomfortable topics. "You're gonna find," he said, rocking back in his chair and rubbing his face and eyes with both hands, "that we've had to institute the harshest possible measures to maintain the cordon sanitaire."

"Meaning what?"

"We don't exterminate them, if that's what you're asking." She waited. "Look, Dr. Miller, I don't have time to justify all the policy decisions we've made since the outbreak. And frankly, it's irritating to have to justify our actions to someone we just rescued from a town that was overrun by Infecteds about an hour after you went wheels up. But I'll give you one. We've got three levels of quarantine. There's the one I just sprung you from for newly arriving people that appear symptom free and have special skills we need, or their immediate family members. There's a second level for people who're suspected of having been exposed. And then there's detention of the clearly infected. That's all. No firing squads, or gas chambers, or ovens. Okay? Do we pass your moral judgment?"

"I'm sorry. I don't mean to be a bitch about it. I just…. Never mind."

Browner sighed deeply. Isabel waited for him to return her gaze. "Alright, look. That third level of detention is…is horrible, okay? And the second level is none too comfy. They're in open-air facilities. Minimal food and water. The medical care is nonexistent. And security is…. You understand that we can't...*police* what's going on inside there. It's all we can do to keep 'em locked up. What they do to each other...." She thought she kept her face neutral, but Browner snapped, "God*dam*mit, Isabel!" startling her.

"But you aren't eradicating yet?" *Turning quarantine camps into death camps?*

"We got the *authority* for it, just not the...will. Yet. There are still people who think Infecteds can be rehabilitated, or resettled on a reservation system, or reintegrated into society. And my subordinate commanders, who are closer to the troops, tell me their units will mutiny if President Anderson gives that order. I haven't seen the president in person since he was sworn in at Raven Rock. He's being kept airborne or at secure locations. So, basically, the plan still seems to be to slouch our way toward Armageddon."

She wanted to ask if Browner led the coup that intentionally infected former President Stoddard, who had adamantly opposed eradication, but a little voice in her head warned against it. "What is it that I can do for you?"

"Plenty." He dug through piles of paper until he found what he wanted. "First, you remember Dr. Rosenbaum? From the NIH hospital?"

It had been less than two months since the two of them had "worked together" in Bethesda. Isabel had studied the effects of *Pandoravirus* on her sister's brain, which she had thought she had been retained to do. Hank Rosenbaum had surreptitiously compared Isabel to her infected identical twin sister. It had been less than one month since their brief and chilly encounter at President Stoddard's competency hearing in Raven Rock Mountain.

"*Ole* Hank. How's he doing?" Her voice dripped with faux concern.

"His family got sick—every last one of them—while he was at Raven Rock."

"Oh." Isabel really should be less judgmental, especially these days. "I'm sorry."

"He's now working with what's left of the government—military, Park Rangers, federal marshals, and FBI, TSA, and Treasury agents—out west. We need you and Townsend to assess whether they can hold on until we can get the vaccine to them, or, if not..."

She waited. "If not...*what*?"

"Can we buy enough additional time through unrestricted strategic bombing?"

"Oh." Isabel found herself longing for the simpler days of life on Virginia roads.

As if reading her mind, Browner said, "We know, by the way, about your sister's experiment. To be honest, I'm rooting for her. But I'm in the minority. To me, if she can maintain order, good on her. But there are others, including POTUS, who think her tactics—mass slaughter of holdout towns and mass execution of her own people arrested for any infraction, no matter how minor—make her irredeemably evil. And I do admit that, long-term, if she stabilizes their economy and raises an army, they are an existential threat."

"Is she raising an army?"

"Her security forces are more *para*military, for now. They issue towns ultimatums—either join or die. If they resist, she cuts loose truckloads of heavily brain damaged Infecteds, who overrun or infect the defenders. She then murders any men, women, or children who survive, infected and uninfected."

Isabel winced, and had to force her eyes back open when Browner continued.

"I'm the one who gets to reject the desperate appeals from little towns in Virginia."

"So why don't you help them?"

It was Browner's turn to wince. "You do know what the *fuck* is goin' on, right? In the world?" She did, of course, but he nevertheless confronted her with hard facts, pulling a piece of paper from its untidy stack as if at random. "Portland," he said, holding the single sheet's corner as if disgusted, "fell yesterday. A convoy of local officials and surviving troops fought its way to the coast. The USS Comfort, a hospital ship, relaxed their screening protocols when the people on shore came under attack. The infection spread from one compartment to the next. Around midnight, the ship ceased responding to orders and set a course south toward who the fuck knows where...and I gave the order for a nuclear hunter-killer submarine to put two torpedoes amidships, may God have mercy on my soul."

Isabel opened her mouth to tell him she got his point, but he pulled another piece of paper from the mess. "That doctor you met in Siberia? Groenewalt? The guy who thought you were your twin sister? He wrangled a military flight back to Cape Town and found his infected wife making dinner and his diabetic daughter buried in their back yard. He used a sat phone to call his partner, that other scientist, Lange, who'd flown Emma down to Khabarovsk to you. Lange is holed up in a bunker outside Paris and listened as Groenewalt shot himself while uninfected neighbors waited to come retrieve his pistol."

"I get it," she mumbled.

"I doubt that you do," Browner shot back. "But that's gonna change. I want you to fly up to Mountain Home Air Force Base in Idaho and meet with Rosenbaum. He's gonna bombard you with requests for assistance, but that's not why you're going."

"Why *am* I going, then?"

"You impressed the National Security Council principals—and me—with your frankness. We need an honest assessment of whether anything can be done to hold the territory between the Rockies and the Pacific. Rosenbaum is going to focus on rescuing pockets of Uninfecteds stranded all the hell over the place, but that's not your brief."

"Okay. What *is* my brief?"

Browner caught Isabel's eye. "There's no Emma out west. It's complete anarchy. The major cities on the West Coast are clinging to toeholds but falling one by one. Refugees, both infected and uninfected, are trying to flee back this way through mountain passes we're blocking and are piling up in camps we can supply only by air drops that instantly become riots. When the virus breaks out, those camps turn overnight with un*speak*able violence. One day we drop food and water. The next day we bomb them. We're slaughtering people, Isabel, by the thousands every single day just to keep them from pouring east through gaps in our lines. If there's no hope of ever reestablishing order out there.... We have to decide whether to start slaughtering them not by the thousands, but by the millions."

It was Isabel's turn to hesitate. "Wait. You mean I'm going out there to help you decide whether to...to *nuke* the western states?"

Browner pressed his thumb and index fingers on closed eyelids. The prior vigor of the Marine general and former Annapolis lineman was long gone. He was tired and old, obviously achy, with gray stubble on his previously clean-shaven chin. "What we can't tell from overflights or from Rosenbaum's memos—we call them *Rosy Reports*—is the human factor. How close to the breaking point are they out West? Do they have a chance in hell of holding out? We need a bitterly honest perspective. Will you help?"

Isabel swallowed hard. Every time she thought the bottom was within sight, a new, lower depth was revealed. But now was the time to be practical. To survive. "What about my family?"

Browner nodded. "We'll settle them. Get them jobs, a house, ration cards."

Isabel was disgusted with everything and everyone, especially herself. But she croaked, "O-... Okay."

Chapter 28

NEW ROANOKE, VIRGINIA
Infection Date 91, 1600 GMT (12:00 p.m. Local)

When the full meeting of The Community council was convened, one thing was immediately apparent to Emma. Everyone present was infected. "What happened with the uninfected representatives? That woman?"

"Jane Finch?" Samantha found in her notebook. "No one can find her."

"Maybe she doesn't like exercise," Sheriff Walcott said.

"Was that a joke?" Samantha asked. It wasn't a challenge, just a question.

"A *joke*? Ah, no, I don't think so. The biggest rule change since we had our last all hands meeting was requiring daily workouts. Maybe she left because of that."

"We lose people every day," Dwayne noted. He had begun wearing camouflage military uniforms, and the latest addition was a black insignia on his collar denoting his rank in the Marine Corps—"Lance Corporal," he had explained, even though he commanded over a thousand troops. When Samantha had suggested he should be a general, or at least a colonel, he hadn't seemed to understand. "But I'm a Lance Corporal."

"How many leave?" Emma asked. Dwayne clearly had no idea. "Maybe we should have them…sign *out* or something? Otherwise, our census won't be accurate."

"Or should we end our policy of allowing people to leave?" Samantha asked.

"No," Emma replied. "It's like a relief valve. If people are trapped, they might rebel. If we give them the option to leave, the most disgruntled will take it. I'd only consider ending the policy if Uninfecteds set up their own community right on our border and leaving was easy. But as it stands now, the Exclusion Zone and the ungoverned areas along our periphery are so dangerous most people are staying put."

Most of the Infecteds around the table said nothing. Emma wasn't even sure they were listening. "We need someone to represent the interests of the Uninfecteds. We need to know what they need—what they *want*—so they don't take up arms against us."

"Entertainment," Samantha said.

"What?"

"I was talking to a boy yesterday—"

"In Copper Hill?"

"Yes. He said they're all really bored."

Walcott surprised Emma by speaking up. "They're lucky to be alive."

"One of our Boards was spray painted with swastikas," Dwayne said as the floodgate of commentary opened. "Last night in Callaway. That's not far from Copper Hill. Maybe it was that boy. Should Sheriff Walcott arrest him?"

Emma scrutinized Samantha. Dwayne's bodyguard/spy had reported that Samantha and the boy had eaten sandwiches near each other during his work break, and that Sam had clearly manufactured several other *chance* meetings with him before they left. But the girl displayed no distress at the suggestion that he be detained and executed.

"No," Emma replied. "And swastikas sound like a political protest. Like we're Nazis." She turned to Samantha. "What kind of entertainment would keep them happy?"

She shrugged. "How should I know? A circus? Carnival rides? He asked if I knew where he could get any weed."

"There's drugs in old police evidence rooms," Walcott noted, "if we need 'em."

Emma said, "This is why we need a representative from them. They could tell us whether drugs would help."

"But I don't trust Uninfecteds," Dwayne said. "We can't speak freely with them in here. Do you think they would listen to an *Infected* if we appointed *her* their representative? I nominate Samantha. She seems to get along with them."

"Hello, I'm twelve. I don't think they'd listen to me."

She was right. With no resolution in sight, they moved on. Walcott reported two violations of density rules. His SE forces had received calls from Uninfecteds about a crowd of about fifty Infecteds in a work detail sent out to Smith Mountain Lake. The infected workers were piled up along a narrow road whose bridge had been felled and were already in a trance-like state, awaiting only a trigger to unleash their rampage. "They didn't respond to commands. But there was a volunteer fire department down the road and we dispersed 'em with firehoses. But the second crowd—"

Dwayne interrupted. "I thought we'd repaired all the bridges after that last storm."

"It wasn't storm damage. The bridge had been blown up. Maybe by some of the uninfected people who called 911, who were tryin' to isolate their little peninsula neighborhood. Or maybe by the army. Do you want me to arrest the residents just in case?"

Emma said, "No. We're trying to avoid killing Uninfecteds if possible to improve their morale. What about the second crowd?"

"Another work detail. About a hun'erd Infecteds cleaning up a hospital, and their boss, the hospital's administrator—an Uninfected—served them lunch in the cafeteria. She phoned to say they weren't eatin', weren't talkin', weren't movin'. When I got there, they was sittin' elbow to elbow at long tables. Most turned to the door where we was standin'. I had the deputies and Uninfecteds tiptoe out and called Dwayne, who brought in some machine guns and fixed the mess. We had to get a second detail to come clean up the first detail. And I don't know if that cafeteria is usable anymore. The Uninfecteds on cleanup duty kept throwin' up from the smells, I guess, or the bodies and the blood and such, then panicked thinkin' they was infected, which they weren't. We hosed 'em down good."

Emma nodded before turning to Samantha. "How are those relaxation classes and anxiety testing procedures coming?"

"I haven't had time to work on them recently."

Because you've been spending your time talking to uninfected boys, came the voice in Emma's head. "We need them. In the meantime, make sure our foremen know not to cram a bunch of Infecteds together. No more than six Infecteds per ten square meters, like the Rules say."

They went through the rest of their agenda. Food stocks were dangerously low but had stabilized. Plenty of military overflights had been observed, including drones loitering over towns, and several mysterious explosions that were probably sabotage but couldn't be traced to ground incursions by military forces. They were still expanding successfully to the south and east, but had not yet reduced the holdouts at Virginia Tech. And they had received franchise applications from as far away as Indianapolis, Indiana, and Binghamton, New York.

When they finished, Emma repeated, "We need someone to represent the Uninfecteds. Someone we can trust, but they can trust also. Any ideas?"

She waited a full minute, but no one said a thing. Samantha had also been surveying the room's blank faces, and finally turned to Emma, tilted her head, and arched her brow. It may have been some kind of silent comment on the futility of Emma's exercise in democracy. Or it could be Samantha simply practicing being expressive like the Uninfecteds.

"Any ideas what kind of person might work...Samantha?"

"Someone famous that they recognize, like a politician."

"Do we have anyone like that?"

Samantha turned to Dwayne. The head of her security forces returned the girl's gaze, mute and blank. "Dwayne? That motorcade? South of Charlottesville?"

"Oh," he finally replied. But that was the end of it.

Samantha gave up and said, "Some Secret Service agents dropped President Stoddard and his family off near one of our checkpoints. They took a job on a farm but I think he wants to be president again. Or his *wife* wants him to be."

"Why wasn't I told this?" Emma asked Dwayne.

"It didn't seem important."

* * * *

Emma had to raise her voice over the rattles and road noise of her poorly insulated 2008 Honda CRV. "How long did it take you to figure out I sent a spy with you to Copper Hill?"

Samantha replied, "About four minutes."

"How long till the spy admitted to you what he was doing?"

"About a minute later. Are you spying on me because I like boys?"

"Yes."

"But you like boys too."

"That's different."

"Why?"

"Because it's sexual. Some men appeal to me because I might want sex with them."

"Not because you want to have their babies? You said we need babies to keep The Community going. And if a boy is really hot—tall, and muscly, and...and really *cute*—he probably has good genes that would make good *babies, right*?"

"Probably. Statistically. And don't forget smart."

"Obviously. It's not different at *all*, really, between you and me. You like handsome men. You had sex with that pilot less than an hour after they put him in our hospital room."

"I thought you were asleep."

"I heard things. And I have questions, like—"

"What does this have to do with you and your crush on that uninfected boy, and on just about every boy you run into? Don't lose your focus. We're barely surviving an apocalypse. We need to work real hard. Plus, longer term, you seem to be developing—" *Shush!* said the voice in Emma's head. *Don't share every thought you have!*

But Samantha somehow already understood the incomplete sentence. "Developing *feelings*?" Was it the girl's keen intellect, or did Emma and Samantha share some bond? Some similar rewiring of their highest functioning postinfection brains. "Is there really much of a difference between sexual urge, and a crush? Aren't they both emotions?"

"You'd have to talk to my sister. That's her thing. I'll answer any epidemiology questions you have."

"I'd *like* to talk to her. I wish she and your brother's family and Jake had joined."

"You liked my nephew."

"He *is* cute, and tall, and has a nice face, and he's my age so we would both live more or less the same length of time if we're not killed first. I hope he's not dead."

"Am I supposed to turn here?" Emma asked.

Samantha confirmed the turn onto the dirt road, which grew bumpier and dustier. "Sex is why there have been so many rapes," Samantha summarized. "But it also holds uninfected families together. Parents have sex and want to keep on having sex. And they take care of children from previously having had sex. That didn't stop *my* parents from making up the story that I was dead, but I had turned and they never came close to me after I killed that navy man. I don't think *they* had sex anymore, but my father *did* have sex with his secretary in his study when my mother was visiting the States. I told her, and my father fired the secretary because she might be a Chinese spy or something."

"We're almost there," Emma interrupted. "Does this story have some kind of end?"

"Should Infecteds get married, and raise kids in families like Uninfecteds? Or should we make a Rule that they have to have a certain number of children and then have The Community raise them so their kids don't starve to death or wander off?"

"You seem interested in the subject. Write me a memo with the pros and cons."

"Okay. And can I hang out with boys?"

"Okay."

"*Un*infected boys?"

"Just uninfected? Why?"

"Like I said already, they're more interesting."

"Okay. I guess. But if you have sex with them—even if you kiss them—they'll get sick, you know."

"I'm not ready for sex. I keep waiting, but I don't feel anything like you do."

They parked amid pickup trucks at the gate. Dwayne had posted armed guards at every farm to prevent theft of food, but they recognized Emma instantly. So did Angela Stoddard, former First Lady of the United States of America. "Oh, thank God." She rose, groaning, from her knees where she had been pulling radishes from the ground and piling them in a wheelbarrow. "Kids, get your stuff and your father! We're outta here."

The woman, whom Emma remembered always being impeccably groomed, wiped sweat from her brow and left a streak of dirt on her forehead. "Dr. Miller, I presume?" Angela Stoddard held out her hand. Emma had trained herself not to infect susceptibles, and had to override her hesitation to shake the hand of a vaccinated and immune person. Samantha surprised the First Lady by holding out her hand too and by shaking it with a pronounced motion. Up walked a young girl about Sam's age—Samantha's wave was returned without hesitation—and a tall and muscular boy who stared not at Samantha, but at Emma. Behind them was President Stoddard, barely visible over his son's broad shoulders.

"Your capital is in Roanoke, right?" Mrs. Stoddard asked. "That's not far. Should we talk title—for my husband, that is? I've got some ideas."

The two Stoddard children were staring at Emma and whispering. The girl pushed her big brother off balance and laughed before their gazes returned to Emma and they averted them. Samantha stared at everything they did, smiling inexpertly when they grinned, practically oblivious to their parents.

"What's *your* title?" asked Angela Stoddard.

"Chief Epidemiologist."

The grimy woman, still exuding a regal bearing, made some indecipherable face and glanced back over her shoulder at the former president. "*I* think this is the beginning of an *excellent* partnership." Mrs.

Stoddard snaked her arm through Emma's and walked her back toward the car just like Emma's sister had done on long walks at the NIH hospital.

"We had your twin sister to the White House for dinner, you know?" Emma peered over her shoulder and caught the First Son staring at her butt. The Stoddard's daughter had fully engaged Samantha in chatter—"I *love* your hair!"—but Sam had seen the Stoddard boy's ogling of Emma and tilted her head as if to reiterate some earlier point about uninfected boys and sex.

Chapter 29

Isabel couldn't discern the source of the fires dotting the landscape on final descent. Were they abandoned buildings left to burn? Bonfires providing illumination to defenders? Beacons guiding bombers? Or funeral pyres fueled by an endless supply of bodies?

The few passengers aboard the Boeing 737 were all military. The economy seats were filled with supplies relocated several times during the civilian pilots' pre-takeoff weight and balance debates.

After landing, but before the plane finished taxiing, its passengers in first class had retrieved their rifles from overhead bins and packs from empty seats and were bracing against bulkheads in the galley. A middle aged army sergeant was tightening the chinstrap of his helmet. Isabel had knotted her still long hair into a tight bun at the back so that her helmet fit snugly.

When the plane's engines were cut, the soldiers by the door began chambering rounds with *clacks*, and Rick and Isabel did the same with both their carbines and their pistols. Rick even loaded a stubby grenade into the short tube beneath his carbine's barrel.

The whines of the engines were replaced by crowd noise. One of the soldiers peered out through the tiny porthole in the door and said, "Jeez," in the tone of, "What next?"

The pilot emerged from the cockpit and opened the door. The noise of some commotion suddenly filled the cabin. They had last heard those sounds—agitation and nerves expressed by masses of desperate people—on the ferry docks in New York.

The soldiers began descending the mobile stairs. In the empty galley, Rick and Isabel shouldered their packs. Though heavy, they seemed feather light compared to the massive loads they had humped across Virginia. Unlike then, they could now count on resupply and didn't need to carry everything they needed on their backs…she hoped.

When they reached the top of the stairs, Isabel instantly wished they had their old cumbersome loads. The scene below was one of barely managed chaos. Across the tarmac snaked a line, four abreast, into the distance, which led to their stairs. On the grass between the taxiways was a squatter's camp of impromptu shelters made of blue FEMA tarpaulins, proper camper's tents, and lean-tos fashioned out of discarded crates, pallets, cardboard, and plastic. The airbase was at the tattered edge of order.

"One Infected," Isabel said to Rick, "and this place turns in a few hours."

"And then, you've got a dense, ready-made mob."

The senior NCO in front of them said, "Best not be here when that happens."

At the bottom of the stairs, Isabel stared into the faces of people who must have thought they were crazy. Who would fly *to* a place like that? But they were silent and meek—hoping against hope that nothing would prevent them from boarding. The disorder grew, Isabel could hear, the farther away you got. A hoarse woman croaked, "How many more flights today?" Men growled, "Fuck you!" "No! Fuck *you*!" There was a, "You said there'd be water!" punctuated by, "Keep your fucking hands *off* her!" "The latrines are unusable!" "Don't you stare back at me like that, you piece of shit weekend warrior!"

"Masks on," rippled down their slim line of unrelated newcomers.

Isabel's hand rose to pull her mask up. She had grown accustomed to its place beneath her chin before being vaccinated. It was an unnecessary pre immunity accessory, like a scarf in summer. The men Isabel followed past the mob toward the hangar pulled on gloves and lowered clear plastic visors from helmets or donned microbe resistant eyewear.

They waited beside the ubiquitous sandbags. She remembered, in the early days, giggling at Rick's witty but so true reply. "Because they work," he'd said when she'd asked him why there were so many sandbags everywhere. Fun times.

"Hydrate," he reminded. So like Rick. She smiled as she drew water from the tube attached to the shoulder strap of her body armor.

"Ahhh," she said, pretending to savor the hours old, body warmed water hinting at overtones of plastic, and got a knowing smile in reply.

After pupil and temperature checks—"We've been *vaccinated*!" but they didn't believe her, or care—they entered a small door past a dozen airmen behind sandbags with one-two-three-four, she counted, machine guns. She held up and waggled four fingers.

"*Good* girl," Rick said, bumping into her pack when she turned and smiled.

"That's sexist." Inside, before their eyes adjusted in the dark corridor, Isabel tilted her head back and to the side so their helmets didn't *clunk* and kissed Rick, more fully and longer than usual. "Always kiss," had been her rule. "Just in case." He hadn't argued.

They emerged onto a depressing scene in the huge hangar. Cannibalistic helicopter mechanics stripped skeletons for parts. Teams with glowing tablets, hand tools, and bright lights extracted avionics from organ donors. No overnight Amazon Prime deliveries up here. Helicopter remains seemed held together only by bundles of exposed wiring. And as best as she could tell, only one aircraft was being repaired. *One.* Men and women lowered a huge engine into its housing. Excessive attention was being lavished on that single transplant as harvested relics were shunted into the darker but growing equipment graveyard along the walls.

"In here," came a mumble from behind a gas mask.

Isabel and Rick left the postindustrial charnel house and entered well-lit offices turned barracks. After a half dozen confusing turns through a makeshift, canvas walled maze, they were ushered into a crowded conference room.

"Isabel," Hank Rosenbaum said. His full beard was gone so his mask would fit. He rose slowly, and not to full height—stooped like a man who'd aged a decade in a month after losing his entire family to infection.

A tear sprung to Isabel's eye despite what she had thought of the man, which was instantly forgotten. "Hank, I'm so, so sorry."

"Your sister caught it first. I wasn't sympathetic enough. I apologize for that. Isabel, I want you to know that, initially, you were just some relative of the lab's first subject. When it turned out you were a twin, an *identical* twin, and a *neuro*scientist…how could I not study the two of you?"

He was deflecting. "Could I, maybe, have a moment with Dr. Rosenbaum? Alone?" She glanced apologetically at Rick and the half dozen other people in the conference room, who departed and closed the door. "Hank. What happened? With your family?"

He looked away. "Why are we talking about this?"

"Because…it happened. How are you doing?"

"How am I *doing*?" She regretted having asked. Hank drew a deep breath and avoided her gaze as he sank, leaden, into his chair. Isabel had to restrain herself from reaching for his hand as she sat and leaned forward. "The Air Force flew me back from Raven Rock on…what? Infection Date 64? The roads were still open, so I hopped in my SUV and drove home. The gate was locked. Everything looked normal. I thought about raising my mask to protect *them. I* was the one who'd ventured out of isolation. But I didn't want to scare them. I pulled up. I could see my wife washing dishes at the sink."

He faltered. "But then I saw the graves. Five of them. Two were…small. No markers. And I knew. No one came out to greet me. No grandchildren came running up. I pulled my mask up and called my wife to the door. Black eyes. No makeup. Randomly dressed. I asked what happened, and when I clarified, she explained. Our youngest, Rachel, met a local boy out hunting, or fishing, or whatever. They rendezvoused a few times. The last time he was sweating a little and in a hurry to get home."

Hank suddenly lowered his mask. The act was no casual relaxation of good hygiene. Barrier discipline was deadly serious business. Hank drew a deep breath of fresh, unfiltered air. A calculated risk, or a death wish? "I considered killing them, you know. I really did. They're gonna starve. I seriously thought about shooting my wife and whichever daughters, sons-in-law, and grandchildren had survived."

"You don't know which ones turned?" *Quit asking questions!*

"Does it matter? If I went around to do a headcount, I'd probably have to shoot someone who got agitated and violent, which could trigger all of them. Or, I could just not shoot. Not mask up. Stay there, with them, come what may." He swiped his glasses from his face and rubbed his eyes, half turning away. Isabel leaned as far over the table as possible, just out of reach of his hand, which she wanted to hold. Another barrier breach, but at least one that might contribute the small comfort of human contact.

"So I drove away." He sounded exhausted. His gaze was downcast. "They weren't tending the vegetables. The growing season is short at elevation. They'll have canned food through the winter, unless someone takes it from them. Then what? They're not going to plant next spring."

"Hank….*Jesus.* I am *so* sorry. You have my deepest and most sincere sympathies. But you've also got to know, don't you, that this is happening everywhere. In *no* way could this *possibly* be considered *your* fault."

"I outlawed family dinners. We isolated by household in three houses. Everyone hated me for it, especially my wife. And in retrospect—" He choked. "In retrospect, I wish we'd had those last times together. On the first night I was away—the day Rachel's boyfriend wasn't feeling well—they all got together and made spaghetti. Drank a bottle or three of wine. Had a great time until Rachel vomited." He fixed his gaze on Isabel, demanding that she visualize it. Attending that dinner in her mind the way he must have countless times. "That wouldn't have happened, obviously, if I'd been there. Maybe *our* house—my wife and I and Rachel—would've been infected, but not the others. They'd have had a chance."

Before she could respond, Hank rose, rounded the table, opened the door, and invited everyone back in, ending her heartfelt torment of him.

The buzz of conversation in the hallway quieted as soldiers and officials retook their seats. Rick flashed Isabel a raised eyebrow. Whatever look she gave him in reply elicited a sympathetic expression and a gentle squeeze of her thigh under the table. Hank noticed, managed a smile through pinched lips, and nodded. She had someone. He didn't raise his mask.

"Alright," Hank said to the gathering mostly clad in camouflage, masks, and gloves. "You all know me. I'm acting Regional Director, FEMA Region Ten. This is Dr. Isabel Miller, a distinguished neuroscientist and aide to the National Security Council and the President. She is here to survey our situation. Let's get her up to speed. The latest count I got was that there are 167 isolated uninfected communities in Idaho, eastern Oregon, and southeastern Washington."

"Today it's 162," amended a man with short, graying hair, probably a soldier.

"Okay. One sixty two. Anchorage has turned, but the outlying areas are protected by distance and low population density. Let's talk instead about how many uninfected people are isolated in the Lower 48? Where are they? *Who* are they? And how long have they got? We want to be at the front of the line when the government starts distributing vaccines next week. Our military and emergency personnel are *critical. They* should get it before inoculating office workers in Houston."

"Hear! Hear!" said a civilian, rapping his knuckles on the wood in applause.

"Before we go through all that," said the probable soldier who'd spoken earlier, "I would like to hear where Houston is on special weapons release."

Isabel had no idea what he meant. "You're authorized," Rick replied, "to deploy fuel air explosives, napalm, cluster munitions, and air and artillery dispersed landmines."

That sounded utterly gruesome to Isabel.

"And that's it?" the officer asked, sounding displeased.

"For now, yes, sir. But I presume you're executing the repositioning order."

"Of course. It's using ninety percent of my air transport. I could be relocating some of those isolated populations to safer places. But that still leaves me with a sufficient number of operational weapons to reduce several dire strategic threats."

"Transport is stressed everywhere. As for special weapons release, you know the channels. I'll write up whatever you show me. You match yields to targets, I'll send that."

Thus began Isabel and Rick's grand tour of hell.

Chapter 30

Chloe's mom parked the piece of crap car, which had been issued to their dad by the air force and had a decal and a parking permit on the windshield, in the teacher's lot on their first day at Chloe's, and Jake's, new school. The main drive through the drop-off lane was filled with Mercedes, Beamers, and Bentleys.

"This looks nice," her mom said as they emerged onto the wooded campus of the private school. "Aren't you glad that I made a fuss? And that your dad got a big job? Houston is a huge city, and the public school you're zoned for seemed sketchy."

"They wear uniforms here?" Jake said, eyeing the students headed inside.

"I'm sure everything will be taken care of," their mom reassured them.

The boys, wearing khaki pants and shirts or sweaters with the school's coat of arms on their chests, checked out Chloe the way boys do. The girls wore polo shirts with the same emblem, plaid skirts, and bitchy looks as they checked out Chloe the way girls do. She reached up to straighten her slow growing hair.

The waiting room in the administrative offices was packed with new students and the occasional bedraggled parent. Chloe's mom strode up to the busy receptionist. "We're here to enroll my two children—Chloe Miller, in tenth, and Jake Miller, in eighth grade."

"In line over there," the woman said without looking up.

Undeterred, Chloe's mom said, "And I've been assigned a job here."

The woman peered up through cat's eye glasses on a lanyard. "Doing what?"

"I don't know. They said to just show up, so here I am."

"Staff got here an hour ago. Do you have your teacher's license?"

Chloe cringed when her mother laughed at the fair question. Chloe and Jake got in line behind a fat girl, who waited in vain for Chloe to acknowledge her.

"I was a college cheerleader." Oh-*my-God!* "Something with the cheer team—"

"PhysEd's full. Go see Mr. Edwards in the custodian's department."

"*Custodian?* I wouldn't think kids brought too many valuables to school."

"Janitorial services. Next!"

Chloe had trouble wiping off her face the grin she'd exchanged with Jake. "There's been some mistake," her mother said. "Are you two okay in line here if I just—"

"*Go,* Mom," Chloe said. *Please!* The other kids watched while pretending not to. Her mother kissed Chloe's cheek, but Jake—forewarned—was too quick.

The receptionist called the next kid in line.

"Where you from?" asked the overweight girl, who seemed stereotypically cheerful.

"D.C.," Chloe replied.

"*Wow.*" Chloe didn't get it. Others looked over. "How'd you get to *Houston?*"

Now, she understood. They'd all watched the capital's violent fall on TV. She knew how to play it. "We fought our way out." She debated saying more, but less was badass.

"*Jeez.* What was it *like?*"

Chloe shrugged. *Ain't nothin' but a thang.* A tall boy in line, cute enough, leaned against the wall. "Hey." He extended his elbow. She bumped it with her own, as did Jake, who gave the boy a wuz-up bob of his head. "Name's Turner. Turner Ash."

"Chloe. Miller. This is Jake."

"S'up?" Jake said, lowering his voice so it wouldn't break.

Chloe had decided to get in with whatever cliques of locals existed. This boy, like everyone else there, was a rootless transfer. He gave up his place in line and silenced the tubby girl by his mere presence as he leaned against the wall next to Chloe. If these were ordinary times, she'd ask where he was from? How had *he* gotten there? But these weren't ordinary times. Another student was called in to be photographed for a school ID.

Chloe looked at her dim reflection in the glass office wall. Her hair was still short, but at least it was clean. She tried placing a few unruly strands into place.

"Need this?" Her new acquaintance offered a compact with a smile.

"Thanks." Chloe took it and did a more professional inspection.

"I can tell you've been outdoors," the pudgy girl said. "I just mean you're...*tanned*. It looks *good* on you! My folks won't let me go outside. I'm as pale as an Infected."

Chloe's face looked wind burned even though she had gotten up early to put on makeup, which she and her mother had scrounged from a bin of half used toiletries before being driven to a crappy apartment next to an adult novelties store and tattoo parlor.

"You kill anybody?" Turner asked. "Out on the road?"

Everyone awaited Chloe's answer, even the receptionist. "Yeah."

"Infecteds?" asked the girl. Chloe returned her compact. "Or Uninfecteds?"

"Both."

Jake snorted. "Killed a whole *lotta* Infecteds that last night." He held out his fist for a bump. Chloe would normally have just rolled her eyes, but Jake was getting the hang of popularity so she returned the gesture. For Chloe to be badass, Jake had to be too. "And then Chloe had to...." Jake said before halting and looking away.

Chloe felt her new persona slip away to reveal the person who'd put a rifle to Margus's head and pulled the trigger when he closed his eyes. She, too, had shut her eyes, but not quickly enough. She'd had to make sure her aim was true. She owed him that.

"Had to what?" Turner asked, alert to the change that had come over Chloe.

The sympathetic girl, whose name Chloe didn't even know, said, "We should talk about something else." Chloe's new best friend lent her a tissue.

"Yeah, never mind," Jake mumbled, not looking at his sister.

After another student was called and the line inched forward, Turner asked, "Was it just you two and your mom?"

"Nah. We had our dad, our aunt, her boyfriend who's a Marine, and.... Yep. So...."

"Is it true that Infecteds growl or whatever when they attack you?"

Chloe thought back. They made noises, but it sounded more like from exertion—like the football team's tackling drills that used to so disturb their cheer practices. Plus, she hadn't paid it too much attention amid all the shooting and reloading. "Sorta. But it's kinda hard to make out 'cause there's so much other noise. Shooting, artillery, tanks, helicopters, shit like that."

Turner nodded sagely. "Next!" barked the receptionist.

A cute younger girl was pushed in the back by a friend. She made a fierce face, but nonetheless approached Jake. "Did your mother say you were in Eighth Grade? Me too." A thousand watt smile lit and never left her face.

"S'up?" Jake said. This time his voice broke midway through his coolness.

Smiling, the girl confirmed that her friend was still watching. Jake began talking too much and asking stupid questions that jeopardized his aloofness. "I'm from Lafayette," the girl replied. "In Louisiana. Have you heard of it?"

"Nope." *Good boy, Jake.*

"This school's supposed to be one of the best in Houston. But I heard they've already taken in a bunch of transfer kids and they're annoyed at being forced to take more."

"Next!"

"What kinda guns did you have?" Turner asked Chloe.

"AR-15s and 9 mils."

He nodded. "My dad has an AR too. Took me shooting the other day." He was as nonchalant as he could be and still show off. "I shot up one whole magazine—*pow-pow-pow*," he demonstrated, complete with closing one eye and aiming with the other, "then as quickly as I could I practiced slapping a new mag in to keep shooting."

"You went to bolt lock?" Chloe asked. He clearly didn't know what that meant. "You fired every last round in your magazine and your bolt locked back?" Turner nodded. Mandy looked on in either awe, or horror, smile forgotten until Jake glanced her way. "Bad policy. Better, when get down to your last few rounds, move to cover, drop the old mag into your dump pouch, and reload a full mag. Never fire your last round if you can help it."

"Okay," Turner said. "Good to know. Anything else come in handy?"

"Cough drops," Jake said. "Lots and lots of cough drops."

After Chloe's new friend and Turner Ash got processed, Chloe's turn came. The line behind Jake and the Louisiana girl—"My dad's a lawyer *too!*"—was just as long as when they'd arrived. Name, date of birth, sign a paper agreeing to follow the school's rules, and the all-important photo. Chloe flashed her selfie smile, then pleaded for a retake. After a big huff, the photographer agreed. Bad asses don't smile after the shit they'd been through.

"I guess I'm next," said the petite Louisiana girl just as their mom returned.

"If you need me," Chloe's mom said, "don't go looking around that janitorial room. *Gross.* Just like Tennessee. I wrangled a job in the nurse's office. It just goes to show—*again*—that you shouldn't take the first thing they offer. There's almost always something better if you just push."

"Mom!" Chloe said. "The *nurse's* office?"

"They had an opening. I don't wanta mop up vomit, or clean toilets. *Ewww!*"

"Of *course* they had an opening, Mom. The nurse's office? If some kid gets sick—with who knows *what*—where's he gonna go?"

"I hadn't thought of that," her mom said, seeming to reconsider everything.

"Hi, Mrs. Miller," said the little dark haired girl from Jake's class.

"Oh, aren't you cute!" Their mom glanced at Jake as if to prod him. "What's her name?" she asked her son, who shrugged.

"Amanda. Flowers. But people just call me Mandy."

"Cuuute." Chloe's mom jabbed her elbow into Jake's ribs.

Turner Ash waited in the hallway and said, to Chloe, "I'll walk you to orientation."

Chloe nearly died when her mother gave her a sly thumbs-up. Jake and Amanda aka "Mandy" accompanied Chloe and Turner to the auditorium. Students not only stared as they passed—they were easily distinguished by the blue jeans they all wore except for Mandy, who was in a skirt with a matching navy blue bow in her hair—they steered a wide path, closed lockers, and pressed against walls, even covering their noses and mouths. The newcomers weren't only social pariahs; they were potentially *diseased* social pariahs.

Chapter 31

For two days, Isabel, Rick, and Hank Rosenbaum had toured isolated outposts of uninfected humanity. Each faced its own bitter end, hovering between mere desperation and the total loss of all hope. Each had its own tale of near death escapes along a path of decline to the brink of collapse. Each was unique in its details, which Isabel dutifully documented in reports to the NSC, but shared its experience with a world in which defenses always failed and the virus always won.

The first hint that Hank had lost all hope was when he asked Isabel, "Where do you want to be at the end? Do you want to be on some Pentagon mission in some strange town? Or do you want to be with loved ones in a familiar, comfortable place?"

But I've been vaccinated, she wanted to say but didn't. Vaccinated people die by violent attack just like anyone else.

The second clue about Hank had come when he refused his own vaccination. "No, no. There are plenty of others who need it more."

The third had been his refusal ever to see any cause for optimism. After Isabel interviewed a perfectly reasonable, black eyed National Guard officer—infected but still wearing his camouflaged uniform and insignia—through the fence of a detention center, she had remarked to Hank that Infecteds and Uninfecteds might someday live together in harmony. *"Isabel,"* Hank had admonished, "he gave you beauty pageant answers. All he wants is world fucking peace. But you did notice, right, that every time you typed his bullshit answers on your iPad his eyes dropped to inventory your gear and weapons."

But she was unprepared for Hank's final act of surrender to fate.

All seemed routine as their helicopter approached the landing zone. Isabel now knew what it felt like when people prepared for combat. Nerves were contagious. The soldiers started getting fidgety. *Their* adrenaline wakes *you* up. You start squirming. Every itch needs scratching. Rivulets of perspiration become objects of obsessive focus. Doomed are any attempts to relax by forced concentration. You might as well begin your checks and rechecks like everyone else.

The thirty round magazine in her carbine was full. Isabel had completed the destruction of her fingernails by loading it herself. She slapped it back into her M4, which hung, stock retracted, across her chest at a downward angle. It was safely safed, which she confirmed, reconfirmed, and re-re-reconfirmed. In between, she checked the surprisingly heavy Sig Sauer P320 9mm in its holster. It had seventeen rounds, she made sure, plus one in the chamber, also with the safety on.

The third time she drew the pistol to check it—better safe than sorry—Rick put his hand on her forearm. She reholstered the weapon and secured it with its quick draw strap. "You've done this before," Rick said at a volume barely exceeding the engine noise. "We can shoot our way outta most situations. Relax. Let your..."

"Let your *training* take over? I've heard that speech. Only I don't *have* any training."

"I was gonna say let your *instincts* take over."

"Which is your speech to people with no training?"

"You have *experience*. You've been through the shit before."

All the young soldiers in the back of the helicopter were keyed up. Only Rick seemed calm...and Hank, who stared vacantly out the window without so much as a pistol or a knife or a mask.

Right before they touched down, Hank held out his hand in the old-fashioned way. Isabel knitted her brow in confusion but shook it. "Good luck," was all Hank said.

Both side doors slid open. Isabel exited into the gale with her eyes squinting against the swirling dust. She and Rick were greeted by what had to be half the population of the hamlet. Looming over their town was a wall of smoke from whose direction also came the crackle of sporadic gunfire. "Where's Hank?" Isabel asked.

She and Rick looked all around. The replacements who'd arrived with them had found waiting guides to their new units. The helicopter crew went through their post and, she suspected, preflight checklists. Hank was nowhere to be seen.

"Setting that fire worked at first," said the mayor of either Tuttle or Wendell, Idaho, Isabel couldn't remember which. "But now it's outta control."

Isabel said, "Wait. Sorry. *What?*"

"That fire worked," the man said, nodding toward the towering cliff of smoke. "It burned the Infecteds out that way to a crisp and saved our asses. But then the wind shifted."

"Are you saying you started that fire on *purpose?*"

"It wiped out the Infecteds to our west and northwest. There were tens of thousands of 'em streamin' down I-84. We diverted 'em in some bloody fighting straight into the inferno. Now, it's backfired, so to speak. And in the other direction, people are jammed up for miles along I-84, and more keep comin' from Twin Falls and Salt Lake City. I feel bad for 'em, I really do. But how are we gonna feed two hundred thousand mostly infected people? There's only 367 of us original residents. We're pinnin' our hopes on...*stronger* measures from President Anderson."

Isabel turned to Rick. *He means nuke I-84.* Rick nodded. "Alright," Isabel said. "We should see what's happening over there."

Everyone turned toward the fire and the sound of desultory, intermittent gunfire. "I'm not so sure that's a good, or a safe idea," the mayor said. "Maybe it'd be best if you just flew on back so you can deliver your report."

"Our report," Isabel said, "is on what your security situation is right now."

"Well...we'll wait for you right here, then."

A few soldiers reluctantly escorted them toward the sound of the guns. Isabel kept looking for Hank. This was no potty break. He had simply vanished into thin air. The smells got to Isabel first. The smoke from the approaching fires. The stench of the echoing guns and explosives. But it was the odor of the dead that stood out most. It was often described as sickly sweet, but to Isabel it was more sickly and led inevitably to a cringe.

"Where the hell did Hank go?" Isabel asked Rick, who shrugged.

Their military escorts began moving tactically, as Rick called it— crossing open spaces, like intersecting streets, at brisk jogs, then halting in a crouch or a kneel behind buildings' walls. All talking subsided. Rifles were raised in heightened readiness. Rick and Isabel emulated their guides. For Isabel, that meant gripping her carbine in both hands and ensuring its muzzle didn't point at anyone friendly. Only belatedly did she will herself to go through, in her head, the steps required to actually fire her weapon.

"One at a time," the National Guard lieutenant directed their small band at the next intersection. "On the double." He sent his own man across the road first. The camo-clad soldier sprinted without incident from the pet store beside which they paused to the insurance agency across the street whose windows were smashed to beads lying in a pretty sparkle on the sidewalk. Another soldier went second. Then Rick. Then it was Isabel's turn.

She ran, too slowly it felt even under the lighter weight of her combat load, but made it across. The sound of the guns was now close. Isabel's eyes and throat stung from the smoke and she popped a lozenge in her mouth to stifle any coughs that might reveal their position. When the soldiers bringing up the rear joined them, they proceeded down the next block in a crouch, from doorway to bicycle rack to ash covered car in short dashes that left Isabel's heart thumping under her body armor.

They stopped before reaching the far end of the block. A captain fell back toward them for a briefing. "Welcome to the end of the world." He turned and pointed. "That forest fire has rousted everybody outta hiding. Most are infected." Every few seconds, the calm was shattered by rifle fire out of sight to the left or the right. In between, shouts and calls could be heard. "At your ten! 150 meters! I count three! One with a long gun!"

"Eyes on!"

"I got 'em too!" came another shout. "Man, woman, child! Could be uninfected!"

"Hold your fire!"

The exhausted captain paid them no mind. "The hardest thing is sorting 'em out. Twice, we let folks approach we thought were uninfected, only to see their eyes when they got close." Isabel didn't have to ask what had happened next. "They lie." *To save their lives,* Isabel thought, with a firestorm bearing down on them. "The second group of Infecteds had even buddied up to *look* like a family, but the quote, unquote *dad* was a twentysomething white dude, the *mom* was a middle-aged Asian, and their *kid*, we saw after we smoked 'em, was a really short but fully grown black guy. They answered all our questions okay from downrange, but it never felt right."

"Let us through!" came a distant plea.

"They're bad!" one soldier, nearer at hand, immediately declared.

"Hold your fire!" yelled another, probably their sergeant.

"They're right behind us!" came the far away shout of a man seeking passage. "Please!" The rising pitch of his voice sounded appropriately distressed. But if they could learn to deceive by forming fake families, they could learn to imitate the tones of desperation, which could be heard everywhere. "They're gathering! Hundreds of 'em! On *purpose*! I think they're getting ready for something! Please let us through!"

"Captain Hodges, sir!" It was the much nearer sergeant type up ahead. Their briefer bear crawled away on all fours toward the last building on their block. Their front line overlooked a downhill sloping, empty field and an early stage construction site before more buildings obscured farther view. Isabel slowly rose to a stoop, went to the far edge of the last building, and climbed hand over hand up the wall of a looted deli until she stood almost fully upright.

A football field away, three cowering people—an intact little nuclear family of Uninfecteds, possibly, or pathogen carrying killers, also possible—huddled behind the shelter of the last wall before the open no-man's-land, which was strewn with dozens of uncollected bodies. But they hid not from the guns of the National Guardsmen, to which they were fully exposed, but instead from whatever or whoever lay beyond them.

Rick surveyed the terrain through binoculars. She could discern no pattern from the masses of dead. Were they charging, or fleeing? Running, or kneeling and begging?

"Captain, sir! We got movement on our left!"

Rick turned his binoculars that way. "Jesus Christ."

"What?"

He handed Isabel the binoculars. Hank Rosenbaum strolled at a leisurely pace across the killing fields toward the three prone civilians. "What the *fuck*?" Hank wove his way between the corpses, but wore no protection against infection. "What's he *doing*?"

When she looked up at Rick, his pinched lips said, *You know what he's doing.*

"They're okay!" Hank shouted back across the empty field as he stood beside the cowering family. "They're uninfected!" The family urged Hank by word and hand gestures to take cover.

"Hank!" Isabel shouted.

But he gave one last wave and disappeared, heading toward the wall of flames.

"What in God's name...?" Isabel intoned slowly.

Rick pulled her back down to one knee. There seemed to be, in that moment, an odd lull. There was no shooting, no shouting, no explosions. Or maybe time had just slowed, or her sense of its passage intensified. "Be ready," Rick whispered. His eyes darted this way and that. His head swiveled toward threats more anticipated than observed.

"Rick, what the hell just happened?"

"It doesn't matter. Put it outta your head." He slowly emphasized each word. "And get...fucking...ready." He pulled two magazines out of her backpack where the emergency supplies resided and slid them underneath her armor against her chest, causing her to squirm. She had six more mags in pouches hanging from her webbing. "Drop your pack and run," he whispered, not wanting to start a panic among the nearby Guardsmen.

She nodded, but got that feeling again. Not exactly guilt. Nothing had happened yet. More a sickening sensation of knowing that, if it came to it—and it felt like it would—they would sacrifice the lives of everyone around them to save her life and Rick's. Gone would be the baby faced infantryman sneaking looks at them around sandbags. Gone would be the boy's comrade whose cheeks were flushed either from the chill, or from barely suppressed mortal terror. Gone would be the male and female EMTs across the street, wearing black body armor and black helmets instead of the military's camo versions over incongruously colorful blue jumpsuits. And gone was Hank, PhD in Neuroscience from Berkeley and patriarch of the doomed Rosenbaum clan.

"Halt!" shouted one of the soldiers. "Halt-halt-halt!" Even fractions of a second seemed, to Isabel, to be measurable intervals. *Bam-bam-bam-bam-bam.* She closed her eyes in preparation for saying a prayer, but Rick grabbed her arm painfully and jerked.

She was instantly back in the moment. The family of three had made a run toward their lines and been shot dead.

"Now. Let's go."

"But...Hank!"

"Now!" Rick dragged her to her feet just as a fusillade of gunfire erupted. She saw hundreds of Infecteds storm into no-man's-land, and even more frighteningly watched Rick strip himself free of his backpack. She hopped over it as they headed back the way they had come without even thinking to shed her own, which Rick did for her. The EMTs across the street also took flight as the howl from an onrushing mob merged with the rising crescendo of machine guns, rifles, and grenade bursts.

Isabel shot a look over her shoulder. The captain grabbed at fleeing machine gunners and their assistants, who had abandoned their valuable but heavy weapons and now fled, wild-eyed, toward at least a chance to argue their way out of a firing squad.

"Iz!" Rick shouted, literally pulling her past him then shoving her toward safety.

Both ran. The firing behind them never quite stopped, but seemed like haphazard potshots taken before flight was resumed or the fleeing soldier was overtaken. When a window shattered right in front of Isabel, she realized some of the firing was *from* the Infecteds, and she and Rick were their intended targets.

A stupendous roar preceded Rick's painful tackle of Isabel onto the pavement. A machine gun raked once, twice, three times across their street. Bullets zipped by inches overhead as Isabel cringed, trying to anticipate the unimaginable blows just moments away. The Infecteds now had the Guardsmen's guns and killed infected attackers and their uninfected prey with no regard for either's lives—the new, infected style of machine gunning.

"This way!" Rick shouted. Both made it to the relative safety of an alley wall. But the male EMT following them from across the street fell. The female paramedic went back for him. "No!" Rick yelled as she knelt at her partner's gushing head, hands held outstretched but motionless—a picture of utter helplessness until a fist sized knot of her torso exploded out of her back. Body armor didn't stop machine gun bullets.

Rick issued repeated two-word commands, which Isabel followed in a daze. "Let's go! Get down! Follow me! Look out!" His claw like hand repeatedly bruised her arms until, finally, with Isabel shaking in complete shock, they found a cop with an ordinary squad car, who almost shot them with his drawn pistol. "Friendly!" Rick called out, removing his hands from his carbine as if in surrender.

The cop was clearly terrified. At the ten-meter limit, Isabel could see his pistol, clenched tightly in both gloved hands, shaking. The cop's eyes above his mask were surely twice their normal size. "Why…why aren't you wearing PPE?"

"We're vaccinated," Rick said. "Calm down. We're immune." In contrast to the panicking cop, Rick's voice was low, like a cowboy slipping a harness over a newly broken horse. "My name is Captain Rick Townsend, United States Marine Corps. This is Dr. Isabel Miller, a neuroscientist from the University of California, Santa Barbara. We've been sent here…." Rick was competing with the distracted cop's increasingly terrified looks toward the shrieking sounds of the approaching mob, the gunfire, and the echoes of explosions coming, seemingly, from all directions. "We've been sent here by the National Security Council—"

"Nobody's gotten the shots yet!" the officer said, his eyes barely pausing on the two suspects on which he held his gun. He took one hand off his pistol to key the shoulder mounted mic of his radio. "Dispatch! Come in, please! Is there anybody there? Over!"

"Calm down, buddy," Rick pled. "I'm begging you. We're from Houston—"

"You're *Infecteds*!"

"No. No. We're not."

"Bullshit!" He again tried his radio, holding the pistol one-handed and less steadily.

Bam!

The cop fell back onto the hood. One hand rose to the hole in his chest but his gaze never focused enough to make out what had happened before he slid to the ground, leaving a blood trail streaked down his squad car.

Smoke curled from the muzzle of Rick's M4. He kicked the pistol from the dead cop's hand and began to rummage through the cop's pockets. *Through his fucking* pockets, Isabel thought in total outrage until she saw Rick extract car keys.

They jumped into the squad car and sped back to their helicopter. Rick said nothing. Isabel avoided looking his way. The Black Hawk's crew had already started the engines.

"It's falling!" was all the door gunner said.

"No shit!" Rick replied. "Let's get back to Mountain Home."

"No! Mountain *Home* is falling! They're recalling everything that can fly for fire missions! We were just about to ditch you here!" Inside the cabin sat the town's mayor and what must have been his wife and two young daughters.

Guilt prevented anyone from saying anything on the short flight. On final approach into the beleaguered airbase that Isabel had earlier thought of as an impregnable refuge, Rick pointed out landmarks through the large side window as firefights slid by underneath like in a video game. A line of tanks turning a corner. Rapid puffs of smoke from the slender gun atop an armored fighting vehicle. A broken line of infantrymen retreating from a huge and ragged crowd of Infecteds. A car plowing through a barricade and into another mob before crashing into a lamppost.

"Pay attention! If the base falls, we head that way," Rick pointed. "North!"

She shivered, literally, at the thought, but nodded again and again. The perimeter of the airbase was engulfed in open warfare. The fences lay somewhere beneath piles of bodies. Soundless explosions were drowned out by the Black Hawk's thundering engines. But the *tings* of rounds striking their fuselage drew the same reaction from both Rick and Isabel, who put their helmets beneath their foldout seats as the mayor and his family huddled amid hugs as best as they could from theirs. As they descended at what seemed too fast a rate, Isabel saw, in complete contrast to the melee around them, what could only be a bomb slowly and with intense care being driven up a brightly lit ramp into a giant Air Force transport plane—probably the last of the nuclear weapons being evacuated.

After the helicopter hit the tarmac hard, bounced twice, and its doors were opened to the tumult of gunfire and explosions, Isabel never saw the mayor or his family again. At the top of the stairs to the waiting 737, they met the copilot, who shouted over the noise that the ground crew had unloaded the supplies they brought in but was having trouble closing the baggage doors, so they hadn't yet boarded anyone. He seemed stumped when Rick asked him whether they could fly with the doors open. Isabel and Rick took first-class seats and felt the thuds through their boots as the baggage doors were slammed, opened, and slammed again.

They now had no backpacks, so their overhead bin was empty. But they kept their rifles at their sides with the muzzles resting on the carpeted floor and removed the magazines and bulky ammo pouches from their webbing so that the seatbelts fit. Isabel copied Rick, tucking the pouches and mags into the seat back in front of her and into the gaps between her thighs and armrests. Rick didn't say why, but both kept their body armor and helmets on.

The civilian copilot, now joined by the older pilot, both still in the uniforms of their respective airlines, came up to Isabel and Rick, bent over, and peered out the side windows at the now raucous and unruly crowd straining against the Guardsmen who prevented them from boarding. "I need some direction," the pilot said. "We unloaded our cargo and burned half our fuel getting here, so we're light. We can fly you two straight back to Houston." He kept looking outside.

"Or...?" Isabel prompted.

"Or we fill every seat, and I'm fairly confident we could make Denver. If you're willing to do some pioneering and risk getting shot fulla arrows, you can still drive it from Denver to Houston. Or you can hang out in Denver till we or someone else gets more fuel."

Neither Isabel nor Rick was willing to speak first. "What would you do?" she asked.

Rick clearly hated answering. "My mission is to keep you safe. Period."

Isabel saw how much Rick was suffering. He'd just had to kill an innocent man, for God's sake. His breath fogged the cool window. It wasn't fair to force him to make this decision. Isabel looked up at the pilot. "Load the plane up and get us to Denver."

"Yes, *ma'am*," he replied with a finger to his forehead in salute.

Chapter 32

"I'm sorry I'm late," Emma announced—satisfied that the apology she had practiced on the drive over sounded appropriate—upon being ushered to the dinner table in the mansion now occupied by the former First Family. "We had some trouble at the New Christiansburg temperament testing center." The infected ex-president, Bill Stoddard, and his wife Angela, eighteen-year-old son Bill Junior, and thirteen-year-old daughter Ginnie stared back at her from their seats as if not knowing how to reply. "We had several people fail at the same time, and before we could get them outside they rioted. It was a big mess."

"They were Infecteds, right?" Angela Stoddard asked.

"Yes. Of course."

"Oh! Good. That sounds like an excellent program, by the way."

An Infected servant filled Emma's water glass. Another Infected servant brought in the soup course. *"Bread,"* Mrs. Stoddard mouthed toward the waiters. A third Infected servant placed a basket on the edge of the table beside Mrs. Stoddard.

"In the center," the former First Lady admonished even though she could have moved it there herself. The expressionless middle aged man returned and placed the basket where directed. To Emma, the former First Lady sighed and shook her head. Her husband noticed nothing as he sat impassively at the head of the table, moving only when Mrs. Stoddard whispered for him to put his napkin in his lap. Ginnie wore a forced smile, which she directed toward Emma every time their eyes met. Her older brother stared at Emma, and specifically at her chest, but only when Emma wasn't returning his gaze. Emma's only bra was drying on the clothes line outside her one room apartment, and the silk blouse that Samantha had found for her to wear for this occasion was too small and too thin.

"It's so nice, isn't it," Mrs. Stoddard said, "to not have to interact with people who are wearing masks and all that getup? To have dinner with people who are vaccinated?"

Emma promptly looked the former president's way, but he remained oblivious to the conversation, more like Dorothy than Dwayne. Despite the medical care available to him on his flying command post, he seemed highly impaired by the damage from infection after being among the 6 percent who contracted *Pandoravirus* from the vaccine.

"So, the president and I," Angela Stoddard said while stirring her mushroom soup to cool it, "have developed some ideas for the uninfected community here." She motioned toward a waiter, who seemed unsure what she wanted. "Those papers I told you to bring?"

She passed the stapled sheaf across the table to Emma. When Emma reached for them, she felt more than saw Bill Junior eyeing her blouse, which opened slightly amid the straining buttons. *He's cute,* said the voice in her head.

"Red or white?" asked the Infected waiter, who held both bottles out to Emma, again drawing a sigh from Mrs. Stoddard.

"Oh, no, thank you."

"Please!" her hostess interjected. "Surely infected people haven't all become *tee*totalers."

"I'll have some red, please," Emma replied in order to be polite.

"Just like your sister," Mrs. Stoddard mumbled, grinning as she sipped soup from her spoon. "Oh! Too much salt." The waiter had no idea what to say in response.

Emma had abandoned all dinnertime etiquette since the outbreak. She normally read memos and reports at the battered countertop in her apartment's kitchenette over plates of macaroni and cheese from the boxes stacked high in her pantry once Sam had learned it was her favorite meal. But without knowing why, exactly, Emma reverted to the proper manners she had learned as a child and took a dollop of butter from its cup with her butter knife, not her dinner knife, and deposited it onto her bread plate, not directly onto her bread. The waiter refilled her wine, but his face revealed nothing. No complaints about mistreatment, or longing to return to some exalted prior life, or desire to escape the service of demanding Uninfecteds. Just a simple Infected, satisfied so long as he was fed and sheltered.

"Where *is* your sister?" It was little Ginnie.

"I don't know. Dead, probably."

"Oh. *Sorry.*" She made some face, curling her upper lip.

Emma looked around the table. The former First Lady stared at her daughter with brow arched. The ex-president gazed at his soup until his wife told him it was cool enough to eat. "You look just *like* her," said Bill Junior.

"Bill!" his mother censured, though Emma was uncertain what he had said that was wrong. She assumed he was referring to Isabel. And they were, after all, identical twins.

"I was just saying they *looked* alike. *Je*sus. Except for their hair and, I guess, ya know, makeup and all."

Emma reached up to her cheek. *Makeup!* She knew she had forgotten something.

"I'm sure Dr. Miller is too busy these days for trips to the salon, right Emma?" Mrs. Stoddard, herself, was well dressed and well coifed. And she was grinning at what must have been a joke. Emma tried smiling. Ginnie laughed on seeing Emma's attempt, turning to her mother as if at some shared joke. Her mother, however, castigated the little girl, again for reasons lost on Emma, then did the same with her son, whose gaze, on Emma's check, was averted from her blouse.

Isabel told you he was a "horny little bastard," the voice in Emma's head reminded—the exact words Isabel had used after her dinner with the First Family in the White House residence. The voice must have been listening. But Bill Junior was also tall, athletic looking, with smart and sparkling green eyes—facts that Isabel had omitted.

"If you'd like a moment to peruse those papers...." Mrs. Stoddard began but didn't complete.

It took Emma a second to realize what papers she was referring to. The wine was settling around her like a warm blanket. "I'll look them over tonight when I get back home."

"Oh, it's going to be far too late for you to be out on the roads. They're too dangerous after dark. We hear stories of roving marauders—looking for food, and *other* things." Emma assumed she meant rape. They executed men, and the occasional woman, every morning for rape. "You'll stay here tonight." She turned to her household staff. "Prepare the guest room for our distinguished visitor." None of the Infected men moved. "The room next to Bill Junior's!"

Off went one of the attendants.

Next came a cold plate of cheeses, meats, and crackers—and more wine. All throughout that course, Mrs. Stoddard—"Please call me Angela"— described her plans for Uninfecteds. Greater supplies and variety of food. Regular entertainment and news oriented toward their needs. Elections for local offices—"But you should probably continue to appoint people to the top offices, like president, or head of state."

Emma was unsure what she meant given that they had established neither office.

Angela then went on about the need for mass quantities of vaccine. "It's really the number one issue for the uninfected community...after food and safety, of course."

By the time the fillet mignon with béarnaise sauce, russet potatoes, and asparagus was served, Emma was fully buzzed from the wine and wondered at, but quickly forgot to ask about, where they had obtained such huge quantities of food.

"And so, if you agree, of course, I'll see to an announcement of the appointment of the president as representative of the uninfected community."

Most of Emma's troubles had melted away with the fourth glass of red wine. "Sure. Fine." Her new friend Angela seemed inordinately pleased by Emma's empty gesture. After all, Emma was still considering Sheriff Walcott's plan to decimate—reduce by 10 percent—the number of Uninfecteds they currently had to feed. Maybe that could be the Stoddards's first official assignment.

It was almost midnight when they finished dessert and went to bed. Emma was shown to her room by Infected household staff, who did not expect or wait for a thank you. As she turned the knob to enter her room, the door next to hers opened and Bill Junior peered out. Emma hesitated there for a moment before she went into her room and didn't shut her door. By the time she reached her plush poster bed, she heard the door close and lock behind her.

Chapter 33

SAN FRANCISCO, CALIFORNIA
Infection Date 97, 2400 GMT (5:00 p.m. Local)

Noah's arrival in San Francisco aboard one of three empty commercial airliners was fortuitously timed. *Pandoravirus horribilis* had arrived just before him.

The ride from the airport to the SoMa office tower was as inconspicuous as a brass band at a funeral. Police sirens wailed and blue lights flashed. Up armored Humvees manned by rooftop gunners screamed *look at me.* Noah and the other screeners rode in heavily tinted, bulletproof black SUVs. No one knew who they were. But every crowd they passed found their appearance to present an opportunity to express their grievances.

A Red Cross tractor trailer in the parking lot of a shuttered grocery store by the intersection at which the motorcade stopped was out of whatever they'd been distributing. Volunteers in official vests stood aside impotently as wiry, shirtless men swung from the trailer's doors and pumped fists in celebration of some imagined victory. Pierced girls in flowing skirts with green, pink, and cherry red hair hurled quilts out the back of the trailer like the ones used to ship furniture to the cheers of the raucous crowd, which chanted, "*We,* the *people,* will never be for*got*ten! *We,* the *people,* will never be for*got*ten!"

When they saw the motorcade, it became the focus of their ire. A swarm of them like an Infected rampage leapt over the hoods of parked cars with the amazing agility of the young and bounded up to pound Noah's SUV with fists and press faces wild with…whatever, just wild, into the side windows. The motorcade accelerated through the red light just as a brick chipped a pit into the window beside Noah.

Three times, they had to abandon their intended route due to large gatherings in the streets. The first appeared to be a peaceful vigil in which people held candles stuck through little paper shields to protect hands from hot wax. The second was looting run wild, with one man in black wearing a black bandanna to cover his face as he kicked repeatedly and apparently futilely at the locked door of a jewelry repair business. The third detour, which required that the entire convoy awkwardly back up to the previous intersection, was due to the road ahead being dotted with flaming piles of furniture, a blazing overturned city bus, and at least three car fires. A half dozen weathered homeless men pushed their shopping carts full of belongings away from the anarchy being wrought by rioters who appeared both better dressed and better fed.

But the worst awaited them at their destination. "Is that the line?" Noah asked the federal marshal in the front seat of the SUV, who simply nodded. The queue, four abreast, snaked around a corner. When the SUV turned, Noah saw that it went on for blocks. The well-behaved people in the line cowered when confronted by angry young men, and some women, who ranted at them and shook handmade signs in their faces, one of which read, "Say no to genocide!" in red paint that ran like blood.

Most of the would-be interviewees had turned away from the harassment and tried not to make eye contact, many staring down at presumably long useless smartphones as their ungroomed tormentors sent spittle flecked abuse their way. Here and there, scuffles erupted over purses or briefcases yanked from shoulders, which were relinquished after only nominal fights so that victims didn't lose their places in line or have to confront someone with nothing to lose. Noah watched as the thieves skipped down the sidewalk, turned the stolen bags upside down, and emptied their contents with grins, tongues stuck out, and glee.

High above the turmoil, Noah had his first interview—a man in his late twenties. The buzz from the packed waiting room, corridor, and elevator banks rose to a crescendo before falling silent as the guy closed the office door and confidently strode toward Noah's desk. "How do you do. Nelson Krause. Senior software engineer. Facebook."

"Take a seat." The guy was close shaved. Gone was what had surely been fashionable facial hair, along presumably with any egalitarian progressive views. He had even found a tie, though not one that matched his blue blazer, check shirt, skinny jeans, sockless ankles, and brown loafers. The candidate settled into his chair, rocked back, and crossed his leg in apparent ease.

The accomplishments listed on his resume were impressive, but brief. The whole thing came in at under three quarters of a page. *Summa cum laude*, computer science, Stanford. Masters at Berkeley. Four jobs in four years, each a promotion at a bigger and badder Silicon Valley titan. Missing were the now unimportant high school varsity letters, club vice presidencies, near perfect SAT scores, and most likely to succeed yearbook votes. "What can *I* do for *you*?" the man-child asked Noah.

Needless to say, Noah didn't like him. "This doesn't mention what computer languages you're proficient in. Did you see the instructions?"

"All of them. Perl. PHP. C-sharp. C-plus-plus. JavaScript. Python. Java."

Shit. "Okay." Noah typed the man's name into his laptop and hand wrote it on a roll of blank airline boarding passes removed from the dead ticket machines at the blacked out SFO counters. The laptop generated a random six digit number, not unlike an airline reservation confirmation, which he added beside the man's name. "Here's your boarding pass." He tore it from the roll. "Welcome to Texas."

The next asylum applicant, or whatever they were properly called, seemed terrified. Maybe it was the tumult on the streets, which if the pattern was repeated would soon clear, as the risk of infection set in, then fill again in a burst of violence some hours after Noah would, he hoped, be airborne.

"It says here you're proficient in C-sharp, JavaScript, and Python. That's an odd combination," Noah said, having no idea whether that statement was true.

"Well, I was sorta…. Sorta *self*-taught."

Noah leafed through the man's five-page resume. "This says you got a CS degree at the University of Washington." The man nodded. "Go fighting…." Noah said. His interviewee stared back blankly. "The school's mascot? Go…*Cougars*?"

"Right. Yeah. Go Cougars."

The Cougars were Washington State. UW were the Huskies. Watching college football was finally paying off for Noah.

"I know the instructions said that these wouldn't be technical interviews, but I've got a little coding challenge here." Noah proffered his laptop without showing the applicant that on its screen was an Excel spreadsheet. "I'd like you to complete it in, say, Python."

The guy's jaw dropped. Turns out he was an Uber driver who thought he'd heard enough backseat chatter to pass for a software engineer. "Look, man, I'll join the army or Peace Corps when I get there. I'll do whatever shit job it takes. I'm a self-starter."

"Sorry, buddy. I've got seats only for designated specialties."

The man bared his teeth in a sneer as he hissed. "Fuckin' *figures* those asswads would get a goddamn charter flight *outta* here, while the rest of us...."

Noah's right hand dropped to the butt of the pistol wedged into the seat cushion beside his right thigh. It almost came out when the boy's chair scraped the floor. But the guy went to the door and flung it open, admitting the noise that abated as he shouted, "Fuck the system!" and shot both middle fingers in all directions and back at Noah.

"Fuck the fucking system!" shouts grew ever fainter as the door closed and the Uber driver turned anarchist paraded away. A petite blond girl entered. Before handing Noah her resume, she reluctantly lowered her mask and gave him her best selfie smile.

"Sit," Noah said as brusquely as possible without reducing the girl to tears. He'd been warned to brace himself for all kinds of offers, especially sexual favors. The girl perched timidly on the front of her chair. Mechanical engineer. Worked at a pre-revenue nanosatellite startup. She looked the part. His BS meter never alerted. Without asking her a single question, he tore a boarding pass off the roll. "Welcome to Texas."

So it went until he handed out his last boarding pass. By prearrangement, Noah pretended to go to the bathroom past the suddenly hushed, smiling, attentive crowd waiting outside his office. He actually *did* go to the bathroom while a police officer retrieved his bag. "Good luck to you," he said to the cop at the landing in the fire escape.

"Don't forget about us out here," were the man's parting words through his mask.

Noah waited in the fire escape until the last of the screeners arrived. The building was still crammed with asylum applicants, but the screeners fled before they broke the news that the three flights were full and no others were planned.

They followed busses of asylum seekers back to the airport. The emergency detours at civil disturbances grew too numerous to count. Looters were the most common, but each block was its own microcosm. On some people swept up after earlier unrest. But most law-abiding citizens seemed to be in hiding from the disease, or the Infecteds' violence, or the lawlessness that preceded both, or all of the above. Rocks peppered Noah's SUV so often the *clunks* lost their shock value. But the female screener in the seat beside him flinched every time and finally said, "Fucking animals." Once, the convoy came to a complete stop, which Noah had learned was a bad thing. Up ahead, young men—it was almost always young men—were pounding on and ultimately rocking a bus full of engineers, scientists, and professors who clutched golden tickets, so close to perceived salvation.

A marshal in the front opened the SUV's skylight with one hand. The woman beside Noah jumped and gasped as the marshal fired his automatic three times into the air. Two spent shell casings rattled off the top of the SUV and one spun to a rest between Noah's feet. But it was the cops in squad cars, who popped tear gas grenades, that cleared the street. That left Noah's eyes watering and the woman beside him coughing and gagging.

Noah should have taken a less risky job, he decided. But it was his nature to provide for his family, and this job had come with a car and better housing.

Chapter 34

Emma, Samantha, Dwayne, and Sheriff Walcott stared out through the lobby windows at the noisy crowd in the street. The former branch bank was their new seat of government after the city hall had mysteriously burned down. Everyone in the street wore some form of mask. Samantha was craning her neck to read their handmade signs.

"Vaccines now," she read in low tones, minus the sign's exclamation mark. Tilting her head to the other side, she read, "Halt the executions." "We are Americans too." She looked over at Emma. Sam was growing taller and was almost Emma's height. The crowd began a spontaneous chant of "U-S-A! U-S-A! U-S-A!"

Pop. Emma started. Something had chipped the window. Dwayne said he had people taking video to identify Rule breakers. Walcott said his men were down the street in case force was needed. "They're breakin' the Rule on gatherin' size."

"That Rule was meant to prevent infected mob violence," Emma replied.

"Yeah, but a rule's a rule."

"Why don't you try talking to them?" Emma suggested. "Ask them to disperse."

Walcott shrugged, straightened his cowboy hat, and walked out onto the front steps. The instant he appeared, there arose a chorus of boos and jeers. Samantha said, "What do you think their problem with *him* is? The arrests and *executions*?"

As Walcott stood there, both hands raised to try to gain their silence, a single shot rang out. Walcott staggered, dropped to one knee, and sat. A red stain spread on the back of his khaki blouse before he keeled over, presumably dead.

Dwayne said, "I'll call his people at the firehouse," and raised his radio to his lips. But Emma held out a hand and stopped him.

Outside, the Uninfecteds were screaming, shouting, and running despite the fact there was no more gunfire. Within seconds, the street was empty. All that was left of the demonstration was discarded signs and Walcott's corpse.

Samantha said, "Well that's one way to quiet a crowd."

"Dwayne," Emma said, "can you establish contact with the military in Norfolk?" He nodded. "Reach out to them and request doses of vaccine. As much as they can spare."

Samantha said, "They won't give us any, will they?"

"No. But we can have Mrs. Stoddard tour the Uninfected communities and report that we asked. Also, Samantha, come up with a list of punishments for Uninfecteds short of execution and propose them to me." Samantha nodded and made a note in her book. "And Dwayne, ID any leaders of that crowd out there from your video and make them disappear, slowly, over the next week or so. Quietly."

"Yes, ma'am," Dwayne replied before departing.

Sam asked, "Should we, like, do something about his body out there?"

"They'll pick it up on the evening run." But Samantha, it seemed to Emma, was concerned about something, and stared at Sheriff Walcott's remains. "What?"

"I was just thinking," the girl prefaced, an unusual sentence construction for an Infected, "we do all these things—the Rules, the executions, the ultimatums to holdout towns and the assaults when their deadlines pass—but why?"

"I don't understand your question."

"I mean, what if you execute *me*?" The girl stared at Walcott as if it were her answer.

"Why would I do that?"

"What if I fail my temperament test tomorrow?" Sam asked.

"Then you didn't design it very well, did you?"

"I told you. I used that scientist lady from the NIH lab to design it."

"You'll pass," Emma said, turning to leave.

"That's not the point." Emma stopped to hear Samantha out. "Aren't we losing sight of what all this is supposed to be about? Isn't it supposed to help us survive? Establish order and security. Restore the economy. Defend ourselves against attacks. That's all about staying alive. But if I fail my test tomorrow, you'll kill me. Or the SE guys will, anyway."

"What's your point?"

Samantha turned and looked straight at Emma. "Are *you* taking the test?"

Emma's anxiety skyrocketed, and she felt compelled to turn away as she balled her fists and felt her jaw clench tightly. After a silence, she decided that the best thing to do was to leave, which she did, stepping over Walcott's corpse on the way to her Honda, returning to Walcott, and taking the sheriff's pistol belt, holster, and automatic.

Chapter 35

The alarm clock on Isabel's iPhone sounded at an ungodly hour. No light filtered into the hotel room through the drapes. Rick snored lightly in the warm bed beside her. "Hey," she said, poking his bare back. "It's time to get up. We've gotta be there in an hour."

"Wake me up five minutes before we leave." He pulled the sheet up to his neck.

Men. Isabel spent forty-five minutes showering, blow drying her hair, brushing her teeth, putting on makeup, and carefully folding her freshly washed clothes. She used the bathroom light to stow them in her backpack before dissolving into tears. When would this all be over? How would it end? *I can't take this for much longer!* She sat on the bed, sighed, and dried her face as Rick slept through it all. She made little noises and wiggled side to side but got zero reaction. She flicked the lamp on the nightstand on and off repeatedly. *Nothing.* But by God if she broke a twig Rick would dive for his fucking rifle.

"Time to get up!" Isabel said more loudly than was necessary.

Rick swung his feet to the floor, pulled up his trousers, laced his boots, pulled on his T-shirt, and buttoned his camo blouse. "Morning," he said with a yawn on the way to the bathroom. She watched in amazement. He brushed his teeth and shaved in less time than she took putting her hair into a bun. "Let's go," he said upon returning.

"Don't wanta hold you up or anything."

"Something wrong?" he asked.

"Newp." She grabbed her carbine from where it was propped against the nightstand.

Rick slept through the three minute drive to army HQ, missing Isabel's eye rolls, shakes of her head, and sighs. She'd slept poorly, eaten poorly, and had no idea where they'd be sent next, or whether she would ever reunite with her family. Oh, and the world was coming to an end. Rick was apparently going to snore through it. His helmet rested comfortably against the Humvee's grimy armored window.

The brakes groaned and squeaked. "Rick! We're *there*!"

He awoke to 100 percent alertness on command. His only confusion was at seeing her shaking head. "So...everything's *okay*?" He arched his eyes wide for a pupil check at the sandbagged entrance.

"I'm fine." She winced in the glare of the pen light. A thermometer rolled across her forehead beeped. "I'm just, you know, enjoying the hell out of life."

That confused him, which was probably the best she could hope for given that he couldn't exactly stop what was happening. They had spent several days waiting on transportation to Texas, passing on several convoys headed south in hopes of catching a flight. It should have been a wonderful few days. They had little to do other than the daily trip to army headquarters and a few inspection trips they made to area troop emplacements, logistics hubs, vehicle depots, *etc.* But was anyone reading their reports? "Here goes nothing." She clicked Send and at least always got a *bing* and green checkmark.

Isabel kept returning to speculation about Hank Rosenbaum's departure. Rick's only response other than a shrug was to suggest that maybe Hank had headed home to be with his family. He was back to shrugs when she bombarded him with legitimate follow-up questions like why he would do that, what could he have been thinking, how did he expect to make it on foot through forest fires and charged crowds of Infecteds.

Once, and only once, she had received a call from a number she didn't recognize. It was General Browner. "Dr. Miller, I'm sending you a video you might find interesting based on your and...and Dr. Plante's research." The mention of Brandon, who had died so selflessly in New York, stabbed at Isabel's heart. "To protect sources and methods, you can only watch it once before it self-encrypts. It was taken with a hidden body camera by an immunized agent we trained to mimic the behavior of Infecteds. He infiltrated a charging crowd out west. If you have any thoughts or comments, you can message me."

After Browner signed off, Isabel called Rick over and they watched the video together. The camera had obviously been mounted somewhere mid torso given that the faces of the Infecteds all around the agent were slightly above the camera's perspective. The eyes of most of the people were black, although a few showed resolving mydriasis indicating they had been infected at least a week earlier. The only sounds were from a distant loudspeaker, which bellowed orders to disperse and warnings of deadly force.

The eerie silence of the Infecteds all around was striking. *"This is your final warning!"* came the amplified voice from afar. The only movement came from the Uninfected agent, who slowly pivoted his torso. Even that slight motion attracted suspicious glances and clearly caused the agent to minimize his movements.

The video jerked the instant the guns erupted. A roar arose from the crowd. Everything was a jumble of wild swings of the camera, fierce visages, bared teeth, and hands raised to claw. The image darkened as the lens pressed against the back of the attacker in front of the agent, replaced by the shuffling feet below as the agent stooped amid the rattling cacophony of gunfire. Every so often, the relentless charge passed a prone attacker, or the agent swung wildly around as if to escape the onslaught and Isabel and Rick caught glimpses of a head explode on impact of a high-powered round, or a body spin and collapse, or an entire swath of attackers collapse after stumbling over the previously fallen.

The wild swings of the camera stilled. The agent, audibly panting, took cover behind an overturned van. The crowd surged past despite heads bursting and bodies falling. Single rounds repeatedly punched through two or even three Infecteds at a time, but the mass's momentum seemed unstoppable.

In a final bit of horror, a blood-splattered face of a black-eyed Infected rose from the ground right in front of the camera. The woman's lips curled into a snarl as she turned to the agent. She raised a bloody hand toward the lens just as the muzzle of a pistol appeared and its flash flung the Infected's head backwards.

Rick and Isabel exchanged a long, silent look each other's way. Isabel could think of nothing to say to General Browner about the awful scenes of the Infected rampage.

* * * *

Denver was near the far northern end of Uninfected America. Their trip to Boulder had been to the true tip of civilization. All along the Interstate had been signs of fighting. It wasn't as bad as their trip down the highway in upstate New York because most refugees from Boulder had made it south to safety. But the route was clearly held open only tenuously, and only with a major commitment of troops, whose attention—and guns—were ominously aimed into the fields and valleys just off the highway.

"I know we're not producing much vaccine in *quantity*," said the head of the Chemical and Biological Engineering Department at the University of Colorado, Boulder. "But the *quality* is excellent, and we've got studies under way that might show reduced rates of adverse reaction." Isabel's hopes had risen and she had asked if that meant fewer people would get infected by vaccination, but had crashed when the doctor made clear he was talking about a reduction in minor aches and injection site itching. Behind him had been a room full of professors and grad students in white lab coats. Isabel's report to the NSC had been hopeful, filled with upbeat but under substantiated conclusions about the efficacy of small labs' work on the vaccine. Rick hadn't shown her his report about the cost of defending Boulder, but from his facial expressions when she asked she had guessed his conclusions weren't as positive.

They headed to the fifth floor of the army headquarters building, past another pupil and temperature check, and into a large conference room filling with soldiers, camo-clad civilians, and more men and women in lab coats. Most no longer wore masks. They, too, must have received the vaccine. *Their* acknowledging nods toward Isabel and Rick seemed more knowing. Greetings from other members of the club.

The dim video on the screen at the front of the conference room was an aerial shot of some smoking, medium sized city. There were numbers and letters in the corner that changed constantly as the aircraft maneuvered, and a box in the center of the image in lieu of crosshairs. No one paid any attention to the desperate defenders of yet another Alamo.

The video switched to General Browner and others taking seats in one room, and President Anderson in another box on the screen. "Okay," the president said. "Reports?"

What proceeded was an hour of anecdotes, with no big picture context. Lists of towns quarantined along the periphery of the *Corridor*, they called Texas-to-Colorado uninfected territory. Not a very inspiring name for a country. Lots of talk about a neck and shoulders that presumably made more sense if you were looking at a map. Albuquerque and Wichita had been lost. Santa Fe was long gone. Colorado Springs and Pueblo were holding, but with potentially unsustainable air support. Amarillo seemed to be the linchpin holding the whole shebang together. Isabel was wondering what kind of flag and anthem was appropriate for a Corridor when she heard her name.

"Dr. Miller?" Browner growled. She rose uncertainly. "There you are." Isabel couldn't imagine what observation in her reports could possibly have warranted discussion. "We got an interesting query. One of our patrols outside of Norfolk came across a billboard with a spray painted sign directing them to a message. It was from that Lance Corporal at the NIH hospital with your sister asking if we could share vaccine for their uninfected population. We're wondering what you might make of that request?"

"I'm sorry, sir, but I have no earthly idea."

The president waited, seemingly impatiently on Browner, who said, "Her little kingdom is growing by leaps and bounds. Based on our overflights, it appears they've established order in southwestern Virginia east of the Appalachians, and they're expanding into North Carolina down to the Winston-Salem, Greensboro, Durham, Raleigh line. They're also sending out feelers to the northeast and northwest to solicit indications of interest to join their Community. And Asheville to the south has already applied to join by filling out some sort of franchising agreement even though they're several uninfected towns distant. And she reduced her territory's last major uninfected lodgment by using biological warfare—infiltrating some recently turned, highly contagious Infecteds—into Virginia Tech, which finally fell yesterday. There's really nothing like her territory anywhere else in North America, although we've heard of some emergent self-organization by Infecteds in Pusan, South Korea, Johannesburg, South Africa, and Aberdeen, Scotland."

She still could think of nothing helpful to say, but she had to speak. "Well, sir, you remember she had all those notebooks full of ideas for communal survival."

"We've had a team analyzing them and acting as a clearing house for intel. She's been remarkably faithful to her plans in organizing an effective Infected government."

"Are they giving you—the military—any trouble?"

"No. No. They're just mercilessly slaughtering whole towns who refuse to join, so most are joining these days. But they've carefully avoided any contact with our forces in the area. They even returned a captured Special Forces team unharmed even though that team had engaged your sister's security forces when they started machine gunning rule breakers. But we understand she has discontinued the practice of mass murder, at least of *un*infected citizens. She now apparently summarily executes only Infecteds."

"I'm sorry," she said, cringing and at a loss.

"You're not your sister's keeper," Browner said. "But you do understand her better than our study group. When you get back to Houston I want you to work with them. As you know, we have some strategic decisions to make."

In Browner-speak, that meant whether or not to vaporize her sister with nuclear weapons. "General Browner, I'm sure you must've learned from digests of her notebooks—"

"I've read them all," Browner interrupted. "Cover to cover. No digests."

"Then you must've seen she doesn't have any grand scheme to take over the world. She just wants enough territory and resources for a rudimentary, self-sustaining economy."

"And to field a military," Browner said, "that has sufficient depth of maneuver space for its defense." All the man with the hammer saw was nails. He was looking for an enemy state, which he was trained to defeat.

"I'd be glad, sir, to help any way I can. But I have to ask, is what's going on in southwest Virginia any worse than what's going on in the Northeast, or Upper Midwest, or west of the Rockies, for God's sake? Vigilantes, militias, berserk mobs of Infecteds, rampant house by house murder, *both* ways? New York *City*?"

"Perhaps," President Anderson interrupted, "you missed the significance of General Browner's summary. They're expanding. Sending recruiting teams all the way up to the Canadian border. Organizing a military. They're the only instance of anyone doing that at scale in North America. And now, they want vaccines for their uninfected *citizens*, and they're attracting applications to join by *un*infected towns."

She understood. They weren't worried about Emma posing a military threat...for now. They were worried that she would succeed where they were failing. Emma might stop the violence and feed the hungry, inducing increasing numbers of people to accept her Faustian offer and choose order and security over rule of the jungle and starvation.

"I'll help any way I can," Isabel mumbled just audibly enough for Browner to hear.

Chapter 36

Chloe's mom had the brilliant idea of organizing a party to introduce themselves to their new neighbors. "Everyone loves a block party."

They had moved out of their sketchy apartment after being granted a permit to live in an abandoned house. It was owned, apparently, by some old couple who had made the fateful decision to flee the safety of Houston to be with children and grandchildren in Michigan. The Millers had agreed to relinquish the home upon the return of its owners, to care for and maintain the house, and to pack away any personal belongings, which they would have done regardless given how creepy it was to see strangers staring back from a multitude of framed photos. The hall closet was jam-packed with their shit.

It was a crappy little one story house with grossly outdated décor smelling of cat litter and old people no matter how much they aired it out. But Chloe's mom seemed proud of her efforts to upgrade their accommodations, which they probably merited only because of her dad and aunt's important government jobs. Most refugees, Chloe had learned at school, were slumming it in roadside motel rooms reeking of cigarettes.

Chloe's life now consisted of school, and foraging for supplies with government ration vouchers. When they eventually got home each day, the leafy suburban streets were empty. The parks abandoned. No one biked, or jogged, or hung out. No skateboarders or kids playing catch or anyone washing a car in the drive. Television consisted of news about the continuing collapse of civilization, like the first outbreak in Darwin, Australia, alternating with hopeful announcements like the recapture of Tulsa. "I didn't know Tulsa had even fallen," her mom had commented. Judging by the smoke rising from the skyline, it looked more like the total destruction of the city formerly known as Tulsa.

It was in the context of that period of malaise that Chloe's mom threw her party.

"When's Dad coming home?" Chloe had asked.

"Dunno. But when he does, it would be nice if we had made some friends."

Her idea proved even more lame than it initially sounded. They had gotten cleaned up—her mom directing Chloe to put on a little eyeliner, her shorthand for trying to look good—and out they had gone with a stack of invitations, printed presumably illegally in the school nurse's office, with a border of party hats, horns, and confetti. "Meet Your Neighbors! 7:30 pm! Friday! Finger Food and Soft Drinks Provided! (BYOB If You Want!)"

"That's too many exclamation marks, Mom. It looks desperate."

"They're already printed. And cheer up. Maybe there'll be some cute boys."

Chloe had rolled her eyes, but her mother ignored her as the three of them gamely hit the sidewalk and approached the first house. Chloe's mom knocked and rang the doorbell before they stepped back a safe distance. Nothing happened. "Must be out," she said, folding one of the invitations and tucking it into the mailbox.

At the second house, they heard hushed voices behind the door. "We're your neighbors!" her mother had called out in a raised tone. "From a couple of doors down! We wanted to invite you to a party!" Nothing happened. Everyone had fallen silent. Her mom opened the clear glass outer door to slip an invitation into it, and Chloe thought she heard the *kerchunk* of a shotgun being pumped from inside.

"Mom," Jake said as they headed to the sidewalk, "this isn't such a good idea."

"Nonsense. Someone has to keep society going. We can't just hide behind our doors." But Chloe could tell from the looks on her mother's face and her furtive glances at the front windows of the next house that she was no longer quite so certain of her plan.

Knock-knock-knock. "Hello?" *Ring-ring-ring.* Nothing. This time, her mother declined to open the glass outer door or the metal mailbox lid and quietly slipped the invitation under a corner of the doormat, on which was printed an out-of-date, "Welcome."

By the time they reached the fifth house, Chloe was feeling exposed without a weapon. What if someone had turned, hidden indoors, and came springing out when they rang the doorbell? They had left the kitchen knives and fireplace poker, previously set aside for last-ditch home defense, behind in their attempt to foster neighborliness.

"Git off our property!" came a shout from the upstairs bay window of the story-and-a-half mansion compared to the less impressive tract homes common to their block.

"We're...." Chloe's mom hesitated when a rifle muzzle appeared in the window. "We're having a block party. I'll just.... We'll leave the invitation—"

"Clear off! Yer trespassin'!"

Chloe's mom in fact declined to leave an invitation. That would show *him*. And though they dutifully and in silence traipsed up one side of the block to the first cross street, and back down the other to the next intersection, thankfully returning to their home without being shot or attacked by crazies, Chloe's mother never again knocked on a door or rang a doorbell. They just left invitations and scurried away.

At the appointed time Friday evening, they swung open their front door. Paper plates and plastic cups—a necessary accommodation to the apocalypse—lay at the ready. Gross refreshments like an orange drink made from packets of powder and ham and sometimes cheese sandwiches—cut into four pieces but stacked by Chloe's mom in artistic mounds to appear festive and bountiful—filled incongruous ornate silver serving dishes. The peanut butter filled crackers in a crystal bowl were too dry to eat, forcing Chloe to consume the orange drink and then spit it all into the toilet in the hallway powder room. "Don't make a mess!" her mom called out.

The front walk was empty, and remained that way. "Turn the music up louder," their mom instructed Jake—his one contribution to the festivities. "Let's go stand in front of the windows." Chloe sighed as she trudged back and forth like a sentry on guard duty. Nothing moved on the street or sidewalk.

Hours seemed to pass, though in truth they were still on the first song on Jake's playlist. Chloe and Jake shared private looks in between glances at their mother, who stared out the front windows and door lest some would-be reveler escape. By the time the next song came on the small speaker Jake had paired with his iPhone, their mother's obsessive checks for approaching crowds of partygoers began to feel unbalanced and finally maniacal.

Chloe exaggerated her strutting past the front windows in hopes her mom would give up. She raised her knees and pumped her arms like a drum major. Every time Chloe passed Jake, he pretended to bob his head to the music and dance like an inflatable man at a used car dealership. Both found their own respective antics hilarious.

Their mom sat on an old-fashioned, upholstered sofa arm, pretty bare shoulders in a halter top fetched from a Salvation Army bin, slumped over, staring, and—Chloe and Jake finally realized—sobbing.

"Mom?" she called out.

"Turn off the music," she said in a thick voice as she dabbed at her eyes and nose without turning as if they wouldn't notice. "Close the door. Lock it."

Chloe did as instructed, then with nods and pointing supervised her brother in preserving the sandwich quarters and peanut butter crackers in sealed plastic containers and zip lock bags. The noxious orange drink went into the fridge.

"When do you think Dad is coming home?" Jake asked.

Chloe's fierce face of rebuke was his only reply. Their mother excused herself and went to her room.

Chapter 37

CAMP PENDLETON, CALIFORNIA
Infection Date 104, 1400 GMT (7:00 a.m. Local)

"Jesus Christ." Noah stooped to gaze at the line that wound its way out of sight down the street. "How many people are out there?"

The Marine major beside him said, "3,679."

Noah arched his aching back. He'd slept on a sofa in the office's waiting room. "Do they understand I've only got 114 passes to hand out?"

The officer in full combat gear shrugged. "They don't know, but they know." A couple of dozen armed Marines slowly patrolled the line, generally ignoring questions shouted their way. Most people awaiting Noah's life changing interview were white or Asian men. About half looked to be in their twenties. There were no children.

Noah drew his 9mm from its holster and pulled the slide back until he saw a brass cartridge nestled snugly in the chamber. "Alright. They'll be on their best behavior as long as there's a chance they'll get a pass. Any trouble is gonna come when they get the no. So here's what we're gonna do." He handed the major a stack of 114 numbered boarding passes for the lone 737 at Noah's disposal. "If they're getting asylum, I'll send them into the corridor through that door on the left. You set up a table, hand them a boarding pass, tie the pass's number to their name in a log, and send them straight onto the busses."

"And the rest?" asked the major.

"I'll send them outside, through that door on the right. What you do with them...that's your business. And I'd like a couple of armed Marines in here with me."

Noah bumped elbows with the arriving sergeant and PFC, who took up positions behind and to either side of Noah's desk. Noah hit the intercom button. "Send the first one in." He and the Marines raised their surgical masks.

A smiling Asian doctor in his mid-forties with his mask hanging beneath his chin handed Noah his CV. He specialized in infectious diseases at the UCSD Medical Center and began a recitation of obscure papers published when Noah interrupted. "That's fine, thanks." He directed the man toward the door on the left. The doctor hesitated. "You're good. You got a pass."

"Wha...what about my family?"

"Sorry. Only you. But once you get to Texas, you can apply for them to join you."

"How will they get there?"

Noah shrugged. Before the door closed behind the man, Noah saw him stop at the folding table with the two, masked Marines and a stack of boarding passes. Noah rested his finger atop the intercom button, but instead of pressing its button went to that door. The two Marines at the table looked his way.

"Did that guy take a boarding pass and get on a bus?"

"Yes, sir," replied a woman Marine.

Noah proceeded with the second, brief interview of a cheerful civil engineer perched on the front edge of his seat, eager to discuss the tensile strength of concrete beams. "Just head on out through the door on the right," Noah said.

"Does that mean I...?" Noah shook his head. "Motherfucker! God*damm*it!" He took one step at Noah and both Marines' carbines rose to the audible sound of *clicks*, freezing the man but not shutting him up. "How does it feel to play God? To decide whether somebody lives or dies based on, what? Thirty seconds? I got my place at the front of the line two *days* ago! They've given me half a sandwich and a bottle of water. That's it."

"Please exit the building, sir," the Marine sergeant said through his mask.

The man's hand fell away from the knob. "You know what? Maybe I won't. Maybe you're gonna have to shoot me, right here. Get it over with. 'Cause I'm dead either way. Why the fuck should I follow your fucking rules, huh? Just march back to the gate on the 5 and good luck?"

"This is your last chance," the sergeant said, "to do this your way."

"*Fffuuuck* you!" The door opened onto brilliant sunlight. "*Yeah*, yeah! Get your fuckin' hands off me!"

Again, Noah followed the departing man to the door he'd exited. The major and a whole squad of armed Marines were instantly alert. "Change of plans," Noah announced. "I'm gonna lie. I'm gonna tell people I send out this door that they're going to Texas. That means *you're* gonna have to deal with their...disappointment." The major checked to ensure a round was chambered in his carbine, and nodded.

Each lie took its toll on Noah and, apparently, on the sergeant and PFC behind him. They were replaced every half an hour by a new team who got the painful "I'm-gonna-lie" orientation until Noah grew numb to the admission of his moral failings.

"So I'm in? I'm good?" asked the blonde nurse, grinning, taking a small hop as she pumped her first. "*Yes!* Thank you. *Thank* you! You won't be sorry! I'm gonna work my tail off." She exited through the door on the right. "Hey! Wait a minute. Wait! Talk to the guy back in there. He said I—" The door closed.

Noah checked his watch. An hour and fifty minutes had passed. The little stick figures on his notepad added up to fourteen left doors, eighty-two right doors. He did the math. If the first ninety-six people in line were representative of the rest, he should only have given boarding passes to three of them, not fourteen. He stretched his back and looked out the window. He hadn't made a noticeable dent in the line outside, whose end he still couldn't see. He needed to speed the process up, and he needed to reject a far higher percentage of the asylum applicants.

Or not. What he *really* needed to do was get the hell out of there before someone in that line started a fight, or began coughing.

A knock on the office door barely preceded its opening. A grimy Marine festooned with combat gear said, "I've got someone who should be on your plane." He opened the door wider to reveal a short, dark skinned woman holding a tiny bundle in a hospital blanket. The Marine wore a mask. The woman didn't.

"I'm sorry, but I can only take people with an enumerated list of specialties."

"Yeah, but you're gonna want to take her and her baby too." Noah held his hands out in invitation for him to explain. "We fought our way down to Scripps hospital. Our CO's wife was there recovering from a car accident. The place was a hodgepodge of barricaded wards. Some had turned, some hadn't, and everybody was fighting everybody. On our way back out with the colonel's wife, we got stopped by a doctor and a nurse who told us to take this woman and her baby, and to guard them with our lives."

"And why is that?" Noah asked, eyeing the silent and impassive woman repeatedly.

"Because, they said, she's immune. She came out of the maternity ward where she'd been sealed up tight with a coupla dozen other women, newborns, and medical staff for almost a full day. Everybody else, other than her and her baby, had caught the *P.* and turned or died. She hadn't. Neither of them had. They tested their blood—twice—and said they were both virus-free. Completely healthy."

"Had she been vaccinated?" Noah asked.

"No. The doctors were positive. They said the blood tests confirmed it. She'd never gotten the vaccine."

"So she's...*naturally* immune?" The young Marine officer shrugged. "I've never heard of that before."

"That's why they said you should take real good care of her...and her baby."

The woman had not said one word. "What's your name?" Noah asked. She looked back up at the Marine who had escorted her there.

"She doesn't speak English. Her name is on her hospital bracelet."

"Where's she from?" Noah asked.

"Papua, New Guinea, they said."

Noah nodded and directed the woman and baby to the door on the left.

Chapter 38

"You never even asked me how my temperament test went," Samantha said.

"I saw you the next day," Emma replied. "So I knew you passed." Samantha didn't seem satisfied by Emma's straightforward answer. "Why am I meeting this guy?"

"You're both professors," the girl replied. "I thought you'd want to hear him out."

"Is he Infected or Uninfected?"

"Un-."

Emma and Sam entered the small office in their headquarters. A stout, graying man in full PPE rose at the far end of a conference table. "How do you do?" Emma said.

"Okay, I guess. I'm Dr. Frank Porter, with the Department of Biological Systems Engineering at Virginia Tech."

"Emma Miller. Professor of Epidemiology at Johns Hopkins. Have a seat." The man seemed nervous and fidgeted. If he had been infected, Emma would've been concerned. "How are things at Virginia Tech these days?"

The man seemed not to know how to answer. "You mean, after…? Most everyone is dead…or infected." That confirmed what Dwayne had reported.

He's looking for sympathy, came the voice in Emma's head. "I'm sorry," she said, more a test of the voice's hypothesis than a desire to put her visitor at ease.

"Thank you." Emma couldn't tell whether he sounded sincere, but doubted that he did. "I've heard that, despite your...*tactics*, you're a reasonable person and not a...a...."

Emma waited, but he failed to complete the thought. "Why are you here?"

"Agriculture." It was a timely subject. The proposal to rebalance food production and consumption by reduction of the population had lost its champion with Walcott's death, but was still on the table. "People are hungry," Dr. Porter said. "This young lady here said you might be willing to work together to improve agricultural output."

Samantha tried her unartful smile. Porter seemed stuck in the preliminaries—establishing that there wasn't enough to eat and determining that Emma was willing to partner with Uninfecteds—which she wanted to get past. "I am. So how do we do it?"

"Thirty-four percent of the state's land is devoted to agriculture," Porter said. "Virginia produces wheat, barley, peanuts, potatoes, snap beans, cucumbers, sweet corn, soybeans. Hay for livestock. We've got poultry, beef, dairy, farm raised fish. We even grow apples and grapes. And we can convert land used for tobacco to growing food crops."

"That's one of the reasons we chose Virginia. Why don't we have enough food?"

"Well, most of the best farmland is south of Richmond—east of here."

"If we expand in that direction," Samantha said, "it'll take us closer to Norfolk."

When Porter didn't seem to understand, Emma explained. "We're trying to avoid open military conflict with the national forces that still remain in and around Norfolk."

"I understand you've got issues."

"*We've* got issues," Samantha replied, "if we're working together."

"Fair enough. But east is where the farmland is. Campbell, Appomattox, Prince Edward, Charlotte, and Halifax Counties. Those aren't that close to the coast."

"There's dirt everywhere," Samantha noted. "Why not just farm where we are?"

That elicited a lecture on the gritty sand best for sugar beets and carrots, intermediate silts, and fine clay more suited to wheat, beans, potatoes, and rapeseed. "The best all-around soil is loam, which is fortyish percent sand, 40 percent silt, and 20 percent clay. That loam lies east of here."

Dr. Porter described the history of the domestication of species like wheat, which had been selectively bred over the millennia to maximize production and nutritional value. "Eighty percent of our food supply, directly or indirectly—via livestock eating grass or grain fodder—comes from cereal crops, which are nothing more than varieties of grass like barley, sorghum, millet, oats, and rye. The *majority* of our food comes from just three cereals—corn, rice, and wheat—which should be our focus. But without active management with herbicides and pesticides, those tamed species would be driven to extinction by hardier wild plants that seize abandoned farm fields.

"Some crops—rhubarb, potatoes, artichokes—can fend off the encroachment. They'll do fine unattended for several seasons. But before we lose entire species forever, we need a seed collection program focusing on heirloom crops, not hybrids, whose seed supply is disrupted." Porter said mankind owes its existence to the earth's thin layer of topsoil, which is disintegrated rock hosting a microbial ecosystem that processes decaying matter and recycles plant nutrients. "Plants need topsoil with four things— water, nitrogen, phosphorus, and potassium—which farming saps from the soil. Ancient Egyptians depended on annual flooding of the Nile, whose silt replenished nutrients, but we use fertilizer. With access to petrochemicals cut off, the land will quickly lose its vitality."

"What should we be growing," Emma asked, "to avoid exhausting the land?"

"Without fertilizer, or letting fields lie fallow for multiple growing seasons to revitalize themselves naturally, which is highly inefficient land management, we've got to revert to older methods of farming. Crop rotation, simpler farm implements, and manure." The Norfolk four course rotation, coincidentally named but originating in Britain, would keep the land fertile. "First you grow legumes, peas, beans, lentils, soy, peanuts, clover, or alfalfa. What you don't harvest for human consumption, you allow livestock to graze on to produce traditional manure, or you plow the crop into the soil for use as *green* manure. Both methods pump nitrogen back into the soil.

"The next year, you plant nitrogen hungry wheat for humans to eat. The following season you plant root crops. That could be potatoes for us to eat, but you could also plant biennials like turnips, rutabagas, or kale, which are flowering plants that take two years to complete their lifecycle. They can be harvested to fatten up livestock over the summer, or kept in the ground until needed for feed during the winter. They're a lot better than energy poor roughage like hay. And cultivating livestock will provide you not only with fresh meat, but also dairy products rich in vitamin D, which is in short supply in dark winter months when your skin can't synthesize it from sunlight.

"In the fourth year, the Norfolk rotation dictates growing barley for animal feed before looping back around to legumes. Not only does that rotation maintain the fertility of the soil, but by varying the species you grow, you break any infestations of pests or pathogens that prey on any one type of plant. Using that method ought to support ten people per five acres of farmland."

For fertilizer they could use the nitrogen from unprocessed animal manure, or human manure cleansed of microorganisms by open, aerated composting, or closed, oxygen starving bioreactors. "Each human produces about a hundred pounds of feces, and ten times as much urine, each year. That'll yield about 450 pounds of cereals." Assuming they lost access to mined calcium phosphate, they could spread crushed bone meal from animal skeletons and teeth, which is rich in phosphorus, and potassium from potash, which they could easily extract from wood ashes.

"Okay," Emma finally said. "You're now the head of our Community's agriculture. Prepare a plan—land and farming equipment needed, seed and animal collection, crop rotation, fertilizers, pesticides, and herbicides needed—and I'll review it."

The man hesitated. "Will I be working for *you*, or for the Stoddards?"

"I can have you report to President Stoddard, if that's what you want."

"*No.* I want to work for you, not...*her. Mrs.* Stoddard."

"I understand," Emma said. "You'll report to me, then."

Chapter 39

FARMINGTON, NEW MEXICO
Infection Date 108, 1400 GMT (8:00 a.m. Local)

"You're gonna need a mask," said the deputy sheriff, a Native American from the Navajo tribe, who halted at the police tape barring the door of the high school gymnasium.

"Oh, no," Isabel replied. "We've been vaccinated."

"It's not for that. It's for…the smell." Isabel and Rick donned the masks he offered without further hesitation, then ducked under the yellow tape.

The interior of the gym was dark. "Wait. Stop," said their escort, wearing a cowboy hat and khaki uniform. Isabel could make out basketball hoops and stands, and large bundles of abandoned camping or other equipment strewn all about the court. Even through the mask, she could detect the faintly putrid, steely smell that permeated the stagnant air.

The deputy flicked on a heavy-duty flashlight. When its beam lit the abandoned piles of gear, Isabel gasped. Rick's grip found her elbow as if to catch her.

It wasn't gear that was scattered everywhere. It was bodies. Body parts, to be more accurate. Hundreds, maybe thousands of people. A headless torso with a single arm. A long string of intestines trailing a blood streaked crawl under the stands. A woman in a fetal curl whose hair hung from shreds of scalp. Stumps where legs should be. Hands slipped from their protective cover of eyes gouged black.

The hardwoods were dark with blood. When Isabel turned to see the revulsion shown in Rick's squinting eyes, her boots stuck to the floor.

The smell resolved into the separate reek of blood, urine, and feces like on Rouses Point Bridge, but enclosed in the stifling gym. The walls were smeared from indistinct slides to the floor and occasionally adorned with bloody handprints like ancient cave drawings or macabre, preschool finger paint. Some had died in huddles—families, friends, schoolmates—others in lone, desperate attempts to escape. A body dangled from the stanchions that held aloft a backboard. Upturned sneakers were all that were visible where a man or woman had tried to wedge their body behind the top row of the stands. Other remnants of people extended outward from gaps in row after row of bench seating running the length of the court on both sides.

Old women. Little children. The sounds of the massacre must have been horrific.

"We found this after the army retook Farmington," said the deputy. "Nobody who saw what happened survived. Whatever Infecteds did this are somewhere else now, or killed in the army's reoccupation. After finding this, the soldiers quit taking infected prisoners and went on a killing spree, shooting Infecteds, even the calm ones, on sight."

"How many...?" Isabel had to swallow bile. "How many died here?"

"Don't know. This was an evacuation shelter. The last count they called in before whatever happened was 1,065, plus Red Cross, city officials, and Guardsmen." Isabel's gaze followed his flashlight's illumination, but she had seen enough. "You mind," he said, "if I ask you a question? You're the expert, right, on Infecteds?" He flicked off the beam. In the darkness, he said, "Why? Why would they do this?"

Jesus, she thought. *How the hell do I know?* "Can we go outside now?"

Rick and Isabel followed the deputy back to the exit. The only sounds were the noisy soles of their sticking boots. The flood of sunlight caused Isabel to squint, but she swiped the mask from her face, breathed deeply of the dry desert air, and hunched over and grabbed her knees, very close to retching. When she looked up, the deputy awaited her answer.

"Before the virus reached here, we'd observed only three categories of Infected violence. They could kill you coldly, rationally, to take your supplies or eliminate you as a threat." She swallowed hard, straightened herself up, and tried to provide the analysis, like this, to people, like the deputy, who did the actual work. "The second reason Infecteds kill is when something triggers an adrenal rage, which is typically anything *but* rational."

Isabel closed her eyes at the recollection of the sights inside and took deep breaths. Rick's arm snaked around her shoulder. "And the third reason they kill is when a crowd forms at a blockade or other chokepoint, their density increases, and their members get immersed psychologically into the crowd. That essentially hypnotizes them and turns them into a unified mob capable of unspeakable violence in overcoming whatever obstacle that mob faces. *That* has seemed like the greatest threat. Individuals or small groups can be dealt with—killed—whether the rational types or the adrenally enraged. But a large enough mob of Infecteds, totally unconcerned by death, can break through almost any barricades and keep up their killing until the crowd disperses and their adrenaline resorbs."

A helicopter gunship less than a mile away made a strafing run—*brrrrrrap*—against some unseen target. It disappeared repeatedly through or behind column after column of black and gray smoke before firing a string of *whooshing* rockets, quickly followed by their *boom-boom-boom-boom*. It wheeled up into the sky and away from whatever carnage lay splattered beneath it. It was a sight not even worth noting these days.

"But since *Pandoravirus* got here, we've been observing more and more what you might classify as a fourth kind of violence, or some hybrid of the three that I just described. Calculated, intentional mass violence. Crowds forming, or being formed by leaders, into sufficient density to cause full psychological immersion, then directed—consciously or instinctively—to unleash their unthinking rampage on a target of that crowd's or those leaders' choosing."

"Like...they're forming an *army*," the deputy asked, "of the insane?"

"Not exactly. An army implies training, organization, and equipment, and some durability to justify those investments. These crowds we're seeing form, *ad hoc*, with or without leadership, for the express purpose of overwhelming Uninfecteds. It's behavior somewhere between psychology, from which should emerge an instinct of survival, and sociology, which could sacrifice individuals in service of that group's goals."

"They mob up," the deputy summarized, "and rip whoever opposes 'em to pieces."

From the deputy's radio came an unintelligible crackle, to which the deputy responded. All Isabel had made out was an address, which was the next stop on their tour of horrors. It was a medical clinic in which four beaten, traumatized women were handcuffed, crying, on cots. Whimpering, begging, they immediately turned their attention to Isabel. "Please! Help us!" "Make them let us go!" "Oh, God, please just kill me!"

Isabel was momentarily stunned into silence. "Wha...what's going on here?"

A nurse in full PPE dragged her away. "They were raped." The woman's low voice was barely audible over the whimpering pleas from the room next door.

"*Please!* Dear *God!*" "*Kill* me, please! I'm *begging* you!"

"By Infecteds?" Isabel asked. The nurse nodded slowly. "And they're sick?" Another nod. Isabel's head fell and eyes closed. "My God."

"What do we do?" the nurse asked urgently. "They've all got fevers. They're all gonna turn...or die. Should we even *try* to save them? The army will just gun them down."

"You're supposed to *help* us!" "We came to *you!*"

Isabel had no idea what to say. Not a single thought popped into her head, and for a moment she imagined that *she* was an Infected. Blank. Mindless. Mute.

"Treat them just like you would anyone else," Rick instructed. "Dress their wounds. Flip them over facedown. Hydrate them."

"And then? If they survive?"

"Hand them over to the army. You've done your job. They'll do theirs." The nurse shook her head vigorously, not in rejection but as if to rid her mind of the image.

They said nothing in the back of the deputy's SUV on the way to their next stop. "Our son couldn't run fast enough," the father said, choking on his words. "He was the oldest, but he was only six. When they caught him and started to.... He kept calling for us—*Mommy! Daddy!*—so I...I shot him. I carried our four-year-old. My wife had the baby." The mother's haunted gaze never left the floor, and she said nothing. Several times Isabel worried for their swaddled baby, clutched too tightly to its traumatized mother.

They drove to a nursing home. The staff had fled on foot. Old folks lay near overturned wheelchairs and toppled walkers. Canes were feeble weapons. Why had they attacked *them*? They were as helpless as babies, an unfortunately prescient thought.

At a smoking hospital, Isabel asked, "Why are we here?", breaking the silence.

"They wanted me to show you the maternity and neonatal wards."

"No." Isabel shook her head continuously. "No. No. No. No."

"Who's *they*?" Rick asked. "Who wants us to see whatever's up there?"

"The army. The commander of the local task force who retook the town."

"The guy," Rick said, "who gave the shoot on sight orders?" The deputy nodded. "You can report back that his point was made."

They drove off. The most affecting anecdote of all—the proverbial final straw—wasn't even planned. While awaiting their flight back to Denver, the ponytailed deputy said, "Some guy wants to talk to you." Isabel was too exhausted to resist. But she barely paid the guy much attention—at first—other than to note the Hispanic man's weathered skin, trembling hands, and tics of his eyes, which he tried to mask by blinking.

"We left Salt Lake City," he said softly, "in our camper van. M-m-my wife and th-th-three children." He looked everywhere but at Isabel. "My wife was t-t-taken when we stopped on a b-b-bathroom break. We searched for her. My oldest, fourteen, f-f-found her...raped and, and.... She had fought so hard. She was dead. Almost. M-m-my two oldest, they convinced me to-to honor her wishes. 'Kill me, kill me, kill me.' So.... Our youngest, who was seven, never spoke to me again. We lost our middle one...I was only thirty yards away. Over a little hill. Filling water jugs. She shouted. Only once. They knifed her to shut her up, I suppose, and took everything she had—pink backpack with some Skittles she was saving, her favorite book, a ratty stuffed animal, her water bottle. My youngest disappeared in the middle of the night two days later. I think he went off to pee, but... We looked for days. Nothing...thank God. And my oldest," his eyes welled up, but not enough for tears to flow, "was brave. He ran off to...to help another family. We were out of bullets so I went to get our baseball bat, but by that time.... They killed everybody. I saw it. When they spotted me, I jumped in the camper but didn't know what to do. They were clawing the doors and scratching the windows, so I drove and drove and drove. By myself. Alone."

The man's deep breath was his story's punctuation. *There. Done.* As his story had progressed, she noticed, his stammering had stopped—released, therapeutically, by its telling. Isabel muttered, "I'm so sorry," a few times. But she had heard so many of these stories that her attempts fell flat. She barely had any empathy left.

"You should kill them all," the man said, suddenly focusing, intently, on Isabel. Boring holes with his gaze. "Nuke them. Gas them. Line them up against a wall and shoot them. There would be more mercy in putting them down like rabid dogs than *they're* capable of. They're not human. They're some kind of *animal* that kills and rapes. You've either got to kill them, *all*, or eventually they're gonna kill all of *you*."

Isabel should have noticed his pronoun choice—*you* instead of *us*—but felt numb and dazed. "Thanks," she said, but felt the opposite sentiment. She resented having to carry yet an additional burden—that man's story—as she shook his proffered hand. She should also have noticed that he was heedless of the infection risk such intimate contact entailed.

He left for the outer lobby in the private aviation terminal, which was crowded with cops and soldiers awaiting evacuation. Isabel took a deep breath, conveyed to Rick in an expression her complaint about how hard her life was in having to listen to yet another such tale of woe, and, after brief shouts of disturbance, jumped when a single shot rang out.

They exited the office with their carbines raised, but it was all over except for the excuses. "He just fuckin' *grabbed* it!" said the cop with an empty pistol holster. The Hispanic man's head lay in a spreading pool of dark blood.

Isabel returned to the office, anesthetized by the cold that settled over her, when her smartphone vibrated, followed seconds later by Rick's. It wasn't an email or text. Those apps were long dead. It was from Browner via the more robust Department of Defense servers. Both read their devices in silence. "Cease all surveys and return to Houston immediately. Transportation is inbound. Acknowledge by prompt reply."

From the face Rick made and his typing, she surmised he'd gotten the same order.

Isabel banged out her reply—"I acknowledge and will comply"—but then added, "I'm ready to start work on the Emma task force. One favor? Please get my brother Noah safely back to Houston also." She didn't have the guts to demand an acknowledgment.

Her research was over anyway. She had no further need for reflection on the issues of the day. The logic of all she had seen was compelling. Dispositive, in fact. Anyone capable of the violence she and Rick had seen was evil. All Infecteds were capable of that kind of violence. Therefore, all Infecteds were evil. Period.

Isabel extracted her cell phone and dashed out a quick report to the NSC. It would be her most pessimistic ever. She concluded it as forcefully as she had ever done before. "I see no possibility to coexist with Infecteds in the west, and we should proceed with their eradication by all military means at our disposal."

Before she could rethink it, she hit Send. *Bing.* Green check mark.

Chapter 40

Noah had waited, and waited, and waited. When the pilot finally arrived, Noah was about to ask, in a passive-aggressive display of annoyance, why military people always wanted to do things so early. But the pilot, looking more natural in his flight suit than Noah, boomed, "I don't know who you are, or why you rate, but *this* is your lucky fucking day."

Lt. Col. Carpenter attempted to crush Noah's hand before he understood the game.

"You got lucky first 'cause I just watched the last of my squadron depart. And second, 'cause my weapons officer apparently had volunteered to fly in here with me just to get to his family, who lives out in the 'burbs, and *he* has opted to jump the fence, stay here in *Vegas*, and suffer with said family a fate worse than its predecessor *Sodom*. That means I've got an empty seat and pretty clear orders to get you the fuck to Texas."

Noah nodded, waited, and shrugged. He had no idea why either. Isabel, probably.

"Awright. We're heading straight in to Ellington. Flying time is none-of-your-fucking-business. There will be no refreshments or inflight entertainment. *This* is an F-15E Strike Eagle." He swept his arm around toward the surprisingly huge but still sleek fighter-bomber, bathed in light from the open hangar door. "Do you know anything about operating the weapons systems of a dual role fighter?" Noah cocked his head. "*So*, in lieu of *weapons*, and my weapons *systems* officer, I'll have sitting in my back seat *you*, a...?"

"Lawyer."

A big nod. "Of course. A lawyer." He took the last swig of his coffee and tossed the cup to the ground. Somehow blatant littering didn't live up to the promise of the pilot's swaggering, tough guy persona. "You have four jobs on this flight. *Uno.* Do not ask me to go to the bathroom. *Dos.* Do not ask me *anything. Tres.* Do not *touch* anything. And *cuatro.* Tuck your elbows in and brace if I punch us out of the airplane. Awright?"

Carpenter and Noah donned their bulky helmets and climbed up ladders to and strapped into the ultimate bucket seats with the help of ground crew. When the engines started with the canopy still open, Noah feared they would damage his hearing. Carpenter taxied all the way out before closing the canopy with a squeak, which plugged Noah's ears. He turned onto the runway without slowing and pinned Noah to the back of his seat by the amazingly smooth but powerful acceleration and climb out.

After gawking at the lights of Las Vegas and fires surrounding it, there was nothing much to see but dark mountains and dusky wilderness. In fulfillment of his duties on that mission, Noah's head bobbed repeatedly before he nodded off to sleep.

"Visor down," woke him with a start. It was still dark outside.

"What?"

"Reach up to your helmet and lower your fucking visor," Carpenter instructed as the aircraft banked into a steep turn to the right. Noah fumbled for a few seconds before he felt something slide. The heavily tinted lens came down into place. Whereas previously he could at least make out the horizon separating ground from sky, it was now totally dark except for glowing screens and buttons around his knees.

A light in the cockpit changed all that. Every knob, switch, and dial came clearly into view except those that lay in the stark but slowly shifting shadows. Carpenter pivoted to look back past Noah over his left shoulder. It was in the reflection of the pilot's tinted visor that Noah first saw the large glowing blob.

He too turned to look behind them. The burning ball had risen through the clouds in the distance and stood atop a thinning stalk. The sky was black. The mountains were gray. But the snowcapped peaks shone brightly. The thin layer of haze beneath them separated to allow passage of the fireball, which kept rising fast until it was far above their altitude.

The F-15 shuddered and shook. Carpenter banked back to the left, returning to their original course as the glow slowly dimmed. "Was that what I think it was?" Noah asked.

"Yep, in case you were wondering whether things could get any worse. And you now have one more job—*cinco*. You saw nothing. *Nada*. It was a boring, uneventful flight. I'm dead eyed serious about this, Miller. You wanta get your ass locked up, start blabbin'."

Chapter 41

The day on which Chloe would save her family's lives five times, but who's counting, began with a start. "Get up! Jake! *Up!*" It was Chloe's mother in her brother's room next door. Chloe reached for the kitchen knife under her pillow. But through one eye, she saw that the sun was bright outside. "We all overslept. Someone's *alarm* didn't go off!" *That* was directed at Chloe, and that was the first time she saved their lives that day.

Chloe pried open her squinting eyes. Her phone was dead. It was plugged in, she confirmed on checking the wall, but it was totally dead. Her mother burst into her room.

"I plugged it *in*," Chloe immediately whined.

"Power went out last night. Get *up*! We're all late." Off her mom ran to dress.

In the back seat of her family's clunker, Chloe sipped on a juice box through its tiny straw and, with great difficulty and intermittent success, tossed peanut butter crackers into her gaping mouth from a crumpled plastic baggy. Her mother criticized her with a glance in the rearview mirror. "Whah?" Chloe replied with a full mouth. "I'm tryin' ta maintain hann hygie, li' they say to!"

Her mother was speeding. So they were late? Who fucking cares? They barely learned anything from the substitute teachers in their overcrowded classes. And her mom was treating her crappy job like it was *important* or something. But, Chloe wondered for the first time in her life, where they would get money or ration cards for food if her mother was fired and her father never came home?

That's when she caught sight of Turner Ash, across the divided lanes of the boulevard leading to the gate of their high school, running down a grassy embankment from their school's sports fields and football stadium.

"Stop," she said to her mother.

Three soldiers ran to the edge of the embankment with rifles at port arms and wearing gas masks and rubber onesies before chasing Turner down the artificial hill.

"Stop! Turn *right. Here!* Turn-turn-*tuuurn!*" Her mother slammed on the brakes and turned. That was the second time Chloe saved their lives.

Her mom clearly had no idea why they detoured—"*Okay*"—until they saw, all around the school's gate and the streets leading to it, flashing blue cop car lights and twirling red ambulance lights. The number of emergency vehicles was dwarfed by the multitude of green army trucks. But all concern about them was erased by the far more terrifying glimpse of dozens of white buses, whose windows were spray painted and totally opaque.

Chloe's mom pulled over to the curb of the side street. "*Christ,*" she said, slumping over the wheel that she death gripped like the pilot of a stricken plane.

"Did they quarantine the *school?*" Jake asked from the front passenger seat.

"What-the-*fuck*, Jake?" Chloe snapped. "Yes! Didn't you see *Turner?*"

"Was that *him* bein' chased down that hill?"

"Yes!"

Their mother threw the car into drive. "They could expand the quarantine," was all she said in explanation as the pitiful engine chugged and they accelerated away, sort of.

Chloe's mom headed what she thought was straight home. But they didn't know the typically gridlike city map well and they meandered through a woodsy neighborhood whose irregular streets followed the undulations of a bayou. Two turns later, they were lost. GPS no longer worked, even if the car had one or if any of their phones held a charge. Gas was precious, but they kept driving. Finally, they saw and followed a sign for I-10.

But before they could reach the manmade landmark and pick the direction toward parts of the city that they knew, they pulled to a stop at the back of a traffic jam. "What's this? What's *this?*" Chloe's mom was antsy. She pulled herself up by the steering wheel to the car's fraying headliner to try in vain to peer around the huge Suburban ahead.

She tried tapping buttons on the car's dashboard while repeating, "Radio. Radio."

"Mom?" Jake said. He grabbed and held her hand gently. It was the first time he'd ever done anything vaguely competent in the human relations sphere. "Calm down, okay?"

"We would've been there," she said with eyes darting across the dash. "And...and we wouldn't have gone back to those nice, clean trailers at the airbase. They're all headed to main quarantine. Outdoors, you know? And everyone in there—"

"We know, Mom," Jake tried interrupting, unsuccessfully.

"And everyone in there *is* sick, or *gets* sick eventually. It's like...it's like a concentration camp, and nobody...*nobody* ever gets out."

No one, Chloe couldn't help but think. It's what her mom would've said...before.

A car raced by them in the direction opposite the one in which they were heading. "...all residents of Harris, Fort Bend, and Montgomery Counties," the radio announced after Jake pressed the correct buttons, "to remain indoors. Avoid interaction with persons not known to you to have maintained effective isolation. HISD has canceled all classes for the remainder of the week."

Another car raced past them. "Mom," Chloe said calmly. "Turn around."

"But the interstate is right ahead. This is just rush hour."

"Turn *around. Now.* Just *do* it."

It could have been Chloe's tone again, or her now proven spidey sense, or the radio news, but her mother began maneuvering the car, forward and back and forward and back, until she could U-turn it. During the time that took, three more cars raced past.

When they pulled into the opposite lane, they saw the entire tableau of quarantine unfolding ahead. Everyone was beginning to turn around. Police cars with lights flashing skidded to stops on side streets, and PPE clad cops exited with shotguns or rifles. Long files of armed soldiers jogged toward them in full chemical warfare gear, confronting drivers or chasing runners who abandoned their rides and sprinted across grassy lawns.

Crack. Crack-crack-crack. Two soldiers, one kneeling, felled a fleeing girl.

They drove away. That was the third time.

No one said a word. Her mom looked terrified. There were omens of worse to come. Cars sped and ignored stop signs. At every traffic slowdown, her mother turned rather than stop. No one spoke, but all presumably pondered the same question. *Is this it?*

The breaking news on the radio was reminiscent of a storm report. "The Department of Homeland Security has issued an outbreak warning for the following counties." But it ended, mid-sentence, with a long, loud—.

Beeeeeeeeep. That was followed by repeated shrill and grating tones. "Attention. Attention," came the recorded voice over the car's tinny speakers. "This is the Emergency Broadcast System. Take shelter immediately. Take shelter immediately. This is not a drill. Repeat. This is not a drill. Multiple reported outbreaks of *Pandoravirus* have been confirmed in the Houston metropolitan area. Take shelter and stay tuned to this frequency for further instructions." There was a long scratch of static, then silence. Not like the station was off the air; like it remained on-air but broadcasting nothing.

"Chloe," her mother said with an eerily incongruous calm as she accelerated through an empty intersection despite its red light, "you go to the kitchen and pack all the food you can fit into the bags that we collected and put under the silverware drawer. Jake, you start loading those big jugs of water. Be careful because they're heavy."

"We shouldn't go back home," Chloe found herself saying on impulse.

"We've gotta get *food*, Chloe. And the hatchet, knives, and axe handle."

"Dad said head straight to the go bags." So maybe this one was partially Chloe's dad's save. But *she* was the one who reminded them. *And* Dad hadn't even been there when they'd stashed the bags, filled with scrounged survival gear, amid brownish brush beneath a dilapidated billboard. "We've got knives in there, too, and tarps for lean-tos and ground cover, and that expired crap in cans. Plus, it's away from the city."

Her mother turned yet again and headed south, toward the go bags.

"Three and a *half* saves," Chloe mumbled as they took a meandering but preplanned route on surface roads leading to Ellington Field. Four saves, if you rounded.

* * * *

The roar of jet engines beyond the fence around Ellington Field punctuated the otherwise clandestine retrieval of their four go bags, which lay undisturbed right where they'd left them. Mom sat motionless behind the wheel. She wasn't crying. She might have been developing a plan, but that seemed unlikely. Jake alternated glances out the front window at the climbing fighter-bombers, down at the half empty gas gauge, over toward their paralyzed mother, and around at Chloe in back.

"Mom?" Chloe said, getting no response. *"Mom?"*

"I don't know what to do. I don't know where to go. Where is it safe *now*? How will your father ever...ever find us, assuming he's still...?"

Jake and Chloe shared a lengthy silent look of concern.

Chloe moistened her dry lips before venturing, "Well, we're right next to that air force base. Where we stayed during quarantine, and...and where Dad flew out of."

"If we just drive up," her mom said, "with what's going on, they'll shoot us."

Chloe had an idea and retrieved her residence permit from her backpack. *Bingo.* It was the fifth time that day that Chloe saved them all.

Five minutes later, they slowly wove between offset concrete barriers meant to slow any approaching traffic. A hundred yards from the base's gates, an unseen loudspeaker at the heavily sandbagged guardhouse boomed, "Unknown vehicle! Halt!" Chloe's mom stopped right beside a sign threatening deadly force against unauthorized attempts to enter. "Remain in your vehicle with your hands in sight and make no sudden movements!"

"Jake, put your hands on the dash. Chloe, put yours on Jake's seat back." All sat frozen as a half dozen airmen in full chemical warfare gear approached with rifles and a German shepherd straining on hind legs from a leash and barking. Their weapons were aimed through the windshield. An air policeman's command was muffled by his gas mask. "Turn off the engine and roll down your windows!"

"What if they're infected," Jake asked, "and hiding popped pupils behind masks?"

"Then we're screwed." In slow motion, their mom complied.

"State your business!" came the command from behind the bug-eyed mask.

"My husband flew out of here on government business. See, the car has air force stickers and a parking pass. We wanta wait here for him." When the air policeman asked how long ago he had left, she replied, "About two weeks ago."

That was the wrong thing to say. The airman swung his rifle to point back toward the road and ordered them to reverse all the way to the exit. Chloe's mom tried telling him that they had been *guests* at the quarantine center and they'd be happy to return to one of the trailers. "We're not takin' refugees, lady. Now *move* it!"

"We've got papers!" Chloe said from the back seat. Three rifles turned her way. "Signed by General Browner!" She shoved the crinkled paper through the open window.

"These are just residence permits," replied the man after studying the form.

"But they're signed by General *Browner*," Chloe's mom argued. "You know who he is, right? He's your boss's, boss's, boss's, *boss's* boss."

The airman stepped away for a sidebar with colleagues as the dog reared up and noisily scratched at the car's fading paint. Each tug of its leash loosed a choked growl.

"If you don't know who General Browner is—" Chloe's mom began.

But the airman said, "I know who the fuck he is." He ordered them to proceed, slowly, and the soldiers kept pace with them and their rifles pointed their way. Chloe had thought their plan had worked until they were directed to a turnoff, which lay outside the gate and its double fence. "You park here! No sudden moves!"

They could see the air policeman on the phone, which he hung up after alternating brief conversations and unseen nods with long waits. The muzzle of the machine gun amid sandbags would make short work of their rickety car. Fighter jets took off. Transports landed. A helicopter lifted an artillery piece into the air by a long cable. Civilian airliners taxied out toward the runway.

In the distance, on the other side of the gate, a Humvee arrived and disgorged two pilots in flight suits. One argued and gesticulated in animated fashion. The other hung back sipping on a cup of coffee. The guards argued back until the second pilot tossed his cup to the ground and said something that, apparently, settled the matter.

The gate rose. The first pilot jogged through it toward them. "Dad?" Jake said.

Their mother released the steering wheel, flung open the door, and embraced and kissed her husband. If anyone was infected, they were all infected. Chloe followed Jake out. In seconds, they were all enveloped in a family hug.

The other man in a flight suit approached. "You can take a trailer in quarantine."

Chloe's dad held out his hand for a shake, but the pilot backed away with hands raised to both sides. "Lieutenant Colonel Carpenter," her dad said, "I can't thank you enough."

"Hey, you fulfilled all your duties on the mission. It was the least I could do. But remember *cinco*."

Chapter 42

"This isn't right," Isabel said to Rick's chest as he hugged her goodbye. "*No.* I can *fix* this. Let me message Browner. He got my family back together in Houston. He can—"

"*No*, Isabel. He's got other things on his mind. You know what they're doing out west. Let the man do his job."

She scoffed. "How hard can it be it to...to *vaporize* a bunch of mental defectives?"

"Very hard. You know it is."

Her eyes were welling up. "But...*why*, Rick? After everything we've been through. With...with everything...falling *apart*. Why are you abandoning me *now*?"

"I've got a job to do. Just like you. Only your job now is back in Houston working with that task force studying your sister. Mine is in the field."

"But even *Houston* is dangerous. They had that outbreak."

"And they contained it to just the cordoned off areas."

She knew better than to beg him to shirk his responsibilities. She needed to appeal to his sense of duty. "It could break out again. If it does, I'll *need* you."

He checked, but they were alone. "I'm not supposed to talk about these things."

"I know. But...where *are* you headed?"

"Wisconsin. Not far from my uncle's farm. Straight recon mission, but.....
There's a small outpost—Guardsmen, airmen, state police, navy boots from
the Great Lakes recruit training center—that's holding on, but they're not
trained for long-range patrolling. I know the area, so I volunteered to lead
a team there. If it works out, I can check on my family."

How could she argue? She had pulled countless strings for the
benefit of *her* family.

"I love you," she said. *I don't want you to go!* she didn't say.

"I love you, too." They kissed until it was time and Isabel boarded the
C-130 for her flight back to Houston...alone.

* * * *

After landing at Ellington Field, Isabel found Noah and his family back
in a trailer there. "Full circle, huh?" She gave them her fantastically bleak
report about the atrocities she had witnessed in the Rockies, to which Noah
added his pessimistic reports from farther west. His one hopeful bit of
news concerned the woman and baby from New Guinea who must have
been naturally immune to *Pandoravirus.*

Isabel said nothing about the nuclear attacks, news of which was totally
suppressed in what seemed like a repeat of the first month of the outbreak.
Noah's family painted a picture of an ominous life under martial law, in
constant dread of a quarantine death sentence, failing daily by degrees
and weekly in sudden step changes, all pointing at only one end. In the
glum lull that followed, Natalie asked, extremely tentatively, about Rick.

When Isabel said he'd been sent on a mission, they all seemed relieved.
Apparently, they had been convinced by his absence that Rick was dead.
"He's *fine*," Isabel assured them. "He'll be back in a week or so." Their
sympathy at so naïve and optimistic a hope led to exaggerated but obviously
disingenuous reassurance that of *course* she was right.

"What's *your* plan?" Isabel asked her brother to interrupt the annoying
sympathy. "If the shit hits the fan here again?"

Noah's well thought out plans systematically ruled out north, south,
and west due to insufficient indigenous resources. The only compass point
remaining at least led back toward fresh water and rich farmland.

"Toward *Emma*?" Isabel asked.

Noah shrugged. "At least they're not bombing Virginia."

"Yet."

Their parting hugs and heartfelt goodbyes left Isabel in quiet tears. She felt she was losing everyone. And why wouldn't she feel that way? The whole world was being lost.

The drive downtown had changed dramatically even since Isabel had last taken it seventeen days earlier. Houston was in the tightest grip of martial law possible. Her Humvee stopped time after time at checkpoints along the interstate, the ramp down from the interstate, and every other intersection on surface roads, and she had to endure temperature and pupil checks at each, and behavioral tests—"Soldier crushed under tank; yuck, how gross"—at most.

"Do those gas masks," Isabel asked one questioner, "even work with the virus?"

"What?" replied the soldier. "They might not *work*?"

He startled Isabel. "I'm…sure they're fine. I mean the army wouldn't have you do something stupid, would they?" That apparently did very little to reassure him.

As the elevator rose in Browner's Pentagon South, Isabel rubbed her eyes, which were sore from the repeated pupil checks. The rates of infection should be falling, if Emma's math was correct, as the number susceptible to infection dwindled due to vaccination or, in the vast majority of cases, infection or death. Most Infecteds now would have perfectly normal pupils, but whatever. She was too exhausted to care.

The pace of activity on the floor to which she was directed felt hectic. Male and lots of female soldiers, sailors, airmen, and Marines, many officers, hurried to-and-fro. When finally she found the numbered interior conference room to which she'd been directed, a handwritten sign was taped to the door: "Task Force Dixie."

Cute, she thought, wondering if they dared hang a confederate flag on the wall to help climb into the mindset of her Yankee sister presiding over an atrocity prone, breakaway southern republic.

The activities of the eight people in the large room all came to a stop when Isabel entered. They must not get many visitors. "Hi. I'm—"

"Dr. *Miller*," said a graying man in camo, who extended an elbow for a bump. A large printout of a screen capture of Emma in her hospital gown from the nationally broadcast DHS video was pinned to the fabric walls. Around that photo were others, like mug shots, presumably from intake at the NIH hospital. The little blond girl Samantha. The African American Marine Lance Corporal Dwayne something. The housewife Dorothy, in an action shot with broom in hand. Sheriff Walcott, with a large X across it. And, to Isabel's immense surprise, former President Stoddard.

As she bumped elbows around the room, the introductions and names flew right over Isabel's head. She was too distracted by maps plotting in red the largely, but not entirely contiguous territory constituting Emma's realm together with distant red dots in New England and the upper Midwest. Other areas were filled with other colors—yellow depicting allied communities, she guessed, some crosshatched presumably to convey partial success in Emma's ongoing annexation campaign. And blue around Norfolk and here and there in small dots, which Isabel concluded, when she finally stopped in front of the map, were U.S. armed forces still in the area.

"They seem to be focusing," said the gray haired army officer—Major Kravets, whose name was helpfully sewn above his breast pocket—"on moving east, to the south of Richmond. There's not much population there, but it's fertile farmland. They've also sent emissaries out as far as Detroit and Montreal to gauge interest in a much larger union. Norfolk is keeping a close watch, and if they turn their way they'll call in USSTRATCOM."

Isabel considered asking what the hell that was, but the context was obvious. *Strategic* had come to mean only one thing: *nuclear.* When Isabel's eyes met his, he turned away. "It's okay, major. She's my sister, but I get what we might have to do. What we *are* doing, out west. Believe me, I've been there and I *completely* understand."

"Was it bad?" he asked. His entire team listened intently.

She let out a deep breath. "It's just…killing. Lots and lots and lots of killing. They rip us to shreds. We blow them to pieces. You almost don't even notice the spread of the disease." *Except those raped women,* came the thought and resulting wince.

"I'm sorry," Kravets apologized. "We've been holed up doing intel, mainly mapping, since this thing started. The Pentagon. Raven Rock. Ft. Campbell. Don't know where else we'd go after here. Maybe Colorado Springs. But we don't get to see what's actually happening out there."

"Consider yourselves lucky." She settled in for a go around the table update they had obviously been preparing. In the month since Isabel, Rick, and Noah's family had made it out of *The Community,* as the task force called Emma's kingdom, it had more than doubled in size. "With the latest gains to the east, we now estimate there are over a million residents—*citizens,* I suppose—of The Community, about half of whom are uninfected."

"How is she feeding them all?" Isabel asked.

An army captain explained what they had been able to piece together. She said that Emma's security forces had seized all remaining, unlooted, communal sources of food—stores, warehouses, granaries, mills—but left private supplies alone for now. The latter had contributed to earning her citizens' loyalty, but the imbalance between haves and have-nots had led to a black-market barter system outside regime control and therefore a "network of potential insurgents with whom we have occasional contact."

Potential insurgents. This task force hadn't been convened to *help* Emma's efforts.

One soldier down the table said, "Your sister has an issue with loyalty. We've been getting regular reports out of her council meetings that—"

"*If* they're to be believed," Major Kravets interrupted. The soldier fell silent.

"She's definitely been executing people every day," said a junior officer, straightening her glasses. "Almost every overflight reveals a new mass grave somewhere."

"Are you sure those aren't casualties of infection, or from fighting?"

"We've got imagery of the killings in progress." He found aerial photos on his tablet, which he cast to the room's projector and screen. In one, men and women used rifles to shoot captives from a distance at what looked like a quarry. In another, troops fired pistols point-blank into the heads of men, women, and children kneeling in front of a fresh trench. In a third, machine guns mowed down masses trapped inside a fence. "We've documented eleven established sites that we check daily by drone. She doesn't do *public* executions, so she's not making a big show of it. That makes us think that, in part, she's culling the population of undesirables she doesn't want to have to feed. We estimate her executions number at least 400 a day, which is in addition to the numbers who refuse her demands to join The Community and are executed *in situ* following her overruns."

Isabel was appalled at Emma, but also at the repeated use of *she* and *her* to refer to mass murder. There were half a million Infecteds in Emma's Community, but their crimes—amid the backdrop of worldwide genocide—were being laid at Emma's feet.

They worked till the wee hours of the next morning. Isabel reviewed photos of a large board on which were posted *Rules*—don't breach the peace, everyone over age fourteen has to work seven days a week, no gatherings of more than six people per ten square meters, *etc.* Isabel argued that the fertilizer and pesticide plants Emma seemed intent on securing were of a piece with her recent seizures of fertile farmland. The soldiers' suspicious minds, however, constantly veered toward fertilizer bombs *a la* Oklahoma City, or Zyklon B for her showers. Isabel's defenses of Emma's Community were half-hearted, but someone needed to play devil's advocate, no matter what their true beliefs.

When one by one the soldiers hit their *racks*, Isabel said, "I don't have a rack," even though she wasn't entirely certain what one was. Major

Kravets found an empty cot for her on the far side of the elevator lobby several floors below. The light in the room was dim, and most of the hundred or so staffers there were asleep and snoring. Outside the floor to ceiling windows, little was visible other than the occasional headlights of a truck or searchlights of a low flying helicopter. There had been more lights on her previous visit.

"What we really need," said Major Kravets in a low voice, avoiding eye contact as Isabel stood beside her cot clutching her blanket and pillow to her chest, "is boots on the ground. I've expended all my capital in begging for daily recon sorties out of Virginia Beach, but at this point aerial reconnaissance and signal intelligence doesn't tell us what we need to know. We need HUMINT. We need somebody to go in there."

"To figure out *what*?" Isabel asked in a low voice meant not to disturb anyone.

"Can we coexist with them? Or do we take them out before they grow too big?"

Isabel curled up, fully dressed, under her blanket. Maybe nuclear annihilation was long overdue. Maybe the North Koreans simply hadn't possessed enough nukes to do the job. She tried to imagine it; Emma working at a modest desk in a small room until a bright light flared around curtains that smoked; all the contents of the room being blasted through the far walls, and the unsupported upper floors collapsing.

Nope. Not shocked anymore. Maybe she was just tired. Her head sank deep into the pillow, and her eyelids closed of their own weight. Or maybe something else had changed. Maybe she had grown to accept what Infecteds were, came the last coherent thought before Isabel began repeating her bedtime mantra—*Rick, Rick, Rick*—and calmed enough to descend into nightmares.

Chapter 43

NEW ROANOKE, VIRGINIA
Infection Date 112, 1330 GMT (9:30 a.m. Local)

"Should we announce it?" Samantha asked.

"Announce what?" Emma replied.

"What I just said. That *Pandoravirus* has reached the southern tip of South America." She referred to her notes. "How do you pronounce T-O-L-H-U-I-N, Argentina?"

"I don't know. But why does it matter?"

Samantha was growing increasingly assertive. And Emma no longer controlled what she did with her days, although Dwayne's spy reported her spending time in Uninfecteds' neighborhoods. "It means the infection has spread to every corner of every continent except Australia. That seems like news everyone would want to know."

Emma dismissed the request. "Most Infecteds only care what work they're assigned, what rations they'll receive, and maybe what the weather is. And most Uninfecteds will just redouble their demands for vaccination, which isn't going to happen."

"You said you *would* vaccinate them," Sam said for some unknown reason.

"I lied. To placate them. Surely you knew that."

Samantha grew agitated and began to pace. Agitation *always* interested Emma. She surreptitiously slid open the desk drawer until she could see the butt of Sheriff Walcott's pistol.

"Why *not* vaccinate them?" Samantha's little fists were balled tight. "You agreed they provide 'creativity and initiative.' I wrote your words down. Was that a lie, too?"

"How is the history project coming?" Emma asked.

"I'd prefer it if you answered my question."

"I *am*. How is it going compiling our history of the pandemic?"

"We're doing 300 interviews a day and summarizing the experiences we record."

"And from all those anecdotes by survivors, if you had to draw one conclusion—just one—about the prospects for Infecteds and Uninfecteds living in peace and harmony together in the future, what would that conclusion be?"

"That we need them because they're smart, and creative, and industrious."

The voice cautioned Emma. *She likes Uninfecteds.* Emma remained silent.

"Are you going to infect them all?" Samantha asked in her girlish voice. "Sheriff Walcott had that plan to taint their food."

Emma rocked back in her chair. "Do you have *feelings* for the Uninfecteds?"

"Feelings? Feelings like, maybe, I wanta marry a boy someday? Maybe an uninfected boy, who makes jokes and acts silly and reads books and stays in shape and cares about looking hot? Or do you mean feelings, like, emotions?"

"I'm not sure what I meant, but I think you've answered the question."

"Are you gonna execute me?" Sam asked, her fists balled tight.

"Should I?"

"I think I'm a good worker," the twelve-year-old replied. Or was she thirteen now?

"I do too. But can I trust you?"

"Yes."

"And if I decide the Uninfecteds are a threat to be eliminated?"

Sam hesitated. "That would be a mistake. Machinery would fail. We'd starve."

"And there would be no more cute, silly boys?"

"*You* like uninfected boys too," Samantha replied.

"I never said I didn't. But I've got to know I can trust you, no matter what happens."

There followed the briefest hesitation. "Sure. Always." Blood was visible on Sam's palms as she left Emma's office abruptly. *She's lying,* said the silent voice in Emma's head.

Chapter 44

ELLINGTON FIELD, HOUSTON, TX
Infection Date 114, 1215 GMT (8:15 a.m. Local)

The vaccination protocols were inviolable. No amount of arguing and begging, respectively, by Noah and Natalie Miller convinced the airbase's medics to allow them to wait out the postinoculation quarantine together, as a family. "You're lucky to be getting this at all," the airman said. "But they ordered Ellington to go 100 percent vaccinated."

Noah hugged and kissed Natalie, Chloe, and Jake. They spoke of their love for each other, the parents' pride in their children, the promise of a better future once risk of infection was behind them—essentially everything but, *"Goodbye."* Each rolled up a sleeve, took the shot, stared at the red mark but declined to touch it as if, to do so, would worsen their infection risk, then went outside where they kept the people who waited.

The scene there was surreal. Noah could see his wife, who returned his wave, and his two children, who did not, in their respective plastic chairs ten yards from their closest neighbor. A bottle of water sat beside each—the only accommodation they were afforded.

The hundred odd chairs filled over time. The sun lay behind a veil of haze and the weather was mild. Noah wondered what they did when it rained as bewildered airmen and civilians joined them. Who the latter were, Noah had no idea. Families of airmen, maybe? Or the relatives of the high and mighty? Or simply people who'd been lucky—or unlucky—enough, like the Millers, to be on base when the vaccines arrived?

Noah's eyes returned repeatedly to his family. He knew the math. Four people, each with a 6 percent chance of infection, meaning each had a 94 percent chance they wouldn't contract *Pandoravirus*. That's 0.94 times 0.94 times 0.94 times 0.94. Jake's iPhone calculation was rerun by both his parents. They all came to the same conclusion. There was a 78 percent chance that none of them would get sick, but that meant there was a 22 percent chance that someone would. Which one? There was no such thing as acceptable losses, but there was a 22 fucking percent chance someone would get sick. Half would die. There was over a one in ten chance that one of Natalie, Chloe, Jake, or Noah would die within hours from that single, one-second injection. Noah tried to think about anything other than that.

Jake kept scratching the site of his shot. Chloe's head darted from side to side in a constant sweep of the basketball courts, presumably looking for anyone showing signs of illness but also, possibly, reflecting anxiety over emerging symptoms. Natalie stared at the ground, minute after minute, without moving. Either she couldn't stand looking at her husband and children for fear that she saw them clutching their stomach or head, or *she* felt pain herself and was trying her mightiest to hide it for as long as possible.

Noah tried to distract himself by counting the number of people sitting in the chairs. He gave up at eighty-six and estimated that there were easily twenty or thirty more. That meant six to seven ought to get sick. There were two elevated platforms keeping watch over them—one, a proper guard tower with opaque tinted windows, bristling with security cameras and antennas. The other was an ordinary cherry picker housing a single, helmeted man behind a machine gun pointed at the courts.

A hand went up. A stout airman rose. Not a sound was uttered, but every head turned his way. A medic in full camo but wearing goggles, mask, gloves, and an apron approached, but not too closely. Two men in chemical warfare gear and carrying assault rifles backed him up. The machine gunner in the cherry picker swiveled his weapon.

The conversation was brief and quiet. The medic produced a white coverall. The airman, maybe in his forties, climbed into it and the mask, hood, gloves, and goggles that followed. He looked all around, apparently knew no one, but waved and received hesitant nods in return from several nearby soldiers and civilians. Then he was gone.

Noah found Natalie staring at him. He raised his fingers to make the okay sign. She did not. *What does* that *mean?* Jake was now hugging himself. Chloe was fidgeting, shifting in her seat, sitting on one foot, swinging the other.

A woman leaned over to one side and vomited. People in chairs nearby rose, but a loudspeaker boomed, "Stay in your places! I repeat. Stay in your places." The medic helped the sobbing woman into her coveralls and escorted her toward a low concrete building in the distance near the earthen mounds Noah assumed were ammo bunkers. *Was that where they killed them?* He had heard no gunshots after the first man departed.

Armed airmen turned the woman's chair upside down and put orange traffic cones around it, and they covered the vomitus with what looked to be finely ground sawdust and, from a large plastic jug, some kind of white powder. Everyone around sat sidesaddle to face—and breathe—in any direction but toward the condemned and contaminated site.

Every time the wind blew from that direction, Noah held his breath. He knew he was supposed to be safe. Every seat was widely spaced—at least the minimum ten meters that would keep you from inhaling the virus in quantities sufficient to overwhelm your body's defenses—but why take chances? One way or another, in a few hours he would never have to worry about infection by *Pandoravirus* again.

Natalie raised her hand. *"Natalie?"* he called out involuntarily.

"Mom?" Chloe added.

The medic approached. Noah rose to his feet. *"Sir,"* came the loudspeaker. "Take your seat immediately!" The medic departed, leaving Natalie where she sat.

"Mom?" Jake called out.

She shook her head and waved both hands in air as if to deflect his concern. But she sat forward, rocking slightly, and pinned her hands beneath her thighs just like Noah's infected sister Emma had done to restrain herself from unspeakable acts of violence.

For the next hour, Noah scanned not the basketball court generally, but his son, his daughter, and especially his wife. Natalie raised her head only to check her kids and to catch Noah's eye, but she made no attempt to communicate her condition despite Noah's repeated, pantomimed attempts to elicit a report.

Natalie's head shot around to another retching civilian—a little boy—before he was taken away despite the cries of parents barely restrained by increasingly threatening loudspeaker calls. Natalie's chair scraped the pavement when she jumped on hearing the wail of an airman, who pounded her thighs with both fists and ignored as long as possible the white coverall extended to her. Minutes later, Natalie could barely look at a teenager, who kept shouting, "Mom! Dad!" as she was led off, and the demands of her parents—"Where the hell are you taking her? What are you going to do?"

Another unlucky man—a camo-clad airman—just stood, raised both hands over his head as if in surrender, and met the medic several paces from his chair. The voice over the loudspeaker said, "Good luck, Master Sergeant."

There was a slender airman, who stamped his feet on the ground and clung to his plastic chair with both hands. Two armed airmen in gas masks tried reasoning with him, then summoned help. Six men finally pried the chair from his grip, held him down, and forcibly gave him an injection. His thrashing and flailing settled into an animal sounding whine. Noah could see, as he lay on his side, that the seat of the man's pants was stained by diarrhea. His masked comrades managed to guide the now more compliant man into his coveralls and onto a stretcher, on which they finally took him to the concrete building.

Natalie was staring at Noah. People all around were crying. Not just the relatives of the sick children, who were doubled over or chanting, "Why? Why? Why?" But people around them, who were sobbing in sympathy, or crushed by the overwhelming sadness of it all.

"Attention. Attention," came from the loudspeaker. "Immunity bracelets are available at the southeast gate. Please place one on the arm in which you received your injection. You are free to return to duty or to your trailers. Quarantine is terminated."

A cheer went up. Not lustily, not unrestrained, and not universal, but a muted *hurrah* at having made it through. Not so, however, one family, which gathered around the matriarch, who collapsed to the ground in the arms of her surviving children and husband.

Another family rushed the airmen at the base of the guard tower. Parents pointed toward the concrete building where their young son had been taken and demanded to see him. One, and only one, airman raised his mask and spoke to the parents sympathetically, but they were having none of it. Finally, the mother took off toward the concrete building, and the airman chased her down, restrained her despite the arguing of her husband and feeble punches of young children. The woman was put in plastic ties and led away shouting, "William! Williaaaaam! Mommy loves you! Mommy will always love you!"

Jake and a teary-eyed Chloe joined Noah for a hug from which they watched the commotion—yet another tragic fate the Miller family had escaped—but Natalie studiously avoided the scenes of tragedy as she dabbed at her eyes with a tissue. "Let's go."

"What was that about when you called the medic over?" Noah asked.

"It was nothing," Natalie said, not making eye contact.

"*Nothing?* You scared the *shit* outta me."

"*Yeah*, Mom," Chloe added. "That wasn't cool."

Natalie ignored them. They got in line at the gate. After last temperature checks, they gave their names and the injection numbers written on their arms, and received green rubber wristbands. They were now in some database. It was official. They were immune.

Noah, however, didn't yet feel like celebrating. Chloe punched Jake's arm on his injection site—"*Ow! Jesus*, that hurt!"—but they were grinning and joking.

"You kids walk ahead," Noah told them. Chloe looked suspiciously at her inscrutable mother before dragging her confused brother out of earshot. In low tones, Noah said, "Natalie, why did you call that medic over?"

She stared at the concrete sliding by beneath their boots. "I had a question."

"You scared the crap outta us because you had a fucking *question*? *What* question?"

She took her time answering. Chloe kept glancing back at them. "Remember when they asked if anyone was pregnant?" They had also asked about immunity compromising diseases like HIV and diabetes. "I was asking about birth defects."

It slowly dawned on Noah what she was implying. "But you're on the *pill*."

"Shhhh." Both kids turned toward them. "I didn't like the way they made me feel."

"You never complained *before*," Noah said in an artificially restrained voice.

"I never had to take the midnight to four watch, Noah."

"So...?"

"It was in Tennessee. In that utility closet, when Rick took the others out on patrol."

"Jesus, Natalie, what were you thinking?"

"I was thinking we were gonna die, Noah! That...that we were never gonna get out of there! We *should* be dead by now. *All* of us. I thought that was the last time we'd ever make love. The last time I'd feel...like a woman, I guess. I was sure we only had one, maybe two days left. Max. I never imagined I'd get *pregnant*."

Noah's arm went around Natalie's shoulder, and her head instantly fell to his chest. Chloe nudged Jake, who turned to take in this latest hint at what was happening.

"Are you sure?" he asked.

"My periods are like the fucking atomic clock. Lucky me, didn't miss a beat even when we got chased outta the Old Place. First night I spent sleeping outdoors. *Ever*. First time I'd shot a gun at a person. *Ever*. First time I'd ever fought fucking zombies. *Ever.* First time I'd killed a half dozen people in a day. *Ever.* And the first time I'd watched my kids and husband almost get killed a dozen fucking times. *Ever.* Most women's cycles would be totally thrown off. Not mine."

"So, you've missed a period?"

Natalie's mouth opened wide. "Oh. You're so *smart.* You figured that out?"

He ignored that. "What did the medic say?"

"She said, and I quote, 'I dunno.' Then she asked me if I was preggers, and I lied and said no."

"Why *didn't* you tell them? About being pregnant? *Before* getting the shot?"

Natalie stopped. "Because, Noah, they wouldn't have *given* me the fucking shot." She took off after the kids. Noah caught up with her and slowed her down.

"Do you wanta...?"

"*Keep* it? It could come out horribly deformed. It could, I don't know, maybe catch the virus and turn, *in utero*, and gouge my eyes out during breastfeeding. Or it could be a perfect, beautiful, healthy baby." She seemed to gauge Noah's view on the subject by studying his face. What did she see there? What did he feel? "How can we terminate this pregnancy, Noah? Billions of people are dying all over the globe. The world needs life."

But if we can't outrun a mob, Noah thought, *or keep a crying baby quiet....* He kept those worries to himself and kissed Natalie long enough for his wife's arms to wrap around his neck and for his kids to return to embrace them both.

"You're pregnant, aren't you?" Chloe said. Her mother nodded, smiling through tears. "See?" Chloe backhanded Jake's injection site. "You owe me five billion bucks."

Jake pulled free and asked, "When the hell did you...?"

"Nope," Natalie interrupted, marching off toward the trailer arm in arm with Noah.

Chapter 45

Isabel had been stopping by General Browner's office every day, and every day had been informed the general wasn't in. Her purported purpose was to talk to him about some thoughts she had on Emma and her kingdom. Her ulterior motive was to ask about Rick.

She wasn't sure what she would say to Browner about Emma if asked. Her Community was a hopeful self-organization that promised to quell the violence, at least the non-state-sponsored kind. But overflight video and still photos of men, women, even children standing in front of a ditch half filled with lye-covered bodies were horrific, even if the victims were Infecteds. *However,* she had reasoned silently on more charitable mornings when life seemed brighter, *the detainees had presumably broken at least one of Emma's Rules—committing murder or rape...or skipping afternoon calisthenics.*

Then, there were the darker times. She hated going to bed alone. She had grown used to Rick's body heat beside her. His smell, even when unshowered, was a comfort. His steady breathing was calming even when he snored. She would always try to edge close enough to him to hear his heart, halting her efforts when he stirred.

These days, things seemed bleaker at bedtime. She had never gotten enough work done, so sleep was an admission of defeat. There were more reports to read. More tangential facts to weigh in assessing just how dangerous a well-organized Infected state would be. Facts like their barbaric slaughter of men, women, children, and the elderly after communities resisted annexation. How could any *one* of those monstrous atrocities be ignored, much less *numerous* documented massacres? *All Infecteds are evil,* she concluded each night as she tossed and turned on the cot in the elevator lobby. Each morning, however, she awoke to the promise that maybe *evil* was too strong a word.

General Browner's aide rose from her stoop over the desk of Browner's camo-clad male secretary and gatekeeper. "Hello, Dr. Miller," Ensign Somebody said.

"I know, I know," Isabel said with a smile, "he's not in."

"No, he's in. But he's in a meeting. Do you want to leave a message?"

She had declined to do so each earlier visit. She had wanted to give Browner the opportunity to update her on Rick's well-being. "Yeah, actually. Major Kravets thinks we need human intelligence out of southwest Virginia and ought to resume our reconnaissance missions there on the ground."

"I'll pass that along to General Browner."

Isabel thanked her and returned to her work. Less than an hour later, Isabel was pouring over a long list of assets big and small located in Community territory—bridges, factories, heavy equipment yards, even the locations of underground storage tanks at corner gas stations. The *assets* looked more and more like a preliminary target list.

The door to the conference room opened behind where she sat. "Aaa-ten-*shun!*" Everyone in the room leapt to their feet. She turned to see General Browner. "Dr. Miller, may I borrow you for a sec?"

Isabel followed Browner into the corridor. People there steered a wide path around the four star Marine general. Isabel had met him days into the pandemic—Infection Date 8, when she had learned about *Pandoravirus* and the Severe Encephalopathic Disease it had caused in her sister. In the three months since, Browner had aged. The bags under his eyes had grown. His ruddy vigor had been replaced by a grayish pallor.

"I came by to see you," Isabel said, "about Major Kravets saying we needed—"

"Captain Townsend is missing in action."

It took Isabel a moment to catch the drift of his comment. To find a handle to latch onto so that she could begin to grasp what he'd said. "What...what does that mean?"

"We know he made it to his drop-off point—"

"The outpost?"

Browner shrugged. He seemed unwilling to describe it as an outpost, even though that hardly sounded as secure as a base or a fort. Isabel didn't collapse or dissolve into tears. She wondered how many times Browner had given similarly bad news.

"Their position was overrun six hours later. We're not sure if Townsend's team was still there. And we're not sure how many survivors there were." *If any,* Isabel heard him imply. "Our only way of contacting Captain Townsend after that Osprey left was a longer range radio set used by the unit that was overrun. Townsend's portable comms are all short range."

"What about a satellite phone?" Isabel picked at details to avoid the main news.

"He doesn't have one. The civilian system has crashed since he used it in Virginia. And our military comms are highest priority only. They didn't have the gear."

She nodded. "He's probably gone to his uncle's farm. It's in Wisconsin. His family is there. Just go pick him *up*."

While torture would be too dramatic a description, her words at least bothered Browner. "We know about his parents' farm *and* his uncle's farm. I'm sorry, Dr. Miller—Isabel—but there's nothing we can do right now."

"You can't fly someone up there to pick him up?"

He sighed. "It would take another Osprey running on high engine hours. Two, to be safe, in case of a mechanical failure. With no fuel at their destination, they'd need midair refueling on the way there, and more on the way back. Those packages would need at least four standby combat search and rescue teams, at least two of those prepositioned in infected territory and holding their ground for the better part of a day. That means fixed-wing ground attack support aircraft waiting on calls, more midair refueling, more CSAR."

"What you're saying is that it *can* be done, but Rick's just not *worth* it."

"I'm saying I'd be putting all those lives at risk on nothing more than a hope that Captain Townsend succeeded in escaping the overrun and in leading his men across a hundred miles of hostile territory to his uncle's farm. He wouldn't even be there yet if they were on foot. And every one of those men and women I'd be sending out there, Isabel, has loved ones worried sick about them, too. Yes, it's a risk/reward or cost/benefit calculation, and it doesn't tilt in favor right now of a rescue attempt and may never. But that's not because I don't value the lives of Captain Townsend and his men. I assure you that I do, very much."

"How about an overflight? Or satellite photos? You've still got satellites, right?"

"Some. One. It's running low on maneuvering fuel, but…I'll check into it."

"He'll be fine," she said to reassure the general, though he looked back at her in sympathy. "He's been through worse. And now he's somewhere in *Wisconsin*, not China."

By the time Browner departed with a gentle squeeze of her arm, Isabel had almost talked herself into optimism. She went to the bathroom, closed the stall door, and waited. Surely now she would cry. She sat on the toilet seat fully clothed, staring at the door. No tears came. Rick was still alive, she realized, and as long as that fact was true she was okay.

Back in the conference room, she replied, "Nothing," repeatedly to questions about General Browner's surprise visit. As the day wore on, however, her dread grew. Night was approaching, and with it...bedtime.

Chapter 46

Emma and Samantha watched people disperse after publication of the daily Rules. "They only read the changes," Samantha said. "And I didn't see anyone who acted like they're leaving. That must mean they were okay with today's Rules."

"The Infecteds don't appreciate what the testing means," Emma suggested, watching the first of the people whose names appeared on the training calendar head for the church. "Once they do, there could be trouble."

"The testing is designed so that their best chance, each step of the way, is to go along with the process to the end."

"Until," Emma noted, "the moment they realize they're failing. It has always bothered me that they fail by getting too agitated to control themselves. Is that the best time to euthanize them? When their adrenal response is surging?"

"Is there a better time?" Samantha had either asked a straightforward question, or learned to use rhetorical remarks in speech...like an Uninfected. Emma couldn't tell which.

"Do you feel more at home with Infecteds," Emma asked the girl, "or Uninfecteds?"

"What does *feel more at home* mean?"

"I don't know. It seemed like a question that made sense. Never mind. Who did you end up putting in charge of the executions of Rule breakers and test failures?"

"Dwayne has temporarily taken over the SE police."

Emma surveyed Samantha. There was something different about her. Granted, Emma increasingly had no contact with other Infecteds or with Uninfecteds. The latter thankless duty—typically listening to some mixture of angry demands and none too veiled threats—she now left to Angela Stoddard. As for meeting Infecteds, Emma realized that she either saw the stumbling, semi-brain-dead condemned on their way to execution, or quiet functionaries like Dwayne doing their uninspired best. Were there Infected geniuses out there plowing the fields? Were any exhibiting the first stirrings of whatever was going on in Samantha's head? A primitive, budding sense of self? The faint distracting call of some long ago feelings like love and admiration and those other words?

"You still seeing that boy?" Emma asked Sam. It was a pretty nimble attempt at subterfuge, Emma thought—and it worked.

"What boy?"

Aha. She is *seeing* some *boy.* Emma tried fishing again. "That *Un*infected boy?"

Samantha couldn't hold Emma's gaze. That seemed odd. What could be preventing her eyes meeting Emma's? "Is there a Rule against Infecteds and Uninfecteds hanging out?"

"Should there be?"

"No."

"What's his name?"

"Why? You're not going to kill him, are you?"

"Why would I do that?"

"I dunno." Samantha's trim shoulders rose and fell.

Sam said *I* a lot. All the time, in fact. "Can I ask what you see in whoever he is?"

"Yes. I'd like to tell you. He's cute. Tall. Has a nice face. He's been teaching me how to smile." Samantha bared her teeth, still squinting. "He likes music. He pretends to play the guitar and drums when there's a loud song on, but I took him to the high school's band room and he didn't know what to do with a real guitar or drums. That's interesting, don't you think?"

"How old is he?"

"Almost sixteen."

"You're going to be careful, right?"

"I know the Rules. I wrote them, remember? But eighteen is kind of old. You said we could use more babies."

"Years from now we can use them. Right now, they're another burden."

"Speaking of babies...." Samantha said, going on to describe Dorothy's progress in setting up an orphanage for Infected children and infants. She had *read Emma's mind*. That's what it seemed like—like that old expression Emma remembered from pre-outbreak. To Emma's knowledge, Samantha was the only Infected with that kind of insight. "I asked Dorothy if we should call it an orphanage if their parents are still alive, but she didn't understand. I suppose, though, that if your parents are Infected, they've sort of automatically abandoned you, right? And abandoned children—"

"Foundlings," Emma supplied from distant memory. "That's what they're called."

"How about calling Dorothy's centers *foundling homes*?"

"Orphanage is fine. No sense wasting resources making up new names for things."

There was a single gunshot from the opposite side of the church. "That was quick," Emma said. "They just got started testing. Wanta go watch the next execution?"

"Sure." Off they went toward the far side of the testing center.

Chapter 47

Task Force Dixie's report to General Browner was as divided as its member's opinions were conflicted. On the whole, Isabel observed, it was an exercise in evenhandedness. On the one hand, Emma was pacifying lawless infected areas. On the other, she was doing it through mass murder. They enumerated reasons to ally themselves with Emma, and to nuke her to smithereens. As important as the decision was—for Emma, for the million odd residents of The Community, and for Isabel—she grew impatient for any news Browner might share with her about Rick, his whereabouts, and whether or not he was still alive.

"So you've achieved no consensus?" Browner summed up.

"Unfortunately, no, sir," said Major Kravets. "The Community's paramilitary forces pose no current threat to our troops, but they are overwhelming holdout uninfected towns with ease, and when a fight does ensue, they're unleashing abhorrent levels of butchery. Their forces will, however, continue to scale up, and we see no natural obstacles restricting their growth throughout the Southeast north of South Florida, west of Norfolk, and east of the Appalachians. That could conceivably entail up to a ten X, even a twenty X growth in population and might ultimately even encompass Atlanta, Charlotte, Jacksonville, and Tampa. That's before we factor in any expansion into the Northeast and Upper Midwest. On the other hand, based on the latest recon out of those areas, it would be difficult to imagine a situation that bad not being improved upon pacification by The Community."

Isabel awaited an eruption of frustration from the Marine general. But Browner remained calm. Perhaps he had known that their conclusions would be equivocal.

"I'm not going to ask for a show of hands," Browner said, "or for a vote on a course of action this nation should take in addressing *The Community*." For whatever reason, his stressing of words put verbal air quotes around the name. Maybe it was simply a new term to those outside Task Force Dixie. Or maybe its continued existence was very much in doubt so why formally recognize it diplomatically or cartographically. "But I do have a thought exercise for you. Assuming that Emma Miller's Community *does* avoid direct conflict with our forces in order to stave off open warfare with us, but assuming also that it expands everywhere across the map that we *aren't*—unconstrained by mountains or rivers or national, state, or county lines—where would *that* leave us?"

Heads turned but ended up staring mutely at their task force's leader. "We would be surrounded, sir," replied the army major, "and vastly outnumbered." Browner scanned the conference table for any disagreement, but that conclusion appeared unanimous. Even Isabel bobbed her head once in agreement.

"And if they surround and outnumber us," Browner said, "with control over all the resources we don't stake out and defend, they will ultimately be capable of challenging and possibly defeating us militarily. If that's the case, the only things missing are their intentions. Emma *Miller's* intentions. Would she be an ally? A neutral third party with whom we could trade and have a reliable nonaggression pact? Or an existential threat to be defeated lest they defeat us first? What do we know about her current plans?"

The task force commander turned to Isabel, but she had no intention of answering. "We don't know anything about her intentions, sir," Major Kravets replied. "It's easy to count vehicles and personnel, track movements and expanding boundaries, monitor economic production, demographics, crops in the fields. But they obviously don't publish white papers, have legislative debates, or produce analyses by a semi informed press or best guess punditry. And given the changes to Infecteds' decision making faculties, it's fair to say we know less about their intentions than we ever did about the Soviet Union, or Communist China, or North Korea. The leaders of those countries were, at least...."

When he faltered, Isabel said, "...*normal*?" She turned to Browner. "I'm afraid I have to concur, sir."

Browner rocked back in his chair at the head of the table while drawing a deep breath. "I presume you all know what the National Security Council will have to advise the president in this situation, don't you? When we know that The Community may soon grow into a peer competitor that has the capability of defeating us militarily, but we have no idea what its intentions are?" His sweeping gaze ended on Isabel.

"Assume the worst?" she replied.

"Exactly. In the absence of intentions, all we've got to go on are capabilities. And given that theirs are rising and ours are falling, time is not on our side. We have to make a go/no go decision soon. We should either engage in diplomacy with them, or prevent their rise before it's too late. That might mean a decapitation strike and materiel support for a follow-on insurgency, unrestricted strategic bombing, or both."

The conference room remained totally silent. No one, especially Isabel, offered Browner any advice. This was far above their pay grades.

"If I wasn't clear," Browner said, "I'm inviting you to propose ways that we can learn Emma's intentions so that I don't, solely due to the absence of that knowledge, have to obliterate the better part of a million people, half *un*infected. So…ideas?"

Kravets gamely gave it a try. "They're getting radio and TV back on the air for several hours a day, and we're monitoring everything they broadcast. But so far it's just news, weather, job postings, and Rules, nothing like analysis or political talk or even propaganda that might hint at their plans. The only anomaly is that they have begun re-airing some old sitcoms, movies, and sporting events, which could only be for the purpose of entertaining their uninfected population. That may suggest that their longer term plans are to cater to the needs of, and to maintain, their uninfected *members*. But as you know, signal intel and overflights don't tell us everything we need to know about intentions. Nor does observation from a distance by ground recon missions. We need better human intel."

Isabel pointedly avoided returning any of the half dozen looks from around the table. She did, however, note that Browner's gaze was not among them.

"Okay," Browner said, pushing back from the table and rising, but not before the dozen or so soldiers in the conference room shot to their feet at rigid attention.

Isabel chased Browner into the corridor. He stopped and waited without even seeing her on his heels. Unbidden, he said, "We had one satellite overpass this morning. I was hopeful, but it was at an extremely oblique angle. They couldn't see anything at the farms of Captain Townsend's parents or uncle. No signs on lawns or fields or messages stamped down onto crops. No reflective panels or mirrors or white sheets. No signs of physical destruction or fighting. It still could be that there's a big, log SOS right behind a hill, or some trees, or a barn, or a house—the imagery's angle was, as I said, at an extreme oblique—but...I'm sorry. There's nothing I can do until I have some reason, any reason, to believe that he's still alive."

"Nothing from the outpost where he landed?"

"Yes, there is. We've counted the bodies, in uniform, uncollected out in the open, which is consistent with 100 percent KIA. And the position appears to have been totally looted by Infecteds. It's possible that people scattered and are—or were—running for their lives." Isabel's eyes rose when he put his big paw on her shoulder. "But Isabel, I'm sorry. This is the way it ends these days. No dogtag collection and graves registration marker. No coffin. No taps. No folded flag. Two thirds of the forces we've lost are labeled 'missing in action presumed killed.' That latter label, *presumed killed*, we added to Captain Townsend's jacket this morning. I'm sorry."

His hand felt warm on her shoulder.

"I'll do it," she said.

"Pardon me?"

"I'll go back to Virginia. To Roanoke. I'll meet with Emma and try to figure out what she's planning."

"Isabel, I can't ask you to do that."

"You're not. I'm volunteering."

"Because of Captain Townsend?"

She shrugged, shaking his hand loose. "Because of Rick. Because I don't really have anything or anyone left. And because I'd like to think I might save my sister and all those people from annihilation if all they're doing is eking out an existence."

"Do you realize how dangerous that mission would be?"

"Yeah, I imagine. But it probably won't be any worse than some of the places I've been recently. And Rick taught me a lot. I know my way around an M4."

Browner smiled, but not in amusement. More in recognition of something he thought he might have seen in her all along. Or so she imagined.

"You know also, don't you," Browner said, "that if you report that we should trust your sister, there are going to be doubters who discount your opinion because they think you're lying to save her." Isabel nodded. "You'll need facts to support *any* conclusion, but *that* conclusion especially. And the first place I'd start is what the hell they're doing in gyms and auditoriums and theaters and churches all over her territory. All we know is that they've been sending military age males and females inside, and they're either being dragged out one by one and getting a bullet, or they're coming out *en masse* at the end of the day and sometimes going for group jogs…in formation. We haven't detected any form of basic military training, outdoors at least where we can observe them, but my fellow chiefs are pretty convinced that's the beginning of a general mobilization. Anything you can find out about what's going on in those buildings would help fill in the blanks. Are you sure you want to try? Captain Townsend could still turn up."

"He will," she said, "but I'll go. At least maybe I'll get to see my sister again."

Browner nodded. "Okay. We'll get you fully briefed and kitted out. We'll drop you as close as we can, but we've got an agreement with your sister that the defined Exclusion Zone in the Appalachians will remain demilitarized. We have reason to believe Emma is sending forces into the Exclusion Zone in violation of that agreement, presumably because they're getting raided constantly by hungry people from there, mostly Infecteds, but we are still honoring our side of that deal. What that means is that your infiltration will require a few days' march from your drop-off point to get through it." She nodded, again accepting the mission despite her growing appreciation of its risks. "You probably oughta say your goodbyes to your family." Another nod. "And one word of fashion advice." She looked up. "I'd cut your hair to match your sister's, which has grown out a little as best as I could tell based on her last TV appearance. It might come in handy."

* * * *

"You cut your hair!" Isabel's niece, Chloe, practically shrieked on opening the trailer door. Isabel hugged each of Noah's children and wife in turn, followed with a long, meaningful, loving embrace by her older brother.

"I've been so worried about you," Noah said. "Come fill us in. What's going on?"

That consumed most of Isabel's time with them before she had to present herself at the airbase's hangar. Her description of what was happening in Emma's Community left Noah and family with the same question as Browner—was that great, or terrifying?

The one subject that wasn't raised but was clearly in everyone's thoughts was Rick. Isabel finally decided to throw it out there. "Rick's missing in action." She couldn't bring herself to append, "and presumed killed." Natalie slid her chair over to the trailer's banquette and wrapped her arms around Isabel. Chloe knelt on the opposite side and did the same. To Isabel's amazement, it actually helped ease her distress enough that tears began to flow. She was safe enough there in their embrace to confront the possibility that Rick's luck had run out and his skill had finally proven insufficient.

It was Noah who put things right again. "Rick Townsend is the most impressive soldier I've ever seen. Or Marine, I guess." Natalie and Chloe released her. "If *anyone* can survive, it's him. And if anyone can find a way back to you, he will. He loves you, and I'm betting on him making it."

"*Thank* you!" Isabel said, throwing her arms around Noah. "Thank you!"

Jake awkwardly patted Isabel's shoulder and got a hug. She forced out a smile to help put a stop to the tears, and wiped her face dry. Noah was right. Rick was a survivor, and he was as in love with her as she was with him. There was hope.

"So...what's up with you?" Isabel asked, sniffling, to change the subject. "Anything new?"

"Mom's preggers," Chloe blurted out.

"*What?*" When Natalie confirmed it with a curt nod and suppressed grin, Isabel congratulated her and embraced her again, and said, "*Jeez*, Noah," in good-natured jest that mostly amused and simultaneously repulsed his children.

"And we're all immune now," Natalie reported. "We got vaccinated."

"Wonderful! It's such a *relief*, isn't it? I mean, I didn't wanta say anything before. But just not having to worry about infection...."

"Now, we just worry about everything else," Noah said. When Isabel checked her watch, Noah said, "You have to go somewhere?" She nodded. "Where?"

She took a deep breath. "I'm not supposed to say, but...Virginia."

"You're kidding," Noah replied. "Isabel, you can't be serious."

"I'm gonna go try to meet with Emma. She and that crew from up at the cabin—her roommates at the NIH hospital, your *clients*—now have over a million people in the territory they're governing, and they're doing a pretty good job of getting their economy going. Towns and cities all around them—or parts of them—are applying to join despite the fact that, well, they're a pretty brutal bunch."

"Don't do it, Iz," Noah said, grabbing both of her hands in his as he leaned over to her from his seat. "Rick will make it back here, and you'll be way off in that hellhole we barely escaped." He looked around at his kids. Natalie nodded at him. "I'm not supposed to say anything about this, but when I was flying back to Houston from Las Vegas, I saw a nuclear detonation. They're *nuking* people—Infecteds—out west, Iz." That was obviously news to the kids, who stared at each other in wide-eyed, slack-jawed silence. "They could start nuking places back east, too."

"I know, Noah. I know. That's why I've got to go. There's a chance that Emma could get everything under control. Who else besides her—besides a freaking ruthless, sociopathic infected control freak—could restore order and security and put a stop to the violence."

"By using even more violence?" Noah pointed out.

"We don't have good intel, but there's a sense that their executions are trending down as the number of crazies are reduced. There are always spikes when there's a new spread of the infection, but what if she culls the most violent Infecteds and the ones who're left are people we can live with? Trade with? Trust to honor pacts and treaties?"

"You believe that's possible?" Natalie asked.

"Treaties are just contracts. Why not?"

"And so," Noah summed up, "some Green Berets or whatever are going to escort you back through all that shit—"

"I'm going alone, after they drop me in. We have a deal with Emma that we won't make incursions into her territory, and the military doesn't want to breach it."

Noah rocked back. "Jesus. Okay. *You*, alone, are gonna fight your way into Infected territory, and if you make it march up to Emma's headquarters and do what?"

She shrugged. "Figure out what she's doing, and report back my opinion about whether we can, you know, get along with them, or whether...."

"Or whether we nuke them? Don't do it, Iz. Don't go. How would you get back?"

"Norfolk isn't that far. And I'll get one of their precious military sat phones. They're gonna give all that stuff to me in a few minutes when I show up at the main hangar."

Isabel suffered through the urgings of Noah and his entire family until she finally said, "*No.* It's decided. *I've* decided. It's something I can do that maybe will help. It maybe will save Emma's life and the lives of those million people who seem to be getting a handle on things. You know what it's like out West. And in the Northeast and Midwest. Basically everywhere the infection has spread *except* Emma's Community. If there's a chance—even a *glimmer* of a chance—that she's on to something and we can coexist with Infecteds, we can't blast them to pieces. We've got to try and help make it work. And no one is better situated than me to go on this mission. It's me, or it's nukes."

After a long silence ensued, she asked—again to change the subject—what Noah was going to do if the outbreaks resumed and Houston fell. "Where would I find you?"

He had an answer. "Because we've been vaccinated, they're letting us come and go from the base...for now, anyway. We went on short rations so we could build a surplus of food. This is Texas, so there are lots of guns. I traded food for four rifles and a pistol. We've repacked and hidden our go bags. If they kick us off the base, or if Houston goes under, we'll grab 'em and hit the road again. Like I said before, my plan is to head east parallel to I-10 until we find someplace. There are still a number of uninfected towns back that way. They've got water and are still farming, I hear. Being vaccinated may make us useful to them. So somewhere along I-10 East is where we'll be...if the worst happens."

The farewells were heartbreaking. Isabel had to endure more pleas of, "Don't go." She knew she might never see them again. But if she were honest, she would've told Noah that the one thing she still sought most from whatever remained of her time on earth was to reestablish some connection—any connection—with her sister. She could save Emma and her Community, and help bridge the divide between Infecteds and Uninfecteds, by rebuilding bonds with her twin. That was Isabel's personal plan.

She waved one last time at the huddle of Noah, Natalie, Chloe, and Jake, who embraced each other inside the quarantine center's gate. The walk in darkness toward the well-lit hangar gave Isabel time to compose herself. To convince herself that she was doing the right thing even though she knew Rick would have totally opposed it. But Rick was probably dead. She knew it. It was bound to happen sooner or later, probably to all of them, if she were honest with herself. You tempt fate, over and over, and win, until you don't and fate finally prevails. At least it hadn't been Isabel or *her* stupid ideas that had gotten Rick killed.

They were waiting when she arrived. An army sergeant issued her weapons and gear. "I'd prefer an M4," she said, nodding at the now familiar carbine. "And a 9mm." An air force lieutenant handed her a rugged military satellite phone. "It has DoD GPS, voice, and data."

There were a series of button pushes that sent codes that she was tasked with memorizing. The first were milestones along the route that a Special Forces captain joined in to teach her. Arrival at checkpoints in the Exclusion Zone, culminating in contact with Emma's forces or officials. "The Exclusion Zone is a demilitarized region in the mountains west of The Community. It's filled with people—infected and uninfected—who fled The Community, and they're now starving and desperate. That's the most dangerous part of your ingress."

Isabel's briefer said Emma's security troops would probably confiscate her equipment, so the next time they'd expect to hear back from her would be when she sent one of two codes. The first—Function, D, 1, Send—meant she was in contact with her sister and able to speak free of duress. The second—Function, D, 2, Send—meant she was under duress, and nothing thereafter that she said was to be trusted unless and until she sent the first code. "There is one more code, however, that you should know about. You can send it at any time, notwithstanding a duress code having previously been transmitted. That's Function, X, 9, Send. You transmit that if, in your opinion, there is no possibility of ever striking any reliable agreements or cooperating in any beneficial way with your sister's Community. Remember this one. Function, X, 9, Send. One more thing you should know. If you send a code indicating entry into your sister's territory or contact with The Community's forces, that starts a twenty-four-hour clock. If you haven't called or sent any other codes in the next twenty-four hours, they're going to assume the worst. It's like it defaults to X9. Twenty-four hours."

"What happens if I send X9?" Isabel asked. "Or if the twenty-four hours lapse?"

The army captain caught the eye of the air force lieutenant but said nothing. Two newly arriving men, both looking out of place in dark suits, entered the room. "I would try to get away from populated areas," one said, "as quickly as I could."

Chapter 48

"Who was the first person you killed?" asked the interviewer in her monotone.

"Do you mean last night?" Isabel replied. "Or ever?"

The Infected bureaucrat on the far side of the bright yellow line, uncaring and yet persistent, said, "Last night." Isabel's count began on a thumb and ended on a pinkie. "The man coming through the door." The typing resumed. "The boy outside. The old man on the stairs. And the girl and old woman in the parking lot. Five."

The expressionless scrivener was both doll-like and grotesque. Brown, helmet-shaped hair, loose clothes draping a scrawny, nondescript figure, no makeup of course, maybe thirty-five, maybe fifty-five. The Infected chic of shabby automata. Spartan shells, like the interview room all drab colors...save the bright, impossible to miss line down its middle. On either side of the optic yellow border, dark hardwoods were worn tan by countless trudges. But the neon boundary between was untrodden. Our side. Their side. Isabel's involuntary reach up found no mask—a defining postapocalyptic twitch.

"Did you kill anyone before The Outbreak?" the Infected woman asked.

"Of course not."

"What were you before The Outbreak?"

"Why?"

The interviewer turned worn, yellowing, laminated pages in the ring binder on her desk across the room. "Is it difficult to talk about 'before the outbreak'?"

"Is that what it says? What to do when they won't talk? 'If they say this, ask that'?" The interviewer stared back, repeatedly blinking. *A tell? Getting jumpy? Welcome to the club.* The door and ground floor windows in what signs said had been a title company were wide open. *That'll help her nerves.* But talking was what she really needed to calm down. Doing her job. Typing mindlessly. "Life was easy." The clacking resumed. "So, *yeah*, it's hard on me. All the *emotions*. You know?"

The interviewer nodded. *No, you don't know shit. You have no idea what that means.* She typed every word, then looked not at her binder, but at a form on a clipboard filled with notes in neat handwriting in multiple colors. *So, Emma knows I'm here.* "It says you have insights into the *Pandoravirus* epidemic. The Outbreak, The Killing, The Schism." *They've* named *everything.* A first draft of their history of the world.

"*What* says that I have insights? What is that on your clipboard?"

"The intake form. Please describe what's happened since The Outbreak."

"I thought this was a trial or whatever. About the five Infecteds last night."

"It's an inquiry," the infected woman replied.

"Into what though?"

Silence. *You know* when *to lie, just not* how. "You can start at Infection Date Zero."

"What? From the beginning, to now?" Isabel asked. "All four months?"

"No? Okay." She turned plastic pages. "How about begin with The Killing?"

"And when was that? It seems to me like the killing began at the very beginning."

"Why don't you describe what happened around the time Vice President Anderson took over?"

"We just call him *President* Anderson." The barb was lost on the woman.

It would get dark early. The fresh smell of rain was in the air. It would make for a choice between a damp, miserable night in the woods, or breaking into a house that every once in a while turned out wasn't abandoned. It wouldn't matter whether its occupants were cold-blooded Infecteds or desperate, bypassed Uninfecteds—you were in for a fight. *Better to get this over with.* "People told stories, you know. Maybe some were made up."

"Lies?" asked the interviewer.

"Very good. *Embellished,* more likely. Learn that word and you'll be ready for your SATs." The infected woman opened her mouth, presumably to correct the record about any impending college boards. "I *know*. You're not taking the SATs. It was a joke."

Apparently, there was a page for jokes. Her finger traced the line as she read. "Please just say what happened." Page 11, Option 24 or whatever, in the binder.

"Well, in the beginning everything was normal." She typed. "No guns, Exclusion Zone, yellow lines. Happy people living happy lives. Then, out of fucking *nowhere*, in four months everything got totally fucking fucked never to be unfucked again. The End."

She typed it all. *Perfect job for an Infected—government make-work.* Was she judging? And, if so, whom and what? The events of last night? Or all Uninfecteds on their record since The Outbreak?

The woman paused, fingers poised, ready to type. What she didn't know was that she was the one being judged. It was her life, and the lives of her fellow Infecteds, that were being decided.

* * * *

Over the hours, the interviewer's questions grew tedious, so Isabel asked, "How do you people get paid? Do you even have money?"

"No. Everything is free. But you've got to have your work card punched."

"Wow. Sounds like a workers' paradise. What if you don't want to work?"

That question agitated her. She looked out the window, or *at* the window. Her escape hatch. Maybe all wasn't perfect in paradise, even for Infecteds. The woman again sat on her hands—literally—and took deep breaths. She was either supposed to lie if asked that question by an Uninfected and she didn't know how to lie, or the answer she concealed by her silence was damning. Regardless, the woman needed calm.

"Okay, I'll talk some more." After many long seconds, the interviewer raised her hands to her keyboard. "You remember, we only had weeks to prepare." Tears welled up in Isabel's eyes. *Goddam tears!* The interviewer had lived through the same trauma. But she was infected and didn't give a shit, about anything, ever again.

Once more, the siren song could almost be heard. It would be so easy to be infected. Like a purgatory for people who couldn't quite commit to suicide. *"To sleep, perchance to dream—ay, there's the rub, For in that sleep of death, what dreams may come...."* The dull gray interviewer looked up when Isabel asked, "You ever read Hamlet?"

Her eyes darted to her ring binder, but it would have nothing in it about Shakespeare. "Hamlet is a play," she replied from some distant memory, almost childlike.

"Good! So you...? Now when I say *you,* that makes sense, right?" The infected woman nodded after a short and telling delay. *No,* you *don't get it 'cause there's no* you *in there.* She was waiting to type. "Never mind. The Outbreak. We prepared, or thought we did. As best we could. But who coulda known, right? Just how bad the worst-case scenario really was? I mean, *you* were there. *You* remember."

The interviewer looked up, confused by the ever elusive *yous,* which left holes in otherwise straightforward sentences. She searched for comfort in her binder, calming her...whatever it was that was not her*self. Quit fucking with her,* a voice urged.

"How many have you killed in total since The Outbreak?" she asked, returning to her script.

"This is just a formality, right? They were in the Exclusion Zone. Plus, they were batshit crazy. Totally black eyes. Just turned. You woulda put 'em down too."

"Who was the first person you killed in your life?" the robotic woman tried asking.

"The first? Oh, my baby nurse when I was an infant. Tripped her on the stairs. Then a couple or three housekeepers in my toddler years using toys labeled, 'Choking Hazard.' Then the youth pastor under a mound of collapsed hymnals. *Oh,* and my first soccer coach! I almost forgot about that rental van *accident*! Wait. You're typing this shit?"

"Was it two or three housekeepers?" the dutiful chronicler asked.

Even now, their mental deficits were surprising. "I was *joking.* Like I said, I didn't kill anyone before The Outbreak." The woman patiently deleted everything, then looked up. Not annoyed. Not expectant. Not anything. She could have sat there like that for hours if things around her remained perfectly still and quiet, with no sense that any time had passed.

"It was a young woman, or a girl, on a bridge, wearing a nightgown and running right at me with a screwdriver in her hand. How about you? I'm sure you killed people before your fine self ended up here, all judge and jury and shit. What's your story?"

The break in routine registered in the interviewer's damaged brain, which was forced to plot a novel course on its own—without a manual— one unenlightened step at a time. In her flat monotone, she said, "It was at a refugee shelter. Soldiers started killing patients. One held his finger to his lips and looked out into the hall where the screaming was. The gun was under the pillow. The bullet hit the back of his head under his helmet. Then, there was the woods, the hunger, getting shot at when eating people's garbage."

This one had no problem with *he*, *she*, or *they*, any more than she did with the synonymous pronoun *it*. Like all Infecteds, she only had trouble with the missing *I*, *me*, *my*. Maybe she wasn't so glib after all. Possibly had a middling score on the tests they reportedly administered to themselves these days.

"Would you say that the first person you killed was a girl, or a woman?"

"How the hell should I know?" Isabel's reply was a little too loud, too alarming. The interviewer ceased typing. Her fists balled. Her fingernails dug into her palms. *Calm the fuck down.* Je*sus.* She's on edge. Who knew how good she was at *self*-control?

No weapon was visible at the woman's dented and scratched desk. She stared at her lap. Her jaw clenched. Cords in her neck and arms stood out. But from the chair across the yellow line to the woman's desk was only about three running strides. Choking would be the way to go. Avoid the spittle out of habit. Although easily excitable, Infecteds didn't panic and counterintuitively actually relaxed once death was inevitable.

Or deescalate? "I'm sorry. When your little border guards with those *SE* patches on their shoulders came to investigate and I agreed to answer a few questions, I thought they would be, you know, about the five dead people at that abandoned motel. Which, FYI, is not very damned abandoned. It's like a halfway house between your side and ours. But here you are, asking me *these* questions. Why?"

"To do an accounting of The Killing." The interviewer turned pages in her ring binder until she found something. "Would you like a cup of coffee or tea before we continue?"

"You have coffee? Seriously?" The interviewer shook her head. "How about tea?" Another no before she resumed her search of the binder. "Why do you even care about the killing, or the missing people? It's not like you want revenge. That's so pre-Outbreak. An emotion. Do you need to look up the definition? R-E-V-E-N-G-E? Or E-M-O-T-I-O-N?"

The interviewer found the right page. "The missing people's jobs need to be filled, and if they're just displaced," she read, "they may return and breach the peace."

Isabel's snort drew the infected woman's notice, but she clearly had no sense of the irony—an Infected concerned about violence after what they'd all just gone through. The historian slash stenographer waited. "I've been wondering about this yellow line?" Isabel said. The infected woman looked down. "Maybe it isn't to keep *us* from getting *infected*. It's to keep *you* safe from *us*? If I were to, say, walk up to the line, would that agitate you?"

The mere mention visibly stirred the interviewer. That good old adrenal boost. Not fear, just primitive survival instinct. Her breathing grew shallower. Her muscles unsustainably taut. She wasn't particularly well suited for a job involving contact with the uninfected. She also wasn't a fighter. This one would probably dash straight for the open window and dive out, or try to. In fact, the women even glanced at it. Considered it. Measured her steps. *Just tackle her and choke.* It'd be quick if her windpipe broke.

The curtains drifted in the breeze. The sky was growing grayer. Outside, boys and girls headed into a large brick church. They weren't boisterous like people should be at their age. They didn't walk together even though all had the same destination—a side door into the sanctuary of some Protestant denomination.

"The yellow line," the interviewer finally said, "is for Uninfecteds."

"I don't see any of your uninfected *citizens* walking the streets out there."

"We call them members. They live in a separate part of town. It was their request."

"I *bet* it was." It was like talking to a preschooler. Infecteds understood only the straightforward. Nuance, irony, and sarcasm completely baffled the less sophisticated of them, which was most. "I see you've got great attendance at that church down the street." The interviewer's chair squeaked. Instead of typing, she sat on her hands, eyes closed, repeating something subvocally. *Never seen that before. Oh, wait, I have. Emma's relaxation classes for her NIH roommates.* Finally, she opened her eyes and took deep breaths in through her nose, and out through pursed lips. Mentioning the church had set her off. Better discuss something that won't evoke any powerful reactions.

"After you murdered the soldier who spared your life, did you kill other people?"

The interviewer didn't answer, but visibly calmed and reverted to her script. "Did The Killing lead to The Schism, or did The Schism lead to The Killing?"

"I don't have a clue what you're talking about," Isabel replied. *"Schism? Killing?"*

"The Killing was the Uninfecteds' mass murder of Infecteds, and—"

"That's what you call it?" The volume of Isabel's reply made the interviewer jump. *Sit back, lower your voice, chill the fuck out.* The woman slowly resumed normal breathing. This must be a high-risk job. The interviewer wasn't scared, but she certainly perceived some budding issues

that might frustrate her urge to continue living. "So," Isabel summarized, "you call what happened when the infection swept through *The Killing*, and by that you mean the policy of eradication? The ten-meter rule? Roadblocks and curfews and quarantines?"

The interviewer was too agitated to speak, but she did manage to nod. She needed a few more seconds. A good, long silence ought to do.

On the street outside, orderly Infecteds passed each other without any greetings. There were no anterograde amnesiacs, ten steps this way, eight steps that, staggering toward exhaustion. No paranoid delusionals jerking their heads at each new sight, unable to make eye contact without perceiving homicidal intent. No stroked out obsessives dragging what was left of their dead dog down the street. Those Infecteds were all long dead from self-neglect, from encounters with Uninfecteds, or from Infecteds tidying them up with industrial scale eugenics. These *keepers* outside were the crème de la crème of Infected society. Maybe their clear skin and loyalty to the regime entitled them to live in the showplace capital like North Korea used to do. High functioning because of superb immune systems, borderline exposure, or good hydration during the acute phase of infection. Or maybe they got their hands on some antivirals to lessen the damage of *Pandoravirus*.

The interviewer was finally ready, and began typing with the first words Isabel spoke. "I guess you'd say that The *Schism*, by which I presume you mean the constitutional crisis, was necessary for The *Killing* to begin. I mean, at its heart, the crisis was *about* eradication." The interviewer *clacked* away. "But it's really galling that you act like *we…!*" *Stay calm.* "What I mean is that it was *you* who were so wildly off the charts violent. And then, when we decide that we need to protect ourselves *from* you, you call that *The Killing* like it was some kind of premeditated holocaust or something."

"Did you support The Killing? The policy of eradication?"

Were there right and wrong answers? Infecteds routinely murdered each other for scraps of supplies or to cull the breed. They would have no problem offing an *Un*infected. "I didn't support it at first," came the truth. "Then I saw where things were headed."

After her transcription caught up, she asked, "Where were things headed?"

"Toward extinction."

The interviewer didn't have to ask what that meant. "Did you only kill Infecteds? Or did you kill Uninfecteds too?"

"Both. How about you? You had a gun. Did you kill before you turned *and* after?"

The interviewer's chair creaked when she looked up. That could end up being a useful forewarning in case the last page of her checklist read, "Now, kill the interviewee." But this poor infected woman stared back with what was almost innocence. She was in desperate need of grooming, as worn as the fraying leather cushions of her chair. She gripped its arms. No emotion, but brimming with urges. *Quit baiting her! Just talk.* Isabel's stories of killing, both Infected and Uninfected, were plentiful and came pouring out.

The only sounds were the keyboard and the slamming side door into the church down the street. Were they exterminating people in there who failed their exam? "Will the following please report to the loading dock?" Or were they raising an army? Young Infecteds milled about outside until the door opened to admit handfuls at a time. More Infecteds streamed up the sidewalk toward the building. Others appeared as they exited via an unseen door on the far side. *Dear God, why did I agree to come here?*

The interviewer searched her ring binder for her next question. A truck drove up to the brick church and disgorged young people at its door. "Those guys who showed up at the motel," Isabel said, "after the shooting—the ones with those SE patches—who were they? What does 'SE' stand for?"

"Selective Eradication," the interviewer replied. "They're necessary for the proper functioning of society."

"Wow. Not very...euphemistic. Kind of lays it right out there. What do *they* do?"

"Some Infecteds are too damaged," the woman explained. "Dangerous, or useless. Feeding, housing, clothing, and confining them would be an unnecessary drain on resources."

"So, you test them to see who's high and who's low functioning?" The woman nodded but looked as if she wasn't certain she should have. "And the SE police kill the latter?"

She perused her book. She *definitely* wasn't supposed to answer *that* question.

"Did *you* take the test?" The interviewer was confused. "There was a test, and that test was passed?" A tentative nod. "Congrats. No wonder you believe in the system. But those whacked-out crazy Infecteds in the Zone wouldn't pass, would they? They'd just turned. Black pupils all."

"Mydriasis," the interviewer supplied without looking in her binder.

"You know that word?"

The interviewer began composing a reply, regrouped, and finally said, in a stilted and careful manner, "*I*...am a scientist. *I* am a biologist."

"Reeeally? And *now* you're a stenographer. You don't seem too fucked up. Did you get your hands on some antivirals?" The woman nodded. "Hm. Where'd you get 'em?"

"From the old job," the interviewer explained. "They were the last of them."

"Makes sense then that you aced your test. You were healthy when exposed and got prompt antivirals. The damage was more limited."

She nodded. "Yes, *I'm* high functioning."

"It's all relative, I guess."

"During the exam," she began before faltering. "When the exam, the one that...." Another failed attempt at composing a sentence. Those pesky pronouns.

"During *your* exam? The one that *you* took?"

She nodded again, but uncertainly. "Seven ran and were shot." Her matter-of-fact tone was the shocking part of that personal anecdote.

"They bolted when they figured out they'd flunk?" The interviewer nodded. "And they shot them right there in the exam room?" She nodded again. "But it obviously didn't bother you too much 'cause you passed." A final nod confirmed the gist of the story.

The interviewer said, "The Selective Eradication police provide security at the exams, do the executions, and also patrol the Exclusion Zone."

"I bet you don't want a knock on the door from *them!*" The interviewer shook her head. "So, you fail a test and it's off to the crematorium?"

"No, they shoot you. No crematoria. There used to be gunshots day and night. Now it's usually only on test days. The executions of Rule breakers are done outside of town."

"So, no jail; you just kill them?"

"The Infecteds, yes. Imprisoning people is a huge drain on—"

"Sure, I get it. Don't get me wrong. I'm with you all the way on this one. Keep on keepin' on. It just seems, I dunno, a tad *harsh*? Litter or jaywalk, and off with your head?"

"No beheading. They use guns. And did you check the Board today? Are there new Rules against littering and jaywalking?"

What a stupid fucking question.

"Do you remember," Isabel asked, "what it was like to have a *soul*?" Her interviewer's gaze was blank and hinted at total incomprehension. "Or a *conscience*, or sense of *self*?" The woman searched her ring binder. "There used to be a *you* in there, but it's gone now. That's why the word *you* can be so confusing. I know, I know. You can think it through; connect the dots and kind of get that I'm talking about the biological organism that encompasses your body. But what I'm *really* talking about is the *person* inside you."

The interviewer found something. "What does your inner voice say to do?" *Kill you and get the fuck outta here.* "Never mind. You asked when I first started thinking about killing Infecteds? It was when I realized you were going to kill every last fucking one of us!" She clearly didn't know what to make of the rising volume of the reply. "Have you *seen* a mob attack? Ever been *in* a mob? You tell me—why the hell do you *do* that? You ask *me* about The *Killing*, like it's some inexplicable fucking atrocity. But have you seen Infecteds sack a neighborhood? Go door-to-door looking for something to steal or someone to rape and stumbling onto a terrified, cowering Uninfected family? Children! Old people! Do you apologize and back your way out? No. You go into a fucking frenzy and rampage through the house, slaughtering them you evil fucking bitch!"

Calm down. Calm down. Breathe. Sit on your hands. But the interviewer was undisturbed, which itself was offensive. "Can't you just leave them alone?" Isabel asked. "Do you have some twisted urge to destroy everything healthy? Are you like rabid dogs who have to bite, or hypersexual syphilis victims compelled to corrupt?"

The woman grew wary and stopped typing. What was the trigger? Her hands gripped the tattered armrests of her chair. She sat at its front edge, ready to bolt. *Should I let her go?* That didn't seem like such a good idea. She might run straight to some SE guy. It would be safer to put her down.

"That isn't…done anymore," she finally said.

"What?" But that was all the infected drone said as she sat there, quivering in a stew of her own adrenaline. "What did you say? Shouldn't you have said, '*We* don't do that anymore'?" The interviewer nodded. "And just what the hell does *that* mean?"

"Violence is…." She didn't complete, or know how to complete, her statement.

"What? Bad? Wrong? Evil? Immoral? You don't give a shit about those things."

"The Board says, 'Do not breach the peace'."

"Oh, The Board does, does it? Well why didn't you *say* so?"

Satisfied, she returned to her ring binder and found her place quickly. "Did you discuss The Killing, and was there dissent?"

"Why do you give a flying fuck about this shit?" The answer to *that* question was clear—she didn't. She was following a script and obeying a Board in order to be fed and avoid being shot—a trusty cog in the infected machine. It was as simple as that. You let me live here, and I follow your

Rules. *What was her question? Oh, yeah.* "You ready to type?" The interviewer seemed to relax.

"So, *hell* yes there was dissent, and debate, and argument, and moral quandaries. But you know, it's not just viruses that follow Darwin's law. Ideas are subject to natural selection too. And people, families, and communities that decided killing Infecteds was immoral—they didn't last long, did they? When did the last sanctuary city go dark? Santa Fe? Infection Date 80 or so? Either people changed their minds about not killing to defend themselves and their loved ones, or that grand idea died with its last adherent, usually when you and yours ripped their eyeballs out. Nature self corrects for piss-poor memes."

"What rules," the methodical woman asked, seemingly uninterested in the substance—or vehemence—of Isabel's reply, "did you follow about killing Infecteds?"

"Rules? Like on your Board? Well, before SED got here, nobody was thinking about killing anybody. We had *laws*. And at first the government said no killing, then natural selection, I guess, played a hand in changing governments—your *Schism*—and the new leaders said kill away. But by then, I don't know who was still following orders other than the military. People did what it took, or they didn't survive. Sometimes the same people would kill every last Infected after a fight in the morning, then let other Infecteds go with food and water in the afternoon. There were no rules. It was life or death on a whim. Nobody had time to think through rules because they kept SED secret so long. You wanta talk about crimes!"

The interviewer calmly transcribed Isabel's condemnation. Isabel knew she shouldn't expect more out of the woman but her indifference contrasted frustratingly with the outrage Isabel felt at the long-ago government cover-up. "How about *you*?" Isabel asked, angry and heedless of her pronoun usage. "Did *you* have enough time to prepare?"

The woman hesitated before finally saying, "The husband got ready."

"Yeah? And how'd that work out?"

"They broke into the house. The family hid in the attic. The husband went out to distract the mob, and it worked. They killed him and stole things, but left the rest alone. The son ran out to his father's body even though he was warned not to. After sneaking across the D.C. cordon to a refugee center in Reston, he threw up and they quarantined him in an adjacent ward."

"Then you got sick, too?" The interviewer blinked repeatedly. "That was where the nice soldier from before got shot in his *head*?" She nodded. She understood pronoun free questions. "Ever think, for even one instant, that murdering someone who showed mercy was a fucking horrendous crime?" The interviewer shook her head. *Of course not.* "What happened to *the* son?"

"He was in a different ward."

"So I heard. Next to the ward *you* were in. And the soldiers started killing Infecteds, and the nice soldier got himself shot, and...then came the *woods*, right?" She nodded again. "But no check next door on *the* son? Of course not. Just left him there." She nodded. "How the hell do you expect to organize a society long-term when people just abandon their children?"

"Parents deliver children to The Community. It's a Rule on the Board."

"*I* see. Part of your 10,000 Commandments or whatever." The impossible-to-miss Board stood near a gazebo in the median along the road into town. "Too bad you didn't have that rule about taking care of children at that refugee center."

She nodded in agreement, then returned to her ring binder. The conclusion Isabel had to draw in her report to General Browner was growing absurdly obvious. *How can you* not *despise them? View them as inherently evil? An abomination? The epitome of everything inhuman?*

Chapter 49

NEW ROANOKE, VIRGINIA
Infection Date 122, 2020 GMT (4:20 pm Local)

It was growing dark and a storm was brewing. "Time to wrap this up," Isabel said.

Throughout the interview, Isabel had quietly dreaded this moment. Several times she had almost convinced herself it was unnecessary and questioned whether she even had the will or the moral right to do it. But the twenty-four hour clock was ticking. She had a mission to accomplish and had been advised repeatedly during her briefing in Houston that speed was essential to her safety. *"Try to be done and gone by sunset,"* had been the CIA agent's repeated urging. And the lawyer from the Justice Department had completed the picture by advising, *"All punishment of homicides has been suspended so long as the deceased was infected."*

Not suspended, however, was Isabel's conscience. She took a deep breath, closed her eyes, and thought—to God or to herself—*Please forgive me.* When she opened her eyes, her jaws were firmly clenched. As detailed for her interviewer, she had killed Infecteds before. Uninfecteds too. Why was this any different?

Her interviewer grew apprehensive when Isabel rose and closed the door. She trapped her hands under her thighs as she watched Isabel shut each window and lower its blinds. The infected woman pinched her eyelids tight and muttered something like a prayer—more likely a calming mantra—then opened her mouth to say something, but couldn't get it out. "Shhh. Shhh," Isabel said. The woman's breathing was ragged. *Better be on guard in case she bolts or calls out.* But there was no one else in the building or on the streets.

The woman opened her eyes to find all possible escape routes closed and her executioner—having crossed the yellow line—standing over her. Isabel was five foot four and now probably well under her normal weight of 120 pounds. But her interviewer was skin and bones—100 pounds, max—and frail to the point of being sickly. It was hard for Isabel to remember that the woman wasn't frightened. They don't feel fear, or sadness, or longing for a life that might have been. That's projecting human emotions onto them—a fatal flaw long since eliminated from the meme pool of surviving Uninfecteds. All they get is agitated. An urge to live bolstered by secretion of adrenaline.

The woman tried to say something, but was so jittery the words came out jumbled.

"Shhh. Shhh."

Her neck was slender. She was significantly undernourished. When she tried to speak again, her vocal chords vibrated, giving away the location of her larynx to Isabel's fingertips. "It'll be over in a minute, I promise. Stay calm and we'll do this quickly. Together."

"Mm-mm know you! Know you!" she said.

Curiosity momentarily delayed the ugly process. Or at least a reluctant Isabel allowed the delay. "What'd you say?"

"I...*I* know you." The woman looked up at Isabel. She didn't even bother to raise her hands defensively. Isabel's grip left her neck and settled onto her shoulders as if for a friendly massage. "We...we've met. At the NIH. On your first day. You were late for Dr. Nielsen's staff meeting. I...I was there. The head of the Tumor Cell Biology Lab. You winked. At...at *me*."

"You had a tan. And a wilting red flower tucked in your ear." The woman nodded. Isabel winced, unseen by her intended victim. "Why the flower?"

The interviewer shrugged under Isabel's hands, which she removed. "I...I don't know. My husband and...and *I*," she bobbed her head each time she correctly used a self-reference, "were on a second honeymoon, on Bora Bora, when the call came about SED."

"Hm. You must have kept the flower, ya know, to hang on to the moment. You must have really loved him. And your son."

The interviewer shrugged again. All those human experiences were receding from her memory. "Your sister thought you'd be less likely to kill the interviewer if you knew her from before."

That made sense. "She was right, I guess. Plus, I thought you and I had become friends here." The poor woman nodded. "I didn't really want to, ya know, *kill* you. It just seemed…less complicated that way." She nodded again. Strangely, she understood what many Uninfecteds might not. Isabel shared that, at least, with the woman. "Tell you what. I propose a contract. Between you and me." The interviewer waited. "You do trust me, right?" The woman shook her head. Her honesty elicited an amused snort. "Well, regardless, here's the offer. I won't kill you if you answer *my* question honestly. Okay?" The interviewer nodded. She might even actually tell the truth because it was a contract. Isabel standing over her clearly made her extremely uneasy, so Isabel remained right there. "What's going on in that church up the street?"

"Meditation," the interviewer responded without hesitation. "Relaxation training. Everyone goes through it before they take their test, but young people need extra training. They're more excitable. One part of the test measures anxiety levels. Meditation helps them stay under control and not breach the peace."

"I don't believe you," Isabel said. "Show me."

The tops of the trees outside were dancing in the freshening wind. They fell in alongside a small group of teenagers headed for the door into the church. The interviewer could have bolted, but she didn't. In fact, she acted no differently toward Isabel than she had before her near-death experience. When they reached the church, the teens waited their turn in several loose and untalkative groups, sufficiently dispersed, Isabel decided, that they wouldn't trigger any crowd reaction from excessive density. Isabel and the interviewer climbed the few steps to the church's side door.

The SE policeman there asked no questions when he saw Isabel. He must have assumed she was Emma. Inside, it took a few seconds for Isabel's eyes to adjust to the dim light. The sanctuary had a movie screen in front, but no seating. She made out a dozen groups of ten teenagers each sitting in circles around an adult who led them through breathing exercises. Lips moved in barely uttered chants and pursed for measured breathing.

On the screen were projected images and short videos. A sneering soldier in combat gear staring through the sights of a rifle pointed straight at the viewer. A newly arrived line of Infecteds standing in front of a pit half filled with dead bodies as a belt of ammunition was loaded into a smoking machine gun. A tank gruesomely crushing members of a crowd under its treads as it "mowed the lawn," she had heard tank drivers call it. A string of bombs ripping through a line of houses in a suburban neighborhood. A mob of uninfected vigilantes running toward the camera.

All the while, speakers spewed jarring audio from fighting and riots. Explosions. Screams. Gunfire. Shouts of, "Halt! Halt!" and "Disperse!

Disperse!" The show was clearly meant to agitate the teenagers. Some rose to their feet and had to be coaxed back into place by SE men the size of bouncers who patrolled the spaces between the circles. One teen was being held down by two men until they finally nodded to each other and led the quivering girl, who was on the verge of losing it, out a door by both elbows.

Soon after the door closed, there was a single, sharp gunshot. Numerous people around the room jumped at the sound. Isabel felt lightheaded. She hadn't imagined there was an even more callous rung on the descending ladder of heartlessness.

But they weren't raising an army, Isabel realized. They were trying to put a stop to the violence. They were culling the breed of Infecteds easily roused by committing murder in service of peace. "Okay. I've seen enough. Take me to my sister," Isabel said.

The skies looked like they would break open as they traversed empty streets through the infected town. The only vehicle they passed was a garbage truck from which arms and legs protruded. The few people they passed exchanged no nods of acknowledgement, no greetings, no glances of curiosity. As advised by the CIA man, Isabel tried to make herself inconspicuous. No smiles. She didn't swivel her head to take in the sights like an uninfected tourist in the capital of the Infecteds. She stifled every question she longed to ask her guide.

They crossed the street to a nondescript four story brick building—a former branch bank, judging by the drive-through teller window. As they headed up the steps, Isabel was shocked to pass former President Stoddard, who looked her right in the eye on his way down.

"President Stoddard?"

He turned. "Hello, Isabel."

She felt momentary surprise at his lack of interest in seeing her again. But of course he wasn't the least bit curious. A black SUV pulled up. Former First Lady Angela Stoddard emerged wearing a stylish pants suit. "I'm going to guess," she said, "by how well fed you are that you're the *other* Dr. Miller!" Mrs. Stoddard removed her movie star sunglasses—a new custom upon meeting—but did not approach Isabel for a handshake. No one did that anymore, even if vaccinated. "Hello, Isabel." Angela Stoddard wore shiny black high heels, a broach, a necklace, a diamond bracelet.

"Mrs. Stoddard? How are you doing?"

"We have our good days and our bad days. I take it you're here to see your sister." She stepped up close to Isabel, but eyed the interviewer. "You can go," she said to the woman, who departed without even a glance at her would-be executioner. *So,* Isabel thought, *you got to live after all.* A small part of her felt happy for the poor interviewer even though the woman herself would never feel happiness again.

Mrs. Stoddard glanced up at the threatening sky. "Why don't you come to dinner at our house? Stay the night, for that matter. It looks like it's gonna pour. The kids would love to see you, and I can't imagine you'd wanta stay in *their* part of town overnight. We've had a little get-together planned. That's why I'm picking *him* up, although of course no one will sit down at the table with an Infected. But the people coming to dinner tonight would *love* to talk to you. You'll be my star guest, and we have a *lot* to talk about. Dinner's at seven. We'll count on you at least by six so, you know, you can get showered and a quick wash of your clothes."

President Stoddard got into the car. "Tell your sister," Mrs. Stoddard said, "that we need our rations increased. I know we already get more caloric intake than the infected side. *Blah, blah, blah.* But a lot of the food is tasteless crap and uninfected people just won't eat it. We don't want anybody going hungry. Hungry people breach the peace. Make sure you tell her that. 'Breach the peace.' Oh, and I'll send the car back for you." She took a step toward it before turning to Isabel. "Would you like me to scrounge up some clothes for you?"

Isabel looked down at her baggy camouflage blouse and trousers. "I've kinda grown accustomed to this." *Plus, you never knew when camo will come in handy.*

"Well bless your heart. You'll find Uninfecteds here like to dress up. Anything to distinguish ourselves from *them.*" The former President sat just inside the SUV's door. "Scoot. Scoot over!" He undid his seatbelt and slid to the other side. Angela Stoddard smiled and waved at Isabel. "See you soon! It's *sorghum* night!" She rolled her eyes.

Isabel climbed the steps to the glass double doors in a daze. Everything about this place felt alien. A fading, hand-printed sign read, "Community Headquarters." Not exactly a monument to Infecteds' achievement. But it was early days. *Their beginning is our end.*

She entered, passing zero security along the way. It was so unlike Houston. The lobby was filled with desks—empty at that hour—but no partitions. Who needed privacy? Infecteds didn't watch porn on their laptops or have telephonic fights with their spouses.

On the far side, Emma caught Isabel's eye before she pressed a button on a photocopier. Isabel's face lit up on seeing her sister, but the only light on Emma's came from the copier. Isabel had to hurry to catch up to her departing sister. "Emma. *Emma!*"

On the door into her sister's cramped, windowless inner office was a handwritten sign. "Dr. Emma Miller, Chief Epidemiologist."

"Impressive title," Isabel said. She had dreamed of a totally different scene filled with hugs and kisses and breathless questions. She so wanted a feeling of connection with her sister. Their shared love of science had always served that purpose in the past. "You might be interested to know, Emma, that we found a woman and her baby who are naturally immune to *Pandoravirus*."

That got Emma's attention. "Where are they from?"

It seemed a strange first question—the first words her identical twin sister had spoken to her. Isabel tried not to betray her hurt feelings, not that her pain would ever have been noticed. "New Guinea, I think."

Emma clearly missed the disappointment evident in the leaden tone of Isabel's voice. "That makes sense," Emma said. "Asia-Pacific Islanders have the most Denisovan DNA of any *Homo sapiens*. Denisovans were in Siberia when *Pandoravirus* last broke out. The immunity must be somewhere in that archaic genetic code."

Emma sat and straightened her sheaf of paper with several taps on her neat, well organized desk, so unlike the mess she'd left behind along with everything else from her old life in Bethesda. Isabel searched for some way to keep the conversation going. "What are those?"

"These papers? It's The List. The latest exam results."

"Oh. *The List.* You people do like naming things. The list of the people who passed the tests? Who don't, you know, get...?" She made a throat cutting motion and sound.

"We don't slit throats. We shoot them."

"But I thought you shot them just outside the door of the testing center?"

"Only the ones who can't even complete the test. The others get scored overnight and picked up first thing in the morning, unless they've run." She put a ratty old notebook in a briefcase.

"Hey! That looks like the notebook you got at the NIH. Your, what, fourth?"

"Fifth," Emma corrected, barely paying attention to Isabel.

"Speaking of the NIH, good call sending that biologist to be my interviewer." Isabel was nervous and rambling. Emma didn't seem to notice. "So what's up with those interviews anyway? What's the point?" Emma hadn't invited her to, but Isabel sat.

"We're trying to decide whether we can trust any treaty with Vice President Anderson."

"We call him *President* Anderson," Isabel corrected. "Funny you should mention that. General Browner is trying to figure out the exact same thing about you."

"Is that the reason you're here?"

"Yeah." Her answer seemed to hold Emma's interest, so Isabel kept talking. "And I see you've got SE guys patrolling the Exclusion Zone. They're armed. Isn't that a violation of your existing agreement?"

"They have to be armed to do their job. If you came in through the Exclusion Zone, you saw what it was like." Isabel had observed and tried to keep her distance from tens, maybe hundreds of thousands there, all starving, all desperate, all violent. "We have to protect ourselves from the raids that come down out of those hills. You can tell General Browner that the forces we're raising are intended only to deal with that lawlessness. We're not raising an army to fight him...even though I get reports almost every day of incursions by Browner's troops. Four nights ago, a hydroelectric plant in Bath County blew up."

"I'm sure you're mistaken. It must've been your own people. Rebels or something."

Emma shook her head. "No. They were U.S. Army." She divided her copies into stacks of ten with paper clips, then said, "Samantha!" Isabel turned just in time to see the girl, now thirteen, with her long blond hair still perfectly straight and in place. She carried a combat helmet, and on the arm of her camouflage blouse was a patch that read, "SE." Emma said, "Could you take these to the stations?"

Samantha took the papers and turned to Isabel. "If you're staying for a while, could you come by my apartment? I've got a question for you."

Isabel said, "Sure. And a belated happy birthday."

To Isabel's amazement, the girl responded with a passable semblance of a smile. "Thank you." She glanced at Emma and the smile faded to sudden blankness.

Emma asked Samantha, "What question?"

"I wanted to ask your sister how to put my hair up in a bun like she used to when her hair was long and pretty so it will fit under this." She raised the heavy and, for her, huge looking Kevlar helmet.

There was obvious tension between the two, which Isabel instinctively sought to de-escalate. "And maybe you can tell me how you keep your hair so pretty and straight."

"My secret is a detangler." Samantha again smiled. She could almost pass.

There was no smile on Emma's face as Samantha left.

"So, she's an SE policewoman now?" Isabel asked.

"She's the new head of the SE force."

"Little Samantha? She's in charge of the *executions*? Won't that make her kind of unpopular? A lightning rod for people who're pissed about them?" *Like Sheriff Walcott?*

"Yes."

When Samantha left the building, a man nodded at Emma and followed the girl out.

That was weird. Emma straightened the paper, pencils, and yellow highlighters on her already tidy desk. She continued packing the briefcase with a pad and pens in multiple colors.

"Are you going somewhere?"

"Yes. I've got a meeting at Agriculture."

"Oh, speaking of, I ran into Angela Stoddard outside. She invited me to dinner." Emma clearly couldn't care less. "She said something about wanting rations raised?" Emma stared back blankly. "Do you need to write that down?"

"No. We can't raise Uninfecteds' rations again without Infected members starving."

"So, you're having problems with your harvests?"

"No. We're banking foodstuffs to trade them for resources we're short on." She wasn't exactly keen on keeping secrets. It was clear she was telling the truth because it was immediately apparent that Emma had lost weight. Sam too. "It would help if our only refinery wasn't periodically destroyed," Emma continued, "so we could use tractors to work the fields and trucks to deliver the food before it rots."

"I don't know what you're talking about. Was there some accident? Someone push the wrong button? I'm sure there are plenty of flammable things at a refinery."

"Seizing that refinery was our closest approach to the coast, and it was shelled by five inch guns from the sea."

All Isabel could do was shrug. "So, are you saying you don't think we're abiding by our existing nonaggression treaty? How do you think we feel when you attack an uninfected neighborhood or town? Or you execute people with machine guns?"

"If you're talking about Uninfecteds, we don't punish that many."

"Except in the towns you overrun."

A flash of lightning lit the twilight, followed by a surprisingly loud peal of thunder. Emma didn't even blink.

"Your car is outside," said a woman Isabel didn't recognize at first. "Dorothy?"

"Yes," the former housewife replied. "Hi."

Emma said to Dorothy, "Don't forget the buckets." Dorothy nodded. Isabel watched her put a hodgepodge of plastic and metal buckets around the lobby—on a desk, in the marble entry, in an office doorway.

Isabel said, "That must mean the Marine embassy guard, Dwayne, is—what?—Chairman of your Joint Chiefs?"

"He's head of our security forces, and he works part-time in Dorothy's nursery."

"Taking care of babies?" Isabel asked, fighting a laugh. Emma didn't see any humor in the job description. Or in anything else. Isabel leaned forward. "We want to trust you, Emma. We don't want a war. There's been way too much killing and dying already. And obviously we have our hands full out West. Everything you've done here with your meditation courses and big Board with its Rules and stuff—there's none of that out there. It's," Isabel chuckled, "the Wild West, and it's fuckin' awful."

Emma nodded. "So we've heard. But it's gotten better, I suppose, since your nuclear strikes?" *How did she know about that?* Isabel wondered. Maybe the anecdotal sightings of *missionaries*, one analyst had called Emma's teams, weren't just paranoia. Maybe Emma was training Infecteds to be backslapping, boisterous spies who crack jokes, or sultry courtesans skilled at the easy art of seducing men. "But it's the east where the population is," Emma said, "and where you're vastly outnumbered."

This wasn't the turn in the discussion for which Isabel had hoped. She had a decision looming—codes to be entered into her sat phone, wherever that was. "We thought we'd see about deescalating tensions. Maybe draft new contracts—treaties—between us. Formal ones. Maybe, for instance, as a show of goodwill you'd consider letting your Uninfecteds come over to us."

"No. We're not interested in that."

"Sending your Uninfecteds over to us," Isabel tried again, "might alleviate your problems with feeding everyone. Especially since Uninfecteds seem to want to eat more."

"Uninfecteds provide us with certain things. They come up with creative solutions to problems. Their young are continuing to study, which will facilitate maintenance of our infrastructure and technology. They have skills and expertise we need."

"And they're hostages. If there's a war, you'll kill or infect them all."

"You're already attacking us and we haven't killed them," Emma rebutted.

Isabel feared that she had been misinformed about the cessation of military incursions into Emma's Community. Then again, they wouldn't have told her anything they didn't want Emma to know before sending

Isabel behind enemy lines. "But we haven't used *all* of our weapons," Isabel said. That struck home. Emma's hands subtly disappeared from the desk, to her lap, and from there snuck under her thighs. "So you know what would happen if we found you raising an army?" Emma tilted her head to the side and pressed her biceps to her bony ribcage. "And we don't want that to happen, do we?"

Emma shook her head.

"Because eventually, you know, we're gonna get control of that mess out West."

Emma said, "You don't have enough people."

"Our maternity wards and nurseries are full," Isabel lied. "Natalie and Noah are expecting a baby." *Kaboom!*

"Our wards are full too," Emma said. She had zero interest in her future niece or nephew. "And I'm pregnant."

Isabel's jaw dropped. "You're *pregnant*?" Emma nodded. In spite of all that had happened, Isabel couldn't help but again feel inadequate in comparison to her sister, who had successfully avoided expiration of her biological clock while simultaneously rising to the office of dictator.

"Is the father that pilot from the NIH lab?"

"No. Bill Stoddard."

"The *President*? The ex-President? You two had *sex*?"

"No. His son Bill."

"You had sex with Bill *Junior*? But he's...he's a *boy*."

"Not anymore."

Isabel took a deep breath and held it, at a total loss. She let it out as a long sigh. "I guess not. What-the-fuck-ever. Are you two...gonna raise your child together?"

"He doesn't know about it. And they take babies away as soon as they're born."

"Where will they take him or her?"

"I'm not sure. You can ask Dorothy or Dwayne."

"So you don't have a clue where they'll take your child?" Isabel asked for reasons she couldn't explain even to herself. "She'll just be out there somewhere?"

"Dorothy will begin sending the older children back to their parents, if they're alive, and make them care for and feed them. We're going to add that to the Rules once the plans are finalized. Parents take care of their children over a certain age; children take care of their parents over a certain age. Samantha came up with the idea that we give parents progress reports on their children four times a year. Age. Weight. Height. Appearance on a one to ten scale. Temperament and intelligence test results. That way parents can prepare for them when they age out of the system, which we think will be somewhere between six and ten years old, and the census can forecast the number of future participants in the labor force. All of which is a long way of saying that I will know those reported things about my child, and I will know something happened to it if I stop receiving reports."

Isabel bit her lip and nodded. "How sweet. Real...*efficient.*" Emma nodded.

Rain began to pelt the tall lobby windows. *What a miserable night to be in the field.* Maybe she would take the First Lady up on her offer to spend the night despite the warnings from the CIA officer to *"get while the getting is good."*

Emma rose with her briefcase and rounded the desk for the door.

That must signal the end of their reunion. Isabel followed her sister out of the office. "Emma, just what is the deal with that interview you put me through? All those questions about The Outbreak, The Killing."

Emma, ever patient, stopped to answer. "Those are standardized names for eras. We're trying to decide whether we can trust you and let you continue in the Houston-Denver corridor. You have an army, an air force, a navy, a Marine Corps. You have weapons. We need to determine whether you will abide by a nonaggression treaty. We don't understand you very well. You don't behave in the ways we expect. We decided the best guide to what you'll do in the future is what you've done in the past, so we're studying your behavior following The Outbreak."

"You just admitted, Emma, that we have a powerful military. But you sound like you're deciding whether to let *us* live. Isn't it the other way around?"

"No. By Infection Date 130 we'll have two million members, net of test failures. By Infection Date 190 it will be between six and ten million. By Infection Date 280 it could be as high as sixty million—all productively employed in restoring economic vitality."

"And you'll raise an army?"

"If necessary."

Isabel had to make best use of the dwindling time her twin sister was giving her as she trailed Emma into the lobby. "To be clear, Emma, about the military situation...I *am* talking to the right person, correct?" Emma nodded. "Then you should know that there are people trying to convince President Anderson that we should wipe you out—every town, every port and factory and grain silo. It would take about fifteen minutes. You understand that, don't you? All those nuclear weapons are in *our* hands. Do I need to be any clearer?"

Emma shook her head.

"Okay then. Why would we let you grow stronger than us? Why would we not use those weapons to incinerate you and everything you've worked so hard to build?"

"Because you don't have the willpower to use them against our uninfected population. We're mixed with them. We live in adjacent neighborhoods. We work elbow to elbow with each other. Unlike out West, where your targets were carefully chosen, we noted, to minimize Uninfecteds' deaths, if you nuke our Community you'll kill one Uninfected for every Infected you kill."

"They may have to be sacrificed," Isabel said, although what she felt was revulsion.

Emma's head tilted as she studied Isabel's expression. "No...you won't do it. Just like you couldn't kill your interviewer. You rationalized and found a reason not to."

Isabel followed Emma toward the glass front doors. "Is that what you've concluded from your interviews? Your history of the new world?"

"Yes," Emma replied without looking back.

Lightning flashed and thunder boomed. Sheets of water began to lash the front steps and, sure enough, trickle into the buckets that Dorothy moved a few inches one way or another to adjust for the downpour.

Just before they reached the foyer, Emma ducked into a small office and lugged Isabel's camo backpack out, dropping it with a thud at Isabel's feet—carbine, pistol, and sat phone included. "You might want to report your findings back to General Browner before dinner at the Stoddards'. I don't want him thinking we killed you." She opened one of the double glass doors, admitting a gust of wind.

"So this is goodbye, then?" Isabel couldn't help but say. Emma nodded. "You're not even gonna ask about the rest of Noah's family? If Chloe and Jake made it or not?"

"No." She headed out, but stopped. "Oh, but I almost forgot. *You* may want to know that we're in contact with people about joining The Community as far away as Quebec and Oregon. I got a message from the acting mayor of Janesville, Wisconsin, who said they have your boyfriend, Captain Townsend, and they're sending him down here at my request."

Isabel gasped for air after ceasing her breathing on hearing *Wisconsin*. "Oh my God! He's...*alive?*" Emma nodded. Isabel grabbed her mouth and began to sob.

Her sister stared back at her and tilted her head, studying her. She then nodded, to no one unless, perhaps, it was to that voice in her head. Emma was agreeing with some prior conclusion or some current inner reasoning.

"You're welcome to stay here, Isabel, and meet him when he arrives in a couple of weeks. Or not. Your choice. Dr. Nielsen should also be getting here soon. The Pearl River plant finally fell, and we're bringing her staff down here to set up a production line for the vaccine. Please say hello to General Browner from me, and whatever other polite things you can think of, and tell him we are willing to conduct negotiations leading to a formal nonaggression treaty and a trade accord, but they have to put an end to their attacks first."

With that, Emma casually walked out into the downpour. No umbrella. No raincoat. She was soaked by the time she got to the bottom of the steps.

Isabel followed, but raced to the waiting car with her equipment and ducked inside. The infected driver's head didn't even turn as she slammed the door. He drove off without a word, presumably toward the Stoddard's house. Isabel raised her hand to the window to wave as they passed her thoroughly drenched sister, but Emma didn't even look.

Isabel retrieved the sat phone from her backpack. It *beeped* when she turned it on. She still had a few hours, but she decided to send her coded message now just to be safe. But what message? If Emma was telling the truth, and she seemed to be, they would quickly grow to outnumber the teetering, ever shrinking United States. Weapons systems would degrade. Serviceable equipment would become ever shorter in supply. Fuel tanks would dry up. Destroying Emma's Community of only a million or two would be a smaller moral outrage than nuking half or more of the former country, not to mention it being a more probable success, militarily.

But those weren't Isabel's concerns. Emma had proposed a nonaggression treaty, and Isabel's mandate was to assess whether they might coexist peacefully. *And if I wait here, I'll be reunited with Rick.* Isabel grimaced. She knew what Emma was doing. And it was working, which made Emma twice as scary. "Function," Isabel said as the button *beeped*. "D," *beep*, "1," *beep*, "Send," *beep*. *No duress; ready to negotiate.*

She caught the infected driver's stare at her in the rearview mirror.

The satellite phone rang almost immediately. It was General Browner's aide, then Browner, President Anderson, and who knew how many others. "Yes, she's willing to open negotiations on a nonaggression treaty, and on a trade deal to swap their excess food production for things they're short on. But Emma says we have to stop our attacks, which I didn't *know* about by the way." There was silence. Isabel considered telling them about Rick, but hesitated for reasons that were unclear to her.

The driver pulled up to a brightly lit, columned mansion. An infected footman of some sort held an umbrella over her car door. "I just arrived at former President Stoddard's house to meet with uninfected members of Emma's Community." Isabel headed for the front porch. "I'll report back afterwards." For the briefest instant, she returned the fixed gaze of the infected footman, then turned away, carried her pack and weapons to the far end of the covered porch, and began whispering. "As a warning, they know a lot more about what's happening around the country than you'd think. They must have, I dunno, spies, maybe everywhere. Be careful. Talk to you later tonight."

She waited, and was relieved when no one instructed her to run for the hills, duck, and cover. *But then, they wouldn't....would they?* said a voice in Isabel's head.

Acknowledgments

My heartfelt thanks go out to my agent, Bob Thixton, at Pinder Lane and Garon-Brooke Associates, Ltd., for his tireless efforts in midwifing these labors of love I produce periodically. I also greatly appreciate the opportunity to work with and the editorial guidance given me by Michaela Hamilton, and the support I have received from James Abbate, at Kensington Publishing, with whom I have thoroughly enjoyed working on the *Pandora* series. And last but certainly not least, I would like to express my sincere gratitude toward every reader who gave these books a chance. I understand the time and emotional effort that goes into reading each novel to which you commit and have endeavored to the best of my abilities to not let you down. Please keep reading, and stay on the lookout for my next effort.

About the Author

Eric L. Harry launched his Pandora series of science fiction thrillers with *Pandora: Outbreak* and continued it with *Pandora: Contagion* and *Pandora: Resistance*. Raised in the small town of Laurel, Mississippi, he graduated from the Marine Military Academy in Texas and studied Russian and Economics at Vanderbilt University, where he also earned a JD and MBA. In addition, he studied in Moscow and Leningrad in the USSR, and at the University of Virginia Law School. He began his legal career in private practice in Houston, negotiated complex multinational mergers and acquisitions around the world, and rose to be general counsel of a Fortune 500 company. He left to raise a private equity fund and cofound a successful oil company. His previous thrillers include *Arc Light, Society of the Mind, Protect and Defend* and *Invasion*. His books have been published in eight countries. He and his wife have three children and divide their time between Houston and San Diego. Contact him on Facebook or visit him online at www.EricLHarry.com.

Pandora: Outbreak

"Harry's vision of an apocalyptic plague is as chilling as it is plausible. This masterful thriller will leave you terrified, enthralled, and desperate for the next entry in the series."
—**Kira Peikoff**, author of *No Time to Die* and *Die Again Tomorrow*, on *Pandora: Outbreak*

"After a devastating epidemic that changes the very nature of humans, two sisters, an epidemiologist and a neurobiologist, hold the key to humanity's survival."
—*Library Journal*

BEGINNING OF THE END

They call it *Pandoravirus*. It attacks the brain. Anyone infected may explode in uncontrollable rage. Blind to pain, empty of emotion, the infected hunt and are hunted. They attack without warning and without mercy. Their numbers spread unchecked. There is no known cure.

Emma Miller studies diseases for a living—until she catches the virus. Now she's the one being studied by the U.S. government and by her twin sister, neuroscientist Isabel Miller. Rival factions debate whether to treat the infected like rabid animals to be put down, or victims deserving compassion. As Isabel fights for her sister's life, the infected are massing for an epic battle of survival. And it looks like Emma is leading the way...

"Harry has a first-rate speculative mind, well grounded in current science. The ideas he puts forth are extremely engaging."
—*Kirkus Reviews*

"A good storyteller...harrowing stuff!"
—*The New York Times Book Review*

"Like Crichton and H.G. Wells, Harry writes stories that entertain roundly while they explore questions of scientific and social import."
—*Publishers Weekly*

See where it all began, in the first book of Eric L. Harry's chilling Pandora series.

PANDORA: OUTBREAK

Keep reading to enjoy a sample excerpt.

Chapter 1

CHUKOTKA AUTONOMOUS OKRUG, SIBERIA
Infection Date 7, 1500 GMT (3:00 a.m. Local)

The sound of the zipper on Emma Miller's tent woke her with a start. Cold air flooded in. Backlit in dim starlight she saw a man, his breath fogged. Her heart raced as she fumbled for her flashlight…and found her pistol. "Who's there?" She flicked the light on. It was the blond Russian soldier who had saved her life hours earlier. His pupils were black and unresponsive. "Stop!" He said nothing. She kicked at him. "Stop-*stop!*" He crawled atop her. She dropped the flashlight while flicking the pistol's safety off.

Bam! In the flash, his head rocked back with a hole in his brow.

Sgt. Sergei Travkin collapsed heavily onto Emma's shins. "Oh-my-*God!*"

A knife stabbed her tent and sliced it open. Men hoisted Emma— whimpering before she thought to hold her breath—into the shockingly cold air. The ever sober young scientist loosed an animal sound. "*Nooo! No!*" Someone wrenched from her grip the pistol Travkin had given her after being infected. The pistol with which she had killed him.

Emma's sobs merged with her shivering. Anonymous men clad in personal protective equipment unzipped her blue jeans and yanked. Goosebumps sprang from bare thighs. A bright lantern blinded her. Her jeans snagged at each ankle. "Sto*ooop!*" she screamed. "P-Please!" Buttons popped off her blouse. "Wait!" An ugly knife sliced through the front of her bra. She covered her breasts. Gloved fingers found the elastic of her panties. She clamped her knees together and stooped in a futile attempt at modesty. Her teeth clenched against an overpowering chatter. She shook from the cold, from the shock of killing a man and from the incapacitating terror at what may lie ahead.

"Would…somebody …?" Frigid spray stung her midriff. She doubled over with a grunt. Three men in gowns, hoods, boots, and gloves sprayed disinfectant through a wand, pumped a cylinder like an exterminator, and scrubbed her roughly with a brush at the end of a telescoping pole. She willed herself to stand upright, raising quivering arms and turning circles in place, as soldiers rolled Emma's tent into a single biohazard bundle.

Travkin's dilated pupils hadn't contracted even in the brilliance of her flashlight. *Did he infect me?* Noxious liquid burned her eyes and fouled her mouth. Despite its awful taste, she swished, gargled, and spat. The pool brush scraped at her hair. She grabbed it and used it to scrub her head and face herself. "He wouldn't stop!" she shouted before coughing and spitting. *He never got closer than my knees. Maybe I'm okay?*

Soldiers hoisted the impermeable crimson bag, covered in prickly black biohazard symbols, by loops at its corners and carried away her tent, parka, and backpack along with Travkin's remains. The faint rays of her flashlight shone blood-red through its plastic.

Buckets of cold water cascaded over her head. "*Jee*-zus!" One after another. "Aaaaw!" Her chest seized so tight she couldn't even breathe.

A tall French medic extended a blanket at the end of the pole. She wrapped herself in it but could force no words past locked jaws. The medic draped a second blanket over her head and waved away Russian soldiers' rifles. In the distance—and upwind—the World Health Organization's Surge Team One, and her own Surge Team Two, which had arrived just that day, watched in grim silence. From the shadows all witnessed their worst fears materialize as the grip of rigid infection control protocols seized a colleague.

"Hang tough, Emma!" "You can do it!" "You can *beat* it!" Their accents were varied, but their theme was consistent. "*Farewell, Emma Miller.*" She cried as she stumbled barefoot across hard ground, her feet already numb. The medic kept his distance but illuminated her path with a lantern. Emma heard disturbing noises with each jarring misstep that must have emanated from her.

She asked where they were going. The French medic replied, "Quarantine." Her destiny was now binary. Either she'd contracted the new disease, whatever the hell it was, or not. Like a prisoner in a Roman colosseum, Emma awaited her thumbs up or thumbs down.

Whirring sounds grew louder—air pumps at quick-erect isolation shelters. Travkin had been hustled into one after fighting off the suicidal attack on their landing zone. Emma had watched from a distance and upwind as he, too, had been stripped and scrubbed. But the shelters had been off-limits when she'd come to thank him. Seven hours later, eyes black, it had been Travkin who visited Emma.

The isolation shelters reminded Emma of the bouncy house her brother rented for her nephew's twelfth birthday. Emma and her twin sister, tipsy from the wine at the grown-ups' table, had giggled and jumped like schoolgirls. But those playpens maintained their shape by positive pressure. Isolation shelters were the opposite—held up by poles as their tainted miasma was sucked out through HEPA filters, removing micron-sized particles one hundred air changes an hour. Negative pressure kept germs from escaping the openings.

"What about the other guy?" she asked in vibrato, shivering. "I don't wanta catch it from him."

"Corp. Leskov died," the medic replied.

Oh, God! Please! I'll be good. Please! Okay. Focus. Concentrate. Science.

"Blown pupils," she said, "c-c-can be from intracranial pressure." Her sister Isabel, a neuroscientist, had once told her about that phenomenon. "How'd Travkin get out?"

"He attacked my medical team," replied a new man, also with a French accent, also in PPE, who arrived to escort them the last few meters to the bouncy houses. "Fractured my doctor's windpipe." The open-air site of the mobile isolation ward was brightly lit. "Eye gouging and asphyxiation for one medic." Emma lay on a gurney, as bidden. "Broken neck for the other." They peeled away her blankets. Emma reflexively covered her breasts and pubis. Gas heaters bathed her in blessed warmth. "You're lucky to be alive." Emma scoffed at any mention of her good fortune, emitting a puff of fogged breath.

A wireless blood pressure cuff squeezed her biceps. A thermometer was clamped to her fingertip. The prick of an IV needle caused her to jump. A drip bag flowed cold into her arm. "Antibiotics," the doctor said.

"Cipro?" He snorted. Better. Last-ditch. Kept out of use to prevent resistance. A doomsday-stopper. But oh, the things epidemiology professors know. Statistically, the new disease was probably a virus—not a bacterium— as impervious to antibiotics as fungi, protists, prions, protozoans, and worms, other tiny predators that ate their prey from the inside.

When she'd asked others on her team earlier how bad the new illness was, it had strangely been a big secret. But she asked again, and as a professional courtesy, or as required by the Hippocratic oath, the French doctor seemed to reply honestly. "Until we get the pathogen's taxonomy done and ICD assigns it a name, we're calling the illness SED: severe encephalopathic disease."

"Severe?" Emma asked. "So, a high initial-case fatality rate?"

"Fifty percent," the doctor replied. *Christ!* An incubation period rivaling cholera. First symptoms around two hours. An even shorter latency period. People are contagious before first symptoms, which are gastroenteritis, chills, nausea, vomiting, respiratory distress, joint pain, high fever peaking at hour four in convulsions and acute intracranial pain. The medic laid a third blanket onto Emma, but it did nothing to stop her trembling. "Direct mortality is between four and six hours of exposure. But survivors then report feeling no discomfort at all."

"Whatta you mean, *direct* mortality?" she barely forced out.

"Well," he explained, "Travkin's death wasn't direct."

"*Oh.*" *Jeeze!* "So, if you survive, what th-then? What does it do?"

The doctor glanced at a nearby unit, different from the others in that its vinyl walls were opaque, not clear. Bright light leaked through the zippered seals of its single doorway. "We don't know a lot yet." Just outside the unit lay the unzipped empty body bag from which protruded the remains of Emma's tent. Her flashlight still shone inside.

"You're doing an autopsy?" Emma said. "Of Travkin?"

"You made a mess of his cranium," the doctor replied in tacit confirmation.

"What's the pathogen's vector?" Emma asked.

"It's not zoonotic. It didn't mutate and leap species. The Russians were drilling for oil when a mud logger caught it. Apparently, as an early test for hydrocarbons before the spectrographic analysis is done, old-timers *taste* the rock cuttings. Our guess is the pathogen was frozen a few dozen meters under the permafrost 30 to 40 thousand years ago. The crew, fifty-one, mostly men, all got sick. The Russians called Geneva. As soon as Surge Team One was assembled here, they declared a sudden-onset emergency and called for your Surge Team Two."

"Fifty-one people?" The other isolation shelters were empty. "Where are they?"

"The half that survived the acute phase... Well, you ran into a few of them when your helicopter landed. The Russians are rounding up the others in the forest."

Jesus! Emma thought. "So, *Encephalopathic*? It causes...b-brain damage?"

In a terrifyingly sympathetic tone, he replied, "To the cerebral cortex," and laid a hand on her shoulder.

"Is the damage reversible?"

He shook his head.

"So, p-permanent brain damage?"

"Structural alterations. In every victim we've studied. I'm sorry."

Oh-God-oh-God-oh-God! Get a grip. Get a grip! But she couldn't. *Science!* "What," she said, choking on her fears, "what does the damage do?"

"Did you note Travkin's lack of emotional responsiveness?" He again put his hand on her now-quaking shoulder. "And they can be very, *very* violent."

The tall medic plunged a syringe into the injection port on Emma's IV.

"What's thaaah—" Emma started to ask just before tumbling into a calm and comfy bliss. She smiled at arriving Russian soldiers, armed and in camouflaged protective gear, so unlike the solid green worn by the *très chic* French. *Change of procedure after Travkin?* she wondered, barely clinging to reality against the undertow.

Emma drifted on a river of euphoria. She was Dr. Miller, epidemiology professor, yeah, Johns Hopkins, on assignment, *for...* for the *NIH*, that's it, and the WHO! That took a lot out of her, so she relaxed into the current. She was Emmy of sunny days playing tennis and swimming, and languid evenings gossiping and flirting. A life in a world-within-a-world, her family's Greenwich country club, in a galaxy far, far away.

In summers, she ventured out of that bubble only for sailing lessons on the Sound, which were the highlights of her poor, poor sister's week. Emma had sports teammates; clubs masquerading as charities for college applications; and boyfriends one after the other, scandalously overlapping. Her identical twin sister, Isabel, in contrast, had mom and *dad*. The three would binge-watch television series and movies, *together*—one of Dad's John Wayne movies or whatever for each of Izzy's romantic comedies. They thus ruined Isabel's scant chance for a social life by providing her refuge from some awkward years.

Both twins, now thirty-two, were five-foot-four, both 110 pounds, both fit, both pretty for God's sake. Both were groomed, educated, and well-raised in a wealthy, high-achieving family. Both had light brown hair that turned blond in summers. But Emma's was cut short for convenience on these grown-up scientific adventures. The tips of her hair now felt frozen and her arm cold as she twirled a strand. It had once been long and lustrous like Isabel's still was. Emma felt envious. A medic placed her arm back under the blanket.

Emma raised her wobbly head. Someone was dissecting Travkin's brain in the opaque bouncy house. Was hers next? She had to warn her siblings. "I wasn't told 'bout the risks."

"You were here," the doctor replied, "to determine whether there were any wildlife hosts or amplifiers. You weren't supposed to be on this side of the isolation barrier."

"Then I got *attacked!* Oops! We're sure it's transmiss'ble human-to-human?" A nod. "Also rel'vant. Listen. You *owe* me. You gotta warn my sister and brother."

"I'm sorry," the doctor replied. "I can't do that. We have strict orders to keep this totally secret." He raised a tablet. "For my report, where did you get the pistol?"

"From Travkin! He knew they turn violent? So he gave me his gun? He was...protective. I thought, you know, he liked me? Pro'lly wanted to make sure I was okay."

The distracted doctor said, "Or he came to rape you. Both women on the rig's catering crew were infected during sexual assaults." He gave orders in French to his staff. Among the uninfected, life went on. A medic read something off a monitor. The doctor typed something on his tablet. But in Emma's world, all was ending. She tried to focus. HEPA filtration. "It's airborne?" The doctor's silence chilled her worse than the Siberian air. "If it passes that easily, just from *breathing*, everyone is...*doomed!* The whole fracking world!" The doctor, medics, and armed Russian soldiers were all listening now.

They helped Emma rise and ushered her to her very own clear plastic cube. The tall medic held the drip bag over her head. The short medic held out earbuds, "To talk." The doctor held out a hand, muttering about needing visual observation. They wanted to watch her change into what Travkin had become. She gave him her blankets and covered herself with her hand and forearm. Her skin was streaked red from scrubbing. The doctor droned on and on about ensuring her a high quality of care. In a small act of defiance, Emma turned away to uncover herself and inserted her earbuds. In the silence that followed, however, her fears quickly overcame her defenses.

A lucky near miss, death or brain damage? Buy a ticket and spin the wheel.

In the cube, a medic hung the bag from a hook beside a bare, metal-framed cot and plugged more tubes into Emma's plumbing before leaving her alone. She then curled up on the plastic floor in the fetal position. *Breathe. Just breathe.* She was trembling. *Science. Science.* On the uninfected side of the transparent walls, they worked in the open. Air would dilute the pathogen, reducing its concentration and the risk of infection.

Emma considered whether the two Russian soldiers who stood outside would shoot if she ran for it, and concluded they would. But would they also shoot her even if she didn't bolt? Should she make a break now before she grew too ill? But to where? Naked in frozen northeastern Siberia? Hunted like the rest of her kind? She tried to focus. *Science.*

"Can I have a clock?" When asked if she wanted local, GMT or time since exposure, she chose the last. *Lab time.* Who cares about local, GMT or time back home?

Which was where? Her sister had fretted endlessly about rootlessness when their parents died in a car wreck their sophomore year of college. After the funeral, they had packed all their belongings into storage units. A month later, their childhood home was sold, and the three siblings were set adrift. No more shrine to childhood memories. No parents celebrating academic accomplishments or consoling broken hearts. Her sister Isabel had spent her next few summers with their big brother, Noah, and his young wife, clinging to family. Emma got a string of jobs—and boyfriends—to fill her school breaks. But now she wasn't at home in her apartment in Maryland or in any of the various guys' places she frequented or in nearby Virginia where Noah lived. Emma had people but no place, she thought, as her incomplete life possibly neared its end.

On the laptop screen, a digital clock counted up past 0:31:43.

A new, tall man arrived in full PPE. "Hello?" he said through a mic into her earbuds. "It's Hermann Lange." He pronounced his name in German fashion—"Err-mahn Lang-uh"—even though he was *French* Swiss. Emma did her best to cover herself. He took his hood off briefly to don a headset and extracted files and a laptop from his satchel.

"Thank God," she said, glad to see a familiar face. Everything had been a blur. The mobilization call the day before. Throwing cold weather gear into a bag she kept packed for the jungles of Africa, Asia, or the Amazon—nature's laboratories—where spillovers usually occurred. The huge US military transport, empty save for its crew and its cargo, Emma, departed Joint Base Andrews, refueled in Alaska, and met up with her team, from all around the globe, at a remote Siberian airport.

During their short helicopter flight, Travkin snuck glances at her. Emma couldn't imagine why, bundled up as she was. When they descended toward the tall oil derrick, Emma should have sensed danger. Apprehensive soldiers loaded rifles. Travkin kissed the Orthodox cross he wore on his gold chain. *I killed him!* She jammed her eyes shut.

After landing with a thud, Emma had climbed out, shielding her eyes against soil churned up by the rotors. As the engine wound down, she heard shouts. A half dozen men charged them at the dead run. Full-auto rips from three Kalashnikovs ended the lives of all but one. Soldiers swung their rifles but couldn't shoot through the scattering scientists. Leskov tackled the attacker fifteen meters from Emma. Travkin stabbed him. Neither were wearing protective gear. A single fountain of blood spurted from his chest. Emma had followed fleeing colleagues. But looking back over her shoulder she was struck by the man's spooky eyes, wide as the last bit of life drained from him, pupils totally fucking black like Travkin's.

"Feel like talking?" asked Hermann. He was a social anthropologist on Surge Team One who studied behaviors that caused diseases to spread, like shaking hands, unprotected sex, or ritual preparation of the dead; or that inhibited their spread like handwashing and social isolation. He was in his late thirties and handsome enough. He had twice hit on Emma, and twice failed. Too much alcohol and pot on his first try, and on the second neither had showered for days in The Congo during a now prosaic seeming Ebola outbreak. Happier times. Would he soon watch her writhe naked in this plastic cage as some parasite, now rapidly reproducing inside her, gnawed away on her brain?

"*Love* to chat," she replied. The haze of narcotics was lifting. "SED has to be more contagious than any pathogen we've ever seen. Infection without coughing, sneezing mucal catastrophes? Droplet nuclei in distal airways? Sub-five microns? So it's viral?"

"It's archaic, and we think it was probably highly evolved back when it was frozen," Hermann said. "It didn't randomly mutate, spill over into us from some distant species and barely survive. It *thrives* in us. If you ask me, it evolved *specifically* to infect humans. It's perfectly adapted to us. It just needed contact, which it got when the permafrost was disrupted, and *boom*. It's off and running."

Oh God, oh God, she thought. But she mustered the strength to shout, "So if it *had* no animal reservoir, why the fuck am I even *here?*"

"We collected wildlife specimens for you to examine," Hermann explained. "Just to be certain. If it turns out there aren't any intermediate hosts or transmission amplifiers—if humans are the only reservoir—we may still beat this one, like smallpox or polio."

"What's the R-nought?" Emma asked.

R_0, pronounced "R-nought," was a disease's basic reproduction rate. How many people in a susceptible population, on average, will one sick person infect? An R_0 of less than one meant the pathogen was not very infectious and its outbreaks should burn out. But an R_0 greater than one was an epidemic threat, and the higher the R_0, the more infectious. Touch a door knob a few minutes after a high-R_0 carrier, then rub your eye or brush a crumb from your lips and you auto-inoculate, injecting the pathogen into yourself.

But Travkin had only breathed on Emma, briefly, from a few feet away. "What's the R-nought, Hermann?" she persisted.

"High. Higher than the Black Death, smallpox, the Spanish Flu, polio, AIDS. We may have found The Next Big One."

Oh-my-God! Heavy chains bound Emma to a dreadful fate. She again curled into a fetal ball. "Or The Next Big One found us," she muttered.

At his laptop, Hermann asked, "Emma, could you list the emotions you're feeling?"

"Emotions? Seriously? Uhm, well, scared out of my fucking *wits* would be number one on my list."

"Anything else?" he asked.

"Really!" Emma sat up. "You're *interviewing* me?" That really pissed her off! She shook the thermometer from her finger and yanked the blood pressure cuff off. The soldiers at the hatch raised their rifles. The short medic radioed the doctor, who burst out of the autopsy lab as Emma carefully removed her IV just ahead of a rush of euphoria. They had injected a sedative remotely into the tube that led into her veins, but she'd been too quick. Her head spun only once. "What the *fuck?*" she shouted. "You tried to knock me *out?*"

"Dr. Miller," the French doctor replied, "you need that IV."

"Bullshit!" Emma snapped. "If antibiotics worked, we wouldn't be here."

"You're also getting antivirals, antiprotozoals, and fluids." Emma stared with sudden clarity through the walls' distorted optics like at survivors of some post-apocalyptic hell. *She* was free. It was the people outside her plastic shelter, from those garbed head-to-toe in PPE, to everyone on Earth beyond, who now needed to cower in fear – not her.

Emma knew the feeling of spending hours in personal protective equipment. Knock headgear aside, you're dead. Prick a finger capping a syringe, dead. Tear gloves disrobing, dead. You get antsy. It's the *un*infected who were visitors to this hostile new world.

"So Hermann," she said, "parasites follow Darwin's law. What adaptive advantage do big black pupils give SED's pathogen?"

"It could allow the infected to identify each other," Hermann ventured. He'd obviously already thought that one up.

"Why? So they,"—*or is it we?*—"can…build human pyramids to top our walls?"

"Natural selection doesn't have a purpose, only results."

"Good one. Level with me, Hermann. Did I catch it? I can't wait hours."

"It may be sooner. Leskov had a head cold. His immune system was weakened. His fever appeared at forty-four minutes. Have *you* been sick recently?"

"No." So Hermann wasn't there as a friend. He'd been with the others too. Interviewed them too. "How can it *possibly* reproduce so quickly?" she asked.

"A high reproductive rate is one reason SED seems highly evolved *and* perfectly adapted to humans. I'm telling you. It evolved to use us, its hosts, to aid its spread. This brain damage isn't random, it's..." The doctor chided him in French, pointing at Emma, who cried and shivered in fear. "I'm sorry, Emma," Hermann said. "I'm very sorry. If you'd allow monitoring, you'd know sooner."

"Would you even *tell* me if the readouts show a temperature spike?" Before he could protest, Emma asked, "What was it like when Travkin went through it?"

"When you turn, you'll get... He got very ill." Hermann's verbal misstep hit Emma like a body blow. She closed her eyes. She *was* infected. Of *course* she was. *Look at how they're fucking* treating *me!* "Physical distress, memory deficits, possibly anterograde amnesia. Deficits in social cognition." Then he again said, "Sooo, I've got some *questions?*"

"What, fill in bubbles with a No. 2 pencil? 'On a scale of one to five, how much do you wanta murder me right now?' Then some ghoul in there saws open my cranium and takes cross-sections!"

"Emma, the pathologist in there is Pieter Groenewalt," pronouncing it, "Gryoo-neh-vahl-t" with a hard German "t" even though the South African Anglicized his name. "You remember him and his wife. He's bitching that he isn't allowed on this side of the isolation barrier to see the infected—alive. But all the data is being rigidly compartmentalized."

Emma no longer cared about Groenewalt, his petty frustrations or their mission's data security rules, or felt any part of Hermann's world. She was Shrödinger's freakin' cat—maybe dead, maybe demented. Over the next hour and a half, as Emma monitored every sensation she felt plus many more imagined, Hermann talked a lot, adding small scary details to the important terrifying facts about SED. She spoke very little, mostly silently recalling the milestones of her too short life to date.

The clock passed two hours. Nothing. But a few minutes later, her head swam as if the world rotated beneath her, then it was gone. Not so the panic. Her chest clutched at her breath, forcing her to inhale deeply to break its hold. A prickly sweat burst out all over. But that was the anxiety. *Wait. Wait. Wait.*

Emma threw up without warning. It shocked her. The short medic entered—keeping his distance, eyeing her warily—and cleaned up the mess with a sprayer/vacuum on his pool-boy pole. Emma was shivering. They raised the thermostat. Minutes later, she was sweating. They lowered it. Tears of the inevitable flowed. She was sick. *Mommy? Daddy? Help me!*

"Emma? Can I ask you a few..."

"*Why?*" she finally shouted, pounding the plastic flooring with both fists. She had tried to deny her churning stomach, waves of dizziness, and deep fatigue. But at 2:13:25, she admitted the worst. Flushed and clammy, she broke down and sobbed.

"Let us help," the doctor pled. The tall medic sank to his knees and crossed himself.

"Bring it all back," Emma mumbled. The medics entered and reinserted the IV and reattached the blood pressure cuff and thermometer. "I have a brother," Emma said to Hermann as they worked on her. "Noah Miller, a lawyer in McLean, Virginia. And a twin sister, Isabel, a professor at UCSB. I want them notified." Hermann suggested she relax and keep calm. "I want them *warned!* You tell them what's coming and to get ready, get *ready*, you *understand*, and I'll answer anything. I'll cooperate. Noah and Isabel Miller!" Emma shouted, sobbing. "They're all I've got! They're all I've..."

Hermann gave her a single nod, unnoticed by the others. She didn't trust him, but it would have to do. Calmness flowed into her veins. She closed her throbbing eyes.

"We're all in this together," Hermann had the gall to say.

"*Spare* me!" Emma replied. But on reflection, he was fucking right. This thing was incredibly rapacious. *You can run, Hermann, but you can't hide.* Stomach cramps elicited a grunt. Hermann asked if she needed more painkillers. "Yes!" she replied. A wave of peace followed. *Let's just get this over with. Come on you little piece of shit virus! Give it your best shot!*

The doctor returned from the opaque morgue. Emma latched onto the spinning Earth, sat up, and asked him for news. "Groenewalt found brain damage unrelated to the trauma from the gunshot. Bleeding. Loss of neuronal mass, particularly in Travkin's right hemisphere. The damage was remarkably similar to the earlier victims."

Emma pressed on her eyelids as pain split her forehead. *It's happening! I was kidding! Please stop!*

"Emma?" she heard Hermann say. "Can you look up at the camera?" She stared into the bullet-shaped cylinder. "Thanks. So, these questions might sound odd, but humor me, okay? When we were in The Congo last year, you told me about having lunch at your country club after tennis, and the busboy was one of your classmates?" Emma was too tired to fight him and nodded. "You remember how you told me you felt?"

"Embarr'ssed," Emma said, slurring.

"Right," Hermann replied. "And do you know *why* you were embarrassed?"

"'Cause I was rich. And when he bussed our table, I was whispering to a girl and she laughed. He thought I'd said something about him. Izzy, my sister, said I'd been rude. But we weren't talking about the boy. I'd invited Izzy along to play doubles 'cause she didn't have any friends and our parents made me. We were laughing about Isabel dying a virgin 'cause she was so uptight. She pro'lly knew, and that was why she got mad."

"The busboy was poor and had to work cleaning tables," Hermann said, clarifying his point for the record. "And you were rich and playing tennis over the school break. That fact made you feel embarrassed in front of your classmate?" She nodded. "And forgive me, but when you shot Sgt. Travkin, the man who'd saved your life, how did you feel?"

That burned through the painkilling haze. "*Fuck* you! He wouldn't stop!" Tears welled up. She began to cry, but Hermann persisted. "I felt terr'ble! *Okay?*"

Before she drifted off, Hermann asked, "Why'd you feel terrible killing Travkin?"

"Why the hell do you *think?* He saved my life, then I shot him… with his own *gun!* He gave me his…his…" She drifted in and out of consciousness. "Remember our deal!" was the last thing she recalled saying. "Remember…!"

* * * *

"Emma? Emma? Emma?"

A penlight streaked across her vision, leaving red smears in her view of the French doctor holding it. Her wrists and ankles were zip-tied to her cot's frame. Coiled plastic IV tubing and her blood pressure cuff and thermometer lay in a pile. When two armed soldiers entered the unit, her heart raced and the plastic ties cut into her skin.

The doctor argued with a Russian officer in English. "She's American! W-H-O! I don't care about your orders! We take full responsibility!" Everyone turned toward the sound of a gunshot outside. Emma's tensed muscles began to quiver.

The doctor said to Emma. "We have to go. Feel up to it?" Another gunshot.

She rose, naked, when cut free. Five men, two armed, stood between her and freedom, and she felt dizzy and unsteady on her feet. The tall medic handed her an impermeable coverall, which she held until he directed her to step into it. He put plastic booties on her feet, latex gloves on her hands, a mask and goggles on her face, and a hood over her wet hair. He then taped her sleeves to her gloves and her pants cuffs to her boots. A heavy, gray wool overcoat was hung on her shoulders. It smelled of body odor.

Outside, she climbed into a huge, open vehicle. Single shots were drowned out by its big engine rumbling to life. Only Hermann sat beside Emma. The doctor, two medics, and two Russian soldiers, one at the front and one by the open rear door, lined the opposite wall. *Jump out!* Her pulse pounded.

As the slow, bumpy ride began, Hermann asked, "Emma, how do you feel?" Tree branches scraped across high metal sides, distracting a guard. A flood of frigid air drenched the benches lining the walls of the open compartment. "How do you feel?" he repeated.

"Fine," came from memory. "How are *you?*" seemed like the thing to say.

Emma couldn't read Hermann's expression. "Well, I sure wish I'd left on the helicopter with Pieter."

The doctor said something in French, shouted, stood, and banged on the metal bulkhead. The vehicle halted. The doctor exited at the rear. Hermann peered out a side hatch and gasped. *"Mein Gott!"* Emma followed his gaze. Oil workers knelt, eyes dilated, and removed hardhats on a command given in Russian. An officer raised a pistol to one man's forehead—*bang! "Mon dieu!"* Hermann cried. Although the workers bore signs of fighting—bloody faces and limbs, torn clothing—they were serene and composed, staring up at the muzzle unflinching as each was shot in turn.

Hermann jumped at each *bang*, muttering in French, his face contorted.

The Russian soldiers on the opposite bench stared at Emma from behind respirators. They would be distracted if their headgear were knocked askew. Deep breathing helped her resist the impulse to lunge, prematurely, for their rifles.

Outside, the French doctor shouted, "Murderers!" in English, at the Russians.

"Do you remember our deal, Emma?" Hermann asked. She nodded. A medic raised a camera. Hermann said, "Subject, Dr. Emma Miller, epidemiology professor, Johns Hopkins University, contracted SED six hours ago." Date, time, location. "Dr. Pieter Groenewalt departed for Geneva two hours ago with eleven brain specimens. We are evacuating to Anadyr in an open-air vehicle to lessen infection risk. Russians are killing all SED survivors except Subject. Repeating questions one and two, Event Log Twelve."

Dive across the aisle between the two soldiers and maybe neither would fire. Claw the face shield loose and yank the rifle from one soldier's lap. If the other hesitated, she could fire first and kill them all. But if the second guard was heedless of harming his comrades and opened fire inside the packed vehicle, she would surely die. Plus, there were all the soldiers outside. It took all her willpower not to obey the intense instinct she felt to flail at the men who threatened her life.

Hermann still flinched at each report from the Russian officer's pistol. "Emma, you told me about," *bang,* "about a lunch at your club after tennis. The busboy was a classmate." The rear door remained open. *Bang.* A headfirst dive outside. The woods were thick. "Do you remember how you felt when he came to your table?"

"Embarrassed," she replied from memory, uncertain what that word actually meant.

"Yes," Hermann typed—*bang!*—and flinched. "*Why* were you embarrassed?"

"Because… Because… She was too fatigued to compose an answer. *Bang!*

The soldier by the rear door checked his safety. It was on the left, beside the trigger. "Were you embarrassed because he was handsome and you were sweaty?"

It had been a cool day. The boy had bad acne. "No."

"Maybe," Hermann ventured, "you were embarrassed because you were rich and played tennis all summer, but he was poor and cleaned tables on his vacation. Is that it?"

She had a trust fund that would pay her millions in a few years. The boy must have been working because he needed money. But… "No," she replied.

Significant looks were exchanged. *Take the scissors protruding from the tall medic's pouch. Jab them through the soldier's face shield. Grab his rifle. Flick the safety to "Fire." Kill everyone.* Too many steps. The second soldier would certainly fire first.

"One more question," Hermann said. "When you shot Sgt. Travkin, the man infected while saving your life yesterday, with his own gun, how did that make you feel?"

"Terrible."

"Okay. Do you know *why* you felt terrible?"

"Because…" She couldn't even recall what feeling terrible meant, and tried to recreate the feeling. He entered the tent. She shot him in the face. There was nothing "terrible" or anything else about it.

The doctor climbed aboard, cursing in French. The rear door slammed shut. The vehicle slowly passed the site of the ongoing slaughter. The French doctor, medics, and armed Russian guards swayed as the vehicle's treads ground across the terrain, and ducked as sticks and leaves rained down from low branches. *Now?* Emma smelled smoke.

Everyone's attention was drawn through hatches to the growing pile of burning bodies. *Now?* In the distance beyond the pyre, a small floatplane rose into the pale blue sky. *Now?* But no one other than Emma seemed to notice the departing aircraft as more bodies were tossed into the crackling flames. *Now?*

Pandora: Contagion

MADNESS HAS GONE VIRAL

The world is not the same since the *Pandoravirus* outbreak changed the essence of human nature. Those affected by the disease are consumed by adrenal rage. They erupt in violence with the slightest provocation. And now, infected scientist Emma Miller is forging them into an army of merciless killers marching across America.

Emma's twin sister, neuroscientist Isabel Miller, is desperate to avert the chaos that threatens to engulf civilization. But her team has its hands full staying one step ahead of the civil unrest that's ravaging the country. Noah Miller, the twins' brother, thought he had created a safe haven for his family in the mountains of Virginia—until the arrival of Emma and her infected followers proved the folly of his plans.

The Millers' conflict is just one of many sweeping the nation. A nation divided into factions. A nation on the precipice of all-out civil war...